R63990

in the Old West

D1610687

ALSO BY JEREMY AGNEW
AND FROM MCFARLAND

Medicine in the Old West:
A History, 1850–1900 (2010)

Entertainment in the Old West

Theater, Music, Circuses, Medicine Shows, Prizefighting and Other Popular Amusements

JEREMY AGNEW

McFarland & Company, Inc., Publishers
Jefferson, North Carolina, and London

790
AGN
– – –

LIBRARY OF CONGRESS CATALOGUING-IN-PUBLICATION DATA

Agnew, Jeremy.
   Entertainment in the Old West : theater, music, circuses,
medicine shows, prizefighting and other popular amusements /
Jeremy Agnew.
      p.   cm.
   Includes bibliographical references and index.

   ISBN 978-0-7864-6280-3
   softcover : 50# alkaline paper ∞

   1. Theater — West (U.S.) — History —19th century.
   2. Performing arts — West (U.S.) — History —19th century.
   3. Amusements — United States — History —19th century.
   I. Title.
   PN2273.W4A36 2011
   791.0978'09041— dc22

                                        2011013292

BRITISH LIBRARY CATALOGUING DATA ARE AVAILABLE

On the cover: Details from 19th and early 20th century circus
poster art (Library of Congress). Front cover by TG Design

Manufactured in the United States of America

McFarland & Company, Inc., Publishers
   Box 611, Jefferson, North Carolina 28640
   www.mcfarlandpub.com

For Gage,
who has entertained me
far more than he knows

Contents

Entertainment Milestones

1841   First pioneers journey to the Northwest along the Oregon Trail.

1847   Several "living picture" shows that simulate classical paintings and sculptures appear in New York.

1848   First news of the gold strike at Sutter's Mill in California; end of the war with Mexico adds large areas of Texas and California to the United States; first known theater presentation in California at Monterey.

1849   Transcontinental gold rush of Forty-Niners to the California gold camps opens opportunity for traveling entertainers; the first professional production in California, *The Bandit Chief*, is given in Sacramento; first circus in the West performs in San Francisco; first professional theater production staged in California at Sacramento.

1850   San Francisco booms as a center for theatrical entertainment in the western United States.

1852   Publication of *Uncle Tom's Cabin* and the first theater adaptation of this long-lasting, popular play.

1853   Founding of the San Francisco Minstrels.

1854   The Grattan Massacre in Wyoming initiates war with the Plains Indians for the next 36 years; publication of *Ten Nights in a Bar-room*.

1859   Major gold rushes to Central City, Colorado, and Bannack, Montana.

1860   First transcontinental mail deliveries via the Pony Express.

1861   Start of the Civil War between the Union and the Confederates; completion of the transcontinental telegraph ends the era of the Pony Express; Adah Menken debuts as Mazeppa in Albany, New York.

1865   Defeat of the Confederacy and the end of the Civil War; the San Francisco Minstrels begin a 19-year stay in New York.

1866   The first of many herds of cattle are driven from Texas to the railheads in Kansas; New York opening of *The Black Crook*, the forerunner of musical comedy and burlesque shows.

1868   Lydia Thompson and her British Blondes present *Ixion*, the forerunner of "leg shows."

1869   Meeting of the Central Pacific and the Union Pacific at Promontory, Utah, completes the transcontinental railroad from the East to California; Michael Leavitt creates Mme. Rentz's Female Minstrels, the first American burlesque show.

1870   Beginning of the worst years of Indian warfare between the U.S. Army and the Plains tribes.

1872   William F. Cody appears in the stage play *The Scouts of the Prairie*.

1876   General George Armstrong Custer and his troops are annihilated at the Battle of the Little Bighorn in Montana; Deadwood emerges to become the center of a gold rush to the Black Hills.

1877   Discovery of silver in southern New Mexico Territory (later south-central Arizona) creates a rush that results in Tombstone.

1880   Leadville booms with silver mining to become the largest city in Colorado after Denver.

1881   The bloody Gunfight at the OK Corral takes place in Tombstone, Arizona.

1882   W.F. Cody organizes the *Old Glory Blowout* Fourth of July celebration in North Platte, Nebraska.

1883   W.F. Cody organizes *Buffalo Bill's Wild West* to commemorate the passing of the Old West.

1885   The end of the cattle drives from Texas and decline of the Kansas cattle towns.

1890   The end of the Indian Wars after the battle at Wounded Knee, South Dakota, between the U.S. Army and the Sioux Indians; gold strikes on the back side of Pikes Peak in central Colorado results in the boomtown of Cripple Creek.

1893   The silver crash and subsequent depression closes many Western theaters; "Little Egypt" introduces the belly dance at the World's Columbian Exposition in Chicago.

1895   The first public showings in Europe of movies of short subjects.

1897   Start of the Klondike Gold Rush, the last of the great gold rushes, and the boom of mining in Dawson, in the Yukon Territory, in the frozen far north.

1900   The rise of movies in the nickelodeons.

1903   *The Great Train Robbery*, the first sophisticated western, is filmed in New Jersey by the Edison Company.

1917   W.F. Cody dies in Denver, Colorado.

Preface

The amusements of a people are the best index of their character.[1]

At one time or another, almost every town in the Old West had a concert saloon, a theater, or an "opera house." This book relates the background and story of the entertainment presented in these places by the actors, actresses, and traveling troupes who criss-crossed the Old West, performing in tents, saloons, fancy theaters, and even the open air. This is the story of the men and women who provided the legendary entertainment of the Old West and left a legacy that provided laughter and tears for several generations of pioneers.

Expansion of the West was spurred by the doctrine of Manifest Destiny, a term coined in the late 1840s. This was the concept that Americans should conquer and settle the United States from coast to coast, supplanting native peoples with the American way of life. Millions of Americans heeded the call, drawn westward by the fertile valleys of the Northwest and the lure of gold discovered in 1848 in what would become northern California.

Early expansion of the American West was the handiwork of a hardy group of men who trapped beaver, dug for gold, herded cattle, cut trees, fought Indians, and farmed the fertile valleys of the Northwest. Some were accompanied by women who braved the unknown to travel with their families to the land of promises in Oregon and California. Toiling hard to wrest a living out of the land, these westerners needed and demanded entertainment after their workday was done. To fill this need, entertainers followed rapidly to provide a laugh, a tear, and escape from the world of daily toil.

The heyday of popular American theater in the Old West lasted from about 1850 until early in the 20th century, a period which generally coincides with the popular perception of the "Old West." Prior to 1850, theater entertainment consisted primarily of dramas that were presented more for elite audiences than for the uneducated masses. Shortly after 1900, motion pictures,

1

which were originally introduced in variety theaters as novelty acts, started to rise in popularity. After about 1920, movies became the primary form of popular entertainment, and legitimate theater returned to the elite.

Professional entertainment in the Old West developed in three sequential phases. The first phase was characterized by itinerant entertainers who traveled from town to town, going wherever they could find an audience, often performing in saloons and tents. As the West became more settled, the second phase was characterized by stock companies, made up of groups of actors who settled in a particular town or city and presented a series of plays in rotation, changing them as audience attendance dwindled when the majority had seen a particular show. When easy and reliable transportation — notably the railroad system — developed, the third phase was characterized by traveling companies of actors who presented the same play at different locations, moving to the next town after a few days or when audience attendance started to fall off.

The theme of this book broadly covers the emergence, growth, and types of entertainment that amused the miners, cowboys, loggers, railroad men, and high society during the golden years of the expansion of the American frontier from St. Louis to the West Coast. Though the main theme covers stage entertainment, the diversions that amused the Westerners covered many different forms, because the lines of entertainment in the Old West were blurred. Circuses and horse acts, for example, were presented indoors in theaters as well as outside in the open. Singers and dancers performed outside on the sidewalk in boomtowns and inside on the stages of theaters. Buffalo Bill Cody performed in plays on the stage but also outside with his *Wild West* show. Preachers and temperance workers were considered by some to be entertainers, even though they tried to impart a worthy message. All these and more made up the fabric of entertainment in the Old West.

When researching what happened in the past, it is sometimes difficult to sort the facts from errors that have crept into source material. I have done my best to verify everything presented in this book but, ultimately, I am responsible for any mistakes that have crept into this narrative.

Incidentally, the spellings "theater" and "theatre" are both correct according to Webster's dictionaries. Each form will be found in different texts and the names for various establishments, consequently both of these different versions have been retained in this book.

ONE

On with the Show

The audience whistled and stomped its collective feet. As the man on the stage tried to deliver his monologue, a member of the audience yelled out the line for him. When another actor nervously launched into a soliloquy from Shakespeare's *Hamlet*, the theater patrons chimed in and recited it along with him.

People banged beer glasses on their tables and clapped their hands to the beat of the music. The audience talked, sang along with performers, recited famous speeches with them, yelled punchlines out loud, and offered various impromptu comments and criticisms of the players. Patrons stomped their feet and some tossed coins up onto the stage to reward a particularly good performer.

On the main floor of the theater, the rowdier element fought among themselves. Drunks staggered into each other and the small tables, slopping their drinks onto one another and the furniture as they passed. Bleary-eyed men sprayed tobacco juice onto the floor, in the process hitting the shoes and trousers of others nearby. Some of the audience slept in their chairs in an alcoholic stupor. Glasses clinked together and beer sloshed onto the tables and floor. Food, liquid, and goodness knows what else rained down from the balcony. Waiter girls in short skirts strutted among the assorted men, delivering a beer here, patting a head there, and avoiding a slap on the bottom whenever they could. Hanging over everything like a sickly miasma was the gamy aroma of greasy food, pungent tobacco smoke, and stale beer. Bizarre as all these goings-on sound, such events were typical of an evening at a low-class variety theater in the West in the mid-to-late 1800s.

Audiences of the mid–19th century dominated the shows and felt it was their due to heckle and interact with players. Their behavior would appall today's theatergoers. There was often a high noise level during the performance and many of the cast's lines were inaudible. The audience cheered and shouted at the actors and delivered resounding applause whenever they felt that it was deserved. They often insisted that clever dialogue or a fancy piece of stage business be repeated — in the case of popular pieces, perhaps several times. Hence the expression "show-stopper."

If the audience did not like the show or the actor, they hissed and booed, and threw whatever was handy. Eggs, cabbage, and potatoes were favorite missiles. At one play in Sacramento, California, in 1856, someone in the audience even hurled a sack of flour onto the stage and another threw a dead goose.[1] Except for throwing things, this form of behavior still exists as the traditional hissing and booing that is practiced by audiences at today's re-created Victorian melodramas.

Audiences were so rough in some theaters that the orchestra played behind knee-high metal screens, which were intended to deflect various missiles hurled by the audience or for protection during a fight on the main floor. Some of the larger and more respectable variety "theaters" had to employ guards to keep order among the patrons. At the Denver House, in Denver, Colorado, the atmosphere was sometimes so wild that the musicians retreated behind an iron barricade if any of the drunken patrons started shooting.[2]

Such antics were not all one-sided, however. Entertainers, in turn, were not retiring. They shouted, sang at the tops of their voices, danced, and gesticulated wildly to keep their audience's attention. In Pueblo, Colorado, in 1875, the insults of a drunken theater patron became too much for one actress trying to deliver her lines in a play. She jumped from the stage into the audience and hit the man several times with a piece of wood. When she was satisfied, she climbed back onto the stage and carried on with her performance.[3]

Rowdy behavior eventually became unacceptable as theater-going became a more genteel activity. The Program for the Elks Opera House in Leadville, Colorado, stated: "Ladies having in charge children who become noisy will be expected to remove them from the theater."[4] The management of one theater even requested that gentlemen not carry cigars or cigarettes in their mouths in the lobby.

Talking during the show gradually became forbidden as the audience struggled to hear lines spoken on stage. Interestingly though, later vaudeville theaters typically placed what was called a "dumb" act — in the sense of no dialogue — at the beginning and end of their programs. Dumb acts, such as animal or acrobatic performances, and in the late 1890s short silent movies, required no listening skills on the part of the audience. This was done because the noise of patrons who rudely entered the theater after the show had begun, or who left early, was enough to drown out important lines of a comedian or actors in a sketch.

Bad manners in the theater didn't totally disappear. For example, in 1896,

Oscar Hammerstein brought a vaudeville act from Iowa to his theater in New York. Officially named the Cherry Sisters, they were known more popularly as the "vegetable girls," because they were showered with debris by the audience, who were quick to show their disapproval.[5]

Humble Beginnings

The start of entertainers criss-crossing the Old West, entertaining miners, loggers, cattlemen, and settlers, had its faltering origins after the discovery of a few small pieces of gold in the millrace of Captain John Augustus Sutter's sawmill in New Helvetia (more commonly called Sutter's Fort), California, on Monday, January 24, 1848. This important event lured a flood of young, single, would-be miners to the Sierra Nevada mountains of California in a mass relocation of population that has not been equaled in the history of the United States. Two hundred thousand hopeful Forty-Niners crowded into the gold fields.[6] Between 1860 and 1870, a million people poured into the West, seeking their fortunes from gold, timber, cattle, and other riches promised by Manifest Destiny.[7] Over the next ten years, two-and-a-half million more joined them.

The rowdy crowd of young men who flooded the California gold fields in the late 1840s and early 1850s soon demanded entertainment to while away their leisure hours. As a result, itinerant performers and minstrels made the rounds of the early gold camps, bringing badly needed entertainment to eager miners. Many of the enthusiastic Forty-Niners and settlers were so hungry for entertainment that they would travel for hours to see a performance — any kind of performance. To fill the void, actors, singers, and dancers, presenting acts that covered a spectrum from serious drama to comedy, mounted rickety stages in wooden buildings all over the West. Entertainers traveled from town to town by foot, wagon, and stagecoach, often putting up with makeshift lodgings and poor meals in primitive mining camps. Some of the plays and performers were perhaps not of the best quality or of particularly long-lasting merit, but they provided popular entertainment for the masses.

Early shows were a combination of songs, dances, and skits that poked fun at topical events. Scripts were sketchy and basic, and often changed from performance to performance depending on the audience and how well the material went over. Part of what made these shows popular was the costumes, the performers' flamboyant styles, the use of highly exaggerated acting gestures, and the actors' rapport with the audience.

Lines in plays might be altered to fit the town where a troupe was appearing. For example, the farce *Wanted: 1,000 Milliners*, adapted from a French vaudeville, was tailored specifically for its presentation in Virginia City, Montana, as *Wanted: A Thousand Young Milliners for the Idaho Gold Diggings*.[8]

Showboats

Before the days of the Forty-Niners in California, traveling performers entertained the settlers of the Western Frontier on showboats arranged as traveling theaters. These showboats commonly plied the Mississippi Rivers in the 1830s, stopping and entertaining at various towns along the river. One of the first, Noah Ludlow's *Noah's Ark*, was an unpowered barge that put to the water in 1817. It drifted down the Ohio and Mississippi Rivers, stopping from time to time to present a show.

The first custom showboat, named *Chapman's Ark* or the *Floating Theatre*, was built and launched in Pittsburgh by William Chapman in 1831.[9] Though the description "showboat" sounds grand, the boat was, in reality, only a crude building on top of a floating flatboat that was 100 feet long by 16 feet wide. It was also unpowered and simply floated down the Mississippi River from Pittsburgh (via the Ohio River) to New Orleans, stopping to provide entertainment on the way, on a strictly one-time trip. In New Orleans, Chapman dismantled the boat and sold the lumber. He and the other actors then returned to Pittsburgh to repeat the process.

Chapman eventually tried a real boat, named the *Temple of the Muses*, which attracted audiences as it sailed up and down rivers in New York. The Chapman family were well known on the traveling entertainment route and went on to perform in San Francisco during the Gold Rush years.

Showboats grew in size and magnificence to one named the *Floating Circus Palace*, built by Gilbert Spaulding and Charles Rogers, and launched in 1852. This was the type of showboat that was mentally conjured up by the name. The boat was 200 feet long, had steam heating, and was lit by 200 gas lamps. The theater had a 42-foot performing ring in the center that presented a variety of circus acts. The central showplace was surrounded by two levels of seats that could hold an audience of 2,400. The boat included a box office, a bar, a concert saloon, a museum, dressing rooms for the performers, and stables for the animals. Spaulding and Rogers' *Floating Circus Palace* did not last long, however, and was destroyed by fire in 1865.

Concert Saloons and Variety Theaters

Theater entertainment was an extremely powerful cultural force in the early West and had a great influence on frontier towns. Mining camps that did not yet have a church or school would somehow manage to have an "opera house." This grand-sounding building may have only been a rough log building with a crude stage, but it signified that a town had "arrived."

Typical was the mining town of Randsburg, California, which built a theater in 1896 when the camp was only a year old.[10] In the late 1870s, Cheyenne, Wyoming, boasted 17 of these theaters serving a population of less than 4,000. Such theaters catered to the need for relaxation for entertainment-hungry settlers of Western towns and attendance at shows was usually very good. The number of stage performances in the Old West went from about 2,000 in 1870 to an estimated 10,000 in 1890.

The essential elements of theaters in mining camps, cattle towns, lumber camps, or other similar settlements, was a small stage, a balcony, reserved boxes along the side for private use, and a well-stocked bar. Private boxes, where customers could dally with "actresses" and waiter girls in private, were a common feature of saloon theaters in the Old West. Theaters with curtained-off boxes for prostitution were colloquially known as "box houses" and the girls who worked in them were known as "box rustlers."[11] Men gained prestige by being seen surrounded by women in one of these boxes. It was a sign of wealth and success.

The larger theaters in cities such as San Francisco and Denver had large stages with good lighting and the ability to make elaborate scene changes. Small theaters in the West might have nothing but a flimsy wooden stage with a backdrop of painted canvas. Itinerant performers traveling a circuit of small towns might sleep in their wagons, in a tent, or on the ground. In small towns without a theater, performances might be given on a makeshift stage at one end of a saloon, church, or meeting hall. In one instance, the actors made do with some boards placed across two billiard tables to make an impromptu stage.

In 1885, the town of Woodland, California, 25 miles from Sacramento, built a new theater at the corner of Second Street and Dead Cat Alley. Previously the 1,500 residents of the town had watched touring shows at either Templar's Hall, Washington Hall, or Central Hall. The new "opera house" was a substantial three-story brick and iron building, dedicated solely to theater entertainment. On the inside was an auditorium, a large stage, and four boxes. Until the theater burned down in 1892, it offered Shakespeare, melodramas, comedies, musicals, farces, lectures, and concerts. Four years later a new opera house was built from brick. For the next 30 years several small touring companies included Woodland on their travel circuits and performed there at least one day a week.

Some theaters did not occupy the entire building in which they were housed, but operated in multi-purpose buildings. In the Waycott Opera

House, for example, in Colorado City, Colorado, the theater occupied only one of the three floors, sharing the building with Mack's ice cream and candy store below it, and a meeting hall for fraternal lodges and office space above.

Some theaters were not very large. The Matthews Opera House in Spearfish, South Dakota, built by Texas cattleman Thomas N. Matthews, had only 260 seats. Even in this small size, Matthews wanted to create a lasting showplace and built a solid stone building out of local sandstone. The small size of the theater did not stop enthusiastic audiences and sometimes as many as 500 people — half of whom could not have had seats — jammed into the tiny theater. This was amazing as the town had only a thousand residents. Like other theaters, the building was used at different times to serve various functions, such as a dance hall, a basketball court, and a shooting range. During World War II the theater housed an assembly line for parachutes. In 1919 it became the Princess Theater, a small movie house with a nine-foot by twelve-foot screen for silent pictures. Like many others, the theater was later abandoned and fell into disrepair. (In the 1980s the building underwent extensive restoration and redecoration, and continues to present live theater as the modern Spearfish Center for the Arts and Humanities.)

The type of theater that was most associated with the Old West and

Portrait of an unknown acting group onstage. Small groups like this, who usually sang, danced, and presented plays and short skits, were common in the West (History Colorado, Aultman Collection, Scan #20010351).

rowdy entertainment was the variety theater. These theaters had their origins in the concert saloons and variety theaters of the East, then moved with the settlers to the emerging West and soon became a fixture in Western towns. Variety theaters played an important part in the development of frontier theater entertainment because they were the direct ancestors of vaudeville theaters. All manner of acts were presented in them, from comedians and acrobats to singers. The unrestrained entertainment found there was often of a somewhat bawdy nature. In spite of the poor reputation of the variety theaters, some of the acts were quite good, consisting of singers with trained voices and comedians with clever routines. Some saloon shows featured talented performers from the East or from Europe.

Entertainment in the variety theaters varied from animal fights to lectures on temperance, from Oscar Wilde to Gilbert and Sullivan, from boxing matches and speeches to Shakespeare. Amelia Bloomer, inventor of the bloomer costume, lectured on clothes for women.[12] Henry Ward Beecher spoke on abolition. P.T. Barnum expounded on temperance and the evils of drink. Other popular acts were song-and-dance teams, tear-jerking melodramas, comedians, acrobats, contortionists, spiritual mediums, fortune tellers, magicians, jugglers, troupes of blackface minstrels, sentimental songs, and dancing. The predominantly male audience also enjoyed comedy, either satire or slapstick routines.[13]

The Keystone saloon on Chestnut Street in Leadville, Colorado, advertised a specialty act in which a man shot apples off his wife's head. In the gold-mining town of Cripple Creek, Colorado, the Cabinet Saloon was the professional home of Madame Vida de Vere, who told fortunes with a crystal ball. Her "act" was quite popular as it was said that she was able to locate rich mines in the district.[14]

Even before variety theaters and concert saloons became popular, saloons were considered to be the place to find entertainment. Entertainment tended to be passive, and often consisted simply of convivial meetings with friends and relaxation through drinking. Often all that was needed to escape from the cares of the work day was a good drink and a good laugh.

As the Western frontier developed, early saloon-keepers showed burgeoning signs of show business and tried to incorporate whatever type of entertainment they thought would attract customers into their watering holes. Lotteries and prizefights were two of the favorites. Showing what would later be a theatrical touch, some saloons became virtual museums, crammed full of whatever the saloon-keeper could collect to draw in patrons. The displays might feature stuffed animals, along with elk and moose heads on the wall, or live animals, such as a trained bear, or a cage with a mountain lion or bobcat. Live rattlesnakes in cages or glass display cases were popular with bar patrons. A saloon might be made into an impromptu performing theater with the gaming tables pushed aside and a backdrop hung from the ceiling. Those with more ghoulish tastes could pay a dollar and view the severed head of a Sioux Indian that was pickled in a barrel of whiskey in Nuttall and Mann's Number Ten Saloon, where Wild Bill Hickok met his end.

This sort of morbid display was considered by some to be very entertaining. In 1853, a Texan named Harry Love was authorized by the California legislature to enlist a group of rangers to hunt down a series of outlaws with the common first name of Joaquin. They were Joaquin Carrillo, Joaquin Valenzula, Joaquin Ocomorenia, Joaquin Botilleras, and Joaquin Murieta (or Murrieta). After a fight with a group of Mexican bandits, the rangers preserved the head of the alleged leader in a glass jar full of alcohol and put it on display in San Francisco. Admission was a dollar. It was never satisfactorily established if the head was that of outlaw Joaquin Murieta or not. The head apparently did not look like contemporary descriptions of Murieta and it was claimed that it belonged to some itinerant Mexican who was in the wrong place at the wrong time when the posse came upon him. Another grisly trophy was the severed hand of an individual alleged to be Manuel "Three-fingered Jack" Garcia. Both gruesome relics were exhibited around Sacramento and San Francisco (typically advertised in garish posters that screamed "FOR ONE DAY ONLY!") until they were lost in the San Francisco earthquake of 1906.

Many of the "music halls," "variety theaters," or "opera houses" in the Old West were basically a concert saloon that accompanied drinking with the acts of a play or a variety turn. This was similar to the saloons in the East that added entertainment during the 1830s and 1840s as an incentive for customers to stay and consume more beer, wine, or whiskey. For the same reason, in the 1850s and 1860s these places turned into saloon theaters with an emphasis on entertainment, but with the pursuit of drinking retained. To encourage customers, these establishments often included gambling tables.

A traveling reporter for the *New York Tribune* described one Western concert saloon like this: "During the performance, several babies and an enterprising dog were running about the floor, and occupants of the gallery amused themselves by tossing apples over the heads to their friends below. Like most of the male spectators, my companion and guide had a navy revolver by his side."[15]

Performers in these concert saloons were expected to dance and drink with the audience after the show. In concert saloons and low-class variety theaters, the singers and dancers became waiter-girls — as they were called — between turns on the stage. In Miles City, Montana, both the Gray Mule and Cosmopolitan saloons had small theaters with bar girls wearing short dresses with low-cut necklines. These waiter-girls mixed with customers between acts, selling drinks and often themselves.

Between 1870 and 1895, the concert saloon became a popular contact point for prostitution, along with brothels. Many of the waiter-girls were prostitutes and their stage performance was a form of advertising. Because of this, a man who saw a woman in a saloon assumed that she was a prostitute. Saloons were a male stronghold. Respectable women were not accepted in saloons and, in some towns, were barred by law from entering one. Some saloons had separate entrances and facilities, such as "wine rooms," for women, but they were few and far between.

Concert saloons appealed primarily to working-class men. As opposed to the constraints of attending a serious play in a legitimate theater, men in the concert saloons could drink, watch a show, and be served by attractive, provocatively dressed women.

A reporter who went into one of these theaters wrote: "After depositing two bits with the door-keeper, I entered a hall filled with old age, middle age, bald-headed age (next to stage), youthful age, and boy age — all sitting around tables drinking promiscuously with the 'cats.' I seated myself at one of them and was surveying the gallery when a dizzy dame came along and seated herself alongside of me and playfully threw her arms around my neck and coaxingly desired me to 'set 'em up.'"[16]

The theater in these saloons was usually located at the back of the building, so that patrons had to pass the bar on the way there and would probably succumb to the temptation of buying a drink as they passed. Profits from the sale of liquor were so high that often the saloon didn't charge for admission to the theater, as long as the patron continued to order drinks.

A typical example of the variety saloon was the Theatre Comique music hall in Butte, Montana, in 1886. This was a two-story building with the primary entrance for working men on Main Street, but with another more discreet entrance for more respectable customers in the alley behind the building. The alley entrance was a stairway that led directly to the upstairs boxes. The door of each box could be bolted from the inside so that a patron having a meeting with a waiter girl would not be interrupted. The front of the box was covered with a fine mesh screen with paintings on the outside. In this way the patron in the box could see out, but the audience in the main auditorium could not see in or see what was going on in the box. To avoid disruptions from the waiter, drinks were slipped through a slot in the door. The Theatre Comique offered variety and burlesque shows until 1898, when competition from legitimate theaters led to a gradual decline of business. Like many other variety theaters, the Comique ended up as a motion picture theater.

Every mining town had a similar establishment. In Durango, Colorado, it was the Phoenix Variety Theater. This showplace was richly appointed with thick rugs and beautiful furniture, and was lit by glittering chandeliers. The theater presented the usual mix of comedy, dramas, and musicals to entertain the local miners. More private entertainment was available on the upper floor where the waiter girls made themselves available.

About 40 miles to the north, in Silverton, Colorado, in the late 1880s, this function was provided by the Alhambra, which was a combination saloon, dance hall, gambling den, and variety theater. As part of its entertainment, the Alhambra at one time presented a trapeze act by a Mr. and Mrs. Bicket. Unfortunately, one night Minnie Bicket missed her hold and fell about 15 feet, knocking out two teeth and bruising herself quite extensively.[17] The competition for the Alhambra was the Temple of Fashion, often called just "The Fashion," which also presented similar variety shows on a small stage.

Wright's Opera House, built in 1888 in Ouray, Colorado, had a large hall for theatrical productions in the upstairs of a two-story building. The

street level was used for retail businesses. As in many small towns, the theater served multiple roles, from dances to town meetings, and was even used in later years as the arena for local high school basketball games.[18] In many of the saloon-theaters like this that were housed in a two-story building with the saloon downstairs and the theater on the second floor of the building, it was customary for the audience and the actors to go downstairs to the saloon for a drink or two at the end of each act. While this practice promoted camaraderie between performers and their audience, the last

Discreet outside stairways sometimes led directly from the street to balcony boxes upstairs in a theater, so that wealthier patrons could enter without going through the main theater and possibly be recognized on their way to a rendezvous with an "actress" (author's collection).

scenes of a play often became somewhat disjointed as inebriated actors struggled to remember their lines.

The distinction between variety hall, "opera house," and concert saloon in the Old West eventually became blurred as their purposes blended together. Because the types of amusements presented there were similar, it was easy for proprietors in small Western towns to move smoothly between the various worlds of male entertainment. Women, of course, were paramount to entertainment, in variety acts, as singers and dancers, and for diversions of a more personal nature.

One of the first madams to open a bordello in the mining town of Silverton, Colorado, was Jane Bowen, who was nicknamed the "Sage Hen." Her husband, William, was involved in mining, while Jane opened and managed a variety theater. The couple went on to expand the entertainment side of their business endeavors, opening a combination saloon, dance hall, and brothel named Westminster Dance Hall. The locals preferred to call it the "Sage Hen's Dance Hall," after Jane.

A dance hall was typically a deep frame building with a bar down one side and a raised platform at the back for the orchestra. The rest of the building consisted of a large open floor for dancing. The women who acted as dance partners were supposed to smile at the customers, as well as talk to them and dance with them, all the while trying to sell drinks.

At the back of a dance hall might be rooms for private entertainment, or a door that led outside to cribs for prostitution at the back or across an alley. All of the women in dance-halls, however, were not necessarily prostitutes. Some were married women who worked as dance partners to earn extra dollars while their husbands worked. Others were widows trying to support themselves.

Sentimental Favorites

Lively music was a part of the concert saloons and variety theaters, and either accompanied singing and dancing, or was presented as entertainment by itself.

Theaters used orchestras for musical accompaniment, but some were less than magnificent. The so-called orchestra that accompanied the first play at the Eagle Theater in Sacramento in 1849 consisted of a fiddle, a flute, a drum, and a triangle that was used to call boarders to dinner at the next-door restaurant.[19]

As part of the musical tradition, songs were very popular as entertainment. Favorite songs among the single men who were far from home were those that reflected tearful laments about mother, personal loneliness, or the perils of poor working girls. Sentimental songs included tear-jerkers such as "The Irish Mother's Lament" and "You Never Miss Your Sainted Mother Till She's Dead and Gone." Other favorites were "Bird in a Gilded Cage," "Only a Pansy Blossom, Only a Faded Flower," and "She's More to be Pitied Than Censured." A few more examples were "Just a Dream of You, Dear," "Silver Threads Among the Gold," and "The Longest Way Around Is the Sweetest Way Home." The list of these heart-wrenching ballads was long.

The effect of music on miners and cowboys who were far from home could be dramatic. Enos Christman, an ex-miner who started a newspaper in the California mining town of Sonora, told an anecdote about two Mexican women who entertained a group of Forty-Niners with music on guitars and a tambourine. When the women played the familiar refrain of "Home, Sweet Home," the hardened miners wept from the memories of their pasts. Knowing full well what they had done, the two women left with their tambourine filled with donations of the miners' gold.[20]

As well as being sung on the stage, these sentimental tearjerkers were often sung in bordellos by any of the girls who might have a good singing voice, because the madams felt that men touched by sentimental ballads were more likely to spend freely and tip generously. (In a sense, these songs of pathos were early versions of the country-western songs perpetuated decades later by singers such as Hank Williams and Webb Pierce. Popular songs of both eras also emphasized the perils of drink.)

The tunes for many of the popular songs that traveled around the Old West were adapted from earlier melodies. The music for "The Streets of Laredo," for example, came originally from a 16th-century London street song about a young man dying of syphilis. As another example, the tune for the popular cowboy song "Red River Valley" was adapted from an 18th-century melody from New York called "The Bright Mohawk Valley."[21] The music for "The Cowboy's Dream" was the same as the older folk song "My Bonnie Lies Over the Ocean."

Music was also used in other ways. In the larger towns, a band often played in front of local theaters or dance halls to attract customers to the show inside. In an enterprising move, Ed Chase, the owner of three of the most popular theaters in Denver, had a brass band ride on a bus through the streets to promote his theaters. An added attraction that always piqued the interest of men was looking at the cancan girls who rode along with the musicians.

Other "teaser" acts might perform outdoors to try to attract potential customers and cajole them to the main show inside. In Leadville, Colorado, during the boom days of the 1880s, tightrope walkers and trapeze artists sometimes performed outdoors, attracting perhaps 2,000 or 3,000 people on a good night. Local newspapers reported that a very large crowd attended one of these performances at the corner of Pine Street and Harrison Avenue, on the south edge of town.

The Theaters Mature

Early theaters in the mining camps of the Old West frequently called themselves "grand," but were more likely to be quite crude in construction. For example, when The People's Theater in Virginia City, Montana, opened its doors, it proudly claimed to have "the most elegant appointments." In reality, the main hall was lined with muslin. In the interests of safety, it was crudely flame-proofed by soaking it in a solution of alum.[22] Uncomfortable wooden benches seated 250 and music was provided by an orchestra of four musicians. Other of the "elegant appointments" were a wood-burning stove and footlights that consisted of five candles. Winter temperatures in Montana frequently reached −40° F and, in spite of the large wood stove, the inside of the theater was often so cold that the shivering audience walked out during the performance. This was not unusual in the Rocky Mountain West. In 1859 the Cibola Minstrels played three nights a week at Reed's Theatre in Denver until the winter weather became so cold that the patrons could not stay warm.

Early Western theater stages were lit by candles or kerosene lamps. In the most primitive theaters, the candles might simply be stuck in empty whiskey bottles and lined up at the front of the stage. As towns grew larger and theaters developed in size and scope, the candles were replaced by chandeliers and stage lamps that used gas. One of the advantages of using gas was that the level of stage lighting could be varied by opening and closing the gas valves, thus raising or lowering the flames. The adjustments, however, were tricky and not always precise. If the operator erred and dimmed the footlights too low, the flames went out and the production had to pause while someone went out on stage to re-light the gas jets.

The use of gas had other hazards as well. At one opera performance in Denver, one of the stage hands turned on the gas to the lamps, but forgot to light them. As a result, the orchestra played the first act in the dark. The other unfortunate aspect was that members of the audience were almost gassed and left the theater complaining of violent headaches.

The invention of limelight, also known as "calcium light," replaced gas light with a more intense form of light that was about 750 times brighter than a candle. Limelight used a flame from a combination of oxygen and hydrogen to heat a cylinder of lime (calcium oxide) to incandescence. This type of lighting was more versatile for use. For example, limelight was used

These unusual theater lighting fixtures could use either illuminating gas (glass globes at top) or the newer electric light bulbs, at bottom (author's collection).

extensively in the popular musical extravaganza *The Black Crook* to simulate sunlight, moonlight, and rainbows.

The first working version was developed by Thomas Drummond, so this type of light was sometimes called a "Drummond Light." Its introduction allowed the development of early spotlights. The apparatus was built inside a metal box fitted with a lens to focus the light. This system was the basis for the expression "the limelight" for show business, and "being in the limelight" for being the focus of attention.

The use of limelight persisted until the arrival of electricity and the development of carbon filament lamps in 1879 by Thomas Edison. Electricity allowed the use of the even more powerful carbon arc spotlights.[23] Colored glass filters were used in front of the lens of the light to alter the color of the light and create different moods. By the turn of the century, all the major theaters were equipped with electric lights. Many large theaters were supplied by a theatrical lighting company founded in 1896 by the Kliegl Brothers, who invented a very bright electric arc light. Theater and motion picture lights are still nicknamed "klieg [sometimes spelled kleig] lights" after them.

As 1910 approached, theaters in large cities, such as Denver and San Francisco, were remodeled to hold from 1,000 seats to perhaps 2,000 or 3,000, in order to maximize profits for the owner and capitalize on the drawing power of major stars. Tickets for performances on the West Coast typically cost between a dollar and two dollars, except for exceptional shows. In this manner, major stars (such as Edwin Forrest) could make as much as $2,000 for a night's performance.

The larger theaters in the West were patterned after designs prevalent in New York. The main floor, which was previously "the pit," later the "parquet" or "parquette," became "the orchestra," containing the very expensive seats. Behind the orchestra, at the back of the theater, was the less-expensive "family circle." The first balcony became "the dress circle," replacing many of the previous patron's boxes. The cheaper seats were in the second balcony or the gallery, which was at the back of the first balcony. The third, or upper balcony in early New York theaters was often reserved for prostitutes and their customers, or for the very cheap seats. Prostitution provided additional income for theater owners.

Entertainers on Tour

In the second half of the 19th century, there were two widely separated theatrical worlds in the United States. One was New York, which was the theatrical capital of show business in America and where careers were made. The legitimate theaters were elegant and the audiences were sophisticated. But part of being a success in New York meant that an actor had to tour the rest of the country and, in particular, California. So, on the other side of the country, a second entertainment world revolved around San Francisco, which was the theatrical capital of the West Coast and paid the highest wages. Almost all famous actors and actresses appeared there at one time or another.

Whether they were stars, singers, family troupes, minstrel shows, or comics, performers had to tour to make money and stay on top of their success. Even major stars like Edwin Booth and Lotta Crabtree had to tour the West. The good part of touring was the fresh audiences in small towns, the enthusiastic applause, and the money. The bad part of touring was stagecoach breakdowns, weather-related and other travel delays, the lengthy time required for travel in the limitless spaces of the West, living temporarily in primitive boardinghouses and cheap hotels, and constantly eating in poor restaurants with equally poor food. Other discouraging components of extensive travel were the possibility of rain and snow, tiredness, companions who drank too much, the loneliness of being on the road, the social prejudice that was often attached to actors — and particularly to actresses — and problems with local theater managers. Another hazard for poorly performing shows was that baggage might be held or confiscated to pay for debts at a rooming house or theater.

As well as the physical surroundings of life on the road, working conditions could be challenging. Rehearsal time might be during the day for a show that same night. An actor or actress in a stock company might have to memorize multiple roles and parts from several different plays and songs for musical productions. The show generally had to go on in spite of tiredness, illness, or the loss of one of the players. Actors had to be good at ad-libbing to cover for others actors who forgot their lines, missed their cues, or went off on a drunken tangent.

Two aspects of life on the road in the Old West that were not easy for entertainers from the "civilized" East were potential Indian attacks and threats from outlaws and bandits who might hold them up. Popular actor Jack Langrishe and his wife were held up by bandits while on their way to Denver in 1862. Luckily for the duo, one of the villains recognized them from a previous stage show he had seen and so the miscreants set them free without robbing them.[24]

Early actors faced rough travel conditions to reach their audiences. Before the completion of the transcontinental railroad in 1868, methods of travel from New York to the West Coast were limited. There were three general ways to reach San Francisco in the 1850s and early 1860s. These were the same options that faced the early hopefuls traveling to the California gold fields. The first was to travel by stagecoach or wagon across the plains from the trailheads at Kanesville (now Council Bluffs), Iowa, and Independence, Missouri, along the Oregon Trail to the California Trail, and then south to the diggings in the Sierra Nevada Mountains. This was a lengthy journey that could take up to six months, and was not appealing to a famous actor or actress. Hail, rain, mud, storms, and other misfortunes and perils of the long journey west overtook many of the pioneers and the trails were littered with cast-off possessions from overloaded wagons and lined with the graves of those who died of disease and deprivation along the way.

The second way to reach San Francisco was to travel by ship from New York, Boston, Baltimore, or a similar Atlantic seaport down the east side of South America, around Cape Horn and its unpredictable weather, and up the west side of the South American continent to San Francisco. This was a mammoth journey of about 13,000 miles that took from five to eight months.

The third option, which was a variation of the second, was to travel by ship down the East Coast to the village of Chagres on the Atlantic side of the Isthmus of Panama, cross the 60 miles over land by boat, train, and mule to Panama City on the Pacific side, then catch another ship up the West Coast to San Francisco. If everything went smoothly, the Panama route cut the travel time to less than two months. Unfortunately, many travelers found that the jungle crossing of the Isthmus, with its high humidity and daily torrential

Before the arrival of the transcontinental railroad, actors and actresses often had to travel between engagements in the West by stagecoach, braving bad roads, uncertain weather, holdups, and possible Indian attacks (Glenn Kinnaman Colorado and Western History Collection).

rains, took far longer than that. Constant hazards to contend with on the way were malaria, cholera, and yellow fever. Hundreds of travelers fell ill with fever, and many died from illness and accidents. None of these three options was particularly appealing to show business people to whom time was money.

In the mid–1800s, acting companies were primarily "stock companies" that were typically repertory companies that had their own theater in a specific town. The company had a series of different melodramas or plays that were presented in rotation by the same actors and actresses, changing the play when audiences began to decline and demand new material. The group might travel to nearby towns, but opportunities for travel were limited by the available methods of transportation.

With the expansion of the railroad in the 1870s, the stock company was generally replaced by the "combination" company. This consisted of a major star, such as Edwin Booth, "combined" with lesser-known supporting actors. Under the combination system, the actors presented only one particular play, but moved rapidly from one town to the next, staying only a few days in each location. They traveled with all the necessary scenery, costumes, and props, requiring only a theater or lecture hall in which to set up and perform.

Consolidation in the 1870s reduced the number of stock companies touring the country presenting dramatic theater. In 1871, more than 50 stock companies were in operation in the larger cities across the country. After a nationwide financial crisis that began in 1873, this number had shrunk to between seven and ten by 1880. But, by 1886, approximately 260 combination companies were on tour across the country.

Luckily for actors, feverish building of railroads took place in the 1860s, primarily because of the needs of Union forces to move troops and supplies with greater efficiency during the Civil War. In 1850, there were about 9,000 miles of track to serve the entire country, but by 1870 this had increased to over 50,000 miles and, by 1880, to 80,000 miles. This massive expansion of the railroad system and completion of the transcontinental railroad made it easier for actors and theatrical troupes to travel to many towns in a short period of time. This made possible the "one-night stand," where performers could play for one performance only in a particular town, thus maximizing the profits for their efforts. The subsequent extensive network of rails that sprang up to connect small towns to the transcontinental route made it possible for theater troupes to go from town to town, week after week. Traveling companies could efficiently travel and perform in short periods of time from North Dakota to Texas and St. Louis to San Francisco. Prominent stars had their own private Pullman cars, while others used regular coaches. Popular actress Lillie Langtry had her own train.

When actress Olga Nethersole traveled the West, she was quoted as saying: "I have taken to the rolling home since leaving the East and I find it so delightful.... When I wish to rest I rest. When it pleases me to dine I dine, and my meals are prepared to please me."[25]

Being away from main railroad lines, however, made it difficult for some towns to host the best shows and actors. Aspen, Colorado, for example, had several theaters, but it was difficult to travel there across the Rocky Mountains from Denver, and it was not able to attract the best of the acts on the circuits until the arrival of the railroad on October 27, 1887. The Wheeler Opera House subsequently attracted some of the best talent on the traveling circuits. The Opera House was built in 1889 by Jerome B. Wheeler, who made his fortune in the East before investing heavily in the silver mining town, developing mines and building a hotel, a silver refinery, and the Opera House. (The theater still stands and is active today in summer theatrical productions.)

In spite of the obstacles involving travel, the latest New York shows toured extensively in the Old West. A motley horde of variety entertainers and touring companies criss-crossed the country, taking advantage of the economical method of rail transportation to travel to remote towns. By the 1870s and 1880s, thousands of actors were visiting the West, performing in melodramas, comedies, farces, and variety shows.

The easy transportation of the railroad made it convenient to make relatively brief stops. Because the potential audience in many towns was small by today's standards, theaters had to have a constant variety of playbills to keep drawing audiences. Small towns often had three different shows a week to keep ticket sales up and the theaters full. Entertainers usually played only three or four performances in any one town; therefore troupes usually spent only two or three days in one place and then moved on.

The alternative for a troupe permanently based in a particular town was to present several different plays each week. This meant that the actors had to remember the lines for three different performances a week, along with the script from any other short skits and songs that they presented.

Another approach was to do what Jack Langrishe did when he leased The People's Theater in Virginia City, Montana. He presented several short runs of shows at selected times of the year when he thought could draw enough audiences that it would be financially worthwhile.

As the volatile boom towns of the mining years faded away in the West and large cities became established, travel around a theater circuit by entertainment troupes declined as they secured permanent home bases. The smaller towns and theaters were visited only by less-skilled acts who came through town offering single performances.

Accommodations

Finding a place to sleep while on the road in a booming mining camp or a cattle town full of cowboys could be a problem. Even rooms for residents were often so hard to find that it was not uncommon for workers in mining towns to share rooms and sleep in shifts when they were off work. One miner might use a bed in a communal dormitory for eight hours, then when he was at work, another man occupied the bed. A third probably had the bed for the remaining eight hours. This made it difficult for traveling actors to find accommodations.

The Tabor Opera House in Leadville came up with a creative solution. The third floor of the theater had 25 hotel rooms that were part of the Clarendon Hotel, next door to the south, to accommodate the players in the theater below. The theater and the hotel were connected by a covered walkway so that theater patrons and actors could cross between the two buildings without going outside in the deep snow of winter.

Even this type of arrangement did not always solve the rooming problems. When entertainer Eddie Foy arrived in Leadville in 1878, the town was booming with growth from silver mining, and lodgings were hard to come by. He found that there were no rooms for rent — a common problem in the bustling town. Foy and some of his fellow actors solved the problem by sleeping on mattresses on the stage after the last performance each night.[26]

Accommodations in a booming town could be chancy at best. One actor who had a room over a saloon when he appeared in Virginia City, Nevada, complained that he could hardly sleep at night for the noise of arguing and fighting in the room below because the patrons drank all night. The last straw for him came one night when a bullet fired from a gun in the saloon below came through the floor and missed his head by a hair's breadth. Literally. It grazed his ear and carried away one of his graying locks in the process.

Two

Entertainment for Everyone

Typical movie renditions of entertainment in the Old West consist of images of attractive, long-legged women in fancy short dresses dancing the cancan in a saloon filled with gamblers, cowboys, and bar girls. While this type of entertainment certainly existed in saloons in cattle towns and mining camps, there was far more to popular entertainment in the Old West. Minstrelsy, burlesque, and variety shows were the predominant forms of light entertainment that were popular after the Civil War. Other forms of entertainment were melodrama, farce, musical comedy, and operas. In the early mining camps, even itinerant preachers and temperance workers were considered to be a type of entertainment.

Not all theater performances consisted of the vulgar dances and skits that were popular in concert saloons and early variety theaters. Many cowboys and miners liked wholesome entertainment rather than bawdy stage romps. Entertainment presented in theaters, therefore, ran the gamut from comedic song-and-dance men to opera and classically trained actors. An enjoyable evening's entertainment might consist of dramatic readings from Shakespeare.

Some of the lighter fare in entertainment that toured the West were the Famous Georgia Minstrels, the New London Gaiety Girls, and the Miners Merry Burlesquers. A typical playbill for the evening entertainment at McDaniels New Theater in Cheyenne, Wyoming, featured a fancy dance by La Petite Lizzie, clog dancing by Walter Parks, ballads by Fannie Garrettson, dances by Mlle. Cerito, songs by Ella Newell, Ella Martell, and Maggie Louise, and short sketches by various entertainers, along with vocal and instrumental entertainment by the entire "ladies and gentlemen of the company."[1]

Even American Indians put on shows. In the winter of 1857, the Washoe Indians of western Nevada faced a critical lack of food. To avoid starvation their leader, Captain Jim, hatched a plot. He spread the word among the local settlers that his tribe was going to put on a fandango, demonstrating Indian

23

Posters such as this attracted male audiences who were eager to see women in tights (Library of Congress).

dancing and pagan rituals.[2] He said that, as a gift of friendship, each attendee should bring two sacks of flour. In return, the tribe would give each of the audience a return gift of friendship that was a tanned deer hide. The local miners and white settlers were thrilled and, on the appointed evening, showed up with their sacks of flour. The Indians put on a good show of dancing, drumming, and singing. After the show, as promised, each miner received a cured, tanned deer skin as a gift of friendship. The tribe warded off starvation with plenty of flour to last the winter. It wasn't until later that the miners realized that they had traded two eight-dollar sacks of flour for a buckskin worth one dollar.

Opera

Contrary to the image of bawdy dances and skits in a saloon theater, opera was a popular form of entertainment that arrived early in the West. The infant town of Denver was only six years old when its first operatic performance was given on December 8, 1864, by a Mr. and Mrs. Gruenwald. The duo, both members of the San Francisco Opera Company, were traveling from San Francisco to New York when they were stranded in Denver by a heavy winter snowstorm. Because they were stuck, they decided that they might as well put on a concert. Culture lovers reportedly enjoyed the performance, but some of the rough and ready miners were not as lavish in their praise of high opera. The Gruenwalds later went on to perform in Central City, which was located in the mountains about 30 miles west of Denver.

Examples of operas that were well-received by Western audiences were *The Bohemian Girl, Maritana, Matilda, Il Trovatore, Fra Diavolo, Olivette,* and *Faust.* Productions of works by Verdi, Donizetti, Rossini, and Mozart were all presented on Western stages.

Light opera was popular, as well as the more serious type. Notable were the comic operas of the talented British team of librettist W.S. Gilbert and composer Arthur Sullivan. Their *H.M.S. Pinafore* successfully debuted in the United States in New York in 1878 and set the standard for comic opera for the rest of the century. This song-filled production debuted on the West Coast in 1879 in San Francisco, where the Tivoli Opera House drew full houses for 63 consecutive nights.

Another popular import from Britain was the musical *Floradora*, which was highlighted by music, dancing, and pretty girls. In 1900 the show ran for more than 500 performances. Starting in 1893, the light operas of Victor Herbert, such as *Mlle. Modiste, Babes in Toyland,* and *Naughty Marietta,* were also well-received.

Legitimate Theater

Legitimate theater, as opposed to the entertainment available in the variety or saloon theater, brought some culture to Western towns. Traveling troupes allowed local audiences to see famous actors and popular plays from the East, and gave some validity and status to an infant mining camp.

Serious plays presented by touring companies ranged from Shakespeare to melodramas. As befitted Victorian times, most plays had a moral and uplifting theme. So much so that early plays were often labeled as "moral lectures," in order to attract and be acceptable to audiences who looked down on "the theater." A series of such plays was presented by James and Louisa Lord, who toured the West in 1869 and 1870 with an accompanying troupe of players.

Actors did not always perform complete Shakespearean plays, but often presented excerpts consisting of the dramatic and comedic highlights of a particular play, such as *Hamlet* or *Julius Caesar,* or from a series of plays. Even though such presentations would seem to create an atmosphere of serious drama, programs were usually balanced by a short farce that concluded the evening's entertainment. The titles of these comedies, such as *A Peep into the Seraglio* or *The Guardian Outwitted*, gives an indication of the lack of seriousness that was presented. Even the somber mood of Shakespeare's darker plays might be broken as jugglers, dancers, acrobats, and singers performed in front of the curtains between acts.

Many English plays were performed on Western stages, because there were no international copyright laws at the time and these plays could be performed without the payment of royalties. As a result, many of the actors who appeared in the West were Shakespearean performers from Great Britain. The popularity of Shakespeare was possibly in part because he wrote for the masses and partly because audiences in the Old West may have identified with some of the plays' values and tastes. Some of the audiences' enthusiasm may also have been due to the flamboyant acting styles of many of the traveling actors and to the ribald material that some of the plays contain. Shakespearean plays were so popular in southwest New Mexico that miners named the town of Shakespeare after him. After touring the U.S. in the 1830s, Alexis de Tocqueville commented that even isolated cabins in the Far West normally contained a book of Shakespeare.[3]

As well as being presented in their original form, Shakespeare's plays were favorite targets for burlesque. Hamlet might appear in a fur cap and snowshoes, and quote the most outrageous parodies of the original lines. These burlesque characters might suddenly break into minstrel melodies, complete with banjo accompaniment. The fact that rough-and-ready Western audiences could easily understand these parodies, and why they were funny in relation to the original plays, says much about the popularity of the original plays.

Shakespearean plays were very popular in the California gold camps, particularly such spectacles as *Richard III*, *Othello*, and *Julius Caesar*. Also popular were productions that featured a particular star, such as Edwin Booth playing King Lear or Edwin Forrest as Macbeth.

Two of the distinguished actors who played in Shakespearean dramatic theater were Junius Brutus Booth and his son Edwin, both of whom played Hamlet all over the West. When Edwin performed for the Forty-Niners, he reportedly made as much as $25,000 a month when he was on tour. This was an amazing amount when one considers that a common miner made $3 a day.

Shakespeare was so popular that even mainstream actresses took on some of the male roles. In spite of the seeming gender difference, it was not unusual for a woman to play a male part in Victorian theater productions — even in Shakespearean plays — in order to prove that their technical acting skills were as good as a man's. The legitimate actress Sarah Bernhardt, for example, frequently played her famous interpretation of Hamlet in a feminized male costume.

Victorian Melodrama

One very popular type of theater in the decades following the Civil War was melodrama. Melodrama was essentially a morality tale in which a situation fraught with peril was resolved by the strong action of the hero, who was the heroine's true love. Melodramas, such as *The Widow's Victim*, *A Husband's Vengeance*, and *Ten Nights in a Bar-room*, had a strong appeal to Victorian morals and principles. To create sensational productions, Victorian melodrama frequently added natural disasters to the staging, such as earthquakes, fires, floods, and tidal waves, or other spectacles, such as horse races,

The Sixth Street Theater in Wallace, Idaho, is housed in the former Lux Building (1891), that was previously a hardware store and had a bordello upstairs from 1899 to 1977. The theater presents melodramas in the summer (author's collection).

trains, and shipwrecks, that challenged the resources of even a large well-equipped theater.

The name "melodrama" comes from Greek words that combine "song" and "drama," because songs and musical accompaniment played a major part in the original form of these productions. The American roots of melodrama were in British theater, but date back as far as classical Greek drama, which combined the actors' words with a musical background. The theatrical form evolved into a drama with sensational action, extravagant acting, and a happy ending. The downward spiral into temptation and shame of one or more of the major characters, followed by their eventual salvation, was considered to be the perfect combination of plotting. Moral stories that involved vices, such as drink, gambling, and temptation of an innocent heroine, were favorite plots.

Later melodrama bordered on the unrealistic by exaggerating highly stereotyped characters and presenting flamboyant staging. These dramas were purposely intended to be an escape from reality and the daily grind of mining, lumbering, or cattle raising, by providing an evening of fantasy and a peek at other people's troubles. The most popular were those that provided emotional conflict and vivid scenic effects, such as Eliza crossing the frozen ice floes on the Ohio River in *Uncle Tom's Cabin*.

The music that accompanied Victorian melodrama was used in two ways. One was that music was used to increase the emotions of the audience and provide dramatic tension. Fast staccato music could heighten suspense at the appropriate times, whereas slower melodies were used as a background to romantic interludes and settings. This mechanism continued on into the musical accompaniment used for early silent movies. The second way that accompanying music was used was to identify various characters with their own musical theme. This was called "signature music," a theatrical device that is still used in motion pictures today.

The stories in melodramas had tight plotting and colorful dialog. They offered reassurance and hope to everyday folks that, after multiple setbacks and near disasters, goodness, right, and justice would prevail. Plots were generally simple and the characters were essentially one-dimensional, either very good or very bad. Evil and corruption in the villain and goodness in the hero and heroine were easy to identify, though occasionally a humorous character was added for some comic relief.

Melodrama became a theatrical art form where virtue and villainy were played against each other in their purest distillation. In this way, the moral qualities of the characters were reduced to their fundamentals. The villain posed a threat that was eventually overcome by the virtue of the heroine and hero. In playing these parts, the actors made their characters larger than life.

The characters' emotions were amplified, their gestures were exaggerated, and their social roles were emphasized, so that the players appeared to be governed by their emotions and the play's conflicts were reduced to essential elements.

The classic plot of Victorian melodrama was that the hero and heroine were in love, but their rightful union was blocked by various obstacles. The heroine was usually forced by circumstances to choose between her feelings of love for the hero and her sense of duty. The themes of dire predicaments and perilous circumstances that plagued the major characters were perfect for the members of the emerging working class of the late 19th century.

The moral theme behind the plots of most melodramas was that the ideal Victorian lifestyle for a woman was true love, with subsequent married life and domestic bliss. Popular themes were sentimentality, patriotism, democracy, moral values, and the virtues of common people. Melodramas also tackled some of the serious issues of the time, such as slavery and the ever-popular themes of temperance and excessive drink.

To understand the theme of virtue prevalent in Victorian melodramas, it is necessary to appreciate the prevailing attitudes towards young women. The Victorians placed a very high value on virginity in a bride; any fall from purity for a young woman was considered to be scandalous and a cause for expulsion from the home. In this light, the morals described in melodramas were clear and simple. The chaste heroine's choice would be between the love of a poor but honest man (miner, logger, farmer, whomever) and her duty to marry the corrupt villain in order to save the family honor or redeem the mortgage. Typically, her virtue (for Victorian times read "virginity") was at stake. The heroine symbolized Virtue (with a capital "V"), goodness, purity, love, and Victorian delicacy. She was an earthly — but innocent — angel, and was highly vulnerable to the scheming villain. Though illicit sex was hinted at in these morality plays, it was never blatant. Victorian morality dictated that the heroine had to be kept in peril of temptation or seduction for several acts, before being rescued at the end of the melodrama.

Classic melodrama dialogue, such as the following, was delivered with a straight face:

VILLAIN (menacingly): You must play the rent.
BLONDE HEROINE (hands held up in horror and eyes wide): No, no. I can't pay the rent.
VILLAIN (smirking and twirling his mustache): Yes, yes. You *must* pay the rent.

The way in which she was able to pay the rent without compromising her virtue and be reunited with her true love was the essence of the story.

A typical plot revolved around the vulnerable heroine, who had been cast out by the landlord or her father, at the same time pursued by a villain attracted by her youth and virtue, and involved temptation in the form of drink, or drugs, or illicit sex. The villain was usually some rich man, such as a scheming landlord, an oppressive boss, an overbearing businessman, or a tyrannical father, thus stereotyping those in power over the so-called "little guy." This type of plot reflected a widespread suspicion by the lower classes of the upper classes.

A stock set of characters usually defined these plays. First, there was the hero: a poor but honest working man who was wronged or falsely accused, but who vanquished his opponents at the end of the play. The heroine was a working girl who was beset by temptations and perilous situations. The villain, supported by various heavies who were his henchmen, was a wealthy businessman who took advantage of the hero and tried to make off with the heroine. Comic relief, between the emotional scenes, was provided by an ethnic character, typically an Irish or German man. He usually paired off with a woman in a secondary role, who was a friend and supporter of the heroine during her trials and tribulations. There was often another secondary female character who was in league with the villain. As some of the dialog was often lost in the noisy theaters of the times, these characters were easier for the audiences to follow if they filled predefined roles as stock characters.

Victorian melodrama presented in the gold camps was typified by a play called *My Partner*, by Bartley Campbell, which was the story of friendship, estrangement, jealousy, and the associated tribulations of life in a mining camp. The play recounts the story of the friendship of two miners, Ned and Joe, and their common love for Mary Brandon, the hotel owner's daughter. Ned, who comes from an upper-class background, impregnates Mary — in itself an unusual plot twist for Victorian times, but note the evil "upper class" categorization — before he is murdered by the villain, Josiah Scraggs. To try to make the situation right for Mary, Joe marries her, but is falsely accused of Ned's murder. Scraggs is eventually revealed as the murderer, and Joe is freed and united again with Mary.

A play called *East Lynne* was a sentimental tear-jerker that drew audiences into the theaters again and again. A billboard announcing its arrival in a mining camp or other small Western town would bring patrons out in droves. The play, based on a best-selling 1861 novel by Ellen (Mrs. Henry) Wood, became one of the most popular plays in U.S. history.

The story revolves around a stately home named East Lynne. In brief, Lady Isabel elopes with her lover, a scoundrel by the name of Sir Francis Levinson, is abandoned by him, then returns to East Lynne disguised as a governess to care for her son Willie, who "dies" onstage with great pathos. In agreement with Victorian morality, which required just retribution for transgressors, she dies at the end of the play. The characters and plot preached to the audience about Victorian domestic ideals and roles, the values of home and family, and the respectability of the Victorian class structure.

Arguably the most popular melodrama of the late 19th century was *Uncle Tom's Cabin; or, Life Among the Lowly.* Harriet Beecher Stowe's novel of the same name was first published in 1852 and sold 300,000 copies in its first year. Stowe refused to give her permission for an adaptation into a play; however, copyright laws being somewhat loose in the 1850s, the plot was rapidly pirated anyway and she did not receive any compensation. The first stage adaptation followed quickly and was performed in Troy, New York, on September 27, 1852. Various other versions appeared on the stage soon after and touring companies were on the road by 1854. Not all of them were faithful adaptations of the original novel. Characters and scenes were added and deleted at will, depending on what the producer thought would be popular. Singers, minstrel acts, tap dancers, animals, and pugilists — even a steamboat race — were added by various adapters. The bloodhounds weren't added until 1879. Interestingly, the obligatory pursuit of Eliza by bloodhounds (usually played by mastiffs or Great Danes[4]) across the frozen Ohio River on the stage was not part of the original novel, but it was probably the scene that made the most impression on theater audiences. In the 1890s, some 400 different troupes were presenting the play across the country.

Uncle Tom's Cabin, along with the temperance plays *The Drunkard* and *Ten Nights in a Bar-room*, had a strong appeal to upright families who did not feel that the theater was an appropriate place for entertainment and enjoyment. Instead, they saw these three shows as uplifting morality messages, and flocked to the theater — and later to performances at traveling medicine shows — to wallow in them.

Given the unpredictable nature of some Western audiences, even *Uncle Tom's Cabin* might involve an unexpected outcome, such as happened in 1882 when the popular play was being presented at the Bird Cage Theatre in Tombstone, Arizona. At the point in the play where Eliza crossed the river with the bloodhounds pursuing her, a drunken cowboy, thinking to "rescue" her, stood up and shot one of the trained dogs who was the "pack" of hounds. The horrified audience grabbed him and beat him up. The next day, the man sobered up, was filled with remorse, and compensated the dog's owner.[5]

This was not the only shooting in the Bird Cage's theater that involved the audience and actors. Western notable Calamity Jane, who appeared in mining camps all over the West, took a shot at a villain on the stage. Luckily, she had so much to drink that she missed him completely.[6]

Between the acts of a play, variety acts were often presented in front of the curtain, in order to keep the audience's attention while the next scene was being prepared. Jugglers, acrobats, trained animals, singers, dancers, and comedians were popular fill-ins. Even legitimate theater wasn't always immune from the needs of the manager to gain and hold the attention of the audience. When Sarah Bernhardt played in *Camille* during her first American tour, she was disturbed to find that the acts of the play were broken up by cancan dancers and a xylophone player.

Minstrel Shows

Not all entertainment presented on the stage was serious drama. As a forerunner to vaudeville, minstrel shows offered exuberant entertainment in rousing form, with shouting and hollering, jokes and laughter, and lively dances. In contrast to melodramas and serious plays, there was no intricate plot to follow or complex characterization to study. The songs, dances, skits, and jokes of the minstrel show provided rousing escapism.

Minstrel shows were a unique form of American show business. The concept of white men in blackface makeup calling themselves "Ethiopian delineators" and claiming to use Negro dialect, songs, dances, and jokes as a form of entertainment would seem to be unusual, to say the least. However,

Show poster for William West's Big Minstrel Jubilee, showing comedian Billy Van with and without his stage make-up (Library of Congress).

minstrel shows turned out to be one of the most popular types of entertainment between the Civil War and the turn of the 20th century.[7] This theatrical form had a major impact on later burlesque and vaudeville.

Minstrel shows also perpetuated stereotypes of Negroes for a long time after this type of show had virtually disappeared. Though the entertainers claimed to authentically portray American Negroes, the shows were a parody of folk characters in America and did not at all accurately reflect the life or culture of black people.

One of the unique features of minstrelsy was the actors' costumes and actions. Though the actors originally claimed to authentically depict Negro songs and dances, their makeup and actions were gross caricatures of any real people. The greasepaint or burnt cork used for "blacking up" was not realistic, even though it was striking in its theatrical impact.[8] The color was exaggerated in its total blackness, because, in reality, it should have been various shades of brown. The result was a type of black-and-white clown makeup with large eyes and gaping mouths, exaggerated at the top by a black wooly wig. Instead of being merely makeup, it was a stark theatrical mask that was intended to be part of the show and emphasize the stereotype.

The rest of the costume was also a caricature, with the clothes made from wildly colored, baggy, mismatched patchwork cloth and the feet encased in huge shoes. Even the actors' movements were highly exaggerated, and consisted of rolling the eyes, cocking the head at odd angles, and twisting the legs, arms, and bodies into jerky, contorted positions. In hindsight, these negative elements were acceptable only if it was clearly understood that the men and women who acted in these shows were merely entertainers trying to amuse the audience and did not represent real racial characteristics. This also has to be taken in the context of contemporary social values. Most white Americans at the time considered that the Civil War had settled the "Negro question" and were not concerned with stereotypes of black performers. Many Northerners felt that minstrel shows were an accurate depiction of the South, and Southerners accepted the image of the happy, singing field worker.

Though minstrel acts had appeared early in the 1820s, the father of American minstrelsy is generally considered to be Thomas Dartmouth "Daddy" Rice, a white entertainer who first performed a blackface song and dance act in 1828. He portrayed an old black slave named Jim Crow, after he supposedly watched an elderly, crippled Negro singing and dancing a peculiar jerky dance.[9] Others feel that Rice may have received his inspiration from Negroes dancing informally in the Bowery district of New York, where he lived. Whatever the source, Rice expanded this material into a solo full-length act that immediately became very popular. By 1832 he was performing a full-length program of blackface songs at New York's Bowery Theatre.

Other similar minstrel acts followed. A major contribution to the expansion of minstrelsy occurred in 1842 when the Rhythm Minstrels put together a complete show of blackface in New York City. The first minstrel groups were small, consisting of four to six performers. In 1842, Daniel Decatur Emmett created a group called The Virginia Minstrels, who presented an entire program of singing and dancing in blackface, accompanied by violin, banjo, tambourine, and bone castanets. The group was made up of Emmett, Frank Brower, Dick Pelham, and Billy Whitlock. Their first public appearance was on February 6, 1843, at the Bowery Amphitheatre. In 1855, Emmett opened the first minstrel hall in Chicago.

By 1850, the minstrel show had evolved into a standardized format of three parts. In the first part, the blackface cast sat in a semicircle with a white-face cast member called the "interlocutor" seated in the center, and two eccentrically dressed blackface comedians placed at either end (thus logically named the "end men"). The interlocutor was the master of ceremonies and the onstage show director. The customary names for the end men were Tambo and Bones, names which referred to the instruments they played. One played the tambourine. The other played the "bones," which were banged together to form a rhythmic, clacking sound, like Spanish castanets.[10] Other accompanying musical instruments were typically a banjo and fiddle. As part of the show, the interlocutor posed questions and riddles to the end men and other members of the company, that led into songs and dances. Probably the most-quoted famous corny joke used was: "Why is the letter T like an island?" The answer: "Because it is in the middle of water!" Another was the hoary old universal joke that asked: "Why did the chicken cross the road?"

The first part of the show typically started with an upbeat song by the entire cast. This was followed by individual songs and dances, though some pieces again featured the entire group. The cast encouraged the audience to join in the performance by clapping their hands, stamping their feet, whistling, shouting, and singing along. The performers wanted audience involvement and most of the songs were easy to sing along with, such as "The Old Grey Goose," "Turkey in the Straw," "Old Dan Tucker," "Sweet Betsy from Pike," and the "Blue Tail Fly." Vigorous audience participation resulted in a distinctive entertainment style that made the entire performance upbeat and raucous. Many of the songs became popular entertainment among settlers and around emigrant campfires precisely because they were popularized by traveling minstrel shows.

Songs ranged from sentimental tear-jerkers to foolish nonsense songs. After the minstrel show became popular, many songs were written by professional white composers, such as Stephen Foster, who knew nothing about authentic southern Negro music. Many of these songs, such as "The Old

Folks at Home," "Camptown Races," and "Oh, Susannah," became very popular and appeared as standards in minstrel shows.

Dances varied from serious dances to lively Irish jigs. These individual performances were interspersed with rapid-fire jokes between the interlocutor and the end men.[11] The interlocutor used precise English, but the end men told their jokes, puns, and riddles colored by a heavy Negro dialect. The first part of the performance closed with another upbeat musical number by the entire group.

Often there was no fixed script for the show, so the interlocutor was able to change the show, depending on his perception of the mood and tastes of the audience during the performance. As a result, the entire group had to be good at ad-libbing and improvisation.

After an intermission, the second part started. This was the olio, which was a musical miscellany. The olio, consisting of a succession of songs and dances interspersed with comedy and novelty acts (some of which involved frantic slapstick and outright farce), often resulting in a wild, uninhibited performance by all. The acts presented depended on the talents of the particular actors in the show. Popular features of this part were a humorously mangled version of a politician's stump speech and a "wench" who sang sentimental or romantic songs in a high falsetto. The wench was played by a white male with blackface make-up and in a woman's costume.[12] Though the wench role had been appearing since the 1840s, this character became a staple of minstrel performances in the 1870s. Because of the light yellow make-up these female impersonators used, they were nicknamed "yaller gals." Males in the audience were fascinated by the cross-gender roles. Women reluctantly admired the fashionable gowns.[13] This was not the traditional female buffoon role, where burly, unshaven men acted female roles for comedy, wearing outlandish outfits and producing obvious parody. Instead, these performers created earnest illusions of female entertainers.

Francis Leon (stage name "Leon") was one actor who began as a minstrel wench, but moved into more serious female impersonation, wearing beautiful costumes and singing light opera in the part of the heroine. Another of the popular female illusionists was William Dalton (stage name Julian Eltinge), who appeared in minstrel shows, and later in vaudeville and musical comedies, as a professional female impersonator. Audiences and reviewers were mixed in their reaction to this obvious display of cross-dressing and gender confusion.

Conversely, women performing serious impersonations of men also appeared on the stage, though this form of entertainment was never particularly popular in America. These were not the burlesque-type of male impersonation, where the women portrayed men while wearing tights and short costumes in order to show off their legs, but were serious attempts to create the persona of a male. One of the most popular was Vesta Tilley from England, who first appeared in vaudeville in New York in 1894. She created the image of a dashing man-about-town and sang light music-hall songs.[14]

The third part of the minstrel show was a one-act comedy sketch, often based on a popular piece of literature or drama.

The olio section of the show later separated and emerged by itself as the variety show. Over a number of years, variety shows evolved into a format that included an opening production number that prominently featured the female members of the company, followed by the individual acts of comedians, jugglers, magicians, and a variety of novelty acts.

Black minstrelsy increased after the Civil War and the popularity of minstrel shows rapidly spread across the country. From about the mid–1840s to the 1870s, minstrelsy was probably the most popular form of entertainment in the United States. A good example of this popularity was the San Francisco Minstrels, starring Charlie Backus and Billy Birch, which was originally founded in San Francisco in 1853 by Tom Maguire. In 1865, the troupe opened in New York and was so popular that they played there for the next 19 years. This was the longest run in one place of any minstrel troupe.[15] Minstrel shows also used burlesque as part of their repertoire. In 1873, Bryant's Minstrels presented the parody *Cinderella in Black*.

Minstrelsy was originally an all-male form of entertainment. This changed as the shows evolved. Musical shows featuring female minstrels were a routine part of New York theaters by the 1870s, though women had sporadically appeared in them earlier. By 1871, 11 all-female troupes were performing. Typically, these shows featured young women in whiteface in dances and minstrel bands, with the end men remaining in blackface.

Less Conventional Forms of Entertainment

GETTING RELIGION

For entertainment-hungry miners, traveling circuit preachers often unwittingly acted as a form of entertainment. Listening to a vibrant parson ranting and raving about saving men's souls was considered by many to be high entertainment. Some of the more vocal of the itinerant preachers were known to ramble on for two or three hours before tiring out.

If an early mining town had no regular church building, these itinerant preachers often used the local saloon. The nude paintings behind the bar would be discreetly draped and the bar covered over for the duration of the service. The "professor," as the piano player in a saloon or bordello was often known, might accompany the hymns on his honky-tonk piano.[16] Most saloon owners didn't particularly mind this interruption of trade as they knew that the audience of miners would be very thirsty again after the preacher was finished.

The outcome of this dose of religion might be more than just entertainment. Two preachers and a band of lady missionaries preached so well in the Close and Patterson Saloon in Las Vegas, New Mexico, that they baptized four gamblers and 15 bar girls.[17] Rather than sporadic events, religious services in saloons were routine occurrences.

Religion affected entertainment in other, more subtle ways. The miners' rowdy entertainment in the boom town of Dawson, in the Yukon Territory, for example, was shut down from midnight every Saturday until 2 A.M. Monday morning in observance of the Sabbath. All saloons, dance halls, theaters, and business houses were shuttered, and no work of any kind was allowed on Sunday. Some theater owners tried to get around these restrictions in a variety of ways. One method was to have "sacred concerts" of religious music and take up a cash collection afterwards.

Listening to a fiery preacher was considered entertainment for bored miners. Church services, featuring hell-fire preachers, were often held in simple wooden buildings, like this chapel (author's collection).

WALKING THE PLANK

One of the stranger forms of entertainment in the early West was the short-lived phenomenon of plank-walking. In December of 1865, "Yankee" Driggs rented Stonewall Hall, in Virginia City, Montana, and sold tickets for people to watch him walk on a wooden plank. For this magnificent feat, he placed an 18-foot-long plank on supports about 18 inches above the floor and walked back and forth on it for 36 hours. Surprisingly, this seemingly repetitive entertainment attracted enough viewers that he made enough money to start his own business in a tin shop.[18] The popularity of the sport did not last long, however. In an even more ambitious move, Driggs decided to stage an endurance contest at Virginia City's Shebang Saloon between himself and C.W. Blunt for what he styled the plank-walking championship of Montana Territory. The marathon started well enough, but the two decided to stop after 49 continuous hours due to lack of interest by spectators — and mostly a lack of ticket sales. After this ignominious end, the peculiar sport of plank-walking was not heard of again in Montana.

A similar contest was held at the Bird Cage Theater in Tombstone when John Forseck and John McGarvin staged a walking competition. They walked around and around the interior of the theater on a specially constructed track for over six hours. This walking contest didn't appeal to the audience and the disappointed management never staged one again.

TEMPERANCE LECTURES

Though drinking was a major form of self-entertainment among early miners, loggers, and cowboys of the Old West, not everyone was in favor of alcohol. Women's groups believed that undesirable male urges were intensified by "demon rum." A typical woman's anti-drinking slogan was: "Lips that touch liquor shall never touch mine."

As civilization spread across the West, anti-saloon leagues sprang up to declaim the evils of drink and drunkenness. Groups, such as the Woman's Christian Temperance Union (WCTU), founded in 1874, were organized to combat the perceived alcohol problem. By 1890, the WCTU had about 160,000 members. Ironically, anti-saloon lectures were often given in saloons, presumably for the lecturer to be close to his audience.

In the 1870s, the residents of Leadville, Colorado, considered their town to have such a drinking problem — which may have been true — that they founded the Blue Ribbon Society, the Leadville Temperance Club, the Praying Orchestra, and the Anti-Treat Society.

Miners and other saloon patrons, who were avid drinkers themselves, loved to listen to lectures that involved their favorite pastime. Crusaders who were particularly popular were those who claimed to have been former drunkards. Vivid descriptions of how a reformed man previously got roaring drunk and either beat his wife or broke the heart of his true love, and spent the money on alcohol that was supposed to feed and clothe the children, were considered to be high entertainment. The speakers tended to launch into hyperbole and exaggerated descriptions that made the lecture all the more engaging.

One of the popular melodramas that made endless rounds of Western towns was *The Drunkard; or, The Fallen Saved*, written by actor William H. Smith and an anonymous co-author. First performed in 1844 at P.T. Barnum's Boston Museum, this was one of the most popular of the melodramas with a temperance message. The play focused on several of the favorite subjects that scandalized proper Victorian folk as it followed the decline of Edward Middleton while he succumbed to the perils of drink. Included were messages about the evils of alcohol, the villainies of city lawyers, the plight of an innocent heroine who marries for love, and a villain who tries to destroy a happy marriage. Typical scenes of the heart-wrenching drama were Edward drinking in a tavern, his wife sewing shirts by candlelight to earn money to feed his daughter, and the child shivering in threadbare rags.

The play included a frighteningly realistic representation of *delirium tremens* (also known in the vernacular as "the horrors," "the rams," or the "jimjams"), where the actor had to scream and writhe on the floor as his character succumbed to the evils of drink. In a typical Victorian melodramatic ending, though, the hero was redeemed from being a drunkard and rejoined his wife and family. The final message was that love and everyday people can win against the evil influences of the villain. The moral was that the protagonist was redeemed after taking The Pledge not to drink.

The early temperance movement led to another of the most popular plays of the Victorian period. Riding on a wave of temperance sentiment, Timothy Shay Arthur from Philadelphia wrote a story called *Ten Nights in a Bar-room*, in 1854. Its stage adaptation (by William W. Pratt) opened in New York in 1858 at the National Theatre. It became one of the most popular plays in America, probably second in popularity only to *Uncle Tom's Cabin*.

The playbill self-righteously proclaimed: "It has reformed many a drunkard." An advertisement for a performance of December 29, 1865, trumpeted that the play was about "folly, misery, madness and crime caused by the brutal, disgusting, and demoralizing vice of drunkenness." When asked by the tavern owner what led to his downfall, the protagonist replies: "You. Rum. Eternal curse on you. Had it not been for your infernal poison shops in our village, I had still been a man."[19] This type of rhetoric appealed strongly to Victorian anti-liquor sentiments, and the play was strongly supported by the Anti-Saloon League and the Woman's Christian Temperance Union.

The play was set primarily in the Sickle and Sheaf, a local tavern, and focused on the descent of Joe Morgan into "vile and debased drunkenness." His daughter Mary came to the saloon every night to plead with him to come home, and sang the famous lines:

> Father, dear father, come home with me now!
> The clock in the steeple strikes one.
> You said you were coming right home from the shop,
> As soon as your day's work was done.[20]

Joe becomes reformed after his "angel child," Little Mary, dies after a quarrel in the saloon that results in her being hit on the head by a rum glass thrown by the saloon-keeper, Slade, and reciting the immortal line: "Father! Dear, father! They have killed me!" Joe returns: "I'll never risk another drop of liquor as long as I live." He then becomes a teetotaler and is reunited with his wife. In another burst of Victorian moral retribution, the saloon owner dies at the hands of his own son who has become a drunkard also, and liquor is banned from the town.

These anti-liquor plays often included a diatribe against alcohol spoken directly to the audience by one of the characters, including a strong suggestion that the town where the play was being presented be voted dry by the populace.

One staunch advocate of temperance was P.T. Barnum. Originally a drinker and wine enthusiast, Barnum's change of heart occurred when he visited Saratoga in 1847 and observed drunkenness among many of the fashionable visitors.[21] After taking The Pledge, he promoted abstinence to his friends, then introduced temperance lectures and plays to his museum.

Not all anti-saloon crusaders were male. One of the first was Sarah Pellet, who journeyed to California in 1854 to save men from themselves. She planned to make her living by giving temperance lectures. She traveled to Weaverville and immediately tried to persuade the townspeople to pass a law prohibiting liquor. Her proposition to them was that if the town would ban alcohol, she would recruit 5,000 young women from the East to be potential wives for the miners. Nothing resulted from either side of the agreement. Pellet didn't deliver any women and the men didn't stop drinking. Pellet took her enthusiasm and lecturing to other towns to continue her relentless campaign against whiskey.

The most famous female crusader was Carry (also sometimes misspelled Carrie by newspaper reporters) Amelia Nation, who was born in Kentucky on November 25, 1846. She came from an odd family. One aunt thought she was a weather vane and Carry had a cousin who insisted late in life that he should crawl on all fours. For a time her mother believed that she was Queen Victoria and only let her family visit her after they had made an appointment. Carry herself had peculiar visions and firmly believed that she could talk to God. At her worst moments, she fasted for days on end, put ashes on her head, and went around the house in a bizarre garment made from sackcloth. As biographer Herbert Asbury wrote: "She followed the well-beaten trail of mental instability and extravagant religious zeal, and she was urged onward, and from her viewpoint upward, by a deep-rooted persecution mania and a highly developed scapegoat complex."[22]

Nation began campaigning against the "demon rum" in 1890 as part of her work for the WCTU. Her first attempts at serious saloon-smashing bloomed into full flower in 1900, when she felt an inner calling and started after Dobson's saloon in Kiowa, Kansas.

She continued her campaign throughout Kansas, smashing saloons wherever she could. She was a formidable figure: 54 years old, almost six feet tall, weighing 175 pounds, and possessing a face that would brook no opposition. She would stride into a saloon swinging her hatchet and happily smash windows, mirrors, beer kegs, whiskey bottles, and the paintings of nude women hanging on the wall behind the bar. She was also known to unexpectedly pull cigars out of men's mouths. Not everybody agreed with her tactics and the

citizens of Topeka made plans to tar and feather her if she tried anything in their town. Her antics were not well tolerated by the police and she was arrested 25 times across the country for destruction of private property and causing unruly crowds to collect.

She soon became a famous figure for her axe-swinging antics, which she called "hatchetation." As a result, she engaged an agent and accepted bookings on the vaudeville circuit. She lectured across the United States, appearing in Atlantic City and Pittsburgh in 1903, and venturing to Canada, England, Ireland, and Scotland to carry her

Temperance zealot Carry Nation carried her saloon-smashing act — and her hatchet — to the stage in her quest to suppress "demon rum" (Library of Congress).

message about the perils of drink, abhorrent modes of dress, and the evils of the corset. Nation was an entertaining speaker and audiences who disagreed with her would hear the sharp side of her tongue. She was particularly entertaining to see in person because she accompanied her lectures with demonstrations with her hatchet.

She even composed songs about temperance. One had the following lyrics, sung to the tune of the popular children's nursery rhyme about blackbirds:

> Sing a song of six joints, with bottles full of rye;
> Four and twenty beer kegs, stacked up on the sly,
> When the kegs were opened, the beer began to sing;
> "Hurrah for Carry Nation, her work beats anything."[23]

On November 10, 1903, Nation appeared in a special version of the temperance play *Ten Nights in a Bar-room*, parts of which were rewritten for her. The climax occurred in the fourth act when she smashed a saloon with her axe, wrecking the stage set at every performance. She insisted on calling the play *Hatchetation*. After each performance she circulated through the audience selling miniature pewter hatchets for 25 cents each, along with photographs and souvenir buttons. She extended her crusading by publishing a bi-weekly newspaper, appropriately named *The Smasher's Mail*. She died on June 2, 1911, at the age of 65 from a disease of the nervous system.

It should be noted, however, that, in the end, the temperance movement had the last laugh, in part influenced by the driving force of Carry Nation. Organizations such as the WCTU to a large extent forced the National Prohibition Act, called the Volstead Act after the Minnesota congressman who sponsored it. Also called "The Noble Experiment," the passage of the Eighteenth Amendment to the constitution in 1918 introduced national Prohibition the following year.

THREE

Women as Actresses

Both entertainment and women were so scarce in the early West that a glimpse of either or both could draw large crowds to a theater. If the entertainer was a woman, the attraction was even greater. At Erickson's saloon in Portland, Oregon, the featured attraction was an eight-piece, all-girl orchestra. The women were so popular that August "Gus" Erickson had to install an electrified rail to keep the enthusiastic loggers and sailors away from the players.

A Definite Lack of Women

Women were in short supply in the early West. An estimate made in 1849 indicated that roughly 43,000 men journeyed to the West, but only 5,000 women. The 1860 census of Colorado showed 32,654 males and only 1,577 females. In 1860 in Virginia City, Nevada, there were 2,857 men, but only 159 women. In 1875, in Dodge City, Kansas, males outnumbered females by six to one.

In the mining camps in the mountains of the Sierras, where some 200,000 lonely men toiled to extract gold from the streams, the percentage of women was very low. The first census of California, performed in 1850, showed that less than eight percent of the white population of California consisted of women.

This shortage of females meant that watching actresses performing in variety shows was one way for men to view women, and so the popularity of female stage performers was high. Going on the stage in the West was an opportunity that beckoned to women, and many were quick to take advantage of it. There were five times as many actresses performing in the West as in the East. Popular as this was, however, being an actress in Victorian times carried a definite stigma.

Patrons who wanted an even closer peek at skimpily dressed actresses could use the technology of opera glasses (author's collection).

While going to a concert hall or opera house was quite acceptable, going to "the theater" was not considered proper. The theater of the late 19th century had a shady reputation, especially among rural people who felt that the perceived glamour of the stage had an immoral taint. Part of this feeling was legitimate as the theater was often linked with sexual images, such as skimpily dressed actresses, cross-dressing, and prostitution, all of which were contrary to the accepted publicly endorsed moral standards of the day. The result was periodic, fervent outbursts against actresses by moral crusaders who based their campaigns more on their own personal beliefs and opinions than on facts. One minister from Chicago, for example, held the extreme opinion that more women had been "ruined" (Victorian parlance for the loss of their chastity) by the theater than by saloons and brothels. Some of this thinking even carried over the footlights to women attending the theater, and it was not until the late 1800s that theater-going became an acceptable pastime for respectable women.

Actresses were considered to be a bold lot. Buffalo Bill Cody had this to say: "Actresses are not a narrow-minded people. They do not go off behind the door or to some dark room if they want to kiss a man. The boldly walk up to him and with their enthusiasm, they are willing to let the world know that they like him and do not hesitate to show it in their voice and by their lips."[1]

To understand these attitudes towards actresses and the theater, it is necessary to look at the view of Victorian culture towards women and their place in contemporary society.

Victorian Attitudes Towards Women

The Victorian period refers to the years 1837 through 1900, corresponding roughly to the time of the reign of Queen Victoria.[2] Both in England and the United States this was a time of a curious combination of public prudery and loose morals, public condemnation of sexual activity and private indulgence in vice. As John Hanners summed it up: "The Nineteenth Century [was] imbued with religious evangelical fever and rigid moral and racial codes."[3] Though many of the fashions and cultural trends of the Victorian period originated in England, the concepts were quick to cross to America to make Victorianism a way of life on both sides of the Atlantic.

It was an era in which the superiority of men and the suppression of women into the home, kitchen, and child-rearing was a way of life. Women were supposed to devote their lives to caring for their husbands and children. As late as 1873, English philosopher Herbert Spencer argued that women represented an arrested state of evolutionary development because females generally had a smaller body size and brain capacity than males. It was true that studies had shown that women's brains weighed on the average four ounces less than men's; but, in spite of increasing evidence that this measure was irrelevant, medical men went to great lengths to theorize that this smaller capacity led to diminished mental ability. One scientist tried to adopt a peculiar measure of intellect that related the weight of the brain to the weight of the thigh bone.[4]

Even as enlightened a scientist as Charles Darwin proposed in his ground-breaking *The Descent of Man* that "the chief distinction in the intellectual powers of the two sexes is shown by man attaining a higher eminence, in whatever he takes up, than woman can attain." He continued: "We may also infer ... that if men are capable of decided eminence over women in many subjects, the average standard of mental power in man must be above that of woman."[5] After another page or so of specious logic and argument, he concluded: "Thus man has ultimately become superior to woman." Viewpoints such as this were used to keep women in their perceived place.

This approach, as one author succinctly put it, was unenlightened: "And so, in a painful progression throughout *The Descent*, the prejudices of middle-class English pomposity, in the guise of established knowledge, condemn to inferiority an extensive list of groups, including all women, the Irish, the physically and mentally afflicted, the poor, and indigenous people in all corners of the globe."[6]

The general view of anthropologists in the 1890s, in both Europe and America, was that women should be placed on the evolutionary scale somewhere between the civilized white male and the primitive savage. At the same time, men were afraid of women's sexuality and tried to suppress it, all the while hypocritically seeking it wherever they could. Respectable women were supposed to be pure, chaste, and romantic. These were the ideals for wives, sweethearts, and daughters. They were supposed to act like ladies, wear proper clothing (i.e., clothes that showed no hint of sexuality), have refined and proper manners, and be subservient to their lord and master — their father before marriage and husband after marriage.[7]

One of the missions of Victorian culture was the public recognition and control of women's sexuality. Men, on the other hand, were allowed to do whatever they wanted, under the male-proposed theory that "boys will be boys." Under the guise of moral reform for women, crusaders saw sexual titillation everywhere. Some, for example, even saw most women's love of dance as an outlet for repressed sexual energy.

This domination of women by men meant that women were not allowed to vote, divorce their husbands, own property by themselves, or work at a wide variety of jobs. There was certainly not a place for them in any intellectual endeavors. The Literary and Philosophical Society in Liverpool, England, did not admit women — even as guests. Even Darwin felt that women should be excluded from the Royal Geological Society.

Author Beatrix Potter spent several years studying fungi and lichens. In 1890, when she sought to present her extensive findings to the Linnaean Society of London, her request was refused. The final insult was that her uncle, the well-known chemist Sir Henry Roscoe, was allowed to present her findings at the same meeting. She tried to continue her research at the British Museum and the Royal Botanical Gardens, but was similarly rebuffed. Finally, in frustration, she abandoned her hopes of working in science and instead turned to writing children's stories.

Career opportunities for working women were limited and consisted primarily of domestic servant, teacher, governess, laundress, seamstress, prostitute — or actress. On the plus side, by 1900, actresses made up about 40 percent of the theatrical profession, which was a far larger female percentage than any other employment opportunity. This has been estimated to be as many as 40,000 individuals.[8]

The View of Actresses

Becoming an actress posed its own set of problems and social conflicts. Acting was considered to be a particularly bad career choice for women. The general public viewed actresses as being immodest and showing themselves off in public for money. In 1827, for example, ladies in the audience left during the performance of French ballet dancer Mme. Francisque Hutin because they felt that her costume was too revealing. She was wearing baggy trousers covered by a silk skirt, but when she twirled, the skirt ballooned out, allowing a peek at the opaque trousers underneath.

There were two sides to this problem. On the one hand, men found the visual draw of watching women perform in skimpy costumes, with a chance to see the outline of a woman's legs and figure unhampered by heavy and confining Victorian clothing, to be very appealing. Consequently, starting in the late 1840s, this led to a rise in popularity of stage entertainment that featured women in abbreviated costumes. This combination of drinking and leering at underdressed "actresses" led the *New York Evening Post* to comment in 1862 that similar concert saloons in that city had become "a truly diabolic form of shameless and avowed Bacchus and Phallus worship."[9]

On the other hand, conventional Victorian morality dictated public prudery about the body in general, and women's bodies in particular. Exhibition of the female form was considered to be immodest; conventional wisdom dictated that women should be well-covered in heavy underclothing, voluminous petticoats, long flowing dresses, and high necklines. Nonetheless, however, Victorian men had already seen and started to enjoy displays of female figures on stage. By 1850, an increasing number of men were going to concert saloons to enjoy the latest songs and lively dances performed by scantily clad women.

Part of these conflicting attitudes towards women was that Victorian

This photograph reflects the public perception of women in show business. The unidentified actress, with her skirt raised and showing a lot of leg and black stocking, poses in front of a log cabin. Her hair is loose and flowing, which was considered at the time to be a sign of independence and wild abandon in women (History Colorado, Buckwalter Collection, Scan #20030598).

marriage gave the husband exclusive sexual rights to a woman, including the right to view his wife's figure in private. According to Victorian mores, when an actress (even if unmarried) displayed herself onstage in a tight-fitting, abbreviated costume, she was exposing a private treasure and was giving away some of a husband's "rights" to a group of men who were willing to pay the appropriate amount of dollars for the privilege. This was considered to be a type of prostitution. Thus, an actress "selling" her body on stage was mentally associated with selling it offstage. As a result, the career of actress went against Puritan principles.

Part of this view was due to the way that actresses dressed on the stage in some shows. Most dressed in exotic fashions. Short skirts, transparent fabrics, tights, low-cut dresses, and the frilly underwear of the cancan dancer were expected and openly displayed on the stage. These were not the everyday clothes of Victorian society, but were extreme fashions that emphasized the bosoms, bottoms, thighs, and legs of the performers. Even if playing cross-dressed parts, actresses wore feminized variations of male costuming, such as tight trousers and form-fitting jackets, that again emphasized the female figure.

All this fuss about abbreviated costumes that emphasized hips, legs, and bosoms was somewhat hypocritical because the newest fashion for women that was imported from Paris in 1867 was the Grecian Bend. This style of dress used a tightly laced corset to mold the body into an S-shape that forced the woman's bosom out at the front and her bottom out at the back, thus producing an emphasis on the female figure that could hardly go unnoticed.[10]

Another strike against actresses was that they wore liberal applications of stage makeup, such as rouge and lipstick, at a time when "proper" ladies did not. Again, this created a mental association among the general public of actresses with prostitutes because these women were the only other ones who routinely wore extravagant makeup. Respectable women were supposed to rely on natural beauty through clean living rather than artificial makeup. Some pioneering women did use modest natural makeup, but only something such as a mild application of beet juice to redden the cheeks. (It was not until the 1920s that the use of makeup became popular for everyday use by women and the sales of cosmetics soared.[11])

The differences between definitions here took on very fine distinctions. Though contemporary sources did not necessarily directly consider actresses to be "prostitutes" in the sense of selling sex for money, some critics did call them whores. The name "whore" is today synonymous with prostitute, but in the second half of the 19th century the term was used in the broader meaning of "lewd" or "lascivious," which *Webster's Dictionary* defines as "tending to excite lustful desires." In this sense, for most men, the word was accurate when used for a half-dressed, pretty young actress. Then again, the name "prostitute" was applied at that time not only to women who engaged literally in sexual commerce, but to those who deviated in any way from the ideal of "pure womanhood." Another problem for moralistic Victorians when describing actresses who popularized song-and-dance in the late 1840s was that these women were healthy, normal-sized women. They were not the frail, retiring, ideal "pure women" of Victorian myth.

Right or wrong, the damage was done, and actresses in general were looked down upon. Because of this stigma, proper Victorian ladies did not socialize with women performers and, often by association, with male actors. Actresses and their relatives were used to being asked if they were "legitimate." The perception among the public of those on the stage became so linked with ladies of the night that the name "actress" became used as a common Victorian euphemism for a prostitute. This attitude lasted through the latter half of the 1800s and actresses did not gain respectability until the early part of the 19th century.

Not only actresses, but show business in general had a shady reputation. Early circuses, for example, attracted confidence men and pickpockets who gave the entertainment world a bad name, often causing respectable families to avoid them. Later circuses hired private detectives and security men to keep the criminal elements away.

Compounding the problem was that actresses often did not help their own cause. Some appeared in provocative poses in photographs used for publicity purposes, as well as being sold as Victorian cheesecake. Pictures of actresses could be found on playing cards, picture postcards, cigarette cards, and visiting cards. Interestingly, the first known cigarette card that appeared in the United States in 1878 was the picture of an actress. The more daring actresses and dancers posed for photographs that were more blatantly erotic. Similar photographs appeared in the weekly and monthly magazines of the time under the guise of "artist's models" and "theatrical beauties." In the magazine world, "insightful" reports on popular actresses and stage beauties — illustrated with photographs, of course — appeared alongside illustrations of bathing girls in bloomers, nudes in art, and "naughty French music hall singers." More decorous pictures appeared on advertising posters for shows and on the covers of sheet music.

Stories about actresses, delivered with a requisite disapproving sniff, were commonly written up in newspapers to boost circulation. Starting in about 1880, spicy stories about the theater and popular burlesque performers, illustrated by pictures of actresses in tights, appeared in publications that specialized in scandalous reporting, such as the *National Police Gazette*, as well as in the popular press. It was also popular to claim that early actresses were the cause of many suicides among frustrated suitors and duels for love.

As is done today, actresses endorsed soap, cosmetics, and other personal products, and were seen posing with these items on billboards and in magazines. The famous actress Lillie Langtry was part of the advertising campaign for Pear's soap. Adelina Patti, a Spanish operatic soprano, also advertised Pear's soap, illustrated by a picture of her in the bath with only a light towel draped over her.

Many self-appointed critics had their say about actresses. The Rev. Ernest A. Bell, one of the fervent crusader against White Slavery,[12] had the following to say about women and the theater: "Other so-called theatres are a part of the combined saloon and den of shame. I have conversed personally many times with girls who were deceived into going to such places, thinking they were going on a reputable stage."[13] Bell claimed that theatrical agents acted as white slave traders, luring young women into brothels with promises of a brilliant career on the stage. In reality, the campaign against White Slavery was founded in a media-generated wave of hysteria and no credible evidence was ever found that white slavery was the dreadful menace to the average American white woman that it was claimed to be.

Just as women were stereotyped, Victorian men were sometimes characterized by descriptions that would be considered to be unusual today. Rugged, virile men were supposed to also possess a few womanly characteristics to provide some balance to their supposed lustful, untamed nature. Thus descriptions are sometimes found in contemporary literature of men with strong, broad shoulders — but the waist of a girl. Other characterizations portray men with "hair like a girl" or "small girlish hands," descriptions that today would ring of either homoerotic admiration or gender confusion.

Good Girls Versus Bad

Though the depiction of the "bad girl" actress was widespread, it was unfair to lump all actresses into one category. There were several levels of "actresses" who appeared on the stages of Western theaters.

At the top of the pyramid were the nationally famous legitimate actresses and singers. These were performers of the caliber of Sarah Bernhardt and Jenny Lind. Many good actresses and singers — whether in the West or the East — were great favorites at the box office. In 1853 tickets to the San Francisco debut of Lola Montez were auctioned off at prices up to 65 dollars.

Many of these actresses, such as singer and dancer Lotta Crabtree, provided light entertainment, which was the most popular theatrical style of the day. Drama and opera stars, however, were also popular. Opera singer Adelina Patti appeared in San Francisco in 1884. Tickets for her premiere were seven dollars. The promoter, James Mapleson, made a tidy profit from her appearance. He was so good at his job that lines for tickets started forming the night before the performance, and even places in line quickly sold for ten dollars. When the performance rapidly sold out, including all the standing room, the waiting crowd soon turned unruly and began vandalizing the box office.

Serious legitimate actresses like these were aware of the dubious reputation of actresses and they worked hard to maintain their integrity and a proper moral image. As part of preserving their reputation, legitimate actresses had to be careful of the parts that they played. The opera *La Traviata* by Giuseppe Verdi was the story of a high-priced prostitute named Violetta, who catered to a wealthy Parisian clientele. In Victorian times, this type of plot that did not consider punishment or redemption for the sinner at the end was considered to be an immoral theme, even for legitimate opera. Actress Emma Abbott wanted to put on the production, but was not happy with the basic plot, so she came up with a sanitized version that was more appropriate to her sensibilities. She renamed the opera *Cecelia's Love*.

Included in the next layer down of actresses were dancers, singers, and other entertainers who appeared in comedies and light dramas. These women might or might not derive their entire income from acting. The association of prostitutes and actresses was, in some cases, justified. Many of the women who traveled as actresses with a show worked as part-time prostitutes, and entertained men after a performance to earn additional income while the show was in town. Sometimes they even entertained backstage in the theater. In 1915 the Sanborn Fire Insurance map for Kellogg, Idaho, showed that there was a brothel just off the dressing rooms of a local vaudeville theater. The Bird Cage Theatre in Tombstone had several small rooms for prostitution located in a gambling area underneath the stage. Obviously, then, there was a strong link between this type of actress and prostitution.

Indeed, in the early days of the theater in New York and other large cities in the 1830s, unabashed prostitutes used theater buildings as a rendezvous point for clients. The upper gallery, or third tier, in theaters was traditionally reserved for the use of prostitutes. The women met their regular clients and new prospects there, and the third tier often had its own separate bar to supply alcoholic drinks. The women were required to use a separate entrance, arrive an hour early, and be up in the third tier before the respectable patrons arrived for their seats in the main floors of the theater. This practice all but disappeared after the Civil War.

The third group of actresses, by far the largest, were those who entertained in saloons and variety theaters in the West, and were prostitutes at the same time.[14] These included the ubiquitous "waiter girls," who performed on stage singing and dancing, then served drinks to patrons and negotiated for sex in the private boxes that often surrounded saloon theaters.

Even though the legitimacy of a large percentage of actresses was questionable, it should not be assumed that all women actresses were bawdy or had loose morals. Women could certainly make a success of show business without compromising their integrity. An example of this was Della Pringle, who owned a small touring entertainment troupe called The Pringle Company. Della was born in 1870, in Iowa. At the age of eight, she played Little Eva in *Uncle Tom's Cabin*. She continued acting through her teenage years and, at age 19, left home with dreams of conquering the entertainment world. She started her own small theatrical company and specialized in clean, lively comedy. She had the appeal for the miners and soldiers of the frontier, as she was an attractive blue-eyed blonde with shapely legs. The company made their first appearance in Boise, Idaho, at the Pinney Theater in 1900. Then she and her company traveled around rural cattle and farming communities, and army posts. Like all the other touring companies, one of their staple performances was the ever-popular *Camille*.

The Pringle Company valiantly performed wherever they could find an audience and a building to put on a show. Sometimes, the theaters in which they were appearing were makeshift. One time, in Wyoming, the only place they could find to put on a play was in a hotel dining room. In 1905, the troupe appeared at the Tabor Opera House in Leadville.

Della was a versatile manager. She was good at sewing and made most of the costumes. She also sang and performed in skits. The troupe continued to play small towns until 1920. But, by then, tastes were changing and movies were becoming the popular form of mass entertainment. So, Della trooped off to Hollywood and performed in comedy roles for a while for producer Mack Sennett, but her time was past. (She died as a charity case at age 82 in the County Hospital in Boise, Idaho, in 1952.)

Another example of a woman who made a success of show business was Laura Keene. She started out as an actress in 1851. She acted in California, in Sacramento, San Francisco, and Stockton, but didn't receive an overwhelming reception, so in 1853 she turned to management of a troupe. She leased the American Theatre in San Francisco in the summer of 1855 and produced *Twelfth Night*, *A Midsummer Night's Dream*, and *The Tempest*. From 1863 to 1873, she managed a touring company. After that, she retired to New York to manage a resident theatrical company.

On the other hand, some of the negative stereotypes of actresses were not totally inaccurate. Dancer Cad Wilson, for example, who performed in San Francisco and later in Dawson in the Yukon Territory, had a popular way of encouraging men to throw money at her. She was not the greatest beauty nor the greatest singer, but she had a great stage personality. She would lift up the skirt of her dress, holding it out like a basket, and run around the stage, encouraging men in the audience to throw in donations of coins. Men responded and threw gold nuggets, coins, watches, and jewelry onto the stage and into her skirt when she performed.[15] Holding her dress out, of course, revealed her attractive ankles, stockings, and petticoats, which encouraged men to throw even more. She even had a belt of huge gold nuggets given to her by admirers. Incidentally, she was billed as receiving the highest salary ever paid to an entertainer on the West Coast. Her theme song, which was peppered with innuendo, was "Such a Nice Girl, Too."

Four

Strutting Their Stuff

As the second half of the 19th century progressed into the early 1900s, bawdy stage entertainment progressed from women performing comic roles in tights and abbreviated costumes, to the blatant sexuality of striptease that reached its peak in the 1930s. Women as sexual objects on the stage went through a progression that started with representations of classical art, progressed through the bawdy shows of the variety theaters and the cancan, and eventually culminated in belly dancing and the cootch. The display of women for entertainment has, of course, not ended even today, as a casual review of current motion pictures and television programs will indicate.

Museums

The bawdy stage shows of the concert saloons and variety theaters that featured actresses primarily for their sex appeal could be said to have started, oddly enough, with museums. The association of museums with entertainment started in the East with the "educational museums." The "educational" aspect was emphasized in order to attract customers who felt that mere amusement was not appropriate for religious people. This was a holdover from the Revolutionary period when many American cities prohibited theatrical performances on the assumption that theaters were breeding grounds for gambling, thievery, and prostitution. Historian Robert Allen has stated that, even as late as 1895, an estimated 70 percent of the American population considered going to the theater to be sinful.[1]

Museums, therefore, offered entertainment in disguise and geared themselves to popular tastes. The "museum" name also added an air of propriety for visitors. While it was not seemly for single ladies to the attend the theater, they could attend an educational museum without being mistaken for a wanton woman. Regardless of the name, these museum were run by showmen whose object was to entertain and make money by doing so.

Part of the popularity of these museums was stimulated by an interest among the American public to learn about the natural world.[2] As a result, museums exhibited natural curiosities, such as stuffed birds, dinosaur bones, geological specimens, and animal skeletons. To augment these static displays, lecture rooms were added and men of science presented discourses on a variety of scientific topics.

Customers in these educational museums were also awed by dioramas, panoramas, jugglers, gypsies, mechanical marvels, freaks, magicians, Indians, singers, dancers, contortionists, ventriloquists, educated dogs, magic lantern shows, trained fleas, and any other peculiarity that might cajole customers to part with a dime.[3] One of the odder forms of "entertainment" involved people breathing nitrous oxide, the "laughing gas" that was to revolutionize dental anesthesia. Participants at these so-called "frolics" staggered around exhibiting odd behavior to the great amusement of the audience.[4]

In the interests of promoting educational values, male customers could be further entertained by representations of anatomical displays of the external and internal aspects of the female body, and those with a truly morbid bent could study diseased organs and other "medical curiosities" pickled in alcohol in glass jars. These museums also often offered special so-called scientific exhibits of belly dancing and *tableaux vivant*.

Wood's Museum and Metropolitan Theatre in New York was typical of the theatrical museums, combining educational lectures, freak shows, and theater entertainment all under one roof. Dwarfs, obese women, two-headed calves, giants, and other "curiosities" shared the stage with singers, variety shows, and serious plays.

The Boston Museum and Gallery of Fine Arts was opened in 1841 by Moses Kimball to present such a display of curiosities. The building had a full concert saloon, which was expanded into a performing theater in 1843. In 1844 Kimball presented *The Drunkard*, the morality play that preached a strong message of temperance, for a lengthy run of 130 performances. Plays offered in these museum theaters were usually listed as "moral lectures" in order to pacify the consciences of those who did not feel that they should enjoy them as mere entertainment.

Phineas Taylor Barnum was an enterprising showman who rose to success specializing in this brand of entertainment. In 1841 he bought John Scudder's American Museum at Broadway and Ann Street in New York and turned it into Barnum's American Museum. There, he exhibited five stories of real and fake curiosities: midgets, giants, Siamese twins, freaks, and other oddities. Crammed into the building were hundreds of thousands of specimens of birds, animals, insects, paintings, statues, mineral specimens, Indian artifacts, and every other sort of curiosity. Barnum ran the museum from 1842 to 1868.

Though Barnum's business was primarily in the East, he was an important player in the story of entertainment in the Old West because he pioneered many of the techniques for attracting customers to traveling shows. Barnum was also later responsible for much of the structure of the circuses that were popular from coast to coast.

Barnum did not invent the curiosities that he displayed in his museum, but he sought them out and engaged in intense promotional campaigns to attract customers. As Barnum put it: "The bigger the humbug, the better the people will like it."[5] Typical of his "humbugs" were the famous Feejee Mermaid, a fake made from sewing the mummified head and upper torso of a monkey onto a fish's tail, and "General" Tom Thumb, a legitimate tiny person who toured with Barnum for years.[6]

One of the museum's humbugs with a Western origin was The Solid Muldoon. This was a hoax perpetuated in 1877, that was declared to be authentic by P.T. Barnum himself. The humbug started when a man named Bob Fitzsimmons found a seven-foot-eight-inch figure of a man made from Portland cement in a warehouse in Denver. He buried it in a muddy location in the mountains of Colorado to give it a suitable patina, then had a friend "find" it. The "body" was displayed as a perfect example of a petrified man. Rumor spread that this was the "missing link" between man and the apes. People came from around the world to view it. Barnum shipped the figure to New York for exhibition, but before he could make full use of it, the man who originally manufactured it (in an icehouse in Connecticut), confessed to his part in the hoax.[7]

Undaunted, Barnum pressed on. In an effort to bring in repeat customers to the museum, he started to present a series of concerts, light entertainment, and variety acts in the Lecture Room, which was, in reality, a large entertainment hall. In 1849, he rebuilt the Lecture Room into a regular performing theater, and in 1850 he increased the seating capacity to 3,000. In 1850, he presented *The Drunkard* for a lengthy run. After its success, Barnum continued to present similar plays with strong moral messages. Also in 1850, Barnum organized the American tour of Swedish singer Jenny Lind, offering her $1,000 a concert. In 1852, he sent the Irish opera singer, soprano Catherine Hayes, on a successful tour of California.

Barnum's first museum was set afire in 1864 by Confederates trying to burn down New York, but was saved. In 1865, the museum burned again, but this time to ruins. Barnum rebuilt, but his second museum building also burned to the ground in 1868. This put Barnum out of the museum business.

In 1871, Barnum entered the circus industry, and later merged with James A. Bailey to create "The Greatest Show on Earth."

Living Pictures

One of the earliest forms of entertainment that highlighted women's figures were the so-called *tableaux vivant*, from the French meaning "living pictures." This form of entertainment started its rise to popularity in the 1830s in the New York museums, opera houses, and theaters, before spreading to the West. In these performances, exhibitors arranged human figures on a stage, with the appropriate scenery and props, to imitate famous classical paintings or statues. The "models" did not move during the show. Popular topics were sentimental subjects and patriotic scenes, such as "A Monument to Washington." Sometimes the models were covered in flour to simulate plaster of Paris or marble, in order to enhance their likeness to real statues. In New York in September 1831, Ada Adams Barrymore used this technique to illustrate a painting named *The Soldier's Widow* by Scheffer.

Each segment of a tableau was fairly brief and followed a set pattern. The stage curtains opened to reveal a scene of motionless models. The "picture" was accompanied by music or by an explanatory narration. After a few minutes of viewing, the curtains were closed again and the stage and the models were rearranged for the next tableau. Other names for the use of living models to represent famous works of art were *poses plastiques* and *living statuary*.

This type of stage performance was first seen in 1826 in New York's Vauxhall Garden, which offered a type of variety entertainment that preceded vaudeville. This entertainment attraction was patterned on the older Vauxhall Gardens in England, which opened in June of 1732 as one of the country's oldest "pleasure gardens."[8] In 1827, a Mr. Scudder appeared in the "frontier" town of New Harmony in Indiana as a living statue.[9]

One of the first recorded exhibitions of *tableaux vivant* in New York was in September 1847, when a Dr. Collyer used living models at The Apollo Rooms to simulate classical sculptures in what he called "model personifications." This form of artistic expression was also used in the legitimate theater where, at certain points in the play, the actors stopped in fixed positions within a dramatic scene to freeze the action.[10]

Enterprising showmen soon realized that audience attendance was far better when the scenes were representations of paintings or statues that contained thinly veiled women. Accordingly, the theme of many of these living pictures shifted from the historic towards famous scenes that displayed partially clothed female models, such as *Venus Rising from the Sea, Suzanna in the Bath, Psyche Going to the Bath,* and *The Three Graces.* In an ironic way, then, *tableaux vivant* resulted in a revival of famous art for the masses. Many men suddenly found that they had an interest in classical art that had heretofore lain dormant.

In the era of Victorian attitudes towards public exhibition of the female figure, there was immediate criticism of these exhibitions when they appeared in the late 1840s. When Palmo's Opera House in New York introduced "living pictures" that featured scantily clad women in 1847, for example, the exhibit was rapidly shut down by city officials. As a result, these types of performances gravitated towards the lower class of entertainment places, such as concert saloons and cheap museums. Another exhibition that provoked a police crackdown was a show at the Eagle Hotel on Canal Street on March 22, 1848, that featured women who danced naked behind a thin film of gauze.[11] This was arguably the first documented example of what would later become striptease.

In New York, in 1847 and 1848, there were probably a dozen taverns, hotels, drinking houses, and saloons that exhibited young women — as well as young men — in minimally dressed poses. In spite of police pressure, the popularity of this type of show was so great that many imitators followed. In a burst of hypocrisy, Biblical scenes, such as *Eve in the Garden of Eden,* turned out to be popular, providing an excuse to exhibit partial nudity while supposedly embracing a serious religious theme.

Though many of these shows advertised nude performances, the women were not the modern perception of totally naked, and they actually showed less bare flesh than the advertising promised. The definition of nudity had a loose interpretation. In the Victorian perception, nude was equated with revealing the female form, but not necessarily with displaying totally nakedness. The women wore tights, which were essentially opaque, flesh-colored, form-fitting body stockings, often covered with a short filmy tunic.[12] This was interpreted by critics as nudity. One contemporary spectator commented on viewing a performance by a trapeze artist: "The only clothing she had on was a blue satin doublet fitting close to her body and having very scanty trunk hose below it. Her arms were all bare; her leg, cased in fleshings, were as good as bare up to the hip."[13]

To the Victorian male, the outline of a female form in tights, even though not naked, was incredibly exciting. Men's views of women's figures in the everyday Victorian world were obscured by voluminous petticoats and skirts. The typical woman's summer dress outfit weighed approximately 15 pounds; her winter outfit might weigh as much as 35 pounds.

If the tights were not exciting enough, *tableaux vivant* that included *total* nakedness were available, but typically as private showings to rich patrons in large cities such as San Francisco. Some prostitutes found that this could be

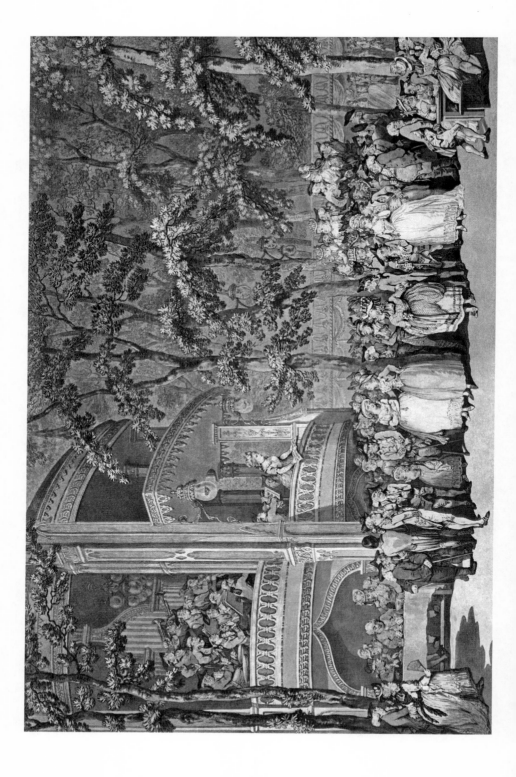

an appealing arrangement, as all had to do was pose, and did not necessarily have to have sex with the customers. A group of these women might band together to put on a naked show for wealthy clients. Erotic postcards and photographs featuring classical living statuary without tights were also available as a form of early Victorian pornography.

One way to circumvent the religious restrictions limiting entertainment on Sundays in some communities was to continue to exhibit "living pictures," but to display only religious scenes. As with the other *tableaux vivant,* the themes were rather loosely adapted from Biblical stories and prominently featured the voluptuous nature of the "performers," who were the usual dance hall girls dressed in tights.

Burlesque and the Leg Shows

Another thinly veiled guise for exposing women's bodies as a part of entertainment was known as "The Leg Show"—for reasons that will become obvious. In a wry reference to women's legs and the Biblical Old Testament story of the golden calf that the Israelites worshipped when Moses was on Mount Sinai, one wag commented that early San Francisco worshipped the calf, although he was referring to women's anatomy, not the golden kind.

On the early American stage, "burlesque" was a legitimate theater form that presented parodies of well-known works of literature or music. Burlesques of literary classics included topical humor and satire, along with songs and dances. The social satire presented often bordered on the scandalous by using pointed barbs at current events. Burlesque was born in the concert saloons, where it was a type of working-class entertainment. What is remembered today as "burlesque"—with strippers performing on a runway that extended into the audience—was a different theatrical form that did not appear until the 1920s.

Early burlesque as a theatrical show was satiric, comic, and full of mischief. For example, several of Shakespeare's popular plays were parodied, or "burlesqued," as *Hamlet and Egglet, Roam-e-eow and Julie-ate,* and *Julius Sneezer. Richard III* was parodied as *Bad Dicky.* One burlesque show, created by impresario Michael Levitt, had a character named Octobus Sweezur. *Ben-Hur* was burlesqued as *Bend Her,* a satire with shapely, skimpily dressed women driving in the famous chariot race. The operettas of Gilbert and Sullivan were frequent targets of burlesque. Their popular operetta *The Pirates of Penzance,*

Opposite: Vauxhall Garden in New York was one of the first theaters to present exhibitions of "living statuary" (Library of Congress).

Poster advertising The Gaiety Dancers in 1900. Dancing groups like these were the forerunners of the female chorus lines of the 1920s (Library of Congress).

for example, became *The Pie Rats of Pen Yan*. Many popular serious operas also didn't escape the rapier wit of burlesque and parody. Donizetti's *Lucia di Lammermoor*, for example, became *Lucy-do-lam-her-more* or *Lucy-did sham-amour*; Rossini's *La Gazza Ladra* became *The Cats in the Larder*.

The first U.S. production of *Camille* was in 1853. In 1863, a burlesque version appeared as *Camille (With the Cracked Heart)*, followed rapidly by another burlesque by Bryant's Minstrels. Another version of *Camille* unintentionally provided some black humor that does not seem to have been noticed by theatergoers. When the Colorado Springs Opera House was opened on April 18, 1881, the debut performance had Maude Granger in the title role. This was a rather poor choice for a resort town in which a large portion of the population was made up of tubercular health seekers.

Two of the pivotal stage shows that were primarily responsible for the later leg shows were *The Black Crook* and *Ixion*. These shows established women wearing tights as a major element of burlesque shows that followed.

THE BLACK CROOK

The Black Crook is considered today to be the forerunner of musical comedy and American burlesque. The show was an elaborate musical spectacle with fanciful scenery and dozens of beautiful dancing girls in flesh-colored body stockings and other revealing costumes. It was the longest-running production in New York in the 1860s, opening on September 12, 1866. It ran for an amazing 474 performances over 16 months in its initial engagement, grossing over $1 million. It appeared at Niblo's Garden and Theatre, possibly one of the finest theaters in the country at the time. Niblo's was started by a tavern-keeper in a converted stable in 1828 as the Sansouci, and grew to be an important dramatic theater. It was one of the most popular locations for entertainment in New York.

The Black Crook was a four-act musical extravaganza written for the stage by Charles Barras. The production that ultimately appeared on the stage had a curious yet serendipitous history. It involved a French ballet company that was stranded in New York when the theater in which they were scheduled to perform — The Academy of Music — burned down. In a last minute shuffle, the troupe of dancers was added to a stage melodrama strongly reminiscent of *Faust*, that was already scheduled for production. Elements of the plot involved a wicked stepmother, an evil hunchback, fairies, demons, the Devil, and assorted monsters. The result was *The Black Crook*, which combined music, dance, spectacular production scenes, and scantily clad dancers to produce five-and-a-half hours of scenic splendor. The combination of ballet sequences intertwined with scenes of melodrama and spectacle involved a cast of literally hundreds of performers, and was the first show to warrant the designation of "extravaganza."

The Black Crook was the story of two lovers, Amina and Rudolph, in a mythical medieval European village. The plot thickens with the entrance of the evil sorcerer Count Herzog, who is called "The Black Crook" because he had a crooked back, or hunchback. In the best traditions of melodrama, he separates the lovers in order to use them to fulfill a pact with the Devil to provide a soul each year in exchange for an extra year of his life. The story evolves with ballet productions, lavish costuming, and spectacular stage effects to the required happy conclusion when the lovers are reunited and Herzog is consigned to the depths of the underworld. The plot was implausible at best, but the extravagant sets, stunning production numbers, and special effects of flying fairies and sets that rose magically out of the floor almost overwhelmed the audience.

Although there was some criticism of the number of women's legs that were displayed, the newspapers and reviewers were generally quite complimentary. Some of the press and the clergy, however, immediately labeled it as unfit for a public audience, which, of course, increased attendance. The editor of the Chicago Times went so far as to ungenerously call the women "ladies of the evening," a harsh Victorian euphemism for prostitutes. Self-styled critic Charles Smyth, a Protestant minister in New York, lambasted the play in a three-hour sermon, during which he described the dancers' costumes and figures in such minute detail that he had obviously studied them and the spectacle very closely.[14] His comments were apparently ignored by the theatergoing public, who continued to flock to each performance. The costumes that he complained about were tights worn under a knee-length ballet tutu and modest short pantaloons. These costumes had been worn with decorum in the ballet on the New York stages for decades, but they did, however, reveal the outlines of the female lower figure that was conventionally concealed under voluminous skirts.

Ballet had been featured for some years in the legitimate theater, but even ballet was not without its critics. Ballet dancers of the time wore quite modest outfits, consisting of loose pantaloons covered by a knee-length skirt. Critics still objected to this, because the audience could see the shape of the dancers' legs outlined by the material of the trousers.

In spite of these criticisms, The Black Crook was one of the most popular and successful stage productions of the second half of the 19th century. It was the longest-running production in New York in the 1860s, then after that, it toured for 20 more years. It was revived eight times in New York alone between 1868 and 1892. The Black Crook was still touring in 1908 when the show appeared at the Tabor Opera House in Leadville. Individual performers in the show came and went, but the success of the basic format proved to be long-lived. The success of *The Black Crook* was so great, in fact, that it spawned a host of imitators. Among them were *The White Crook*, *The Red Crook*, *The Black Rook*, *The Black Rook with a Crook*, *The Golden Crook*, and *The Black Crook, Jr.*

IXION; OR, THE MAN AT THE WHEEL

The other show that had a major impact on stage entertainment in the late 1800s was *Ixion*, the forerunner of the later "leg shows" that featured women in tights playing the role of men. The American burlesque show, as a theater form, started in 1868 with Lydia Thompson and her British Blonde Burlesque Troupe. The official name for the performing group was the Lydia Thompson Troupe. In 1869, the newspapers, including the *New York Times*, started to refer to them as the "British Blondes," and that was the name that stuck — even though they were not all blondes.

Thompson had premiered the play *Ixion* in London in 1863 with blonde co-stars Pauline Markham, Alice Logan, Ada Harland (who wore a blonde wig to match the others), Lisa Weber, and Harry Beckett. The success of the play in London took them to New York in 1868.

The eye-opener for Victorian audiences was that the women wore costumes that consisted of opaque flesh-colored tights, covered by a type of tunic, like a short, filmy, knee-length dress with a high neckline. The outfit was completed with lightweight boots. By wearing these revealing outfits, the British Blondes made women's bodies, rather than their talent, a requirement for future performers.

Lydia Thompson and her group were a shock to the traditional theater. Using bawdy jokes and sketches, these scantily clad female performers catered primarily to males in the audiences. With much of its origins in minstrelsy, this type of entertainment also had its roots in England in the 1840s, when dance routines separated from the ballet to become a distinct type of entertainment. So Lydia Thompson did not invent the theatrical form, but merely brought it to America. Members of the troupe wore the typical costumes from the British pantomime, in which women with full figures and long legs wore short tunics and tights to play male roles.[15]

In this musical play, a lampoon of Greek culture featuring characters from classical Greek mythology, Lydia Thompson played Ixion, the King of Thessaly. The basic plot of this extravaganza was that Ixion, a mortal, accompanied by Mercury, goes to dine with Jupiter, and flirts with the Greek goddesses Juno (played by Logan) and Venus (played by Markham). All of the supporting roles, except for one, were played by women. The only male in the cast, Harry Beckett, ironically, played the part of a woman. Thompson dressed as a man and performed vigorous dances traditionally executed by men.

The British Blondes used suggestive poses and topical dialogue to strut their sexuality and mock masculine authority. They figuratively thumbed their collective noses at Victorian propriety and provided conflicting images of prostitute and lady. Victorian males were fascinated as these actresses shattered polite expectations of the way that women should talk and display their bodies in public. The usual naysayers, of course, immediately declared their actions to be improper and not at all respectable.[16] Part of this criticism arose because these women appeared in cross-dressed roles, wooing other women playing the female roles, and talking and joking about the interaction between the sexes. The cross-gender role-playing was naughty but fascinating to Victorian males.

The show opened at Wood's Museum and Metropolitan Theater in New York on September 28, 1868. *Ixion* was a resounding success and took in $46,000 in October alone. In December, the show moved to Niblo's Garden. The advance publicity was so good that the show was sold out on opening night.

Interestingly, *Ixion* involved no special effects or magnificent sets like *The Black Crook*. Most of the success of the play was because it featured attractive women dressed in tights, singing, joking, and dancing in the manner of burlesque. Thompson used the traditional elements of burlesque, such as parody, songs, dances, and topical humor, but she added the spectacle of scantily dressed, attractive women. The costumes emphasized the entertainers' legs, hips, and bosoms.

The *New York Times* of October 1, 1868, glowingly stated: "Miss Thompson is a blonde of the purest type, saucy, blue-eyed, golden-haired and of elegant figure.... It is hard to judge her as an actress, in a disguise that robs her sex of all its charms, for Miss. Thompson has to swear, swagger, and be otherwise masculine as Ixion ... but she is lively, vivacious, and spirited."

This show had an impact in several different ways. One was that it challenged the way that women could act and display themselves. The second was that it challenged the way that women could participate in what was previously an all-male entertainment form. As minstrelsy and burlesque originally used all-male casts, with men playing both men's and women's parts, critics were concerned that this new theater form that featured cross-dressed women would take over what were traditionally male roles. Considered especially radical was that these brash women challenged the contemporary view that women should be pure, pious, and dependent on men, with their natural role being wife and mother.

Some other critics could not see beyond the women's brief clothing to the entertainment value of the production, and made their criticism known immediately. The *New York Times* of February 5, 1869, ranted about the undressed performers, the singing that resembled screaming, and the "incoherent ravings called puns." One disgruntled New York critic in *The Spirit of the Times* on February 13, 1869, unkindly wrote: "Brains would be a tiresome encumbrance, and the absence of lungs would be a positive relief, since the ... singing that is attempted is ... diabolically bad." Another commented in *Appletons' Journal* in 1869: "One is dazzled with ... beautiful faces and startled at the coarse songs, the vile jargon, the low wit, and the abandoned manners of the characters." The criticism of "nudity" probably helped to ensure the success of the show. But the public loved Lydia Thompson's British Blondes and the spectacle they presented, and the show grossed $40,000 in its first month.

Encouraged by the public and financial success of *Ixion*, Thompson continued on in a series of burlesque spectacles that included *The Forty Thieves; or, Striking Oil in Family Jars, Sinbad the Sailor; or, The Ungenial Genii and the Cabin Boy*, and *Pippin; or, The King of the Gold Mine*. As before, most of the principal roles, including all 40 "male" thieves, their 40 female companions, and miscellaneous fairies, were all played by women.

After her success on the East coast, Thompson launched an extensive tour of the United States in 1869 which included theaters in California. When she arrived in San Francisco in June of 1870, she found that Weber, Harland, and Beckett had preceded her in another troupe, this one called the British Blonde Burlesque Troupe, and were appearing at Maguires Opera House. Both groups followed with separate tours of California and the gold fields.

The British Blondes were such a sensation that several imitation troupes sprang up almost immediately. The first American burlesque show was created by Michael B. Leavitt in 1869 as Mme. (Madame) Rentz's Female Minstrels, a combination of female minstrels and vaudeville that he called "burlesque." The show featured variety acts, short comic sketches, and musical numbers — along with scantily clad women. His show became the model for burlesque shows in the 1880s and 1890s. The act was renamed in 1879 as the Rentz-Santley Novelty and Burlesque Company, after the star of the show Mabel Santley.

As burlesque shows became more popular, productions became lavish musical extravaganzas, featuring processions of chorus girls playing various parts. As the popularity of the leg shows grew, these women's initial pioneering role was taken over by male theatrical producers and booking agents who reduced burlesque primarily to the display of the female body. The plots were not always the most sophisticated and mainly consisted primarily of troupes

Typical cancan maneuver with the girls' knees raised while they rotated their lower legs to the music (author's collection).

of women doing parodies or "burlesques," while wearing revealing men's clothing. The stage directions for some of these leg shows might be quite loose, consisting of vague instructions in the script such as: "dance by principals interspersed with tableaux."

THE CANCAN

Among the many types of dance performed by women that were popular in saloons and variety theaters, the cancan stood out. The cancan originated in France as a dance for couples that was performed in the style of the galop — a lively dance. The cancan, as performed in the variety theaters, was a wild, noisy dance performed by several women at the same time. The name "cancan," also sometimes spelled in two words as "can can" or hyphenated as "can-can," came from a French word that described a scandal or an indecent dance, hence the eventual meaning of "a scandalous dance."

The dance itself consisted of vigorous high kicking, rotating the lower leg with the knee raised and the skirt held up, and rotating on one leg with the other held straight up in the air while grasped by the ankle. The cancan was accompanied by fast, lively music, and often by screams and yelps from the dancers.[17] The appeal for men was that the energetic high kicks revealed the dancers' legs, black stockings, and frilly underwear.[18] The dance could be performed by a single dancer or by several at the same time in a synchronized chorus line.

Like most entertainment that spread out across the West, the cancan appeared first in the East. The introduction of the cancan to America has been credited to Giuseppina Morlacchi, the wife of Texas Jack Omohundro, who performed the dance in a play called *The Devil's Auction*, in Boston on December 23, 1867. She later used the cancan as her signature dance when she appeared in stage productions. The dance was performed in New York as early as 1869 when it was performed at the Waverly Theater. The popularity of the cancan spread rapidly and it appeared at theaters in all the entertainment capitals across the West.

In 1879, articles in the San Francisco *Chronicle* that hinted of scandalous goings-on in the theaters forced the police to investigate the cancan, which was by then being performed in almost every concert saloon and theater on the Barbary Coast, San Francisco's brothel and saloon district.[19] After looking carefully at the matter — so to speak — the police prohibited the performance of the cancan in San Francisco.

As part of the "investigation," they arrested Mabel Santley of the Rentz-Santley Novelty and Burlesque Company in March of 1879, while she was performing at the Standard, which was a relatively high-class theater. She was accused of indecent exposure. Her skirts were long enough in the police's view, but the problem was that she didn't keep them down around her ankles. She was hauled into court and fined $200.[20] That action apparently satisfied local moralists, because it seemed that everybody promptly forgot about the perils of seeing women's legs and the lively strains of the cancan reappeared even more vigorously on the Barbary Coast.

References to the dance came from other sources as well. Tombstone, Arizona, had an eating establishment named the Cancan Restaurant. The townspeople, however, claimed with wry humor that the name was appropriate because all the food came from tin cans.[21]

Another change to burlesque that occurred in the 1870s, after the introduction of the British Blondes, was that women performers started to become more voluptuous. The tastes of Victorian men ran towards women with hefty thighs and wide hips. A weight of 160 or 170 pounds (when the height of the average woman was about five feet three inches) was not unusual. The popularity of buxom women in the 1890s was typified by May Howard and her troupe, the May Howard Company, in which each of the women weighed more than 150 pounds. Howard had previously performed with the Rentz-Santley troupe.

In 1899, burlesque comedian W.B. "Billy" Watson managed a troupe called Billy Watson's Beef Trust. It was built around large performers, some of whom weighed more than 200 pounds.[22] They were made to visually appear even larger by wearing tights with horizontal stripes.

In order to be popular, some performers who were not quite as voluptuous as Billy Watson's women were reported to wear padding on their hips and thighs underneath their costumes.[23] It was not until the early 1900s that men's tastes in women went from large busts, plump thighs, and broad hips, to slender, long-legged women, and a slimmer look in actresses started to become popular with the public.[24]

Vaudeville

From about 1880 to 1920, vaudeville was the most popular form of entertainment in the United States. Vaudeville had its origins in France, where the term referred to light comic plays with musical interludes.

The name "vaudeville" came originally from a 15th-century French name, *Vaux-de-Vire*, as applied to a series of songs from the Vire Valley. The name was later corrupted to *Voix-de-Ville*, meaning the "voice of the town," and eventually to *vaudeville*, as the generic name for a ballad or a light comedy. The early French form of vaudeville consisted of a farcical play, accompanied by songs set to popular tunes.

The early American form of vaudeville catered to an all-male audience of the variety theaters, concert saloons, and beer gardens. Later American vaudeville developed out of these variety shows as an attempt to clean up and legitimize the bawdy acts that were presented in concert saloons by waiter girls and prostitutes.

American vaudeville developed in the 1860s along the same lines as the British institution of the Music Hall. Between about 1870 and 1890, the presentation of respectable variety acts broke away from its origins. By 1890, the part of the concert saloon form of variety entertainment that featured broad comedy and lively song and dance, but with clean variety acts, had been consolidated as a separate type of entertainment which retained the name of vaudeville.

In 1881, Tony Pastor's Fourteenth Street Theatre opened to present "clean" variety shows that catered to families. This is often considered to be the origin of vaudeville.[25] One promotion that Pastor used to attract women to his theater was to give away sewing kits and dress patterns.

In essence, variety turned into vaudeville under theater manager Benjamin F. Keith. The first theater exclusively devoted to vaudeville was opened in Boston by Keith and Edward F. Albee. They eliminated offensive material from the acts and fined offenders as they tried to reintegrate audiences that had been forgotten in the 1850s with the concert saloon. The vaudeville that came from the variety show and theater catered not only to men who drank and smoked, but had acts to appeal to women and children. Vaudeville theaters eventually became known as the "Sunday School Circuit," because nothing was presented that would be offensive to churchgoers. Though "good, clean entertainment" persisted in vaudeville, some questionable material started to creep back in by around 1908.[26]

One of the vast untapped audiences for entertainment was made up of middle-class women and the family members they could bring. By trying to remove the earlier scandalous image of stage entertainment, Keith and Albee tried to tap into this untouched potential reservoir of theatergoers. The waiter girls were out and matinees for women and children were in.

This later type of vaudeville show became standardized as eight to twelve acts that lasted from seven to 20 minutes each. These short, fast-paced acts followed one another in rapid succession, so if the audience did not like a particular act, they had only to wait a few minutes, because it was soon followed by something that they might like more. Typical vaudeville acts consisted of song, dance, magic acts, fire-eaters, animals, acrobats, ventriloquists, jugglers, sword-swallowers, and male and female impersonators. Comic sketches dealt with everyday life, such as dealing with landlords and marital problems at home. Keith and Albee also introduced the concept of continually repeating shows between 9:30 A.M. and 10:30 P.M., making it possible for patrons to drop in and see a complete show at any time. Typical of these shows was the Great Vaudeville Company, which played in Weisiger's Hall in Louisville, Kentucky.

Starting in the 1870s, burlesque as an entertainment form also changed as the bawdier acts in variety entertainment separated from vaudeville and became a new form of burlesque. This type of burlesque was more suggestive, and a major part of the entertainment featured the display of women's bodies. Burlesque continued to cater to white working-class men out for a night with the boys. It answered the need of masculine entertainment for miners, loggers, cowboys, and other single males of the American West.

Where burlesque had started as a legitimate satire or parody of a popular comedy or drama, it had now changed into the leg shows that started with *The Black Crook* and Lydia Thompson's British Blondes. By the 1890s, burlesque had changed so much that even Lydia Thompson claimed that it was totally different than what she had helped to pioneer in the 1860s. The more rowdy, raucous shows that primarily featured women, sometime called "dirty burlesque" or "the turkey show," were especially popular in Western saloons.

The new vaudeville included every type of act except scantily dressed women and offensive material, two of the staples of the new burlesque. Vaudeville tried to attract audiences to a clean act that women and children could attend. Even though a differentiation into vaudeville and the new type of burlesque took place, burlesque and variety troupes played to many of the same types of audiences in the same theaters, along many of the same circuits. At the same time, some acts might play in both burlesque shows and variety houses, but to different audiences.

Belly Dancing

Another way of exhibiting women's bodies was with belly dancing. The belly dance was introduced to America at the World's Columbian Exposition in Chicago in 1893. Intended to be a showcase for technological and cultural programs, the Exposition was arranged to commemorate the 400th anniversary of the discovery of the New World by Columbus. The fair was made up of 65,000 exhibits, displayed on 686 acres of reclaimed swampland on the shore of Lake Michigan, about five miles south of the city center. The exposition operated for six months and drew 27.5 million visitors. It has been estimated that between five and ten percent of the entire population of the United States at the time visited the fair.

The exposition consisted of two separate sites. White City was the formal site, the more "proper" and educational side of the displays. Featured exhibits there ran the gamut from commerce to fine art. Commercial entertainment and popular attractions were located in Midway Plaisance. This side of the exposition was intended to produce income for concessionaires.

Part of the exposition was planned to present and explain the new scientific field of anthropology to the public. Accordingly, the fair built villages that featured cultures from around the world. In reality, the displays emphasized the contemporary American view that non-white cultures were barbaric and primitive. The villages and exhibits were arranged in what contemporary scientists felt were a descending order of "civilization," based on the brain-weight measures discussed in the previous chapter. The displays ranged from German and Irish exhibits at the beginning, to African and American Indians at the other end. About half way down this presumed evolutionary chain were the "Streets of Cairo," along with Algerian, Egyptian, and Persian exhibits. This was where women performed the *danse du ventre*, which translated from the French literally means "dance of the stomach" or "belly dance."

Unlike the leg shows, such as *The Black Crook*, that featured extravagant underdressed chorus lines, the belly dance was performed by a solo dancer. Long lines formed as fairgoers — presumably caught up in the spirit of scientific inquiry — thronged to see the native women dance this latest sensation. Belly dancing quickly became nicknamed the "cooch," "cootch dancing," the "hootchy-kootchy," or some combination of these names and spellings.

In spite of exaggerated advertising claims, belly dancers performed in quite modest costumes. They typically wore simple baggy trousers and midriff-length tops, though perhaps with exotic designs on them. One salacious aspect for most men was that these women typically wore their hair long and loose while performing. This was considered to be a symbol of wild abandon in an era when respectable American women wore their hair pinned up in public.

The simple rising-and-falling tune (usually played on a flute) that is heard in movies to accompany the belly dance has been attributed to Sol Bloom, the entrepreneur who had obtained the rights to display the Algerian Village. When his group was invited to preview the dance to the Press Club of Chicago, Bloom realized that he had no music. In a flash of inspiration, he improvised a series of notes that are now traditionally associated with the mysterious Middle East. Bloom later regretted that he had not copyrighted the music.

A lady visitor to the Chicago Exposition, a Mrs. D.C. Taylor, gave her impression upon seeing the belly dance for the first time: "She takes a few light steps to one side, pauses, strikes the castanets, then the same to the other side; advances a few steps, pauses, and causes her abdomen to rise and fall several times in exact time to the music, without moving a muscle in any other part of her body, with incredible rapidity, at the same time holding her head and feet perfectly rigid."[27]

After the Chicago Exposition closed, the belly dance exhibition went on to New York, where it continued to be met with popular acclaim. A cooch dancer by the name of Omeena performed at the St. Louis World's Fair of 1896. In 1896, a "Little Egypt" dancer, thought to be Ashea Wabe, created a scandal by performing supposedly "nude" in New York. Because of the scandalous connotations, burlesque troupes quickly added a "Fatima," a "Little

Egypt," or a "Zora" to their shows and, by 1900, the cooch dance was a standard feature of burlesque companies. By 1904, at least five Little Egypts were touring the country, horrifying yet fascinating audiences everywhere with their abandoned dancing style.

Arguably the first "Little Egypt" was Farida Mazar Spyropoulos (different sources give her name as Fahruda Manzar and Farida Mazhar), who danced at the Chicago Exposition. She later performed in Skagway, Alaska, and Dawson, in the Yukon Territories, during the gold rush to the north. Another "Little Egypt" was Freda Maloof, a Greek girl billed as the "Turkish Whirlwind Danseuse." She tried to repeat Little Egypt's belly dance in Dawson, but the local superintendent of the Northwest Mounted Police rapidly stopped the dance as being too suggestive for the locals.[28]

Belly dancing continued after the beginning of the 20th century as part of carnival sideshows that toured the country. In the early 1900s, belly dancing appeared in brief films in nickelodeons and peep-show machines.

The belly dance was the sexual display of a single female performer. There was no drama, no plot, no company of performers — just the exhibition of one woman. As such, the cooch dance was another forerunner of the striptease.

The Skirt Dance

Skirt dancing was a form of female display that started in the mid–1870s and was very popular until about 1910. This was generally a less erotic form of dancing than belly dancing, because the skirt of the costume contained up to 60 feet of fabric. The dance involved acrobatic kicking, revolving, hopping, gliding, and graceful turning while controlling the material in the skirt. Like some other forms of dancing, skirt dancing became such a rage that it was commonly performed by non-professionals at home. The dance was so popular that one of the early Kinetoscope films produced by Thomas Edison's studio was of a skirt dance.[29]

The skirt dance was subject to many variations in tempo, style, and athletic performance. One variation was similar to the cancan, featuring acrobatic high kicks that showed enough leg to be appealing to the males in the audience. In the 1890s, dancer Charlotte Collins performed an uninhibited version of the skirt dance to the song and music of "Ta-ra-ra-boom-de-ay," revealing her stockings, garters, and some bare thigh during the high kicks. This act appealed to men and was the type of performance that was responsible for what has been referred to as the "Naughty Nineties." On the other hand, when English actress Letty Lind (Letitia Rudge) performed her version of the skirt dance in America in 1888, audiences were surprised that she did not reveal her legs or bosom.[30]

Striptease

In the early 20th century, burlesque turned more to the vulgar display of women, and focused more and more on the exhibition of the female figure. The erotic gyrations of the belly dance eventually changed into the shimmy, then the striptease dances of the 1920s and 1930s. Victorian theater did not condone nudity, as defined as total nakedness. Stripping in the Victorian sense was the removal of the outer garments to reveal tights or a circus-type of acrobatic costume.

Striptease did not become a part of burlesque until the mid–1920s, at a time when burlesque was already in decline. In the 1930s, striptease became a separate form of entertainment with such headliners as Gypsy Rose Lee and Ann Corio appearing in lavish costumes. The parodies that had started in burlesque, however, continued as even the dancers' names, such as Tempest Storm and Candy Barr, were exotic and tinged with a sense of humor.

The outfits were designed in more and more exotic fashion so that the actual stripping could be prolonged, thus creating more tips and revenue from alcohol from the customers. A runway that extended into the center of the audience was added in 1917 to bring the performers closer to audience and promote verbal interplay between the two, thus again prolonging the performance. Dancers were intended to be seductive and the dances were intended to be a slow tease rather than a rush to nakedness. Similar to the earlier living picture and leg shows, strippers did not undress to the point of nakedness, but ended with a minimal cover of G-string and pasties.

The downfall of this type of burlesque started in 1934 when New York Mayor Fiorello LaGuardia and Paul Moss, the commissioner of licenses, revoked the licenses of a series of burlesque theaters. This action led to the decline and eventual disappearance of striptease in the 1930s, though theaters in many large cities showed stag films interspersed with strip dances and baggy-pants comedians as late as the 1960s, as they tried to hold onto decreasing audiences.

FIVE

Bright Lights of the Pacific Coast

The combination of the annexation of California to the United States and the discovery of gold brought large crowds of single men to the Sierra Nevada Mountains, where the rough-and-ready miners demanded rough-and-ready entertainment. After a hard day of sluicing gravel for gold or cutting trees for lumber, miners, loggers, and other active single men didn't want to stay in their bachelor cabins in the evening. They wanted bright lights and entertainment — accompanied by drinking, of course.

The audience was not always particular about what the entertainment was. As a result, the *Mountain Democrat* newspaper of Placerville opined on October 10, 1857: "A California audience is generally not a very severe or critical one." All the men there asked was that the entertainers did their best.[1]

The Early Fandangos

Before the days of the gold rush of 1849, entertainment in California had a down-to-earth nature. When California was still an outpost of Mexico, bullfights, gambling halls, and fandangos were the popular forms of entertainment. Fandangos, in the parlance of the Forty-Niners, were dance houses.

Before the gold rush, the name "fandango" referred to a dance event, rather than the place in which it was held. The term eventually changed to "fandango house," meaning a dance hall, then became shortened to the simple name of "fandango." An early observer, Josiah Gregg, commented that the name fandango "is never applied to any particular dance, but is the usual designation for those ordinary assemblies where dancing and frolicking are carried on."[2] Fandangos were popular among the poorer inhabitants of Mexican California and New Mexico, many of whom often went to watch American men dancing with Mexican women.

The town of Sonora, high in the Sierra Nevada Mountains of California, had five fandango saloons during the gold rush years. Foreshadowing the later rise of impropriety in variety theaters, the local newspaper noted that at evening's end the men often left with the women dancers, and hinted not too subtly of the poor moral character found in these places. The offended reporter also prudishly noted that men and women danced very close.

James Pattie, attending a fandango in Santa Fe, New Mexico, in 1827 noted: "When the ball broke up, it seemed to be expected of us, that we should each escort a lady home, in whose company we passed the night, and we none of us brought charges of severity against our fair companions."[3]

Fandango houses were periodically the scene of violence. Crime followed the Forty-Niners to the fandango houses as it did everywhere. In the mining town of Volcano, the paper reported that a "Spanish dance house" was closed when the owner was arrested for grand larceny.

The *San Joaquin Republican* of July 30, 1851, reported on a murder that had taken place at Casa de los Amigos, a fandango house in Stockton, which was then a mining supply town. Apparently, Caleb Ruggles and James McCabe hadn't realized that they were in an establishment that in Spanish meant "The House of the Friends," and quarreled over who would go home with dancer Luz Parilla. The subsequent fight involved a Bowie knife and a gun, with the result being that McCabe shot Ruggles. Even though the event was discussed locally as self defense, a year later a new city ordinance prohibiting fandangos went into effect.

Gold Rush Days

Some of the first entertainers in California were traveling minstrels who performed wherever they could, appearing in tents or saloons in the gold fields. The so-called theater might be a false-fronted building with canvas walls. For lack of a place to perform, some entertainers played their acts on the street. Others performed in a saloon, splitting the profits with the saloon's owner.

Songs might be accompanied by solitary instruments, such as a piano, a flute, a violin, or a guitar. The music might even be supplied by an accordion, nicknamed a "stomach Steinway." When entertainers worked alone, they provided their own accompaniment. In the smaller places, if there was an orchestra, it perhaps played only on weekends. Often musicians were paid by passing the hat.

The **Pinos Altos Opera House** claims over the door to be established in "the late 60s" — but was actually the late *1960s*. This authentic-looking reproduction theater was used by the local Melodrama Company to host tourist melodramas (author's collection).

Entertainers presented a wide variety of material on the Forty-Niner's stages. Lotta Crabtree entertained with songs and dances. Edwin Booth recited Shakespeare. Methodist revival preacher the Rev. Adam Bland held forth on a street corner and then passed the hat (the audience reportedly gave freely). The Forty-Niners could watch prize fights, dog fights, bullfights, badger fights, and horse races. Adah Menken rode a horse across the stage in *Mazeppa*. J. Ross Browne presented a travelogue entitled *A Trip to Iceland*. Noted explorer William Burton gave his impressions of the Middle-East in *Arabia*. Cancan dancers kicked their legs in the air and showed their underwear. Burly miners held their collective breath as they watched Eliza escape across the ice floes in *Uncle Tom's Cabin*. Most playbills were as varied as the Fallon House theater in the gold-mining town of Columbia when Edwin Booth topped the bill in the serious production of Shakespeare's *Richard III*, followed by Lola Montez and her wildly gyrating Spider Dance.

Music was always popular and the miners liked robust songs, dances, and plays that appealed to the middle classes, performed by actors who portrayed everyday folk characters. The men also enjoyed romantic and nostalgic songs, because these reminded them of home, and the wives and sweethearts that they had left behind them in the East.

One popular musical revue that toured the California goldfields in 1849 was called *Seeing the Elephant*. Written and staged by Dr. David G. Robinson, this was a good-natured parody of mining in California.[4] It featured Robinson's popular song of the same name, which chronicled the ups and downs (mostly downs) of the gold miners. Robinson opened the Dramatic Museum in San Francisco on July 4, 1850. He continued to present *Seeing the Elephant*, and started the first school of drama in the city.

In the late 1840s, the catchphrase "seeing the elephant" was used to imply the excitement and disappointment of chasing the lure of California's elusive gold. The symbolism is said to have originated with a story of an Eastern farmer who had never seen an elephant, but wanted to do so. When a circus came to a nearby town, he decided to find out what the excitement was all about. On his way to town, he met the circus parade. The elephant scared the farmer's horse, scattering all the goods in his wagon. The farmer was not impressed, but figured he had "seen the elephant."

On October 20, 1851, Robinson opened the American Theatre in San Francisco, at Sansome and Halleck streets. It was one of the first brick buildings to be erected on the shallow fill that was pushed into San Francisco Bay to add to salable real estate in the city.[5] The theater was large enough to seat 2,000 patrons.

San Francisco

San Francisco was the theatrical capital of the West and was at the cultural center of the theatrical industry on the West Coast. By the end of the 1850s, booming San Francisco had almost as many theaters as Philadelphia, which had a population that was about six time as large.

The first known theater presentation in California was given in Spanish and took place in a converted lodging house in Monterey in 1848. At that time almost all of the Californian residents were still Spanish-speaking citizens

Blackface entertainers in minstrel shows were known as "Ethiopians" or "Ethiopian delineators." Some of the men in this troupe are dressed to play the parts of women (History Colorado, Garrison Collection, Scan #20005957).

of Mexico. The first English-language performance recorded in California was *The Golden Farmer* by Benjamin Webster which was presented to American soldiers stationed in Sonoma.

Entertainers of all sorts soon started to tread the boards. In the fall of 1849, the Aguila del Oro in San Francisco presented a chorus of "Ethiopians"— the contemporary term for blackface entertainers in minstrel shows — who sang Negro spirituals. The Verandah offered a one-man band who presented a solo musical performance playing the pipes, accompanied by drums and cymbals attached to his arms and back. As if this weren't enough, he danced to the music at the same time that he played.[6] More sedate establishments offered women performers playing the harp or piano. One woman, who played the violin at the Alhambra, was paid two ounces of gold dust daily, at the time worth $32.[7] Another young female musician took in $4,000 over a period of five or six months.[8]

Not as important in stature as San Francisco as the hub of theater entertainment in the West in the 1850s, but still a major part of West Coast theater, were the towns of Stockton and Sacramento. From San Francisco and Sacramento various theatrical groups played a circuit of the smaller mining camps in the Sierra Nevada Mountains, from Marysville and Nevada City to Placerville.

At first, there were few dedicated theater buildings on the touring circuit. Theater buildings were considered unnecessary because most towns already had some sort of a public hall that seated from 800 to 1,400 people. These halls were multi-purpose and were used for stage entertainment, lectures, concerts, music, dancing, and anything else that required a large space. When a touring group came to town, these buildings became temporary theaters.

Between 1850 and 1859, over 50 theaters and variety halls were built in San Francisco. Many were ramshackle wooden structures that were soon lost to fire. In this same time period there were a little over 1,100 performances of plays and melodramas (907), operas (48), and minstrel shows (66). Respected acting groups, including the Chapman family from the earlier Mississippi showboats, moved to San Francisco and performed there.

Sacramento beat San Francisco in building a dedicated theater. The first structure in California created specifically as a theater was the Eagle Theatre in Sacramento, built by Z. Hubbard as part of his saloon. The theater was basically a tent that was 30 feet wide by 65 feet deep, with a stage that was 15 feet deep. The "theater" could seat 300, with another hundred in the balcony. Admission was $2 on the main floor and $3 for a box. The first professional theater production in California, *The Bandit Chief; or, The Spectre of the Forest*, was presented there on October 18, 1849.

The building was not as grand as it sounded. Actors had to enter the stage through the saloon, and patrons with seats in the balcony had to climb up a ladder on the outside of the building. Canvas strips were nailed under the ladder to preserve the modesty of female patrons in skirts.[9] The theater did not last long, as it was destroyed by a flood on January 7, 1850.

The first dedicated theater in San Francisco was on the second floor of Washington Hall. A wooden structure that had a saloon on the ground level, it was located in Portsmouth Square, in the center of town at Kearny and Washington Streets.[10] The first theatrical show was a double bill, consisting of *The Wife* and *Charles the Second*, given by Sacramento's Eagle Theater actors on January 16, 1850. The price of seats was expensive — as much as $5 for the best. This performance was followed in April by several performances from a French vaudeville troupe, who performed in a new theater built at Washington Street near Montgomery. Washington Hall eventually became one of San Francisco's most elegant brothels.

The first circus to appear on the West Coast was Joseph Andrew Rowe's *Olympic Circus*, which premiered in San Francisco on October 4, 1849. Rowe was a versatile performer. He performed in *Othello* on February 4, 1850, and later alternated shows between Shakespeare and the circus.[11]

A building was not an issue for this first circus. Because plenty of space was needed for trick riders to jump through hoops and acrobats to fling themselves into the air, the initial performance was held on a vacant lot on Kearny Street near Clay. The performers played out their acts in a tent, with the audience seated on wooden benches. Prices were high, even for gold-rush San Francisco. The audience paid $3 for the pit, $5 for seats in the stalls, and a whopping $55 for a private box.[12] Similar circuses appeared in 1850 and 1851.

Theater entertainment caught on quickly with San Franciscans and a group of amateur actors presented various plays during the summer of 1850 at Robinson's new Dramatic Museum. The dominant theater in San Francisco in the early days was The Metropolitan Theatre, opened in 1853 by Catharine Sinclair. When Wade's Opera House was built in San Francisco in 1876, it was the largest in the city and the third largest in the country. It contained a third tier that may have been included for prostitutes to entertain clients.

The cruder forms of entertainment were presented in variety and music halls, such as the Bella Union, the Pacific Melodeon, Bert's New Idea Melodeon, the Temple of Music, the Adelphi, and Gilbert's Melodeon. Gilbert's, which later became The Olympic, located at Clay and Kearny streets, advertised itself as having "freedom from constrained etiquette"[13]—a description that piques the imagination. The programs were certainly vulgar, but not necessarily obscene. No dancing, no pretty waiter girls, and no robberies were tolerated on the premises, but female performers were required to sell drinks between stage appearances. Revenue came from a nominal admission charge and the sale of liquor.

San Francisco was not all bawdy shows. Between October 1851 and December 1854, 14 Shakespeare plays were presented and enjoyed by patrons of all tastes.

The Bella Union originally opened as gambling house in 1849, then presented the first minstrel show in San Francisco, by the Philadelphia Minstrels in October of that year. Typical of the varied types of entertainment that appeared at the Bella Union were a Mexican quintet, consisting of two harps, two guitars, and a flute, and Charley Schultze, who played the violin and sang.

The Bella Union presented occasional theatrical performances during the gold rush days, but it remained primarily a gambling house until 1856. Then it was reopened as a theater by Samuel Tetlow. His tenure lasted until 1880, when he shot and killed his partner, Billy Skeantlebury. After that, he sold the Bella Union, took up with a chorus girl, and was quickly reduced to poverty. Ned Foster took over the saloon in 1887 and ran it successfully until 1892 when the city passed legislation prohibiting the sale of liquor in theaters. The loss of revenue forced most of the Barbary Coast theaters out of business.

The type of shows presented at the Bella Union gradually degenerated and, in 1869, the San Francisco *Call* described one current show as consisting of "songs and dances of licentious and profane character," and claimed that the saloon presented "all that can pander to that morbid desire of the rabble for obscenity."

The Bella Union building was destroyed several times by fire, but was quickly rebuilt each time. When it was rebuilt in 1868, the building lasted until the great San Francisco earthquake of 1906. In later years, the Bella Union became the Haymarket Theatre, then the Imperial Concert Hall, and finally a waxworks called the Eden Museum.

In 1875, the management of the Bella Union decided to change its approach. They wanted to get away from the variety hall's sordid reputation and make it into a reputable theater. Their new advertising assured potential customers that there would be no indecent behavior on the stage or in the audience. In spite of these affirmations, the theater continued to rent private boxes for $55, while seats on the main floor sold for $3.

Many of the actors and singers who appeared at the Bella Union and other San Francisco theaters became stars of drama, vaudeville, or musical comedy later in their careers. Edward "Ned" Harrigan — who later teamed with Tony Hart to become the celebrated song-and-dance team of Harrigan and Hart — started his career singing with Lotta Crabtree in 1861. He earned his living by caulking ships before he appeared as a singer at Gilbert's Melodeon. He did not have an auspicious start there, but he persevered at show business and finally became a success when he moved to the Bella Union. After a year he was making $50 a week, which was a good salary for a new entertainer. His partner, Tony Hart, was a talented comedian who had sung and danced in San Francisco's saloons for several years previously. One of his specialties was wench impersonations in minstrel shows. He joined Mme. Rentz's Female Minstrels in 1870 and teamed up with Harrigan in 1871. The two went on to great success and acclaim in a series of musical ethnic plays based on a collection of stereotypical Irish characters and the paramilitary organizations to which they belonged. The first was *The Mulligan Guard*, which opened in New York in 1879.[14] One of the series, *Cordelia's Aspirations*, ran for 176 performances. The last of their shows to feature the Mulligans was *Reilly and the Far Hundred*.

Dance halls and concert saloons were popular in early San Francisco. They followed the typical saloon building design, being a long rectangular room with a low ceiling and a bar down one side, a clear space in the center for dancing, and a raised platform at one end for the orchestra. In the low-

This is a re-creation of the Long Branch saloon in Dodge City, Kansas. Though not intended to be an accurate reproduction of the original, it is representative of Western saloon-theaters of the late 1800s. The bar is along the left wall, with a piano and small stage at the left rear, chairs and tables for drinking, and gambling on the right (author's collection).

class places, this consisted of only a piano. In others there might some combination of instruments, such as a fiddle, a trombone, and a clarinet.

Among the worst saloons in San Francisco was the Opera Comique at Jackson and Kearny streets, a street-corner so dangerous that it was nicknamed "Murderers' Corner." The Opera Comique offered the bawdiest and most obscene shows on the Barbary Coast. It was owned by Happy Jack Harrington, who was known for dressing in high fashion, complete with top hat, frock coat, and white shirts with ruffles down the front. He ran the theater for several years with a woman called Dutch Louise, who was also known as Big Louise.[15]

Harrington, it turned out, was a heavy drinker and drank up most of the profits. After one particularly severe bout of drinking, he found religion and renounced his wild ways. As part of his conversion, he sold the theater and bought a restaurant. Big Louise wasn't ready for the restaurant business, so she married a rich miner and left San Francisco. She may have made the correct choice, because Jack was later found drunk and clutching a Bible in the gutter in front of his restaurant. The restaurant was subsequently sold at a sheriff's sale in 1878 and Happy Jack went back to his old trade. He made enough money at gambling to open another saloon, this time at Pacific and Sansome streets. His location was again in the worst part of town. Pacific Street contained such a large collection of saloons and bordellos that its local nickname was "Terrific Street."

Jack was so bitter about losing his original saloon, restaurant, and all his money that he rented a lecture hall and railed on against the salvation group that had "saved" him from temptation. His audience of only seven — six newspaper reporters and a drunk with nothing better to do — didn't really care.

Top-rate theater entertainment started in San Francisco when Thomas "Tom" Maguire built Maguire's Opera House in 1856. It was a magnificent building — 55 feet wide by 137 feet deep, with a seating capacity of 1,000. The interior was white and gold, complemented by crimson and gold draperies, and brightly colored cushions. Lighting was by gas, with the highlight being a huge, specially manufactured chandelier that was suspended from the top of the interior of the building.

Maguire's first entertainment consisted of the standard minstrel shows, novelty acts, and stock companies. The theater was so successful that he eventually brought in stars from all over the world, offering the best of comedy, drama, and Shakespeare. In 1859, Maguire refurbished the Opera House and started to offer authentic opera.

Maguire owned three different buildings named the Jenny Lind Theatre, the first two of which burned down. The first Jenny Lind opened in September 1850; it was located on Kearny Street above the Parker House saloon, which was also owned by Maguire. Described as being a "handsome" theater, it could seat an audience of 800. Popular presentations were *Hamlet* and *King Lear*. The theater was destroyed by fire (as happened to many theaters) on June 22, 1851, along with the rest of the wooden structure. Maguire rapidly rebuilt, but this second theater, even though it was advertised as being fireproof, also burned down shortly after it opened.

Showing great perseverance, Maguire rebuilt again, but this time out of white sandstone brought from Australia. This was the largest of the three theaters, 75 feet wide and 140 feet deep, with seating for 2,000. The two upper stories had floor-to-ceiling windows and included a balcony, several galleries, and a few private boxes. This magnificent structure was opened on October 4, 1851. For two weeks in 1852, Junius Brutus Booth played in *Hamlet*, *Macbeth*, *Othello*, and *Richard III* to packed houses.

Like the first two, this Jenny Lind Theater also did not last long. In the summer of 1852, the city bought the building for $200,000 and turned it into the city hall.[16]

Maguire was the leading producer of stage shows for the San Francisco theaters. He was born in New York in 1820 and worked there as a hackney (horse-drawn cab) driver and bartender before moving west with the gold rush in 1849. He had no theater experience, but was attracted by the potential of profit and was a good enough businessman that he succeeded. After finding success in San Francisco, however, Maguire lost his fortune and died in poverty in New York.

One of the best theaters in town was the California Theatre, which presented first-rate productions and attracted major stars to its stage. The theater opened on January 18, 1869, with Edward Bulwer-Lytton's popular comedy *Money*.[17] One of the best-known Victorian comedies, the play was a satire of social greed and arrogance, but was balanced by Victorian sentimentality and romance. The building was torn down in 1888.

After the completion of the transcontinental railroad in 1869, the freewheeling early days of San Francisco theater ended. Actors and traveling troupes could now easily travel from the East, bringing theatrical culture and the latest shows. In the 1870s San Francisco became one of the largest and wealthiest cities in the United States, fueled by the outpouring of gold and silver from the Sierra Nevada mines and the Washoe district of southwest Nevada.[18]

Seattle

Theater in Seattle, Washington, which was originally settled in 1851, developed later than the northern California circuit, but the town was another important theatrical center on the West Coast. Much of Seattle's growth occurred because it was a recreation center for the Northwest's logging industry and later because it was one of the major stepping-off points for the turn-of-the-century Alaska gold rushes.

Theater in Seattle had its first stumbling steps when Henry Yesler, one of the founding fathers of Seattle, built a 30-foot by 100-foot building called Yesler Hall in 1861. This building replaced earlier theater space in makeshift quarters in the dining room of Yesler's sawmill. The new hall had multiple uses, including a place for performances by itinerant entertainers, and soon it became the center of Seattle's entertainment activity. In 1865, Yesler replaced the hall with Yesler's Pavilion, at Cherry Street and First Avenue.

Traveling companies started to appear in Seattle in the 1870s, presenting the usual mix of shows. On July 24, 1871, for example, Dr. C. Pinkham gave a lecture on phrenology, physiology, physiognomy, and other subjects. He supplemented his views on how to pass desirable traits on to one's children with an onstage examination of two heads. Also in 1871, the first professional play in Seattle, *Uncle Tom's Cabin*, was presented. This popular play kept coming back to Seattle in various versions — one as an operetta, one with an all-colored cast, and one with two Little Evas and two packs of bloodhounds.[19]

In 1874, actress Edith Mitchell was marooned in Seattle, waiting for a boat to Hawaii, so she staged a theatrical performance. She rented a small hall over Charles Plummer's store and gave a recitation of excerpts from Shakespeare and various popular poems. In 1875, the Fanny Morgan Phelps Dramatic Company came to Seattle to perform several plays, including the obligatory *Uncle Tom's Cabin*.

There appeared to be enough public support for entertainment in Seattle for a local troupe to be organized. The result was the John Jack Theatrical Company. Their premier performance was the ever-popular tear-jerker *East Lynne*. Unfortunately, the evening was marred by the performance of the child actor playing the part of Willie, who refused to die a suitable stage death, according to the script. As a result, the manager was forced to ring down the curtain prematurely.[20]

The theatrical troupe struggled on in spite of a generally lukewarm reception to their performances, and were hindered by a series of other difficulties that arose from time to time. In Victoria, British Columbia, for example, two of the performers became so drunk that they refused to play their parts.

The troupe tried what they thought would be more entertaining for the locals with a play called *Captain Jack; or, A Life on the Border*. After seeing the play, a reviewer for the *Puget Sound Dispatch* described it as "of the dime-novel melodrama description, and consisted of four abductions, one attempted poisoning, two bowie-knife combats, one chloroforming, and twenty-four homicides, and from the beginning to the end there was a running fire of revolvers." In spite of this lively attempt to regain audiences, John Jack finally went bankrupt and the troupe was dissolved.

Despite these misfires, theater in Seattle continued to grow. Frye's Opera House, completed in 1885, was the largest theater north of San Francisco at the time. It had a seating capacity of 1,300. Vaudeville on the West Coast was presented by John Cordray in Seattle in 1888.

One of the best-known of the Seattle theatrical entrepreneurs was John Considine, who came to Seattle from Chicago in 1889. As happened in many towns across the West, Considine combined elements of the theater, saloon, and bawdy house into the People's Theater in 1891. The idea for this combination of elements was certainly not new, but Considine did add one new twist. In most of these "theaters" women sang, danced, and then sold drinks and themselves between acts. Considine's approach was different. He hired performers with respectable talents specifically to sing and dance on the stage, and designated other women to the specific job of entertaining customers in the boxes. Admission was ten cents.

Local anti-liquor sentiment forced the closing of The People's Theatre in 1894. But, in 1897, when the Klondike Gold Rush started, Seattle was a major port for ships headed north and the City of Seattle decided to reconsider its anti-liquor ordinance. Considine was allowed to reopen. He hired Ashea Wabe, one of the Little Egypts performing around the country, to perform the notorious belly dance. Wabe had been arrested for dancing nude — in the Victorian sense — at Sherry's in New York for a fancy bachelor party in 1896. She danced to tremendous applause. She was found innocent when she explained to the judge that she wasn't actually naked. Another Little Egypt, Fahruda Manzar, has also been credited as the one who danced at Sherry's — but dressed in nothing at all.

Considine was so successful in his approach to entertainment that he later left the seedier part of the theater business and went into more legitimate forms of entertainment. He eventually turned his single original theater into the nation's first vaudeville circuit. At one point, Considine paid Sarah Bernhardt $7,000 a week to perform.

In 1909, in the wake of the Alaska gold rush, Seattle staged the Alaska-Yukon-Pacific Exposition to commemorate the annexing of Alaska. A Little Egypt troupe entertained there, providing a certain amount of titillation for the attendees.

Like anywhere else, it was not always easy to find success in Seattle's theatrical business. One theater was successively known as the Madison Street Theater (which opened with *H.M.S. Pinafore* in 1890), the Cordray (where Sarah Bernhardt played in *Fédora* in 1891), and, finally, as the Third Avenue Theater, before being torn down during urban reconstruction.

Spokane, in eastern Washington, drew from Seattle's success. The town enjoyed various operettas and variety shows after Emma Abbott appeared in 1883 in *The Bohemian Girl*. She performed in a warehouse with seats for the performance costing $2. Other theaters in Spokane were The Fall City and Concordia Theaters.

Dawson

Though the gold rush to the Klondike River of the Yukon was both geographically separate from and occurred at a later time than the gold rushes to the western states of the lower 48 states, it was philosophically a part of the great gold rushes to the West; it had many of the same characteristics, and many of the same people participated. Ed Schieffelin from Tombstone prospected up the Yukon River in 1882. Nellie Cashman, who ran a boarding house in Tombstone, ran one in the Klondike. Wyatt Earp, Soapy Smith, Arizona Charlie Meadows, and Kate Rockwell all appeared there from time to time. The list goes on and on. Because Seattle was the closest major port of embarcation for the gold fields, Dawson, Skagway, and Seattle shared many of the same entertainers.

The first of the gold rushes to the Far North started when modest amounts of gold were found on Birch Creek, not far south of the Arctic Circle. In response, a town named Circle City was founded in 1893. By 1896 gold production was greater than $1 million, and the town — known as the "Paris of Alaska" — had grown to 1,200 inhabitants. The residents were entertained by a music hall, two theaters, eight dance halls, and 28 saloons.

Entertaining the public was not always easy. One troupe of vaudeville players with a limited repertoire didn't plan very well and became unexpectedly stuck in town for the winter by bad weather. They performed the same routines every night for seven months until even the entertainment-hungry miners became bored.

Circle City collapsed as fast as it had grown and, by the end of the winter of 1896, it had become a virtual ghost town. The miners bailed out for the next promise of riches on Rabbit Creek, and the great Klondike Gold Rush of 1897–99 was on.

Dawson, which was founded on this, the last of the great gold rushes at the turn of the century, became the center of entertainment for the north. By June 1898, Dawson's population had grown to about 28,000 people. Like Circle City, however, Dawson's fame and fortune came and went in an eyeblink. Dawson lasted as a boomtown for only a year, from July of 1898 to July of 1899. Before that it was a small frontier town; later it became a virtual ghost town.

Gold-rush Dawson was the hub of frenzied activity and even the most outlandish schemes were proposed in all seriousness. The Trans-Alaskan Gopher Company, for example, planned to contract the digging of tunnels in the Klondike by using trained gophers. Another peculiar scheme (proposed by a company with the impressive name of The Klondike and Cuba Ice Towing and Anti–Yellow Fever Company) was to tow icebergs from Alaska to the South Seas to make cooling compresses for fever victims.[21]

While it lasted, Dawson was a wild meeting place for exuberant miners who demanded entertainment. Drinking and gambling continued 24 hours a day, except on Sunday. As would be expected, dance halls and saloons saw most of their business from 8 P.M. to about 6 or 7 A.M. The dancing was preceded by stage entertainment, which lasted until around midnight. The formal part of the entertainment might be a dramatic play, followed by a series of vaudeville acts. These stage shows were often crude, but they drew in large audiences six nights a week.

After the shows were over, the dance floors were cleared and the orchestra — perhaps a piano, violin, trombone, and cornet — started to play around 1 A.M. A dance typically cost $1 for thirty seconds to a minute of whirling around the floor. At this rate, the men could go through their money fast. Wages for a common laborer were $10 to $20 a day. Dance hall girls in Dawson typically earned $100 a night. The popular dances were waltzes, schottisches, square dances, quadrilles, and polkas. After a short whirl to a sprightly tune with a dancer, the leader on the stage told the men to head to the bar and buy their partners a drink. All tunes were lively music designed for lots of movement in order to create a thirst. At this point the men bought drinks for the women or accompanied them back to their rooms for a short interlude.

Dancing with the shady ladies was popular. Roddy Conners, a short, thickset Irishman, danced away between $500 and $2,000 a night and, as a result, ended up penniless. Some of the women went down in Dawson history. Gertie Lovejoy, for example, had a diamond set between her two front teeth and became Diamond-Tooth Gertie.

Though Dawson's star was short-lived, its boom and bust was phenomenal. George "Tex" Rickard, a former marshal from Texas, went to Dawson and invested $60,000 in a gambling hall and saloon named the Northern Saloon. In only four months he made $155,000.[22] Other popular theaters in Dawson were the Tivoli, the Monte Carlo, and Alexander Pantage's Orpheum. The best-known pianist in town was the Rag Time Kid, who played at the Dominion Saloon. He boasted that he could play any song requested.[23]

Although geographically remote, Dawson was up-to-date. Acetylene lights were used in the theaters, which later converted to electricity. In some establishments, the bar, the dance hall, the gambling tables, and the stage entertainment were run as separate concessions. The building owner simply leased out space for these different enterprises and made his money from collecting the rents.

Theatrical productions in Dawson were not always the most lavish, and producers often had to make do with whatever was available in the distant frontier town. The productions of both *Pygmalion* and *Galatea* called for a fawn. The closest animal that the producer could find was a stuffed and mounted malemute dog.

Malemutes were often called upon to play stage roles, because they were commonly available in Canada and the Yukon as sled-dogs. In one production of *Uncle Tom's Cabin*, for example, the role of the pack of bloodhounds was played by a single malemute puppy. Apparently, he was not amused at being thrust into an acting role because he howled in protest all through his part as he was guided across the stage by wires.[24] This was not the only substitution in this low-budget production. The ice floes in the Ohio River that Eliza crossed as she escaped from her slave-trader pursuers were made of crumpled newspaper. The more conventional approach was to make them out of heavy cardboard and paint them to look like ice.

Women entertainers of all ages were popular on the stage in Dawson, whether they were actresses, singers, or dancers. As in other gold camps, female performers were of two kinds. One was the legitimate dramatic actress, who sang and danced. The other was the variety entertainer in a low-class music hall, who visited with customers after performing in the show.

The entertainment was varied, and not always sophisticated. At the Grand Opera House, George Snow, an entrepreneur and part-time miner, produced Shakespearean plays and vaudeville shows. Snow's children performed and the miners were so desperate for entertainment that they threw gold nuggets onto the stage to show their appreciation. At one performance in Dawson, Monte Snow and his sister picked up $142 on stage after they danced and sang. Nine-year-old Margie Newman, "The Princess of the Klondike," was overwhelmed with gold nuggets after she sang a sentimental song that brought tears to the eyes of miners far from wives and children.[25]

In the spring of 1898, "Klondike Mike" Mahoney, and a troupe known as the Sunny Sampson Sisters Sextette, tried to bring a small piano over Chilkoot Pass from Skagway for Hal Henry of Henry's Theatrical Enterprises. The group was turned back at the Canadian border because the Mounties said that the trek over the pass was too rough for females. The troupe went back to Skagway and performed for six months in Soapy Smith's saloon.[26]

Jefferson Randolph "Soapy" Smith was one of the ultimate con men of the far north. He gained his start in Leadville, Colorado, entertaining miners as he sold them bars of soap on the street corner. As Smith wrapped the bars in front of the customers, he tucked an occasional $10 or $20 bill into the wrapping while he prattled on to skeptical onlookers. A confederate would wander up and purchase a bar of soap. (Guess which one.) The confederate would open the wrapping, whoop out loudly, and wave a $20 bill in the air. Sales of bars of soap were brisk after that. Strangely enough, none of the purchasers ever found money in their soap.

Smith moved on from Leadville to Creede, Colorado, where he and his henchmen basically ran the town. Before he was run out of town, he joined the gold rush to Alaska. He tried to run Dawson the same as he had run Creede, but was not as successful and was shot to death there on July 8, 1898.

One who went on to prosper with vaudeville was Alexander Pantages.

He was originally born around 1871 in the Greek Islands as Pericles Pantages, but in a moment of self-aggrandizement he renamed himself after Alexander the Great. Pantages was an illiterate Greek immigrant who could hardly speak English.[27] He joined the gold rush of 1898 to the Klondike, hoping to make his fortune. When he reached Skagway he realized that he could make more money by entertaining than by digging for gold. He quickly had the bright idea that the local miners would pay to hear the latest news. Because he could not read, Pantages hired a man to read the copy of the Seattle *Post-Intelligencer* that he had brought with him in a local dance hall. He charged $1 a head for admission and made $350.[28]

Pantages became a bartender and then a waiter, before becoming stage manager at Charlie Meadows's Monte Carlo Saloon. He also started a small theatrical company presenting the usual popular plays, such as *Uncle Tom's Cabin* and *East Lynne*.

Pantages prospered in show business in Dawson because he had a knack for figuring out what audiences wanted and then providing it. He brought in the best entertainment that he could, though it often consisted of the usual mix of singers, dancers, jugglers, comedians, and good-looking women in abbreviated costumes. He made a fortune by combining women and earthy comedy, and adding extravagant dance numbers and sentimental ballads to the mix. He stuck to the fundamentals of the variety show business, keeping the pace fast and leaving the audience wanting more. He offered the best and most successful show in town at $12.50 a table. At peak times, he grossed $8,000 a day.

In 1900, Pantages fell in love with Kathleen "Kitty" Rockwell, better known by her nickname of "Klondike Kate." She was a teenaged dancer who wore a $1,500 satin gown in one show, had a belt of $20 gold pieces, and once appeared wearing a head-dress decorated by 50 lighted candles. Kate and Pantages entered into a personal relationship and she became the headliner at Pantages's Orpheum theater. The Orpheum was destroyed by fire three times, but Pantages rebuilt it at once. Eventually the Pantages chain of show houses spread to Seattle, Portland, Los Angeles, San Francisco, and many other cities and towns all over the West. At the peak, he owned 22 vaudeville theaters and had a controlling interest in another 28.

Not all the entrepreneurs in Dawson were as successful. Charlie Kimball, who was a success as miner and wanted to branch out, built The Pavilion dance hall for $100,000. Off to a good start on opening night in June of 1898, he took in $12,000. Unfortunately, he spent money as fast as he made it and lost everything, including his dance hall.

Not all the entertainment was indoors in the theaters. The pretty, petite Oatley Sisters, Polly and Lottie, were popular performers who had previously appeared nationally in the lower 48 states. For their act, the girls entertained every evening on a canvas-covered platform, just off the main street of Dawson. The two girls danced and sang, accompanied by a portable organ. They were sometimes also accompanied by their dog, Tiny, who was reported to have a fine soprano "singing voice." They had been performing for a number of years before arriving in Dawson, as one of their earlier appearances was in Victor, Colorado, in 1896.

The girls sang lively songs and danced all night, but were well paid for their exhausting efforts. They also sang sad songs, such as "Break the News to Mother," "A Bird in a Gilded Cage," and other sentimental ballads of the day which brought tears to the eyes of the hardened miners. When the weather was bad, the girls took their act inside at the Regina Saloon.

Like elsewhere, the lines between actress and prostitute were sometime blurred as the girls of Dawson struggled to make a living. Fanny Hall, for example, was a performing actress who was also known to work as a prostitute. The local paper reported in January of 1900 that she was working in the dance halls under an assumed name.

Further south, in Victoria, British Columbia, was one of the jumping-off points for the Klondike, where men pushed, shoved, and brawled to get on the overcrowded ships for the north before the other gold seekers. In the spring of 1900, the owners of the Savoy theater, in Victoria, organized a large burlesque and theatrical company to go to Dawson. It was the largest to go to the Klondike, comprised of 173 singers, dancers, actors, actresses, jugglers, comedians, and all their supporting staff and musicians. In Dawson, they opened the Savoy saloon and dance hall. The building, lit by oil lamps and heated by pot-bellied stoves, soon became the liveliest spot in town. The band, which consisted primarily of trumpets and violins, played lively melodies while the chorus line danced the naughty, high-kicking cancan. More sedate entertainment was provided by a male barbershop quartet. As in other theaters of this type, the benches were moved from the floor after the show to make space for dancing.

Hollywood depicts dance halls as being splendidly furnished. The reality in Dawson was that all the furniture, and much of the wood, had to be packed over the mountains. As a result, saloon furnishings were plain, sturdy, and serviceable. A typical combination of saloon and theater was the Monte Carlo. It consisted of a deep, dark room heated by a sheet iron stove, with a bar running the length of the left wall. The bartenders were splendidly outfitted in white aprons and starched shirts with diamond stickpins. Behind the saloon area was the gambling room, where faro, poker, dice, and roulette were played 24 hours a day. Beyond this was the theater itself. The main auditorium on the ground floor had movable benches, which were removed for dancing.

Above the auditorium floor were a balcony and a small curtained stage. The upper floor also had boxes used for private entertainment, which could be rented for a night or a week. Champagne cost $60 a quart.

One of the men who drifted in and out of show business in Dawson was a character named "Swiftwater Bill" Gates. Gates started as a dishwasher in Circle City, then followed the next gold rush to Dawson. He was one of the lucky ones. He struck gold and was soon wearing a Prince Albert coat, a top hat, and a magnificent diamond stickpin. Hoping to increase his fortunes, he went into business with Jack Smith. Smith was an experienced businessman who owned several saloons and entertainment halls before he opened the Monte Carlo in a tent on Front Street. Together, Smith and Gates started the Monte Carlo Dance Hall and Saloon in a permanent building.

Gates went to San Francisco to buy liquor and arrange for girls for the dance hall. Unfortunately, Bill had a habit of spending money very freely. While Jack waited patiently in Dawson, Bill rented a suite of rooms at the Baldwin Hotel in San Francisco. He called himself the "King of the Klondike" and started spreading gold dust all over town. When he started to run out of money, he persuaded a Dr. Wolf to invest $20,000 in the saloon. Meanwhile, he continued to parade around town, spending the money with the girls who were supposed to be headed north for the Klondike and a career at the Monte Carlo. Wolf finally realized what was happening and demanded his money back — or else. Gates somehow raised some money and paid off the irate Wolf.

Meanwhile, in Dawson, Gates's partner, Jack Smith, realizing what was happening, attached liens to Gates's mining profits and his share of the ownership of the dance hall. Bill continued to play the role of a spender for the rest of his life, chasing young women, making fortunes and losing them just as fast, until he died in 1935 in Peru, after somehow finagling a huge silver mining concession.

Gates's antics were so famous that he became a caricature. John Mulligan and his wife, Carrie, had been staging vaudeville and burlesque shows on the Pacific Coast. Their show consisted of a series of bawdy and satirical skits of contemporary issues. They wrote *The Adventures of Stillwater Willie* as a satire of the life of Swiftwater Bill.[29] They produced the show in the Tivoli and later at the Monte Carlo. Rather than being angry or insulted, Bill was one of the greatest enthusiasts of the show. He watched performance after performance, applauding heartily each time.

SIX

Theaters Across the Old West

Actors, actresses, theatrical troupes, and entertainers of all sorts traveled the theaters of the West, particularly after expansion of the railroad system allowed easy travel across the wide open spaces. It was still, however, primarily the big cities like San Francisco, Denver, and Virginia City, Nevada, that could afford to build the magnificent theaters and could draw on large enough audiences to attract top-notch entertainers. Small towns had small theater buildings and small audiences that could only attract traveling troupes for a few days at a time. For this reason, this look at theaters in the West is a selective one that concentrates primarily on entertainment in several of the larger cities.

The second factor that influenced this particular choice of theatrical centers was that cities — such as Tombstone in Arizona, Leadville in Colorado, and Deadwood in South Dakota — were wide-open boomtowns founded in their early stages by a young, predominantly male population who worked hard and expected to be entertained in a similarly unrestrained fashion. The result of this uneven population distribution was that top-notch theater entertainment was concentrated in a relatively few large cities. The large, first-class theaters offered the best salaries and working conditions, whereas the minor circuit of small theaters in out-of-the-way towns hired underpaid performers. As one humorous example, the *Ouray Times* reported on October 22, 1881, that the local production of the show *The Charcoal Burner* was attended by a "large crowd." The number was apparently relative for this small mining town in Colorado, because the total box office receipts were only $11.25.

Virginia City, Nevada

In the 1860s and 1870s, Virginia City, Nevada, grew to become one of the most important towns in the West for entertainers. Many of the owners of large mines lived in San Francisco, so essentially Virginia City was economically and philosophically a suburb tied to the city by the bay.

Small amounts of gold had been found on Sun Mountain, just east of the California-Nevada border, in 1849, but they didn't amount to much. In 1859, an analysis of a blue clay that was interfering with gold-sluicing showed large amounts of silver and a new mining rush to western Nevada was on. By 1861, the population of Virginia City had grown to a little over 3,000 people. At the district's peak in 1875, estimates placed the population at around 20,000.

Virginia City quickly sprouted several theaters. In February 1861, a hall with 1,000 seats was built. The Alhambra Theater was a showplace that featured bawdy burlesque musicals that consisted mainly of voluptuous actresses displaying their figures in scanty costumes. The women were generally available for further private entertainment after the show.

Tom Maguire, one of the most successful of the San Francisco theatrical showmen, saw an opportunity in the booming silver camp and built Maguire's New Opera House in 1863 as a showplace for popular entertainment for the miners of Virginia City. Combined with his San Francisco theater, he was able to book top acts for tours. Minstrels, dog fights, *The Black Crook*, and the exotic Adah Menken appeared there. The interior of Maguire's new theater was bigger than his opera house in San Francisco. It featured gas chandeliers of glittering crystal, and gas footlights. At either side of the stage was a double tier of boxes, furnished with rich woven scarlet drapes, gilt chairs, and velvet railings. The stage curtain showed a magnificent view of nearby Lake Tahoe from the top of the intervening mountains. The theater also had several billiard parlors, a cigar stand, smoking rooms, a magnificent bar, and gaming tables.

The opening play was Edward Bulwer-Lytton's comedy *Money*, with Julia Dean Hayne and Walter Lehman in the lead roles. One of Hayne's early notable roles was as Lucretia Borgia in Victor Hugo's play of the same name. The opening night of Maguire's theater was marred somewhat by a one-sided shoot-out between a gunman named Howard and a man named Jack McNab. McNab was unarmed, but Howard shot at him anyway, from the balcony across the theater. While patrons ducked, McNab jumped down onto the stage and disappeared behind the curtains. Luckily, McNab escaped, and the play continued.

The McNab-Howard fight, it seemed, was not the only unwanted occurrence on opening night. As Hayne was reading a poem to commemorate the grand opening, a Washoe Zephyr, one of the howling windstorms for which Virginia City was famous blew down the canyon and rattled the building. Indeed, Washoe Zephyrs were not something to ignore. As Mark Twain eloquently put it: "A Washoe wind is by no means a trifling matter. It blows flimsy houses down, lifts shingle roofs occasionally, rolls up tin ones like sheet music, now and then blows a stagecoach over and spills the passengers; and tradition says the reason there are so many bald people there is, that the wind blows the hair off their heads while they are looking skyward after their hats."[1] In this case, the wind died down as quickly as it had started, and the performance continued with no further interruptions.

John Piper acquired Maguire's Opera House in 1868 and changed the name to Piper's Opera House. Under Piper's management, the opera house became one of the most impressive theaters in the West. It stood out among the others and became a required stop for touring musicians, lecturers, actors, and performers of all sorts.

Other theaters in Virginia City were Topliffe's Theater, E.W. Carey's La Plata Hall, The Temple of Comedy, the Niagara Concert Hall, Henry Sutcliff's Music Hall, and the Gold Hill Theater.

Deadwood, South Dakota

A rich gold strike in 1875 along Deadwood Creek in the Black Hills of South Dakota led to the founding of the town of Deadwood. Two dance halls soon appeared, followed by a series of variety theaters. By 1877, there were 75 saloons, gambling dens, and brothels to provide entertainment for the local gold miners.

One of the most popular variety theaters in Deadwood was the Gem Theater on lower Main Street. The Gem, managed by Alfred Ellis Swearingen, appeared early in the town's development and provided entertainment for everyone. Deadwood pioneer Estelline Bennett vividly recalled the raucous sounds that drifted out of the theater. "The Gem Theater for nearly a quarter of a century was a clangorous, tangling, insidious part of Deadwood's nightly life. The raucous tones of its ballyhooing brass-band in the street outside threaded through the pealing church bells like an obligato. They shrieked in blatant brass the interdependence of the good and bad in Deadwood Gulch."[2]

Opening night at the Gem featured operatic singers, banjo players, comedians, clog dancers, and an exhibition of trick shooting. For a variety theater, the Gem presented some of the top-notch performers playing the Western theater circuits at the time. Along with quality entertainment, men went there to seek the simple pleasures of drinking, dancing, and the earthy entertainment by the Gem's waiter girls and prostitutes.

Over the years of its existence, the theater featured a wide variety of stage presentations, including trapeze acts, boxing matches, stage plays, danc-

The Gem Theater was considered to be the most popular entertainment place in roaring Deadwood during the gold rush years (Glenn Kinnaman Colorado and Western History Collection).

ing, vaudeville acts, and even exhibitions of war dances and scalp dances by local Sioux Indians. The original theater building burned in 1879, and was rebuilt almost immediately. The auditorium of the new Gem Theater was 30 feet by 70 feet, with a 24-foot ceiling. The auditorium was surrounded by 19 curtained boxes where patrons could order whiskey and beer, and dally with the waitresses. The stage was 20 feet by 30 feet, with dressing rooms underneath. After the dancing and singing acts on the stage were over, the patrons cleared the main floor and used the open space for dancing. To promote the sales of alcohol, the building had a bar area in the front, and next door was a dance hall and wine rooms. This combination must have worked well as the Gem reportedly brought in about $5,000 a night.

A series of nightly performance by the Gem Band, outside on the balcony, was used effectively as advertising to attract customers, though the local paper once complained that it wished that the group would find some new tunes to play. Hiring a band to play and advertise the opening of a saloon or theater was a common practice. When the Head Quarters Saloon was built several months after Cheyenne, Wyoming, was founded, the owners used a brass band to call attention to their place.

The Gem recruited stage acts from the East, as well as recruiting girls to work as waitresses at the theater. Not all the recruiting was totally explicit about the job's duties. It was not unusual to have women hired from Chicago or New York arrive for work, only to find that the "work" entailed more intimate physical activity than they had expected as actresses. This was reportedly the cause for the suicide of at least one teenaged girl who thought she was entering a legitimate theatrical career.[3] The Gem was finished off for good by a second disastrous fire on December 19, 1899.

Another combination theater and brothel in Deadwood was the Green Front Theatre, which was located close to the Gem on lower Main Street. Like other theaters of its type, the Green Front was well known for brawls, suicides, and fights.

Similar to the Gem was the Bella Union. Like the Gem, the Bella Union also presented variety acts and dancing on a stage, while offering gambling on the main floor and 17 curtained boxes above for more personalized entertainment by waitresses and other saloon women. The Bella Union was the scene of several shootings and killings. In one unusual incident in 1876, a stranger walked in and watched a woman singing, accompanied by a man on a piano. After the song was over, the man shot at both of them, but missed. The piano player shot back and mortally wounded the man, who turned out to be the woman's husband. The dying man made witnesses to the shooting promise that they would make the piano player marry the woman as soon as he was dead.[4]

In another unusual incident, Fanny Garrettson and Richard Brown were performing when a man named Ed Shaunessey from Cheyenne suddenly rose up out of the audience and threw an axe at the two. Brown calmly pulled out a gun and shot the man dead. It turned out that Shaunessey had been living with Garrettson for three years. She had left him and he was hoping to either win her back or gain some measure of revenge.

Deadwood's theaters were rough, tough places and even the audiences of hardened miners could sometimes be surprised. During the 130 nights that the music of Gilbert and Sullivan played at Deadwood's Bella Union, eight spectators were shot.[5]

On the other end of the entertainment scale was Jack Langrishe. In 1876 Langrishe leased the McDaniels Theater on Main Street to present legitimate theater performances of comedy and drama. The opening presentation was *The Banker's Daughter.* Unfortunately, the building, which had log walls with a canvas roof, was not waterproof and a torrential downpour dampened the enthusiasm of the opening crowd.

The McDaniels Theater was next to the No. 10 Saloon where Wild Bill Hickok was killed, and was ultimately used for the trial of Hickok's slayer, Jack McCall. Langrishe later rebuilt a better theater, but it burned down soon afterwards. Jack and Jeanette Langrishe did so well that they built another theater in Deadwood and theaters in nearby Lead and Central City.

Leadville, Colorado

Gold was discovered in California Gulch in central Colorado in 1860, and limited placer mining started around a small settlement called Oro City.[6] The gold soon played out and the mining district declined. Then a curious blue material in the ground was assayed and found to contain a very high percentage of silver, creating a new mining boom and the town of Leadville. By 1880, the area's population had mushroomed to close to 15,000 residents. Leadville grew to second only in population to Denver as the largest city in the state and, for a while, there was even talk of making Leadville the capital city of the state.

After 1880, when the railroad arrived in town, it was easier for the better types of theater talent — such as Eddie Foy, Jack Langrishe, and Charles Vivian — to travel there easily. Previously, various troupes had to travel from the railhead in Denver to Leadville across the intervening mountains by stage-coach, a journey of about a hundred jolting miles. One distraught actor commented that his stagecoach had overturned a total of six times during the journey from Denver. A typical theatrical circuit in Colorado in the 1880s consisted of one-nighters in Fort Collins and Boulder, Denver for three nights, Leadville for three nights, Colorado Springs for one night, Pueblo for one night, and Trinidad for one night. A grueling schedule of travel indeed.

The miners of Leadville, like those of other boom towns, demanded entertainment to fill their hours away from work. Though entertainment tended towards drinking and bawdy stage shows, Leadville developed as a major stop on the Western theater circuit, and many of the major stars of the day performed there. The quality of the shows in Leadville covered a range from high-class entertainment at Tabor's Opera House and Tom Kemp's Grand Central Theater, to the poor taste of the variety theaters, such as the Coliseum, the Comique, and the New Theater.

The first theaters were built in Leadville in 1877 and 1878. Most were variety theaters, which featured drinking and women. The New Theater advertised specifically for "waiter girls" to appear in "short clothes." If the girls refused to wear short dresses, they were not hired.[7] In this context, however, "short" only meant skirts that were above the ankle, instead of floor-length.

A stir was created when serving girls were asked to wear really short skirts that came to just below the knee. As this was considered absolutely scandalous for the time, most of the women refused.

Typical of the rowdy theaters was the Theater Comique on State Street (now Second Street). In 1879 the rent was what would seem to be a staggering $1,700 a month, but the box-office receipts were $1,200 a day. During the shows that ran from 9 P.M. to 2 A.M., the atmosphere could turn wild. Customers in the balcony were known to throw food and liquor bottles at the patrons seated on the main floor.

Not all the entertainment was as rowdy, however. The Chestnut Street Theater, also known as Wood's Opera House after its owner Ben Wood, emphasized family entertainment. On Wednesdays afternoons the bar was closed and Wood put on matinees for women and children.[8]

The Tabor Opera House in Leadville, Colorado. The third floor consisted of hotel rooms that were connected to the next-door Clarendon Hotel (now razed) by an enclosed third-floor walkway between the two buildings. The lower front of the Opera House was occupied by commercial businesses. The Furmans, who operated an appliance store on the left, still own the building (author's collection).

From 1881 to 1886, Charles E. "Pap" Wyman ran a combination saloon, dance hall, gambling house, and theater at the corner of Harrison Avenue and State Street. Pap paid actors at the theater $75 a week and his musicians $35 a week. Waiter girls were only paid $10 a week, but they were supposed to make most of their money in tips and commissions on drinks.

Wyman's place had more decorum than many of the other variety theaters and featured an open Bible on a shelf behind the bar. A large sign requested no swearing by customers. Married men were not allowed to gamble, and drinkers who were obviously intoxicated would not be served more liquor. On the other hand, the waiter girls could sit on a miner's lap to try to sell drinks (though nothing further than that was allowed), and Pap was reputed to carry his spare change in a coin purse made from a human scrotum.[9]

Tom Kemp had one of the largest and most successful theaters in the mining camp. The auditorium was 55 feet wide by 100 feet deep. The stage was 35 feet deep by 55 feet wide. At the back of the auditorium were 45 private boxes, in two tiers, each of them elegantly furnished. The front of the building had six wine rooms on the second floor.

Sophisticated entertainment came to Leadville with the opening of Tabor's Opera House. Built by Horace Tabor, it was thought to be the largest and grandest opera house west of the Mississippi. Solidly constructed out of stone and brick, the Tabor Opera House had its grand opening on November 20, 1878. When successful plays and performers from New York toured the country, Leadville and the Tabor Opera House were regular stops. Some of the famous performers who appeared there over the years were magician Houdini, composer and bandleader John Philip Sousa, Sarah Bernhardt, Oscar Wilde, Lillian Russell, Anna Held (one of Ziegfeld's beauties), Helena Modjeska, and boxer Jack Dempsey. Rival theater owner Tom Kemp occasionally stole talent from Tabor, and Tabor returned the compliment by stealing from Kemp.

Horace Austin Warner Tabor — known commonly as "HAW" Tabor — was one of the instant millionaires that sprang from the riches of the fabulous silver camp. Tabor had humble enough beginnings. He and his wife, Augusta, first opened a mercantile store in Oro City in 1859. To supplement the family income, Augusta opened a boarding house. Over the next few years, Tabor and his wife moved back and forth across the mountains to various small mining camps.

In 1878, back in Oro City again, Tabor grubstaked two prospectors, August Rische and George Hook, to $60 worth of supplies in exchange for 30 percent of their profits — if they struck gold. They did, and Tabor was on his way to incredible riches. Tabor invested well — or, perhaps, mostly through luck — in other mining properties and made millions from the flow of silver from his mines. His Little Pittsburg mine alone produced at the rate of $8,000 a week.

Tabor's Leadville Opera House cost an estimated $78,000 to build. The construction took place in an amazingly short time — one hundred days — considering that all the materials had to be freighted across the mountains to Leadville by wagon before the arrival of the railroad. Tabor spared no expense in building the theater and insisted on the finest furnishings. The interior color scheme was a stunning combination of red, gold, white, and sky-blue. The auditorium was 57 feet wide by 65 feet deep. The theater could accommodate 880 patrons and contained seats covered with scarlet plush velvet. This was a luxury for the audience, because the seats in most theaters of the time were simple wooden chairs without any padding. The horseshoe-shaped dress circle, which was reached by an upper flight of stairs, could seat 400 people. On either side of the stage were two private boxes, one reserved for Tabor, the other for his wife, Augusta, after they divorced. The dressing rooms were located below the stage.

For the times, the technical aspects of the stage productions that could be accommodated was quite amazing. The stage was an impressive 34 feet deep by 57 feet wide with a ceiling three stories high, and was even equipped with a trapdoor for magicians to disappear and for stage shows requiring dramatic entrances. One remarkable production at The Tabor Opera House was *Ben-Hur*. The famous chariot race was performed on stage with six live horses and a real chariot. The horses ran on a revolving treadmill that made them gallop at high speed. Though well planned, the staging was not without hazards. One night, one of the chariot wheels flew off, narrowly missing members of the orchestra. Luckily, nobody was injured and, after stage hands replaced the errant wheel, the race was on again. The use of a giant treadmill accompanied the production all over the country.

The interior of the theater was lit by 72 gas jets, the first building in Leadville to be so lit. Around the front of the stage were an additional 30 gas lights that served as footlights. Tabor was ever the entrepreneur and the coal gas came, naturally, from Tabor's Leadville Illuminating Gas Company.[10] A few years later the lights were converted to electricity.

The entire theater was heated by a massive coal-fired furnace, which was an excellent idea for the chilly winter nights at the 10,200-foot elevation of Leadville. By contrast, many early theaters were not heated, except by the warmth of the audience's bodies. This made the atmosphere decidedly brisk for actresses in skimpy costumes.

Jack Langrishe and his popular group of players performed on opening night at the Tabor Opera House. The featured attraction was the three-act comedy *Serious Family*, supplemented by a farce called *Who's Who?* The hanging of two lot-jumpers, one named Edward Frodsham and the other named Stewart (by vigilantes in a building across the street from the theater the day before opening night) may have detracted somewhat from the luster of the new theater, but nobody seemed to complain.

Maude Adams, daughter of actress Annie Adams, was the first American actress to play the part of Sir James Barrie's Peter Pan; she appeared at the Tabor Opera House many times during her stage career. Adams was born Maude Kiskadden in Salt Lake City in 1872, and started acting in San Francisco at the age of five. She was an accomplished actress by the age of six, loved the theater life, and went on to have an accomplished career. She joined a traveling stock company when she was 15 and spent several successful years perfecting her art as she performed in small communities throughout the West, before going on to further fame and popularity on the stages of New York. She preferred California, but, like other actresses, she went to New York because that was the center of American theater. She first played the role of Peter Pan in 1905, then played the same part for several years as she toured the so-called "silver circuit," which consisted of theaters in San Francisco, Salt Lake City, Denver, and Leadville. Adams retired at age 51.

Tabor's rags-to-riches story did not end happily. With high living and poor investments, his fortunes shrank in the early 1890s. When silver mining collapsed in 1893, the rest of Tabor's fortune went with it.[11] The ensuing depression forced the closure of many Western theaters. Tabor ended his days as the postmaster of Denver, a menial position obtained for him by friends.

After Tabor lost his fortune, the Tabor Opera House was purchased by state senator Algernon Weston and became the Weston Opera House. In late 1901, the building was sold to the Elks fraternal organization, was extensively remodeled, and reopened a year later, under the new name of the Elks Opera House. The theater was renovated and the sleeping rooms on the third floor that were originally part of the Clarendon Hotel were remodeled into a ballroom. Other suitable space was remodeled into lodge rooms, and the street level was rented to retail businesses.

The connection of the theater with the Elks was not as remote as it might seem. The Benevolent Protective Order of the Elks was originally founded in New York in 1868 by Charles Algernon Sidney Vivian. Originally known as the "Jolly Corks," it was primarily a social organization. Vivian was a singer and dancer, and appeared many times at the Tabor Opera House and other theaters in Leadville. The Jolly Corks name was changed in 1869 to the Elks. Vivian arrived in Leadville in 1880 and formed a stock theatrical company. He invested in a theater that later went bankrupt — possibly because it did not offer liquor, dancing, and prostitution, three of the staples of entertainment in contemporary Leadville. Vivian died unexpectedly of pneumonia on March 20, 1881, and his funeral was held in the Opera House.

During the hard financial times of the 1890s, performances at the theater were cut to one night a week, but still presented the best performers and shows. The Elks Opera House continued as a center of entertainment in Leadville for the next 50 years. In addition to its primary function of hosting entertainment, the theater was occasionally used for funerals for famous people and served as the location for commencement exercises for the local high school until 1960. As in many other towns, theaters in Leadville were dark on Sunday, as this was considered to be a day of rest.

The association of the Elks with a theater was not unusual. In 1904, Elk Lodge #330 in Prescott, Arizona, decided to add an opera house to the building they had under construction. Local residents raised $15,000 for construction of the theater, which had 900 seats and eight dressing rooms. The grand opening took place on February 20, 1905, with Florence Roberts starring in *Marta of the Lowlands*. Admission was $2.50 with the price of boxes being $20. Along with stage entertainment, the theater was used for dances, high school graduations, and civic functions. Prescott also turned out to be a convenient stopover for companies traveling between the East and the West Coast, and the theater hosted such notables as Scottish entertainer Harry Lauder and John Philip Sousa.

Denver

By the late 1800s, Denver grew to be the second-largest city in the West, after San Francisco, and was able to draw entertainment headliners.

Denver was founded after the discovery of small amounts of placer gold at the junction of Cherry Creek and the South Platte River in June of 1858. The town grew from the uniting of a crude collection of tents and log cabins, called Auraria, on the west side of Cherry Creek, and a similar group of thrown-together rough buildings on the east side called Denver City. The gold "strike" turned out to be negligible and Denver's strength grew as a supply center and jumping-off point for the rich gold strikes in the mountains to the west. Though the community only had 4,759 permanent residents in 1870, tens of thousands of men passed through the city, either going to the gold fields, purchasing supplies for mining, or wintering over when the mountain weather became too severe. These young, mostly unattached men wanted to be entertained.

Entertainment was not long in arriving. In July of 1859, the year after Denver was founded, the first theatrical performance was given in Apollo Hall on Larimer Street. Owned by Harry Gunnell, Apollo Hall was a combination saloon, gambling hall, restaurant, and billiard parlor, with a theater upstairs. Attending the premiere were 350 hardy Denver pioneers who sat on rough wooden benches to see Shakespeare's *Richard III*. The stage was lit by twelve candles that served as footlights.

On October 3, 1859, Colonel Charles Thorne's Star Company from Leavenworth, Kansas, presented *Cross of Gold: or, The Maid of Croisay* at Apollo Hall. The play was followed by a farce called *The Two Gregories*. Apparently, Denver was not to Colonel Thorne's liking, because he and his son William afterwards abandoned the rest of their company and took the stagecoach back to Leavenworth. They never returned.

The Thornes' one-week run was followed on November 8, 1859, by the Haydee Sisters, accompanied by comedian Mike Dougherty, all of whom were remnants of Colonel Thorne's Company. The players of the new Haydee Star Company were apparently more stable than the two Thornes, and the three Haydee Sisters (real names Rose, Flora, and Louise Wakely) and Dougherty continued to entertain in the Colorado gold fields for the next several years. Dougherty entertained in Denver between mining stints in the nearby mountains.

Apollo Hall was a good example of the multiple purposes for which these establishments were used. As well as serving as a theater, the hall was used as a gathering place for the first legislative meeting of the provisional government of the new territory before the state capitol building was completed. The legislators were so used to having a drink (conveniently available at the Apollo's bar) that this tradition carried on into the new capitol. Actor Jack Langrishe and his Langrishe Dramatic Company debuted in Apollo Hall on September 28, 1860, with *His Last Legs* and *The Youth Who Never Saw a Woman*. A performance of several plays, including the farce *The Barber Shop*, on July 29, 1861, attracted an audience of 600.

Theater in early Denver adapted easily to the local customs and times. For example, gold dust was such a common medium of exchange in early Denver that it was accepted at Apollo Hall's box office as admission. When "The Anvil Chorus" from Giuseppe Verdi's *Il Trovatore* was being performed, the program acknowledged a Mr. Myers for the loan of six anvils to make the performance "more effective." Similarly, when a military overture was played, a Colonel Potter loaned a cannon to the theater to make the opening salvo more realistic.

Apollo Hall's location over a saloon was a typical location for an early theater. Another was Criterion Hall, which started as one of Denver's first saloons before the second floor was remodeled into a theater with a seating capacity of 650. For opening night, the owner, Charles Harrison, stole the

Converse and Petrie Ethiopian Minstrels from the competition at Apollo Hall.

Between 1859 and 1876, Denver had approximately 60 "theaters," and nearly all of them were located in saloons. The acts they presented were typical of saloon theaters of the time. One featured act at the Diana Saloon was Signor Franco, whose curious act consisted of swallowing stones. The Blake Street Bowling Alley featured a Professor Wilson, who performed nightly on a trapeze.

Cibola Hall, owned by James Reid, offered gambling, along with light entertainment. The Cibola Minstrels drew crowds of several hundred every night at 50 cents a head. On off-nights the audience listened to music or a girl singer. As in other music halls, girls were available for dancing or for back-room activities that earned the theater the nickname of a "brothel dance-hall."[12]

One of the popular lower-class variety theaters in Denver was the Central Theater on Market Street, at the center of Denver's red light district. As well as shows and dances, the Central offered cock fights, dog fights, and boxing matches. It was also well known for the "key game." To work this confidence game, women who entertained in the boxes at the theaters sold keys to their rooms to customers eager to pursue further bedroom action. Of course, the keys fitted no such rooms in any local hotel or boarding house. A good worker could sell 10 to 12 keys each evening for three to five dollars a key.

On July 16, 1861, Apollo Hall was remodeled and opened under a new name: Criterion Concert Hall. A blackface troupe called the Criterion Minstrels performed, along with various performers imported from the East. The Criterion Saloon featured Mademoiselle Carolista, a petite tightrope walker who sometimes performed her act blindfolded as she walked from the stage to the balcony of the theater. She also pushed a wheelbarrow from one end of the rope to the other. On July 18, 1861, as a publicity stunt to promote the theater, she walked on a tightrope for 300 feet, 50 feet above the ground, across Larimer Street from the Criterion to the New York Store across the street.

The location of Denver, which was originally off the main rail lines, meant that a journey there for entertainers was not financially feasible, causing many early touring theater companies to bypass the city. In 1870, railroads arrived in Denver from Cheyenne and Kansas City, and made access to Denver easier. Later entertainment circuits went from Omaha and Kansas City to San Francisco, via Cheyenne, Denver, Salt Lake City, Virginia City (Nevada), and Sacramento.

In 1869, the Howson Opera Company, consisting of four members of the Howson family, performed at the Denver Theater. Among other offerings, they presented a burlesque of Verdi's *Il Trovatore*, which they called *Ill-treated Il Trovatore*.

Following up on his Leadville theatrical success, Horace Tabor built a magnificent opera house in Denver at 16th Street and Curtis in 1881. Tabor wanted the town to have the finest opera house in the West so, as he did with his Leadville theater, he spared no expense on the furniture and carpeting. The estimate for the final cost was between $750,000 and $850,000.

The opening performers for the Tabor Grand Opera House were the Emma Abbott Opera Company, who performed *Maritana* on September 5, 1881. Again, willing to spare no expense, Tabor guaranteed her $20,000 for the engagement and $3,000 for travel expenses. His ploy was a success, though, because the opening crowd numbered 1,500. The total receipts for the first week were $14,404, which was an average of $2,000 for each performance.

Over the next ten years, the theater mostly presented plays, but also put on shows that ran the gamut from opera to a succession of variety and minstrel shows. Shakespearean plays were popular, including such favorites as *Julius Caesar*, *As You Like It*, *The Merchant of Venice*, and *Romeo and Juliet*, with *Othello* being presented 17 times.

The success of the Tabor Grand lasted for about nine years, then the theater lost much of its business to the Broadway Theater, which opened on August 18, 1890, at 16th Street and Broadway. The opening show was *Carmen*, played by the Emma Juch Grand English Opera Company. In an ironic twist of fate, Tabor later acquired the Broadway Theater and turned it over to his brother-in-law to manage. Expanding his theatrical interests, Tabor bought the People's Theater on 15th Street, but the building seemed to be jinxed and the theater never did well. It burned in 1891 and the remaining standing walls formed an eerie landmark for many years.

After Tabor's fortunes sank, he sold the Tabor Grand in 1896. The fortunes of the theater building gradually declined also. It became a decrepit movie house and was ignominiously torn down in 1964 during urban renewal.

The Tabor Grand was not the only serious theater in Denver. The Denver Theater was a large two-story wooden structure at Lawrence and 16th Street. The stage was 30 feet by 30 feet. The auditorium seated 1,500.

Among the burlesque theaters and saloons offering stage entertainment was the Alcazar on Market Street, operated by Louis Klipfel. Several noted actors, including Eddie Foy, appeared there.

One of the prime characters in the Denver theater world was Edward "Big Ed" Chase, who was born in upstate New York in 1838. After a brief interval as a theater owner in Virginia City, Montana, during the gold rush, Chase came to Denver in 1860. In the winter of 1869, Chase and his brother John opened the Cricket, which was a gambling house, but offered a variety show in the building next door to attract customers. It was also known as the Blake Street Opera House.

In 1872, Chase, in partnership with Francis "Hub" Heatley (sometimes spelled Heatly) opened the Progressive, a frame building on Blake Street. Like the Cricket, the Progressive was primarily a gambling house, but also presented variety shows. The ground floor was 25 feet by 100 feet, and included the inevitable bar. The upper floor was divided into private rooms, which were primarily used by high-stakes gamblers. The Progressive offered shows, music, gambling, and drinking. Heatley lost his share when he gambled away the payroll allocated to a theatrical troupe of which he was part owner.[13] He subsequently bought back his ownership.

Chase went on to replace the Progressive with the Palace, a two-story brick building that housed a variety theater and gambling rooms, on Blake Street between 14th and 15th streets. The building's large theater could seat an audience of 750 and the gambling hall could accommodate 200 more. Curtained private boxes lined the second and third floors. The variety theater primarily featured leg shows, with waiter girls performing in the shows as well as serving drinks. The Palace Theater boldly advertised itself as "the Gold Mine of the West" with "delighted audiences." One playbill for 1880 described the theater as a "Palace of Real Pleasure and Voluptuous Art, where Lovely Women fascinate the heart."[14] Good was mixed in with the mundane. Noted comedian Eddie Foy appeared at the Palace.

The gambling side of the Palace was the scene of several fatal disputes. One of them occurred when David Stubblefield shot and killed John Martin on February 27, 1879.[15] Another occurred when Daniel Burke was killed on June 4, 1888. In this instance, the killer was acquitted. Tragedies of this sort were common. On November 13, 1887, 17-year-old showgirl Effie Moore was shot four times at the Palace with a British Bulldog revolver by 19-year-old gambler Charles Henry, who had become obsessed with the young woman.[16]

In 1874, showman P.T. Barnum tried to make his mark on Denver by investing heavily in the Denver Villa Park Association to promote and sell 765 acres in a real estate venture that was planned for 9,000 housing lots. The whole scheme failed and Barnum felt that he had been swindled. He also had real estate investments in Greeley and Pueblo, Colorado.[17]

About 30 miles west of Denver, in the eastern foothills of the Rocky Mountains, the citizens of Central City were anxious to build a new theater that they felt was appropriate to their growth and status. The Central City Opera House was opened in 1878 at a cost of $22,000 that was raised by subscription. The building was 55 feet by 115 feet, made from cut stone with walls that were four feet thick. The stage was 40 feet by 50 feet. The combination of the main floor and dress circle seated 426, the gallery 126 more.

Officially named the Teller Opera House, the theater took advantage of the circuit of actors who traveled between theaters in New York and San Fran-

The Teller Opera House in Central City, just west of Denver, was solidly built from cut stone in 1878. Its location took advantage of the many theatrical troupes traveling between Denver and San Francisco (author's collection).

cisco and appeared in nearby Denver. A host of notables appeared there, including Edwin Booth and Henry Ward Beecher.

When the Tabor Grand Opera House opened in Denver, many of the first-rate touring groups did not want to journey up the steep, winding road through the mountains to Central City, particularly in winter. As a result, the Opera House became a venue mainly for lectures, political rallies, and church socials. The theater fell into disrepair in 1900, but the building was restored in 1932 and still hosts summer operas.

Tombstone, Arizona

Tombstone, Arizona, was another rowdy mining town that was founded on silver after prospector Ed Schieffelin located the Tombstone and the Graveyard claims in the San Pedro Valley southeast of Tucson in 1877. When Schieffelin set out into the Arizona desert hoping to find his fortune, he was told by the soldiers at Fort Huachuca that all he would find was Indians and his tombstone, so the names of the claims seemed appropriate in a grim sort of way. Schieffelin had the last laugh, because the mines and subsequent town prospered, and by 1882 an estimated 10,000 people made up the mining district.

Due to a nearby railroad, Tombstone was a popular stop for variety troupes in the 1880s. Entertainers traveled on the main line of the Southern Pacific Railroad to Benson, 26 miles to the north, and then rode the stagecoach to the theaters of Tombstone.

One performance of note occurred in December of 1879 when Gilbert and Sullivan's *H.M.S. Pinafore* had a one-week run. Among the cast was an 18-year-old minor performer named May Bell. Her real name was Josephine Sarah Marcus, and she went on to spark rivalry between Sheriff Johnny Behan and Deputy Marshal Wyatt Earp. Behan and Earp eventually ended up on opposite sides of the conflict that led to the bloody 30-second Gunfight at the OK Corral on October 25, 1881. While she was in Tombstone, Marcus performed in plays but was at the same time licensed (signed by Wyatt Earp himself) for business in a bordello at Sixth and Allen streets.[16]

Professional entertainment in Tombstone was presented primarily in two theaters. One was Schieffelin Hall, which tended towards legitimate theater entertainment, such as plays, concerts, lectures, variety acts, operas, and the better-quality musical and variety shows. It was acclaimed as the best known in the West and was second only in size to some of the larger theaters in San Francisco.

Schieffelin Hall was built by Ed Schieffelin's brother Al. The two-story

The Bird Cage theater in Tombstone was considered to be the wildest place between New Orleans and San Francisco. One hundred and forty bullet holes in the ceiling would seem to confirm its reputation (author's collection).

building was constructed from adobe and was supposedly the largest adobe building in the United States.[19] As well as the theater, the building housed — and still houses — the local Masonic Lodge. At the time, the stage and interior of the theater were said to be as good as any of the theaters in the East. The inside of the hall was 130 feet long, seated 700 patrons, and had a 24-foot ceiling. The stage, at 40 feet wide, was large for a town like this. The hall opened on St. Patrick's Day, March 17, 1881, with an Irish Ball. For some reason — odd for an Arizona theater — the drop curtain contained a scene of Colorado. It was, however, hailed by the Tucson newspapers as a work of art.

On September 15, 1881, the first serious theatrical production presented in the hall was *The Ticket-of-Leave Man*, performed by a local amateur group, the Tombstone Dramatic Relief Association. The proceeds from the production were used to purchase a bell for the local fire company. The Tombstone Dramatic Relief Association also went on tour in the southern Arizona area, performing in Tucson and other nearby towns.

The first professional performance at Schieffelin Hall was a drama, *The Banker's Daughter*, presented by the Nellie Boyd Dramatic Company on December 5, 1881. Boyd and her company had previously appeared at Richie's

Hall in *Fanchon the Cricket* on November 29, 1880, for a three-week stay. She was well received, and the theater was packed for the entire run.

Theater performances followed over the next few years with a string of New York plays starring first-rate actors and actresses. Performers who were reputed to have visited Tombstone, but who did not in reality, included Lotta Crabtree, Lillian Russell, and Jenny Lind.

The other popular theater in Tombstone was the Bird Cage Theatre. Unlike Schieffelin Hall, the Bird Cage presented a series of earthier entertainments, including leg shows, bawdy humorists, and fast-paced variety acts. Typical of the variety acts were The Happy Hottentots, who presented a program of "Grotesque Dancing, Leg Mania and Contortion Feats."[20] As well as these two entertainment centers, there were several saloons that offered drinking and variety entertainment in the style of the concert saloon, such as the Crystal Palace Saloon and the Oriental Saloon. Other theaters in Tombstone were Richie's Hall, which was up the street from the Crystal Palace, and Turn Verein Hall, directly across Fourth Street from Schieffelin Hall. Both of these were used by traveling troupes of actors, as well as for dances and meetings. Danner & Owens Hall had a large auditorium and a stage constructed for theatrical performances.

The Bird Cage was opened on December 26, 1881, by proprietor William J. "Billy" Hutchinson. His wife, Lottie, was a singer and performer, and he had previously managed the Sixth Street Opera House (officially called the E. Fontana Dance Hall, but also known as the Free and Easy) next door at Allen and Sixth streets. Hutchinson, previously a variety performer, had seen how large crowds flocked to variety halls in San Francisco, and decided to create the same atmosphere in Tombstone. He originally intended the theater to present respectable shows and family entertainment. Part of his promotion was to offer a ladies' night, which the respectable women of Tombstone could attend for free. However, economic circumstances were beyond his control and, to survive, the entertainment style turned towards women and leg shows. The local population of lusty young miners preferred bawdier types of entertainment, rendering ladies' night a failure.

The Bird Cage operated around the clock, and featured dancing girls who were bar maids and prostitutes between acts. Stage shows at the Bird Cage started at 9 P.M. and continued until 1 A.M. or so the next morning. Waiter girls in short dresses with low-cut necklines peddled as many drinks as they could. Beer was 50 cents on the main floor and a dollar in the curtained boxes. The primary entertainment consisted of bawdy skits, singers in short skirts and vividly colored striped stockings, and comedians with risqué stories and jokes. The cancan was, of course, always popular. Sentimental, heartrending ballads about lost love, such as "In the Evening by the Moonlight," and mournful songs about mother and home were well received by the miners.

Along with a reputation as the rowdiest entertainment place in Tombstone, the Bird Cage Theatre was reputed to be the wickedest theater between New Orleans and San Francisco. Under Hutchinson's guidance, additional offerings at the Birdcage were masquerade balls, which featured cross-dressing entertainers, such as comedians David Waters and Will Curlew, in the most outrageous female costumes, performing offbeat antics and singing raunchy ballads.[21]

The layout of the theater was typical for the times. Just inside the main entrance was a large wooden bar that catered to the audience's thirst. To set the tenor of the place, there was a painting of a buxom belly-dancer named Fatima in an exotic Oriental outfit behind the bar. (The painting is still hanging there today. There are still six bullet holes and a knife slash in the canvas, which illustrates the rowdy nature of the men who went to the Bird Cage.)[22]

Once inside the front doors, patrons picked up drinks and went through the bar area and into the theater. Women danced and sang on a stage that was about 15 feet wide and 15 feet deep, located about five feet above the main floor. The stage was lit by a row of gas jets along the front side. The evening's entertainment typically started with a variety show then, after the performance was over, the wooden benches were stacked up and the audience danced and drank until dawn. Those miners with the most stamina caroused all night at the Bird Cage and then went off to their jobs when the sun came up.

At the sides of the theater, high up on the wall, were 14 private boxes where waitresses could entertain in private. Heavy red velvet drapes could be drawn over the openings into the theater to ensure privacy. Patrons entered the boxes via a narrow stairway that led directly from the bar area at the front of the theater and a hallway that ran the length of the building behind the boxes. In the cellar, under the theater and stage area, were a gambling table, another bar, and several rooms for prostitution.

One of the first leading attractions at the Birdcage was Mademoiselle De Granville, who performed feats of strength. Also known as the "Female Hercules" and "the woman with the iron jaw," her special talent was to pick up heavy objects with her teeth.[23] Others who appeared in the varied shows at the Birdcage were the Irish comic duo of Burns and Trayers, the comic singer Irene Baker, and Carrie Delmar, a serious opera singer. One notable who appeared at the Bird Cage in 1883 was comedienne Nola Forest. A local bookkeeper named J.P. Wells was so taken with her that he embezzled $800 from his employer, the Boston Mill Company, to buy jewelry for her. She was not impressed — and he was caught.[24]

Acrobats and women performing on a trapeze in abbreviated costumes were popular with Victorian audiences.[25] A similar popular attraction was Lizette, nicknamed "The Flying Nymph," who "flew" from one side of the theater to the other suspended by a rope.[26] Lizette arrived in Tombstone with a traveling road show which she eventually left to become a madam in a bordello. Ella Richter, who used the stage name Mademoiselle Zazel and was nicknamed "The Human Cannonball," was shot 60 feet out of a cannon by concealed springs — a very popular act.[25]

One of the more unusual acts at the Birdcage in 1889 was called "The Human Fly" in which women (dressed in the usual theatrical tights and abbreviated costumes) walked upside-down on the ceiling over the stage. It was not an illusion — they actually were suspended above the stage. This type of act gained some popularity in theaters around the West for a short while. The trick was that their shoes had special clamps on them that fitted into holes bored in the ceiling to support them. Unfortunately, one of the performers was killed when one of the clamps slipped and she fell to her death. In another version of the "human fly," women wore suction cups on their feet as they walked upside-down on a platform high above the stage. Like the accident at the Bird Cage, the contraptions did not always work, and several performers died from injuries when they fell.[28]

Tombstone did not last long as a booming mining town. By 1881, water had appeared in the mines. Pumps were installed, but, by 1883, the equipment couldn't keep up with the incoming water, even though 2.5 million gallons a day were being pumped out of the deepest shafts. With business fading away, Billy Hutchinson sold the Bird Cage to Hugh McCrum and John Stroufe.

The building was sold again, in January 1886, to Joe Bignon, an entrepreneur who had formerly managed the Theatre Comique in San Francisco. He had also previously performed in blackface minstrel routines and clog dances. Bignon refurbished the building, renamed it the Elite Theatre, and hired new acts that he interspersed with bawdy entertainment.

Bignon's wife, Maulda, better known as "Big Minnie," was also an entertainer. She sang, danced, and played the piano. She was a large woman, standing six feet tall in her pink tights and weighing 230 pounds. Because of her size, she occasionally acted as the theater's bouncer, as well as taking on the job of acting as a madam for the waiter girls who serviced men in the curtained boxes.

In spite of the Bignons' attempts to keep the Bird Cage going, Tombstone was in a terminal decline. In 1886, fire destroyed one of the pumps and water took over the lower levels of many of the mines. Consequently, the ability to mine silver plummeted and many of the miners drifted away in the early 1890s to work in other mining towns. The Bird Cage closed in 1892.

Cripple Creek, Colorado

Cripple Creek started as a mining town later than many in the West. Though prospectors had combed the back slopes of Pikes Peak in central Colorado for years, gold was not discovered in paying quantities until 1890. After that the town boomed, producing over $450 million until mining declined in the 1960s.

The song "There'll Be a Hot Time in the Old Town Tonight," written by Theodore Metz, was supposedly inspired in Cripple Creek when the author heard a colored prostitute singing something similar in the Red Light District.

Though Cripple Creek supported the usual assortment of variety theaters, nearby Victor, four miles away to the southeast, had the largest mines. The Grand Opera House was an attractive red brick building. Even though the town, located at 9,700 feet in the mountains behind Pikes Peak, was off the main theater circuit, it attracted performances by Sousa's Band, Primrose and Dockstader's Minstrels, and many other first-rate acts and plays. One circumstance that helped Victor's theaters to attract this type of talent was that

Even the ravages of time cannot completely mask the fancy exterior of the Grand Opera House, which hosted the best in melodramas, musical concerts, boxing matches, revival meetings, and political rallies in Cripple Creek, Colorado, around the turn of the century (Glenn Kinnaman Colorado and Western History Collection).

the city of Denver did not allow Sunday performances. The city of Victor had no such qualms and the Opera House was thus able to book some excellent acts and musicals for Sunday evenings.

One notable performance was the touring production of Victor Herbert's light opera, *Mlle. Modiste*. The leading lady, Fritzi Scheff, a popular Vienna-born actress and soprano, traveled with her own 15-piece orchestra and its conductor. On opening night, the conductor suffered a mild heart attack due to Victor's high altitude, and had to be taken down to a lower elevation in Denver. Luckily, an acclaimed violinist named Hans Albert had settled in Victor and was able to take over the task of conductor at short notice and the show went on to rousing success.

Victor was also known for its seamier entertainment. Stage shows, accompanied by drinking, fighting, shooting, and prostitution, were the highlights at the Union Theater on Third Street, which proudly called itself "the hottest burlesque theater in the West." A burlesque act by "Cleo the Egyptian Belly Dancer" was reported by the local newspaper to be so indecent that it shocked even the audience of blasé miners, so they ran her out of town.[29]

Dodge City, Kansas

Dodge City developed as a result of the Texas cattle trade. The entertainment characteristics of most of the cattle towns in Kansas, such as Caldwell, Newton, Abilene, and Ellsworth, were similar.

The shows in variety theaters typically started around 9 P.M. and ran until 2 or 3 in the morning. The crowds were often drunk, boisterous, and in the mood for bawdy entertainment. Fights and other disturbances were common, through frequently created by a drunken cowboy who tried to shoot out the lights or put a hole in someone's hat.

The saloons on the north side of the main street, Front Street, were relatively respectable and entertainment consisted of moderate drinking, billiards, and gambling. Saloons on the south side of the street were the rowdy places. The Lady Gay, opened in April 1877 at Second Avenue by Ben Springer and Jim Masterson, had a raised platform for the orchestra. The Lady Gay regularly presented traveling minstrel shows and performing troupes. Next door was the Comique Theater, which presented mostly burlesque skits, but also serious plays, such as *Romeo and Juliet*, *Rip van Winkle*, and *Uncle Tom's Cabin*. Though the Comique was built as a theater, it also had gambling tables, curtained boxes, and waiter girls. The bar was at one end of the room with the stage at the other. After the show, the band played the rest of the night for dancing.

Down the block was the Varieties Dance Hall, which introduced the cancan to Dodge City. The theater opened in 1878, owned by Hamilton "Ham" Bell. The Varieties was replaced by Rowdy Kate's Green Front Saloon, which was said to cater to the lowest tastes.

The Billiard Saloon, also known as the Main Street Saloon, was built in 1872 by A.J. Peacock. In 1876, it was purchased by Chalkley M. "Chalk" Beeson and William H. Harris, who changed the name to the Saratoga for the resort town of Saratoga, New York. This was a high-class establishment that served only the finest liquor. Its fancy interior attracted the leading citizens, along with visiting cattle barons and railroad men. Beeson was a proficient violin player and provided music for the customers while Harris took care of the gambling and liquor sales.

Beeson and Harris sold the Saratoga in 1878 and bought the Long Branch Saloon, which had originally been built by A.J. Peacock and Charlie Bassett (Ford County's first sheriff) in 1873. The Long Branch was built with a bar and billiard tables in the front. Behind them was a private room for gambling and, at the back of the building, was a room where drunks were allowed to "sleep it off."

Beeson hired four other musicians — a violinist, trombonist, cornetist, and pianist — to make up a five-piece orchestra that played in the summer and fall when the cattle business was at its peak. This was strictly entertainment and Beeson did not tolerate dancing, bar girls, or prostitution. Not everybody in Dodge, however, appreciated music. Next door was the Alamo, which had a strict policy of no music. The *Dodge City Times* welcomed it on June 2, 1877, with the comment: "Those who resort to its well kept parlor can hear themselves talk as well as think."

Cowboys who attended the theaters in Dodge City sometimes became rowdy. It was not unknown for them to shoot their guns at the ceiling or to lasso the performers. One cowboy, who roped an actress he admired and pulled her onto his lap, caused a shootout among jealous members of the audience.

Underscoring the uninhibited nature of audiences in Dodge was the time when the appropriately named Dr. J. Graves Brown gave a lecture on the occult in the Lady Gay saloon. As he was lecturing, someone yelled out, "You lie!" He responded in what seemed to him to be an appropriate fashion, only to receive the same insulting reply. Sheriff Bat Masterson jumped up, along with half-a-dozen other men and gunfire broke out. The audience yelled with appropriate vigor, and ran outside. The shaken Dr. Brown left town without realizing that the cartridges were blanks and the audience was having a little fun with him.

SEVEN

A Few of the Famous

Entertainment provided a living for many people in the Old West. The 1870 census for Virginia City, Nevada, for example, listed ten professional actors, a "tragedian," three others who made their living in the theatrical business, and two gymnasts. The census also listed 14 professional musicians who supplied music for the local stages, and two music teachers.[1]

Men as Entertainers

In the early part of the 19th century, theater audiences were primarily male, and men dominated as entertainers. Women actresses did not become popular until around the middle of the century.

Entertainer Stephen C. Massett, a stout little red-faced Englishman who used the professional stage name of Jeems Pipes of Pipesville, was a popular entertainer in the early California gold camps.[2] Pipesville was his name for his little house on swampy Mission Street in San Francisco. Massett composed his own songs, and had a wide vocal range, from a fine baritone to a high falsetto, depending on the mood he wanted to convey. He also performed brief burlesque skits, often using different voices to portray separate characters. As acting wasn't profitable enough to be a full-time activity, in his spare time Massett also practiced law, was a notary public, acted as an auctioneer, and doubled as a journalist.

Massett first appeared in San Francisco in June 22, 1849, when he rented a schoolhouse on Portsmouth Square, borrowed a piano, and put on a lively show of songs. He charged an admission fee of $3 per person and made $500 for his efforts. He left San Francisco in 1852 to perform in a tour of the East. By then, San Francisco had matured in size and scope. Massett's farewell performance was given in a formal concert hall, and was accompanied by a full orchestra.

Another singer, though not of the professional caliber of Massett, was John A. Stone, who called himself by the stage name of "Old Put." Stone's songs appealed more to the level of miners wanting lively entertainment. Popular songs of his included "Hangtown Gals," about the Sierra Nevada gold mining town of Placerville, and "Joachin the Horse Thief," which had the following peculiar first verse:

> Joachin to the mountains was advancing
> When he saw Lola Montez a-dancing;
> When she danced the spider dance, he was bound to run her off,
> And he'd feed her eggs and chickens, make her cackle, crow, and cough.[3]

Artemus Ward, whose real name was Charles Farrar Browne, was a nationally known humorist. He lectured at the New Opera House in Virginia City, Nevada, in December of 1863. He specialized in jokes, nonsense patter, and absurd, dry wit — all told with a grave and somber face, so that the audience couldn't always tell if he was serious or not. He provided inspiration for Samuel Clemens, who worked as a reporter for a local newspaper, the *Territorial Enterprise*, while he was on his way to becoming famous as Mark Twain. Ward was supposed to stay in Virginia City for only a few days, but he and Clemens and some of the other local newspaper men got on so well that Ward ended up staying for three weeks. The story is told that Ward was so popular that when he played at Big Creek, Nevada, he drew a house of 300. That was considered not too bad for a town with a population of 300.

Teams

Husband-and-wife entertainment duos were popular. Eddie Foy and Jack Langrishe were just a few of the singers and dancers who performed with their wives. Husband-and-wife teams, however, didn't always work successfully on the stage. Arizona Charlie Meadows, a former Indian fighter, cowboy, and circus and rodeo performer who popped up from time to time providing entertainment in many of the upstart towns in the west, moved to Dawson during the gold rush and built the Grand Palace dance hall and theater. It was one of the most lavish entertainment spots in Dawson. Like every other theater, Charlie also produced a version of *Camille*. The run was not a total success because George Hillier, the actor who played Armand Duval, was the divorced husband of Babette Pyne, the dancehall girl who played Camille. The friction between them on stage was unfortunately quite evident to the audience.

A problem of a different sort occurred one night with one of the waiter girls, Nellie Lewis, who entertained in the theater's boxes when she was not appearing as an actress. During one performance, Babette, playing Camille, called out a cue for Prudence to appear. Nothing happened. After the cue was repeated several times, Lewis — the dance hall girl who was playing the part of Prudence — stuck her head out of the curtains of one of the upper boxes and yelled out, "Madam Prudence isn't here!" She was eventually persuaded to come out of the box, but steadfastly refused to go on stage.[4]

Arizona Charlie also ran into a bit of a problem with his wife. Charlie occasionally entertained by exhibiting his shooting skills from his old rodeo days. One of his tricks was to shoot and break glass balls that were held between the thumb and forefinger of his pretty blonde wife. One night he missed the ball and grazed her thumb. After that she refused to be in the act.

The Chapmans, a popular acting team who started in show business aboard a steamboat on the Mississippi River, traveled to the California gold fields on mules. Caroline Chapman, who was popular on the California circuit, was born in London, like some other popular actresses in the West, in 1818. She came to America at the age of nine with her father, George, and his family, in 1827. Her early experience was in family theater on Chapman's *Floating Theatre*, where she learned to play a variety of roles until her father died in 1843. She played large theaters in the East, but also loved to entertain in the smaller towns of the West.

In 1846, Caroline and her brother William, nicknamed "Uncle Billy," went to New York, and two years later joined the gold seekers in the California Gold Rush of 1848. She was an excellent entertainer, nicknamed the "Sweetheart of the West." Her brother returned to New York in 1852, while she went on to the Sierra Nevada gold camps of Sonora, Grass Valley, and Columbia. She played comedy in Sacramento and at the Jenny Lind Theatre in San Francisco. She retired in 1871, and died in 1876.

Families frequently formed an entire traveling act. Such was the case with the Lyric Bards, which consisted of James M. DeMoss and his wife, along with their two sons and three daughters. Collectively they were the entire ensemble of the DeMoss Concert Entertainers, who lived in eastern Oregon. Home-grown entertainers like this were not, however, limited to amateur status. The DeMoss group traveled extensively throughout the United States, Canada, and Europe. One of the specialties of George DeMoss was that he could play two cornets at the same time, one with each hand.

The Bad with the Good

Due to a shortage of women in the early West, actresses were always popular and had to be very bad to receive less than hearty applause. One popular practice was for fire engine companies to buy a whole block of seats at auction. When Catherine Hayes appeared in San Francisco, the Empire Engine Company paid $1,150 for the best box in the house.[5]

Female singers, dancers, and actresses had an advantage just by being women. By contrast, men who were poor actors might be pelted with eggs and vegetables.

Because women entertainers could pack a theater in the West, even mediocre entertainment was often received with enthusiasm. The Melodeon in Virginia City, Nevada, proudly announced the arrival of Antoinette Adams, a singer from Boston. The miners, in turn, looked forward with eager anticipation to her arrival. Unfortunately for their fantasies, Adams was not young or glamorous and, as it turned out, could barely sing. She was almost six feet tall, with a long neck, faded blue eyes, a Roman nose, a crooked mouth, and faded blonde hair. She was also somewhat older than they had all imagined. After a good look at her, the locals nicknamed her "Aunty Antoinette."

For her first song — and as it turned out her last — she had chosen "Under the Willow," a popular, sentimental ballad of the day. The audience soon realized that she was not a very good singer. After she was finished, the glum miners, showing good-natured humor at the joke they thought had been played on them, went ahead and cheered and applauded. Adams was so surprised at this lively reception that she sang the same song again. Again they cheered. Again she sang. The miners decided that she was so bad that they should help her retire from the stage, so they showered her with coins. They applauded and hollered every time she repeated the song. Again and again they threw money at her. They made her sing "Under the Willow" until she was hoarse and breathless, as they kept on throwing money at her. She collected enough money that she did indeed retire and left town on the stage the next morning.[6]

Like Adams, not all women entertainers were raving beauties. Some were tall. Some were homely. And some were so big and heavy that even stuffing them into a heavy-duty corset couldn't get them a fashionable 22-inch waist. But audiences gave them the benefit of the doubt and felt that all women were beautiful, though often helped by stage makeup and a fancy costume.

By the same token, not all women were good entertainers. In the mid–1870s, several appalling acts appeared on the Barbary Coast of San Francisco. One featured two large sisters (and former washerwomen) named the Galloping Cow and the Dancing Heifer. During their act, the two lumbered

Opposite: Maude Adams was propelled to stardom by the role of Peter Pan in J.M. Barrie's play of the same name. Immensely popular, she was the first American actress to play the part (Library of Congress).

around the stage, supposedly performing classical dance. Another singing act was The Roaring Gimlet, a woman who was very tall, very thin, and had a dreadful singing voice. Lady Jane Gray was a sad-faced, middle-aged woman who wore a coronet made from cardboard decorated with pieces of colored glass. She claimed to be the illegitimate daughter of an English earl. The Waddling Duck was an overweight woman who claimed to sing in two keys at the same time, but, in reality, simply screeched her lyrics. The Little Lost Chicken was younger, perhaps somewhere in her mid-twenties. She knew only one ballad, which she sang in such a sentimental fashion that she burst into tears at the end. The men who offered to console her quickly found out that she was also a very clever pickpocket.[7]

Like some of the later novelty acts, the stars of these entertainers rose and fell like meteors, but these hardened performers could pretty much take care of themselves. The Galloping Cow, for example, made enough money to open a saloon on Pacific Street in San Francisco in 1878. Due to her size, she was quite able to run and police the place by herself. When she didn't like the attentions of one man who flirted with her, she broke a beer bottle over his head and flung him over the balcony. The fall, unfortunately, caused the man to break his back.

A Few of the Famous

So many popular and notable actors, actresses, and other performers trod the boards of the stages of the Old West that only a few of the more famous will have to serve as examples.

EDWIN FORREST (1806–1872)

Born in Philadelphia, Edwin Forrest was arguably America's premiere actor of his day and the first recognized star of the theater. He was a first-rate Shakespearean actor, appearing to great acclaim as Macbeth, King Lear, and Othello.

Forrest's stage career had a curious beginning. He first appeared at the South Street Theatre in female costume, when the actress playing in *Randolph; or, The Robber of Calabria* became ill. He found that he enjoyed performing and so studied acting. He joined a theater company and played in *Richard III* at the tender age of sixteen. In 1836, he appeared in London in *Spartacus*, one of his most popular roles. In December 1851, he made headlines when he was involved in a contentious divorce trial with his wife, Catherine Sinclair, who was an actress and the manager of the Metropolitan theater.

Forrest's greatest rival on the stage was English actor William Charles Macready. Their resentment of each other became so intense that, at one point when Macready was playing Hamlet in Edinburgh, Scotland, Forrest hissed at him from the audience — one of the worst insults to an actor. The magazines of the day that specialized in scandalous information about theater stars made much of this.

Their rivalry came to a head at the famous Astor Place Riot on May 10, 1849, when anti–British sentiment among the Irish immigrants in New York led to a major riot at the Astor Place Opera House, where Macready was appearing as Macbeth. Some 22 people died and 144 were wounded when the militia fired point-blank at rioters after being pelted by rocks. Though neither actor directly incited the riot, the crowd used their rivalry as an excuse to settle other scores.

LOLA MONTEZ (1818–1861)

Actress Lola Montez arrived in San Francisco, California, in May of 1853. She played the part of Lady Teazle in *The School for Scandal* at the American Theater. At the age of 35, she had three marriages and a trail of scandalous liaisons. Audiences were so eager to see her, because of her reputation, that seats for her performances sold at auction for up to $65.

Lola Montez was born Marie Dolores Eliza Rosanna Gilbert in Limerick, Ireland, to a father who was a junior army officer, and to a mother who claimed Spanish ancestry.[8] The "Lola" was derived from her middle name of Dolores. She later "re-invented" herself and talked fondly of her Spanish ancestors and her supposed girlhood in Seville.[9]

Lola traveled to Europe, where she immersed herself in the exciting art and literary world of Paris. After a brief marriage that failed, she decided to become a dancer on the stage and performed in London and Brussels. In France, she fell in love with Alexandre Henri Dujarier, editor of the magazine *La Presse*.[10] He was killed on March 11, 1845, fighting a duel in defense of her honor.

For a short while Montez was the mistress of Franz Liszt, the Hungarian composer. She went on to have a scandalous affair with King Ludwig I of Bavaria in 1847, which was likely a contributing factor to his later abdication. Ludwig dubbed her the "The Countess of Landsfeld," a meaningless title, but one she delighted in using for the rest of her life. She made her American debut in 1851 in New York, in *Betley the Tyrolean*.

In the spring of 1853, she journeyed to San Francisco where she performed for three weeks in what became her specialty, the Spider Dance. During the course of this dance she pretended to find a spider made of cork, rubber, and whalebone in her clothing and performed wild gyrations as she tried to shake it and others from her dress.[11] The rousing performance involved lifting her skirts and showing off her petticoats and attractive legs.

Her subsequent tour of the California mining towns was not particularly well received. Her reputation had led the miners to expect a different type of performer and she, in turn, was temperamental and not impressed by the rough-and-ready miners. Her singing talents were questioned by theater critics, but she was beautiful and charming, and her sensational spider dance attracted men to the theater.

Lola wrote and performed in an autobiographical play, *Lola Montez in Bavaria*, that dramatized her real-life affair with King Ludwig I. Her performance was not notable, so brother-and-sister performers Caroline and William Chapman put together a burlesque of the play and called it *Who's Got the Countess?; or, The Rival Houses*. As part of the satire, William dressed up in a female costume and presented his own burlesque version of the Spider Dance, named the "Spy-Dear Dance."

During her stormy career, Montez threatened one unfriendly newspaper editor with a horse whipping and challenged another to a duel. While she was in San Francisco, she married Patrick Purdy Hull, the wealthy newspaper publisher of the *San Francisco Whig*. Her marriage was not by any means a bed of roses. The Sacramento newspaper reported that in the mining town of Marysville she pushed her husband down the hotel stairs and tossed his luggage out of a window. She kept his name, however, occasionally signing herself by the peculiar title of Marie de Landsfeld Hull.

She finally settled in a small cottage in Grass Valley, in California's gold country, in 1853.[12] Most of the women of the town were not particularly friendly toward her, because of her reputation from the theater. Flamboyant as ever, she kept multiple cats, parrots, a goat, and a pet grizzly bear cub, and organized regular meetings in her home, hosting notables from the worlds of art, literature and the theater.

Lola left Grass Valley in 1855 to visit Australia, then returned for a few performances in San Francisco. She went on to New York, where she died from pneumonia on January 17, 1861, at the age of 42, following a severe stroke.

JENNY LIND (1820–1887)

Jenny Lind, born Johanna Maria Lind, was a popular singer from Stockholm, who came to the United States with a considerable European reputation. She was arguably the greatest soprano of her time. Many singing stars from Europe toured the United States, because they considered this an easy way to make money. Lind had a fine operatic voice, and was appropriately nicknamed the "Swedish Nightingale" by British audiences. She also had a reputation for high moral values and was a good example of feminine piety. And indeed, the popular singer had a modest and generous nature, usually giving part of her earnings to charity in the cities in which she performed. She often gave complete performances to benefit local charities, without charging a fee.

In the fall of 1849, promoter P.T. Barnum offered Lind a concert tour of the United States. Barnum tempted her with an unprecedented $1,000 a concert for 150 concerts, plus expenses for her and two servants. As a gesture of good faith, Barnum deposited $187,500 in Baring Brothers Bank in London in early 1850, before the tour began.

Because Lind was not well known in America at the time, Barnum carefully orchestrated a large amount of advance publicity for the tour and made the 1850 tour of 93 concerts a great success. She toured New York, Philadelphia, and Boston, along with a series of Western cities, before a return to the East Coast.[13] For his efforts, Barnum grossed more than $700,000. He planted stories in the newspapers and magazines emphasizing her upstanding character and her donations to charity. True to form, she gave part of her concert earnings of $176,000 to charity.[14]

As part of the promotion, Barnum sold Jenny Lind memorabilia, such as hats, shawls, gloves, and even Jenny Lind chairs and pianos. The American tour lasted from September 11, 1850, until May of 1852. Barnum managed her tour until June 1851, then she changed to a different manager. After the tour she returned to Europe.

EDWIN THOMAS BOOTH (1833–1893)

Born on a farm in Maryland on November 13, 1833, Edwin Booth was one of the premier actors of Shakespearean roles in the Old West, and indeed in all of America. He originally planned to be a cabinet-maker, before deciding to follow his father onto the stage. He made his debut at age 16 in 1849 at the Boston Museum, in a minor role supporting his father, Junius Brutus Booth, playing the part of Tressel in Shakespeare's *Richard III*.

Both father and son went to California in 1852, where Edwin gained valuable experience in the Sierra Nevada gold camps, playing a variety of roles from Hamlet to blackface parts, at times accompanying himself on the banjo. He first played Hamlet in San Francisco on April 2, 1853. He played Hamlet — probably his greatest role — from 1853 to 1893. In 1864, he played the role for 100 consecutive nights.

In an unfortunate coincidence, five of Booth's appearances in various gold camps were followed by major fires. When he reached the town of Downieville, the superstitious townspeople asked him to leave before he had a chance to perform.

Fire eventually destroyed Booth's career as a theater manager. In 1866, he was managing the Winter Garden Theatre when a devastating fire destroyed all the scenery and costumes. He then built the Booth Theatre, but went bankrupt due to poor management and a shady business partner. After this setback he stuck to acting and was considered by many to be the leading Shakespearean interpreter of his time.

In the West, Edwin performed in San Francisco, Sacramento, and the smaller mining camps in the mountains, then toured with English actress Laura Keene to Australia in 1854. He was famous for his roles as Hamlet and Iago, which he played all over the West. His popularity was so great that he appeared in New York, Boston, England, and Germany.

Edwin had nine brothers, one of whom was John Wilkes Booth, who assassinated President Abraham Lincoln on April 14, 1865, at Ford's Theatre in Washington, D.C. John Wilkes Booth started his ill-fated career in 1854 at the Charles Street Theatre in Baltimore playing Richard in *Richard III*. Edwin's elder brother, Junius Booth, Jr., was also an actor, but spent most of his theatrical career as a manager and producer. The only time that the three brothers appeared together was in a production of *Julius Caesar* in New York in 1864.

ADAH MENKEN (1835–1868)

Adah Isaacs Menken was a popular actress who appeared on stages in New York, London, and Paris. Her given name was not Adah (sometimes spelled Ada), but Adelaide. Her origins are somewhat clouded as, later in life, she changed the details several times, manufacturing an exotic biography to better promote herself. Her birthplace appears to have been in or near New Orleans, on June 15, 1835. She could have been Creole, Spanish, or Jewish. It is unclear whether she was born to Jewish parents or whether she became Jewish after marriage. The Jewish heritage she talked about apparently came either from her stepfather or from her first husband.

Her theatrical career started at age 17. When her stepfather died, she turned to the stage to support herself and became a dancer and singer at the French Opera House in New Orleans. In 1856, when she was 21, she married Alexander Isaacs Menken, from whom she took her middle and last names. He was an orchestra conductor in Galveston, Texas, and was the first of her four husbands. By age 33, she had been married four times, and divorced three. Another of her husbands was John Carmel "Benecia Boy" Heenan, a popular prizefighter of the time.[15] Apparently she took to heart one of her own mottos, which was to "marry young and often," because she divorced Heenan in 1861, and married Robert Henry Newell.

In 1861, she starred in *Mazeppa; or, The Wild Horse of Tartary*, which was her most sensational role. Adah Menken first appeared as Mazeppa in Albany, New York, at the Green Street Theatre. She debuted Mazeppa in New York on June 13, 1861, at the Broadway Theater, where the play ran for eight months. It was the role that made her famous and earned her the reputation of the "Naked Lady."[16] At the time, her performance as Mazeppa was thought to be the most daring act yet performed by a woman.

The play *Mazeppa* was a drama, a love story, loosely adapted from a poem by Lord Byron. (Even though Mazeppa was a male character, it was common for actresses to play this type of role.) The basic plot was that nobleman Ivan Mazeppa, a young Tartar prince (played by Menken), falls in love with beautiful Olinska, the daughter of a Polish nobleman, who owns the local castle. The problem is that Olinska is already betrothed to the evil and cowardly Count Palatine. Mazeppa challenges the count to a duel, wins, and wounds his rival. Mazeppa offers the count his life in exchange for safe passage from the castle. The count at first agrees, then changes his mind and orders his men to strip Mazeppa naked and tie him face upwards on the back of a wild stallion. The horse is driven away into the mountains where the count presumably hopes that Mazeppa will starve or die of exposure. Mazeppa escapes, of course, returns, vanquishes the count, and rescues his beloved.

The drama in Menken's interpretation was that she used a real horse on stage when Mazeppa was carried off into the mountains. The audience's anticipation was fueled by the following dramatic lines from the villain Count Palatine that was typical of Victorian melodrama: "Lead the vile Tartar hence. Strip him of that garb he has degraded. Lead out the fiery, untamed steed. Prepare strong hempen lashings around the villain's loins. Let every beacon-fire on the mountaintop be lighted — and torches like a blazing forest cast their glare across the night. This moment let my vengeance be accomplished. Away!"[17]

Apart from this stirring dialog, what made Menken's version sensational was that she performed the ride herself. Male actors, dummies, and stunt doubles had previously been used in other versions of the play. In addition, Menken was advertised as riding nude, though in reality she wore a flesh-colored body stocking covered by a light, filmy tunic, so that the appearance to many of the eager men in the audience was that she was indeed nude. The ride on horseback — even though the horse was trained — was not without risk, however. While performing in Albany, Menken fell and injured herself. In another stage mishap, the horse kicked her and broke several of her ribs.

Following her success as Mazeppa in the East, Menken traveled to San

Francisco in 1863 to appear in the same role at Tom Maguire's Opera House. She made $9,000 for her tour at Maguire's, which was a large amount of money for the time. Her nine-month tour of California and Nevada earned her more than $100,000.

While she was in San Francisco, she also appeared in other plays, such as *The French Spy* and *Black-Eyed Susan*, playing her parts in tight-fitting costumes, both to enhance her racy reputation and to keep the audience happy. She also played burlesque. In a musical comedy called *Three Fast Women*, which parodied San Francisco's Barbary Coast, Menken played multiple roles, two female and four male, among which were a minstrel and a sailor.

A rather unusual burlesque of Menken's performance as Mazeppa was presented in San Francisco by an overweight actress known simply as Big Bertha. This production used a small donkey instead of Menken's horse. Unfortunately, Big Bertha was as big as her name implied and one night the poor overburdened animal collapsed and fell off the stage into the orchestra. The accident almost ended the careers of both Bertha and the donkey. They survived, but from then on Bertha limited her act to singing.[18]

In 1864, Menken went on to Maguire's opera house in Virginia City, Nevada. On opening night the theater was full and the audience waited in eager anticipation. They were not disappointed. It was a shocking performance for Victorian times, but the burly miners of Virginia City loved it. They were so overcome that after one performance they presented her with a gold bar worth $2,000.

Menken was so popular in Virginia City that a mine, suggestively known as The Menken Shaft and Tunnel Company, was named after her.[19] The stock certificate had an engraving on it of a naked woman tied to the back of a stallion. As another honor, a new mining district was named "The Menken" after her. In yet another rare tribute, the firemen of American Engine Company Number Two elected her an honorary member.

By performing the under-dressed part of Mazeppa in some of the best theaters in Europe and America, Adah Menken helped to promote female sexuality as part of mainstream show business. Her appearance in tights on the London stage shocked Victorian audiences in England. But her performances in the early 1860s led to more overt suggestiveness in later theater presentations, which eventually helped to pave the way for the popular burlesque shows of the late 1860s. Others tried to imitate her, but there was something about her and her performance that was never surpassed.

Along the way, Menken used her career to promote her Bohemian lifestyle. She was friendly with several famous contemporary authors, including Dante Rossetti, Charles Dickens, George Sand, Henry Wadsworth Longfellow, and Walt Whitman. She was well educated and spoke French, Spanish, German, Latin, and Greek, in addition to her native English. Menken started to write poetry after the death of her infant son with John Heenan, and also acted as a literary critic. She was the mistress of both Alexandre Dumas, the famous French author, and Algernon Charles Swinburne, the English poet and critic.[20]

Menken returned to New York in 1864, but wasn't able to recapture her initial popularity. She tried Mazeppa again briefly on Broadway in 1866, then went on to Paris and London. While in Europe, she suffered a sudden collapse that was thought to be a result of tuberculosis. She died in Paris on August 10, 1868, and was buried there.

JACK LANGRISHE (1836 -1895)

John S. "Jack" Langrishe was an actor, a showman, and playwright for the Western stage. An Irishman formerly employed by the *New York Tribune*, he was lured to the West by the news of the discovery of gold. He arrived in Denver in 1859 and organized a theatrical troupe that played there for the next 20 years. Langrishe and his wife, Jeanette, played in many of the mining camps around Denver during the 1860s, as well as sending traveling troupes to entertain in remote gold camps in Colorado, Montana, Wyoming, Idaho, and South Dakota. He and his troupe traveled from town to town to find large enough audiences to make it worth his while.

The Langrishes built a theater in Denver at Lawrence and 16th streets, where they starred with a stock theater company, presenting the best comedies and dramas of the day. Jack was described as having a "long nose and a powerful voice." In 1871, the Langrishes left Denver to play the theater circuits in the East and West. Jack went on to manage a theater in Chicago, but took a large financial loss due to the Great Fire. After that, he managed a company of *The Black Crook*, which toured New England in 1873. In 1876, he leased the McDaniels Theatre in Deadwood and opened with the play *Trodden Down* on July 29. In 1878, he went to Leadville to run the Tabor Opera House. He returned briefly to Denver between 1881 and 1885, then moved permanently to Idaho where he became a state senator. He published a local newspaper in Wardner, Idaho, until his death on December 6, 1895.

LYDIA THOMPSON (1836–1908)

Lydia Thompson was born in London on February 19, 1836. She debuted as a dancer on the London stage in 1852, and soon became established as a popular dancer and comedienne. She toured Europe in 1856.

She was married in 1863 for a short time to John Christian Tilbury, who was killed in a riding accident in 1864. In 1866, she married Alexander Henderson, who also acted as her manager. Part of the sensationalized publicity he generated included Lydia's reputation as a heart-breaking beauty, the infatuation she instilled in male members of the audience, and the supposed suicide of at least one admirer who despaired of unrequited love for her.

Thompson was best known for her part in *Ixion*, which brought burlesque to the American stage. She premiered *Ixion* in London in 1863, in New York in 1868, and in July of 1869 took *Ixion* on the road to St. Louis, Chicago, and New Orleans. She went on to play many more burlesque roles in tights and a short tunic, such as the title role in the satire *Robin Hood; or, The Maid That Was Arch and the Youth That Was Archer.* She died in London on November 17, 1908.

DORA HAND (1844–1878)

Dora Hand was not a famous actress of the stature of the others in this chapter, but she retains a place in the history of the Old West for her unusual and untimely death in Dodge City, Kansas. It was a case of simply being at the wrong place at the wrong time.

Not much is known about Hand's life before she appeared in Dodge City in 1878, but she was thought to have previously been an opera singer. It is known that she had performed as a singer in New Orleans, Memphis, and St. Louis. Her real name was Fannie Keenan. She was known as "The Queen of the Fairy Belles," which was a nickname for dance hall women. She was apparently well liked around Dodge City and would often come to the aid of those in need. In July of 1878, she appeared as a singer at Dodge City's Comique theater, along with Nola Forest and Eddie Foy. In August, she moved to the theater at Hamilton "Ham" Bell's Varieties.

Sometime in July or August of 1878, James H. "Dog" Kelley, the half-owner of the Alhambra Saloon and Gambling House, where Dora also sang, got into an argument with James W. "Spike" Kenedy. Kenedy (also spelled in the local newspapers as Kennedy) was the son of wealthy cattleman Mifflin Kenedy, former co-owner of the vast King Ranch in Texas.[21] At the time of the disagreement, the younger Kenedy was drunk, paying too much attention to showgirl Hand, and was causing a disturbance, so Kelley threw him bodily out of the saloon. Kenedy paid a fine and left town. Seeking revenge, Kenedy carefully planned an attack to ambush Kelley. Kelley lived in a small two-room frame house behind the Great Western Hotel, also known as the Western House, in Dodge City. Unknown to Kenedy, however, Kelley had been ill and had sought treatment from Dr. W.S. Tremaine of Fort Dodge, five miles away. Dora Hand and Fannie Garrettson, a fellow singer from the Comique, were living in the back room at Kelly's place. With Kelley temporarily gone, Garrettson occupied the front room at night; Hand slept in the back room.

About four o'clock in the morning of October 4, Kenedy rode up to the house, fired two shots into the door, and rode out of town toward Fort Dodge. Assistant city marshal Wyatt Earp and Officer Jim Masterson (brother of Bat Masterson) heard the shots and ran to investigate. The first shot had miraculously missed both women and lodged in the wall. The second shot had gone through the front door, narrowly passed over the sleeping Garrettson, went through the plaster wall dividing the rooms, and struck Hand in the side of the chest, killing her almost instantly.

Sheriff Bat Masterson, Wyatt Earp, City Marshal Charlie Bassett, and several others set out in pursuit. They eventually caught up with Kenedy about 35 miles southwest of Dodge City and captured him, seriously wounding his arm in the process. When Kenedy found out that he had killed Hand instead of Kelley, he was furious.

Kenedy eventually went to trial, but was found not guilty because there was no eyewitness to the shooting. Kenedy then returned to his father's ranch in Texas. Three years later, he was either shot or died from complications of his wound. The innocent victim, Dora Hand, was buried in Prairie Grove Cemetery in Dodge City.

SARAH BERNHARDT (1844–1923)

Sarah Bernhardt was born in Paris on October 23, 1844, though her baptismal certificate lists September 25. She first went on the stage in 1862. She was a legendary star of the stage in Paris, and appeared in theatrical productions from coast to coast in the United States, including in New York, St. Louis, Denver, and San Francisco. She made her first American tour in 1880, playing in more than 50 theaters and giving more than 150 performances. American audiences considered her a great actress, but critics felt that the subject matter of her plays were perhaps better suited to risqué Parisian stages than American ones. In spite of these opinions, *Camille* was a huge success in New York and broke records for attendance. She returned for five more tours over the next 25 years. She loved the scenery, the vitality of the audiences, and the excitement — and considered American men to be ideal. When she appeared in San Francisco for two weeks in 1887, she again played Marguerite in *Camille*.

After the transcontinental railroad made the journey easier for entertainers who performed on both coasts, she traveled in a private Pullman car on her own train, nicknamed "The Bernhardt Special," accompanied by a support staff that included a chef and a personal maid. Worried by the tales she had heard about widespread Western hold-up men, she always kept a small pistol by her side for protection. One of her other little eccentricities was that she reportedly kept the skeleton of a man who was said to have committed suicide because of unrequited love for her.

Bernhardt appeared on the stage until she was well into her seventies and was even tempted into the movies when they became a popular entertainment medium, starring in a production of *Queen Elizabeth* in 1912. She died in Paris on March 26, 1923.

LOTTA CRABTREE (1847–1924)

Charlotte "Lotta" Crabtree was a popular entertainer who eventually sang and danced her way to become one of the top comediennes in New York, London, and Paris. Her origins, though, were humble. Born in New York, she grew up as a miner's daughter in Grass Valley, California. Her father, John Crabtree, was a former book-seller-turned-prospector who never quite struck it rich, but kept on wandering, prospecting, and hoping. Her mother, Mary Ann, an English woman, ran a boarding house to provide the family with a steady income.

When Lotta was six years old, she met performer Lola Montez, who supposedly taught the child some song-and-dance routines. It is more likely that she learned the songs from local saloon-owner Mart Taylor and the dances from J.B. Robinson's dancing school, which had opened in Grass Valley in 1853. In the mid–1850s, Lotta toured in the Sierra Nevada mining camps of northern California, where her singing and dancing became very popular with the miners. Child performers like Lotta were often referred to as "fairy stars." At one time, attending performances by these child actors became a California obsession.

Though John Crabtree had a notable lack of success prospecting around Grass Valley, he continued to dream of making his fortune, and moved his family to nearby Rabbit Creek (now La Porte, California). In spite of his continued dreams, he still didn't strike gold, so wife Mary Ann ran a boarding-house again to make ends meet. In Rabbit Creek, Lotta took singing lessons from Mart Taylor, who was a nominal entertainer and part-time saloon keeper. His specialties were song, dance, recitations, and fast-paced humor. To supplement his income, he was also a part-time cobbler.

As a moderately successful saloon owner, Taylor had a small building with a makeshift stage that he rented to visiting performers. When he felt that Lotta was ready, at age eight, he put her on the stage in a performance of dancing and singing. In a clever move that he felt would appeal to the local Irish miners, Taylor dressed her in a green Irish costume with knee breeches and a green hat. As part of the program, she danced Irish jigs and sang one of the tearjerking ballads of the day. The audience was suitably delighted and showered her with dollar bills and gold nuggets.

Lotta's popularity grew. She toured the local gold camps, and then beginning in 1859, she went on to perform in some of the leading theaters in San Francisco. At age 17, in the 1860s, she wore short skirts that showed her legs and smoked cigarettes during her performances on stage — two actions that women who were considered ladies would not do at the time. She rose to stardom in shows that were crafted for her particular talents in which she danced, sang, and played the banjo. Her popularity continued and she went on to perform in New York from 1867 to 1891, when she retired at age 44.

She never married. Lotta Crabtree died in 1924 at the age of 77. At the time she was the highest-paid American actress and left an estate estimated to be worth $4 million.

LILLIE LANGTRY (1853–1929)

Lillie Langtry was born Emile Charlotte Le Breton on October 13, 1853, on the island of Jersey, in the Channel Islands between England and France. She was nicknamed Lillie in childhood. When she reached adulthood, she had red hair, a good figure, and a small waist. At five feet seven inches, she was tall for the time. She had such a nice shape that a model of Victorian corset was named after her in 1877.[22] One of its more curious features was that it was advertised as retaining its shape even when the wearer was lying down.

She married Edward Langtry in 1874, moved to London, and went on the stage. She appeared at the Theatre Royal in London in 1881. Though perhaps not a great actress, she was a popular performer and entertained on stages in Scotland, Paris, and South Africa. As happened with some of the other famous actresses, she became the mistress of a famous man — in this case, very famous — the future Edward VII of England.

In 1882, she debuted in New York and later toured America. She was pictured one time holding a Jersey lily and so she took the stage nickname of "The Jersey Lily." Among other theaters in the West, she appeared at Piper's Opera House in Virginia City, Nevada.

While Lillie was in America she traveled to Langtry, Texas, to meet Roy Bean, the eccentric judge who was obsessed with her, even though he had never seen her in person. He so admired her, in fact, that he changed the name of his town from Vinegaroon to Langtry, and changed the name of the saloon where he held court to "The Jersey Lilly" (note the misspelling). In the end she never met the judge, as he had died six months before her visit.

Judge Roy Bean (seated on the porch, with a white hat and beard) was so infatuated with actress Lillie Langtry that he named his combination courthouse and saloon in Langtry, Texas, the Jersey Lilly. Note the extra "L" in the saloon's name (National Archives).

Lillie bought a ranch and settled in California and, in 1887, became an American citizen. She died in her villa at Monte Carlo on February 12, 1929, at the age of 76.

OSCAR WILDE (1856–1900)

One of the more curious figures who entertained on the Old West lecture circuit was the Irish poet, playwright, lecturer, and author Oscar Wilde, who was born as Oscar Fingal O'Flahertie Wills Wilde.

Wilde traveled the Western lecture circuit in 1882, speaking on Aestheticism, in which he proposed the idea of art for art's sake. His manner of speaking was somewhat affected, being sprinkled with phrases like "too too" and "too utterly utterly." He tolerated the barbed remarks and jokes at his expense with good humor, because he was making about $1,000 a month from his speaking engagements.

Surviving publicity pictures show him as a man with long hair, wearing a velvet jacket, knee breeches, and silk stockings. During his lectures in the East, the sole stage decoration was often a lily, and some contemporary photographs showed him gazing fondly at it. He also had a great liking for sunflowers which, in Victorian times, were symbols for pure and lofty thoughts.[23] As a result, the residents of Denver were not quite sure what to make of him when he was scheduled to appear at the Tabor Grand Opera House on June 13 and 15, 1882. The madams and prostitutes of Denver's Holladay Street red light district, who were used to more masculine ideas from Western men, staged incidents in downtown Denver, such as wearing huge sunflowers as hats, that poked fun at Wilde's manner of dress and speech.

The local reporters who interviewed Wilde when he arrived were surprised to discover that he was wearing long trousers and other conventional clothing. For his speaking engagement at the Opera House, however, he used his stage costume, which consisted of a black velvet suit with knee breeches and black silk stockings. The lecture had the long-winded title of "The Practical Application of the Aesthetic Theory to Exterior and Interior House Decoration, with Observations on Dress and Personal Ornament." The lecture was not well received — or really understood — by either the audience or the newspaper critics.

On June 14, the day between lectures in Denver, Wilde went to Leadville, where he received a different kind of reception. Several of the miners in town had heard about their outlandish visitor and thought they would play a practical joke on him. They took him underground in an ore bucket on a tour of the Matchless Mine, one of the rich silver-producers in the area. At the bottom of the mine they proposed a toast, thinking that their Irish guest would not be able to hold his liquor at that high altitude. As it turned out, he could hold it better than they could and Wilde outdrank the miners. In spite of this turning of the tables, the miners bore no grudge. Wilde liked the people of Leadville, and they liked him.[24]

Wilde started out from Leadville on Saturday, June 15, to fulfill his second engagement in Denver. Wilde's train from Leadville, however, was late. To fill the void, Gene Field, a reporter for the *Tribune* newspaper, agreed to impersonate Wilde, so that the anticipated crowds were not disappointed. A hairdresser who served some of the Holladay Street ladies of the evening supplied Field with an outrageous wig, on top of which he placed a huge wide-brimmed hat. His outfit was completed with a heavy overcoat. As an added touch, he tucked a lace handkerchief into his sleeve.

In this improbable outfit he was driven by Wilde's press agent, Charles Locke, through the streets of Denver in a carriage drawn by six horses. Field played his part to the hilt as he waved languidly to the crowd in what he felt was the best Oscar Wilde manner. Again, the staring crowds who lined the planned route did not know what to make of what they were seeing.

The plan was that when the carriage reached the offices of the *Tribune*, F.J. Skiff, the business manager of the newspaper would shake hands and welcome Wilde to Denver. Skiff, however, recognized Field and threw a broom at him. This knocked the wig off and exposed the joke. When Wilde finally arrived and heard what had happened, he did not see the humor in the joke and left Denver that night by train, without giving his lecture.[25]

Although a married man, Wilde created a scandal in England when he was jailed for a homosexual affair with Lord Alfred Douglas.

EDDIE FOY (1856–1928)

Comedian Eddie Foy was born Edwin Fitzgerald in New York on March 9, 1856. Adopting the stage name of Eddie Foy, he became a popular entertainer who traveled all over the West. His specialty was clowning around and entertaining with humorous songs. His early career was spent in New York and Chicago, where he performed in blackface, either as a solo act or with one of several partners. He spent 56 years entertaining on the stage, singing songs, and doing jigs, clog routines, and other eccentric dances.

In July of 1878, Foy and his partner, Jim Thompson, appeared in Dodge City, Kansas, at the Comique (pronounced *comm-ick-kew* by the local cowboys), which was a combination saloon, dance hall, gambling hall, and theater. He entertained with a song-and-dance act, doing blackface routines and Irish humor. During his first performance, Foy made some jokes about the local cowboys that they considered to be offensive. In retaliation, they roped him and pretended that they were going to lynch him. Showing remarkable good humor, the 22-year-old Foy took their prank in stride and offered to buy them a round of drinks at the Long Branch saloon. The cowboys were suitably impressed by his courage and amiable temperament and, after this, they grew to like him and his act. As a result, he played Dodge City all summer to packed houses. His specialty was the song "Kalamazoo in Michigan," which was a great favorite of the cowboys.

After this success, he toured the West. He was so impressed with Dodge City, however, that he returned to play there the following summer. When the Comique closed as the annual cattle trade ended in September of 1878, he went to Leadville, Colorado, and performed at the Theater Comique. While Foy was in Leadville, he courted and married a concert singer, Rose Howland, one of the two singing Howland Sisters, in the winter of 1879. He married four times. Three of his wives, Rose (who died in childbirth), Lola Sefton (died 1894), and Madeline Morando (died 1918) all died young. He married Marie Reilly Coombs in 1923. Foy died on February 16, 1928, in Kansas City, Missouri.

LILLIAN RUSSELL (1861–1922)

Lillian Russell was a popular comic singing star. She was born on December 4, 1861, in Clinton, Iowa, as Helen Louise Leonard. She later became known as "Diamond Lil," because wealthy men, such as her friend "Diamond Jim" Brady, showered her with diamonds.

In 1878, her parents moved to New York, because they thought she would do well in the theater. Her parents assumed that she would make the most of her fine singing voice and wanted a career for her in the opera. Lillian, however, preferred the lighter lyrics of Gilbert and Sullivan and joined the chorus of a production of *H.M.S. Pinafore*. After seeing her perform at the Park Theatre in 1879, theater owner and producer Tony Pastor changed her name to Lillian Russell and sent her with his traveling troupe on tour to San Francisco and other western mining towns. She created a sensation and was very popular. The critics of the San Francisco newspapers were less kind and called her "Airy-fairy Lillian."

In 1882, at the age of 21, she returned to the theaters of New York, then went on to perform in the theater in London. In 1886, her marriage fell apart and she went back to the Pacific Coast in Gilbert and Sullivan's *Iolanthe*. She became a star much in demand for comic opera, burlesque, vaudeville, and dramatic presentations.

At age 25 she was a golden blonde. She had a full figure, weighing 165 pounds for a height of five feet six inches. By age 34, she had blossomed to 185 pounds, possibly because she loved steaks and corn-on-the-cob. Because she was a good-sized woman, she refused to appear in tights like other actresses were required to do. She was one of America's favorite actresses for 43 years, then retired at the age of 57. She died at age 61 on June 6, 1922, in Pittsburgh.

ANNA HELD (1873–1918)

Anna Held belongs in this listing of stage personalities because she is an interesting contrast to Jenny Lind. Both women were relative unknowns who were imported from Europe, and both became famous in the United States due to heavy promotion and publicity. What is significant is the difference in the way in which they were promoted. In the 1850s, Barnum emphasized purity, charity, and national spirit in Jenny Lind's promotion. Fifty years later, with the change in perceptions about actresses and women as sexual beings on the stage, Anna Held was promoted by Broadway impresario Florenz "Flo" Ziegfeld as a beautiful and seductive woman.

Anna Held was born in Warsaw, Poland, on March 8, 1873 (though her birth year has been variously claimed by researchers to be between 1865 and 1873). In 1881, her family moved to Paris, where Anna worked as a singer and an actress.

Ziegfeld first saw her in Paris, singing "Come and Play with Me," a song with which she had some success. He brought her to the United States and

Anna Held, a protégée of Flo Ziegfeld, was a rare beauty with a classic Victorian figure that emphasized a tiny waist and broad hips (Library of Congress).

started a massive publicity campaign to make her his first female star. Ziegfeld dressed her in lavish $20,000 gowns and promoted her hourglass figure, with the rumors that she wore jeweled garters and lace corsets. As part of her image, he promoted a line of clothing under her name. He also orchestrated her in a series of publicity stunts, including rumors that she took daily milk baths for her complexion. In other publicity moves, Ziegfeld put her in a kissing-endurance contest (she only made it to number 150—hardly a record), and promoted her in a car race from Philadelphia to New York. As a result, by the time she opened on the stage in *Parlor Match*, she was already a celebrity.

Ziegfeld fell in love with Held and the two moved in together in 1897, ostensibly as man and wife. Held, however, had been married previously in 1894 and never divorced, so the two never formally married. They were later "divorced," however, after a court ruling that theirs was a common-law marriage.[26]

In 1907, Ziegfeld started producing a series of yearly spectaculars, called the *Ziegfeld Follies*, primarily to highlight Held's attractiveness and beauty. These were a type of revue loosely based on the *Folies Bergère* shows of Paris. Each revue was more lavish than the previous year. Plots and music were of dubious quality, but the shows were a resounding success because they featured beautiful women in revealing costumes. In one role, for example, Held changed her costume on stage behind a shield of chorus girls, but still revealed glimpses of corset and stockings to the audience.

During World War I, Held performed for the troops and raised money for the war effort. She was widely praised for her work because she insisted on entertaining right at the front lines. She later returned to New York and collapsed onstage in 1918. She died of cancer on August 12, and was buried in New York.

KLONDIKE KATE (1876–1957)

Klondike Kate was born Kathleen "Kitty" Rockwell on October 4, 1876. She was vague about her birthplace, at times claiming Oswego, Kansas, and at other times Junction City, Kansas. When she was 16, she worked in a chorus line at the amusement park on Coney Island, New York. After gaining some theatrical experience, she moved on to legitimate vaudeville houses in New York, and then to a variety theater in Spokane, Washington, where she hustled drinks to customers for a percentage of the profits. She moved north to Victoria, British Columbia, to the Savoy, a legitimate vaudeville house, where she sang and danced. She rejoined her former employers from the Savoy to play with a 173-member troupe in Dawson at a newly reopened theater that was also named the Savoy.

She hit her peak in popularity as an entertainer during the Yukon gold rush. The miners in Dawson nicknamed her the "Queen of the Klondike" and the "Belle of Dawson." Kate's specialty was the Flame Dance, in which she whirled 'round and 'round, spinning 200 yards of chiffon in the air.[27] The dance itself was quite spectacular, but it didn't hurt her popularity that she wore revealing pink tights while she performed. After her solo performance, Kate received 25 percent on the cost of drinks she enticed miners to buy, and

Kathleen Rockwell, known under her stage name of "Klondike Kate," was a popular entertainer during the Yukon gold rush at the turn of the 20th century. Her specialty was the Flame Dance, in which she swirled 200 yards of chiffon around her (Library of Congress).

received 50 percent on dances with the miners. Her typical take was at least $100 a night. Reportedly, the highest take she made for one evening was $750.[28]

She met Alexander Pantages in Dawson, moved in with him, and became the headliner in his show at the Orpheum theater. They drifted apart when Pantages moved to Seattle to start the movie chain that eventually grew to be his national empire of Pantages theaters. She eventually dropped out of show business and lived in a remote area of Oregon until her death in 1957.

EIGHT

The Amateurs

When professional entertainment was not available to amuse the men and women of the Old West, they had to make do with their own. In winter, in many places in the mountains and on the plains, deep snow and bitter cold kept people indoors for months on end, and boredom often prevailed. Pioneers organized literary societies, reading groups, amateur dramatics, parties, balls, and sledding groups to entertain themselves. For lack of other musical entertainment, local townspeople might get together and form their own band. Some were good, some were not. The local newspaper in Ketchum, Idaho, described the local brass band as sounding like "a regiment of tom-cats with their tails tied together."[1]

Mountain Men

Before formal entertainment was available, life on the early frontier in the West created the storyteller as an entertainer. As a result, some of the earliest "entertainers" in the Old West were the hardy mountain men who crisscrossed the West creating the fur trade. Fur trapper Joe Meek, for example, paid for his passage on a steamboat journey by spinning yarns and charging the other passengers to listen to him. Included in the entertainment of these mountain men was the telling of tall tales that developed frontier legends such as those of Davy Crockett and riverboat man Mike Fink.

At the peak of the fur trade, in the 1830s, hardy trappers roamed the streams and meadows of the Northwest and Mountain West, trapping beaver and gathering the pelts to send to Eastern markets for gentlemen's hats. These trappers delighted in their ability to spin yarns and tell tall tales to entertain each other and the "tenderfeet" who gathered around to hear their stories. One such tall tale was told by mountain man and scout Jim Bridger. He mesmerized his audience of rapt listeners at his trading post at Fort Bridger, Wyoming, with a complicated tale of his pursuit by several hostile Indians. As the story progressed, Bridger worked himself into a more and more impossible situation that had as its climax a hand-to-hand knife fight with a fierce Indian while the two teetered on the edge of a deep chasm. Finally, a listener asked how the dreadful fight ended. Bridger calmly replied: "The Injun killed me."[2]

Bridger was so well-known for telling tall tales that his early accounts of the area of geysers and hot springs in the aptly named Firehole Valley of Wyoming were discounted as mere exaggerations. Part of this was because Bridger tended to go overboard in telling a good story. When he talked about the steaming geysers, the boiling mud pots, streams of water shooting high into the air, and pools of water that were scalding hot, he also described petrified elk and bears that he claimed were found there, and even petrified flowers. His many exaggerations, such as the petrified birds singing petrified songs in petrified trees were hardly believable, even to the most gullible. The general public, particularly newspapermen, did not put much stock in his stories. But, in reality, Bridger was partly telling the truth about this fantastic area that would later become known as Yellowstone National Park. Among Bridger's stories that bordered on fact was his description of catching a trout on the shores of Yellowstone Lake and cooking it at the same time in one of the boiling springs that that emptied out into the lake. It wasn't until the Montana gold rush of 1859 (as similar tales filtered back to the East) that some of the earlier descriptions were believed.

When fellow mountain man John Colter described the boiling thermal springs, bubbling mud pots, and steaming hydrogen sulfide gas vents that he saw near Cody, Wyoming, he was also dismissed as a teller of tall tales. It wasn't until the discovery by a government expedition of similar features in the area that eventually became Yellowstone National Park that he was credited with his discovery. Because the smell of hydrogen sulfide or "brimstone" was traditionally associated with the sulfurous smell of Hell, the area became known as "Colter's Hell."

Because nobody really believed these men's stories anyway, the more garrulous of the mountain men tended to build on their outlandish tales until they really did become unbelievable. Such was Jim Bridger's story of the time that he had fired his rifle several times at an elk in the Yellowstone area and was unable to bring it down. His explanation — told with a perfectly straight face — was that there was a thick wall of transparent volcanic glass between them that acted as a telescope and had magnified the image of an elk 25 miles away. This mirage was supposedly at what he had been shooting. The story had a vaguely factual link as he was describing Obsidian Cliff, a real mountain of black volcanic glass between Mammoth Hot Springs and Norris Junction in Yellowstone National Park.[3] Obsidian is a volcanic glass containing magnetite crystals (black iron oxide) that turn it black.

Along the same lines, Bridger would tell the story of Crystal Mountain, which was so transparent that it could not be seen with the naked eye. The only way that people knew it was there was by a ring of corpses of animals and birds that had run into the mountain and were heaped up around it. Bridger's veracity wasn't helped when dime novelist Ned Buntline picked up on some of Bridger's stories and "improved" on them even further.

Other entertainment for the mountain men could be found at the yearly blowout that they called the rendezvous. The earliest fur trappers operated as employees of various fur companies. The men were paid a yearly salary and were sent out into the valleys of the West to trap beaver and bring the skins back to St. Louis. In 1823, William Henry Ashley of St. Louis, the first lieutenant-governor of Missouri, with his partner Andrew Henry, developed a new method of fur collection and trade. Ashley outfitted small groups of independent trappers with enough supplies for a year and sent them into the West over the winter to collect beaver wherever and however they could, and told them where he would meet them the following summer. In return for outfitting the men, Ashley took half of the furs they trapped. The trappers were then free to sell or trade the other half for whatever they could get.

Ashley's plan was to meet the trappers once a year in a predetermined place in the West to collect his portion of the furs and to reprovision the trappers for the next year in the mountains. Ashley's annual trading spree with the trappers was called the *rendezvous*, a French word meaning "meeting." Beaver pelts and buffalo skins were at their prime in the late fall and early spring, the seasons during which the trapping took place. The rendezvous took place in the summer when the pelts were not as good and the trappers had time to restock their supplies and enjoy some moments of leisure.

The first rendezvous took place in July of 1825, just north of today's Utah–Wyoming border, in a flat meadow where Birch Creek empties into Henry's Fork near Flaming Gorge reservoir. Ashley named Henry's Creek "Randavouze Creek" for the rendezvous, but the name apparently wasn't popular and didn't stick. Between 100 and 120 trappers — the exact number has not been authenticated — showed up at the appointed place and met Ashley's wagon train of trade goods.

This first meeting in 1825 was a rather quiet one. Ashley claimed his share of the furs and traded goods he had brought to keep the trappers going for the following year. But there was no liquor. Ashley quickly realized that, after a year in the wilderness, the men craved alcohol and he could have profited by bringing whiskey. None of the later supply trains made that same mistake.

Ashley's partner, Andrew Henry, bowed out of the partnership after the first year, but Ashley continued to meet the men and trade with them. This system worked so well that Ashley sold out to mountain man Jedediah Smith and retired from the fur trade in 1826. Ashley realized at the initial rendezvous that the trappers wanted to stay in the mountains and he could make a profit by bringing them all the supplies they required to last through the next winter in the mountains. The trappers were content to remain in the West rather than bring their furs to St. Louis, so Ashley's job was to keep them happy and supplied for the next year. He did that by providing trade goods and a rendezvous that served liquor.

Ashley primarily brought domestic staples, such as sewing needles, thread, soap, and other items, such as combs, ribbons, and vermilion, that the trappers could use as gifts for their women or to trade with friendly Indians. Most of the supplies were practical, including knives, guns, axes, beaver traps, cooking utensils, lead for bullets, and food required to survive in the wilderness. He also brought along luxury items, such as sugar, tobacco, and coffee. He and other traders brought supplies for trade with the Indians, such as ribbons, beads, small mirrors, and combs.

Profits for the traders at the rendezvous were high. It has been estimated that the selling prices for trade goods were about 20 times higher than their original cost. Ashley traded furs for roughly half the going price in St. Louis. A pound of tobacco that cost a few cents in St. Louis might be traded for a pound of beaver fur, which was worth about four dollars. Tobacco sold outright for about two dollars a pound, and coffee for between one and two dollars a pound. Whiskey that cost 15 cents a gallon in St. Louis brought 30 dollars a gallon when sold by the drink at the rendezvous. In all fairness, though, the traders faced a difficult journey by wagon train from Independence, Missouri, over mostly uncharted territory along the Platte River, to what is now known as South Pass in Wyoming, and down into the valley of the Green River. Then, after trading for furs, the trader had to somehow get them back to St. Louis and sell them. Huge profits could be made, but the trader had to work hard in order to achieve this.

The 1826 summer meeting, which was held in Willow Valley near the Utah-Idaho border, did not have the shortcoming of being "dry" and the participants at the rendezvous welcomed the opportunity to drink. As James Beckwourth put it: "The unpacking of the medicine water contributed not a little to the heightening of our festivities."[4]

The mountain man spent most of the year in a solitary or semi-solitary existence, so the opportunity to meet with fellow trappers and traders eventually turned the later rendezvous into debauches of epic proportions. Formal entertainment was lacking, so the mountain men provided their own in this once-a-year blowout. The trappers entertained themselves by singing, running, jumping, dancing, trading gossip, story-telling, bragging about their abilities and adventures, card-playing, and general frolicking. Music from fiddles and guitars have been mentioned in contemporary accounts. Other leisure activities included hunting, fishing, foot-racing, and target shooting. Church services and Bible readings were not unknown, and many enjoyed the simple entertainment of meeting old friends. Reading newspapers, even though they might be several months old and creased and worn, provided entertainment — then often provoked heated discussions among the men.

In 1834, John Townsend described his impressions of a typical gathering: "These people, with their obstreperous mirth, their whooping, and howling, and quarrelling, added to the mounted Indians, who are constantly dashing into and through our camp, yelling like fiends, the barking and baying of savage wolf-dogs, and the incessant cracking of rifles and carbines, render our camp a perfect bedlam."[5]

Trappers bragged, raced horses, participated in wrestling matches, fought duels, held shooting contests, and gambled. There were contests of horsemanship and feats of strength. Other entertainment consisted of impromptu dances, drinking, fighting, games, trading, and consorting with willing squaws. (Many of the trappers had Indian wives, but those who did not could usually find a willing partner at the rendezvous.) Gambling might involve card games or a wager on a horse race or shooting contest. Stakes for gambling often involved the trapper's prize possessions, such as his winter's catch of pelts, his horses, or even his squaw. Losers had the double defeat of losing all their possessions and then not having enough to trade for the next year's supplies.

Drinking played a large part in the trapper's self-entertainment because alcohol was not available to them for much of the year. As Maguire has pointed out, the rendezvous was one of the few times that the trappers could safely relax their constant vigilance and become roaring drunk — a practice that would be unsafe if a man were on his own, exposed to the dangerous cold of winter or potentially hostile Indians.[6]

Two types of liquor were popular. One was rum. The other was pure ethyl alcohol that was diluted with water — or not, as the drinker was inclined.[7] The "rum" might be homemade and consist simply of ethyl alcohol with some blackstrap molasses added for flavoring and coloring. One of the more unusual alcoholic drinks made by the mountain man was to peel some bark from one of the aspen trees that commonly grew in the trapping areas and soak it in sarsaparilla. After the requisite length of time, the bark was removed and an equal measure of whiskey was added to the remaining liquid. The resulting drink was said to make an "invigorating tonic."[8]

Another peculiar drink enjoyed by the mountain men, when alcohol was not available, was a mixture of water and buffalo gall — the bitter bile secretion from the liver stored in the animal's gall bladder. Why some mountain man would think to be the first to drink this concoction is a mystery. Apparently, persistence was the key. Newspaperman Rufus Sage commented that "to a stomach unaccustomed to its use it may at first create a slightly noisesome sensation, like the inceptive effects of an emetic; and, to one strongly bilious, it might cause vomiting; but on the second or third trial, the stomach attains a taste for it, and receives it with no inconsiderable relish."[9]

Alcohol, and more conventional drinking, soon became a powerful tool that was exploited by the fur traders. First, the sale of rum and whiskey was extremely profitable. Second, it kept many trappers constantly in debt to the traders, because they tended to squander away their previous year's earnings on drink. Third, the sale or trade of alcohol to the Indians was a low-cost way to trade for buffalo robes or beaver pelts.

Friendly Indians eventually came to the rendezvous to trade, but also to enjoy the drinking, general festivities, and gifts. They would participate with the white trappers in horse races, shooting contests, and fur trading. For the Indians, the preliminary step to trading was to receive some "gifts" from the trader to supposedly "put them in a good mood" for trading. Beads, small mirrors, and other cheap trinkets served the purpose. Trade with friendly Indians involved furs exchanged for knives, tobacco, beads, mirrors, and bright-colored cloth.

Alcohol fueled fights among the men over the slightest provocation. What started out as friendly banter or trading exaggerated stories might quickly turn into a drunken brawl. A typical sequence of events was described by Paul Kane: "As soon as the men got their allowance, they commenced all sorts of athletic games; running, jumping, wrestling, etc.… The whole thing was exceedingly grotesque and ridiculous, and elicited peals of laughter from the audience." But then a somber note intruded. "As the rum began to take effect, the brigades … began to boast of their deeds of daring and endurance. This gradually led on to trying which was the best man. Numberless fights ensued; black eyes and bloody noses became plentiful."[10] Afterwards, however, there might be no hard feelings and the participants made up and toasted each other with more drink.

The trappers liked to play jokes on one another. As the participants became more intoxicated, however, some of the pranks could get out of hand. A joke that may have started out innocently enough might even end in serious harm to one of the participants. Mountain man and rendezvous attendee Joe Meeks described what happened during one of the wilder frolics: "One of their number seized a kettle of alcohol, and poured it over the head of a tall, lank, redheaded fellow, repeating as he did so the baptismal ceremony. No sooner had he concluded than another man with a lighted stick, touched him with the blaze, when in an instant he was enveloped in flames."[11] Luckily some of the other men, suddenly realizing what was happening, beat out the flames with nearby pack-saddles. The poor victim was burned and bruised, but survived.

But even misfortune was often laced with humor. Mountain man Thomas Smith suffered a shattered ankle in a fight with Indians, probably from a bullet wound. To prevent death from infection, the leg was amputated by his companions in a rather gruesome, amateur operation. This probably saved his life, but he afterwards had to use a wooden leg, which gave him the nickname of "Pegleg" Smith. Smith found that this wasn't always a disadvantage, though, as he claimed he could quickly remove the wooden prosthesis and use it as a club during barroom fights.

The men also found it very entertaining to play jokes on the Indians who attended the rendezvous. Mountain man Dick Wootton recalled an incident that involved a man named Belzy Dodd at Bent's Fort, a popular gathering and supply center in Colorado for mountain men. It so happened that Dodd was completely bald and wore a wig to disguise the fact. One day he decided to have some fun with some Indians who were hanging around the fort. Dodd stalked up and down for a while, glaring at the Indians. Finally, he gave a series of war whoops and ran at them and, at the same time, pulled off his wig and threw it at their feet. The horrified Indians assumed that Dodd had pulled off his own scalp, and they ran terrified from the fort. After that incident they called him "the-white-man-who-scalps-himself."[12]

The era of the great rendezvous lasted from 1825 to 1840. Most of these yearly gatherings were held in the general area where the present states of Utah, Idaho, and Wyoming come together. Many were held in the Green River valley of Wyoming. By the 1832 rendezvous, which was held at Pierre's Hole on the Jackson River in Northern Wyoming, the gathering had grown in size to include almost all the trappers in the Rocky Mountain West. Trappers from the American Fur Company, the Rocky Mountain Fur Company, and the Hudson's Bay Company were present. This rendezvous was one of the largest, with about 1,000 present, including Nez Perce and Flathead Indians. Trade with Indians included hoop iron for making arrowheads, knives, blankets, and trinkets — collectively known as "foofaraws" or "frofraws" — for the women.

The last great rendezvous took place in 1837 near Horse Creek, in Wyoming's Green River country. By the time this event — the 13th great rendezvous — took place, alcohol was playing a major role in the meeting. The assembled trappers were eagerly awaiting the American Fur Company's wagon train to start their festivities.

Rendezvous were subsequently held in 1838, 1839, and 1840, but by then, beaver trapping was in serious decline. By 1840, most of the high mountain streams had been trapped out, and the dictates of changing fashions had substituted silk for beaver felt in men's hats.

Native American Indians

Native American Indians entertained themselves with activities similar to those of the mountain men, including playing games, singing, and athletic events. As with the mountain men, storytelling was a popular form of entertainment. Games, such as wrestling and horsemanship, were similar to those played by the mountain men, but for the Indians, besides serving a recreational and entertainment purpose, games for boys and young men also served to develop many of the skills required to be a successful hunter and warrior.

There were two general categories of games played for entertainment. One group was games of chance; the other involved games of dexterity.[13] Games of chance were governed by luck and were characterized by gambling and guessing games. Games of dexterity served to practice and increase the skills required as youths grew into men. Songs and dances accompanied almost all games.

Games, such as contests involving a bow and arrow, helped to hone skills required for hunting and battle. A target might be either stationary or moving, and might include a buffalo hide, a bundle of sticks, or a ball of leaves dragged across the ground. Variations included throwing a target up into the air and then trying to hit it before it fell to the ground.

Men, women, and children participated in competitive games for the sheer joy of the sport. Ball games were played on large courts. The prehistoric Sinagua Indians of the Wupatki dwellings near Flagstaff in northern Arizona, for example, built a large masonry ballcourt from sandstone with a clay-based mortar. Built around A.D. 500, this large structure is similar to those found farther south in Mesoamerica.

Games played by Native American Indians varied from kicking a ball through a goal in a team game (vaguely like modern football) to running a race while kicking a ball. Ball games included throwing games, kicking games, back-and-forth tossing games, and ball-bouncing games. Another ball game that was popular was a type of lacrosse. The specific version varied from tribe to tribe. Both men and women of the Sioux played lacrosse, for example, but only the men of the Cherokee were allowed by tribal custom to play. One peculiar sport was the kicking match, where the object was for each contestant to jump as high into the air as possible, then kick his opponent.

Also popular were throwing games that used spears and hoops. Though there were many variations of this game, the general goal was to place an object into the opponent's hoop and thus "capture" it. One variation was to catch a hoop or ring on a stick, or to shoot an arrow or throw a spear through it.

Another game played for entertainment involved one of the players hiding a small object, such as a decorated piece of wood, in one hand and the other player trying to guess which hand was holding it. In variations of this game, the object might be hidden in a container or under a pile of straw or grass. This might also be played as a communal game, with two teams passing — or not — the object from player to player and each team accumulating points, depending on how good the players were at concealing and out-bluffing the other team. Contestants tried to confuse their opponents by making strange faces or contorting their bodies to distract them. Many of these games were accompanied by various chants and songs. Drummers or singers for each side tried to add to the distraction by making as much noise as they could. Though this sounds like a child's game, the stakes for the players could be high. Typical wagers on these games were horses, guns, or buffalo robes.

Gambling for entertainment was popular and used large seeds, fruit stones, animal teeth, wooden discs, pieces of bone, or small pebbles with symbols painted on them, in games similar to modern games where dice are thrown. Various markings on the thrown objects determined the winner or loser, depending on the combination of marks. Men, women, and children would all participate. Decks of playing cards, introduced when American settlers came to the West, were also used for gambling.

A popular game among women of the Plains Indian tribes was the awl game, which was somewhat similar to some of today's board games. The players moved an awl (a pointed tool used to make holes in buffalo hides) into different holes around the outside of a blanket in sequence, depending on the throw of "dice," which were objects with special markings on them. Other "board" games used similar techniques, in which various objects were moved around in a circle or square, according to the throw of the "dice."

Rough competitive games with horses were common entertainment. These horseback skills were vital for a warrior to chase food, such as buffalo or deer, or to fight the whites or other tribes. Races with wagers were a common way of proving the skills of both the horse and the rider. In one Sioux game, two warriors would charge each other on horseback — like jousting knights of old — and try to wrestle each other to the ground. Horse racing was also popular, and poor wagers on these races could cost a warrior everything. Kiowa, Comanche, and Sioux all engaged in these contests of speed and skill.

In the fall, after the winter supplies were gathered, the Indians tended to relax. It was a time for gossip, games, and storytelling. Gambling was a popular pastime, and family horses, dogs, stored food, and clothing might be wagered and lost. In winter, the men made sleds from buffalo ribs and wood lashed together with strips of rawhide and went sledding if there was enough snow.

On the Trail

Some of the first amateur entertainment for the whites came to the West with the wagon trains. Minstrel songs by composers Stephen Foster and Daniel Decatur Emmett, such as "Oh! Susanna" and "Old Dan Tucker," were sung around the campfire by emigrants traveling the Santa Fe Trail and Oregon Trail. Musical accompaniment might only be a banjo or fiddle, if one of the travelers was musically inclined. These songs had been popularized in the East in the 1840s by traveling minstrel troupes and accompanied the pioneers to newly settled areas.

Another group of what could be called amateur entertainers were cowboys on the trail. After supper it was common for off-duty trail herders to entertain their fellow cowboys with stories, songs, or music. The stories might consist of tall tales, such as the cowboy who rode a giant sheep or the exploits of the legendary Pecos Bill. Songs might be accompanied by musical instruments, even if that included only a harmonica or Jew's harp. Fiddle music was popular and a good player could belt out "Cotton-eyed Joe," "The Arkansas Traveler," "Sally Gooden," or "The Devil's Dream" with gusto, to the delight of his companions.

Songs were sung to pass the time on the trail or in the bunkhouse back at the ranch. Cowboys would also sing for the entertainment of others in saloons. Guy Logsdon at the University of Tucson has claimed that many of these songs that were sung for other cowboys at stag parties contained much bawdy material, some of the songs being obscene as they "dealt with phallic size and virility, venereal disease, and sodomy."[14]

A common form of entertainment, particularly during the cold winter months in mining towns in the mountains, were a series of lectures. The speakers were local or brought in from the outside. The lectures might be sponsored by a local literary or debating society and often led afterwards to a series of debates on the lecturer's topic. In Tombstone, Arizona, for example, Dr. Goodfellow, an amateur geologist as well as a medical doctor, gave a well-received lecture on February 8, 1888, on a severe earthquake that had occurred the year before in Mexico.

Debating societies might discuss literature, politics, or questions con-

Those who wanted the Western equivalent of Coney Island to entertain the entire family could find one option at Pinnacle Park in Cameron, Colorado. The amusement park, served by two railroads, offered rides, a dance pavilion, restaurants, a picnic area, and a small zoo complete with bears. Admission was ten cents, but this did not deter the more than 9,000 visitors who enjoyed the park on Labor Day 1900 (Glenn Kinnaman Colorado and Western History Collection).

sidered to be of burning importance to the audience. This was obviously the case when such a society in Virginia City, Montana, debated the difficult dilemma for the miners: "The love of woman has more influence on the mind of man than the love of gold."[15]

Other local amateur talent, such as singers, poets, glee clubs, concerts, operas, and plays, graced the stages of many small mining towns in the West. Early Colorado Springs, Colorado, for example, was a typical hotbed of organized entertainment clubs. Among them were the Minstrel Company, the Galaxy Club (reading), the Troubadours, the Rocky Mountain Minstrel Troupe, the Choral Society, the Mozart Club, and many others. Another source of amateur music was local churches. Methodists, Presbyterians, Episcopalians, and other denominations often sponsored organ concerts, choral groups, and Sunday School singing groups.

Amateur dramatic groups were popular. A group in Tombstone, Arizona, named the Tombstone Amateur Dramatic Club, included the newspaper edi-

THE O.K. SHOE AND CLOTHING HOUSE

BARRY. BAND. COMING IN TO

CRIPPLE CREEK NOV 24TH 92.

tor and mayor of the time, John P. Clum. As part of their activities, the group raised money for civic projects. One play they performed, *The Toddles*, raised $120. The city also hosted the Tombstone Glee Club, formed in 1880. Mayor Clum returned for a Presbyterian Church benefit to recite "The Spirit of Wine" and sing in a quartet. Following a town fire in 1881, the Tombstone Dramatic Relief Association put on a benefit performance of *The Ticket-of-Leave Man* and raised more than $400 towards a town fire bell. Amateur groups in Tombstone performed many times for other charitable events.

Gunnison, Colorado, built a fancy opera house in 1882, and named it Smith's Opera House after one of the owners. The opening was a presentation of *The Turn of the Tide*, performed by a group of local amateurs, the Gunnison Dramatic Club, on January 3, 1883. After this auspicious beginning, the theater was host to a series of fine theatrical attractions.

Amateur Musicians

Amateur musical groups were often organized early in the development of a town or mining camp. Brass bands, usually consisting of eight to a dozen players, were popular — if enough musically inclined participants could be found. Amateur bands like these were always popular and played in parades, Fourth of July dances, and local concerts. The Tombstone City Band was typical of those that gave numerous free concerts and played for dances that were held in town. Bands were often organized under the auspices of the owner of a rich local mine or mill, who might provide them with uniforms, instruments, and music.

Typical of sponsored bands was the Colorado Midland Band, which was supported by the Colorado Midland Railway. The group was comprised of regular employees of the railroad, except for the leaders, who were professional musicians. The 31-member band was organized in 1894, and was made up almost entirely of men from the railroad shops in Colorado City, Colorado. It was not practical to use men from the far reaches of the railroad, because they would not always be available for practice and to play in regularly scheduled local concerts. Some of the men were amateur musicians; however, some were merely enthusiastic and couldn't play a note before they joined the band. The leaders taught many of the men how to play their individual instruments and coached them on how to sound like a cohesive group. The railroad

Opposite: The town band from Barry, Colorado, marches down the main street of Cripple Creek, Colorado, during a parade in 1892. Local bands provided a popular form of entertainment and performed at parades, dances, weddings, funerals, and picnics (Glenn Kinnaman Colorado and Western History Collection).

purchased the instruments and uniforms. The early uniforms were made from buckskin and styled as Indian garb. This outfit was later replaced by more traditional dark-blue uniforms with brass buttons, though the buckskins were used for special occasions.[16]

As part of the railroad's public relations efforts, the band played at functions all along the Midland's route, and offered regular concerts in parks around the railroad's home town and neighboring communities in the Pikes Peak Region. The band had a fine reputation and created a feeling of goodwill towards the company. The band played regularly on summer Sundays at Stratton Park, one of the local amusement parks at the south edge of Colorado Springs. The band also played as far away as Washington, D.C., in the inaugural parade for Teddy Roosevelt, who had earlier traveled on the Midland Railway. The band and its members faded away as the parent railroad closed in 1918, though some of the musicians continued to play in other local bands.

One well-known band in the Old West was the Dodge City Cowboy Band, led by Jack Sinclair. It was organized as the Dodge City Silver Cornet Band in 1878 after the town put on a fund-raiser to purchase instruments. The name was later changed to the Dodge City Brass Band. In 1880, the name was changed again, this time to become the Dodge City Cowboy Band. The band performed at social events in Dodge City, such as fairs, concerts, parades, funerals, and the Dodge City bullfight of 1884. The group became

Fraternal organizations, such as the Elks, often put on dances, picnics, and charity concerts in their spacious meeting halls (Glenn Kinnaman Colorado and Western History Collection).

nationally renowned for playing high-quality music, and performed around the Midwest, including in Chicago, St. Louis, and Kansas City. The band even went to Washington, D.C., to play at the inauguration of President Benjamin Harrison in 1889.

Each musician had a cowboy uniform that included a broad-brimmed hat, chaps, boots, spurs, a cartridge belt, and a gun. Sinclair conducted the band using a heavy gold-and-silver baton that was encrusted with jewels. He occasionally also used his Colt single-action revolver to lead the band. The gun was plated with gold and silver, and was similarly emblazoned with jewels and turquoise, with his name "Jack" woven in fancy script on the mother-of-pearl grips. The band lasted until 1890, when it was — so to speak — disbanded.

Singing was a popular musical pastime, particularly in the cold-weather months of winter in the West, when outside activities are traditionally curtailed. On December 17, 1870, some of the residents of Denver organized the Denver Maennechor, a German singing society, under the direction of Professor L. Schurmeyer. Their first public concert was presented in Sigi Hall on April 10, 1871. They were well received and subsequently performed at picnics, dances, outings, and other entertainment opportunities. They also toured the rest of the state, and performed in Colorado Springs and Manitou Springs. In the 1880s, the presentation of musical shows in private homes, that had started in Denver, became a popular form of entertainment.

Although Leadville, Colorado, had numerous professional theaters, not all the musical entertainers came from outside the town, as local talent was quite popular. Bob Swartz, Bill McCabe, and Bingham Graves, for example, were miners who played part-time at local dances and wrote music to while away the long winter evenings. Several other amateur groups presented concerts and other forms of entertainment. The Blue Ribbon Comedy Company, which consisted of eight men and four women, often entertained around town. A local group, called the Apollo Club, gave musical presentations. Another group called the Tabor Light Cavalry sponsored plays. A popular drama based on the local scene was called *The Streets of Leadville*.

Amateur musical groups did their best, and often had to overcome unexpected circumstances. In 1888, a club in Topeka, Kansas, put on a performance of Gilbert and Sullivan's *H.M.S. Pinafore* on a boat anchored in a local creek. The show provided an additional unexpected thrill and element of realism for the audience when it sprang a leak and sank during the last act. Luckily, none of the actors or band were injured, and the boat was later raised out of the water.

One of the more unusual locations for music occurred when a choral group of Cornish miners in Virginia City, Nevada, presented an underground concert on April 19, 1879, at the New York Mine.[17] They put on a dance in a 14-foot by 36-foot chamber located a thousand feet below the surface. It must have been a popular event, because over a hundred people enjoyed music, dancing, and food in this unusual setting.

More conventional places for amateur entertainment in the gold camps were the local Miner's union halls. Typically associated with the Western Federation of Miners, these buildings held an important place in the social life of many of the mining camps. Fourth of July balls, Christmas parties, amateur theatricals, debates, and lectures were held in these buildings. If there was no theater or "opera house" in town — a rare event indeed — touring theatrical companies often performed in these halls.

The Miner's Union Hall in Garnet, Montana, had a fine dance floor made from maple spring board. The stage was equipped with a grand piano to accompany the so-called orchestra. During the community dances that were held there every Saturday night, the high ceilings were gaily decorated with bunting hanging from the rafters.

Similar to the miner's unions were the fraternal organizations. Members of groups such as the British Benevolent Association, the Welsh Club, the Friends of Poland, and the Scandinavian Society banded together and put on balls, picnics, and benefits for charity.

Entertaining the Army

Women in the East had access to a variety of entertainment, including concerts, plays, and lectures. Women at a frontier army fort, however, had to develop their own entertainment. Soldiers had to make do with whatever they could and use local talent to entertain one another. Much of their entertainment ran towards outdoor activities, such as riding, skating, fishing, and target shooting. Also available were amateur theatricals and concerts presented by military bands. Entertainment for troops and their families at an army post was more difficult than most situations in the West, because of the isolation of many frontier forts.

Amateur theatricals followed the soldiers out West. Theater entertainment arrived with American troops as early as 1846, when Stephen Watts Kearny and his 1,700 men marched into Santa Fe to seize New Mexico at the start of the war with Mexico. Some of the troops remained in Santa Fe while Kearny moved the rest westwards to take over California. Even though much of the day was taken up by drills, the men who were left behind had so much spare time that they became bored and decided to put on the theatrical play *She Stoops to Conquer*. One of the unit's tailors made the costumes and another soldier with artistic ability painted the backdrops.

The performance, put on in the Palace of the Governors in the town plaza in Santa Fe, was well attended, both by soldiers and the local population. The play was followed by a minstrel show, which was the highlight of the evening, at least according to the Spanish-speaking members of the audience, as it contained more energetic visual elements.

Musical entertainment was often provided by the troops themselves in the form of singing, solo dancing, and playing musical instruments. Banjo, fiddle, and harmonica were used to entertain fellow troops, either as a solo performance or with the players blending together for an informal concert. Counted among amateur entertainment would also have to be organized sports, such as horse racing, foot races, and baseball.[18]

Most frontier forts had some sort of large building that could be used as the need arose for a ballroom, theater, or chapel. Many of these saw little use as a chapel or theater, but received most of their use as a ballroom. Military bands played for dances, which were so popular at some posts that one was held each week. Due to a perpetual shortage of female dancing partners, the fort and any nearby towns and ranches were scoured for women to attend. Officers' wives and enlisted men's wives, the few female servants on post, laundresses, and women from town all mixed freely without the usual military caste system, in order to provide partners.

To relieve boredom, wives at military posts in the West often staged their own entertainment. Though traveling shows did sometimes visit the larger forts on the frontier, many of the posts were so isolated in Indian country that entertainment from the outside world was not possible. At Fort Clark in Texas the soldiers' wives organized their own theatrical troupe. To make do, they used furniture and other props scrounged from their own quarters to mount the productions. Entertainment was so scarce that they played to packed houses. Eventually they made enough money to renovate the makeshift theater, which was also used as the post chapel and schoolhouse.

In a reverse twist of culture, white officers and their wives at Fort Davis in Texas presented a minstrel show to entertain the black troops of the Tenth Cavalry. The soldiers felt that the show was one of the most popular that had been presented at the fort.

The theater at Fort Rice in North Dakota was previously a sawmill. Performances given there were used to purchase recreation equipment for the soldiers. At Fort Shaw in Montana, families came from miles away to attend theatrical performances, even when the snowdrifts surrounding the theater were higher than the audience's heads.

Fort Union in New Mexico had an active program of amateur theatricals and concerts. In 1883, the newspaper in nearby Las Vegas, New Mexico, the *Las Vegas Optic*, praised the local amateur dramatic club as a first class organization worthy of appearing on the legitimate stage. In 1884, the post had an active comedy company to entertain the troops and their families. In 1885, the 23rd Infantry Band gave three open air concerts every week.

MILITARY BANDS

Soldiers who were stationed at regimental headquarters were lucky enough to be able to attend concerts provided by army bands. The band at Fort Shaw presented a concert for the soldiers and their families every Friday evening. Military bands might be pressed into service to play hymns and other music during religious services at the fort.

Severe cutbacks in cavalry and infantry musicians during the 1860s meant that the composition of a band might be limited. To increase the size, the company commander might demand a donation from the officers and soldiers in order to be able to purchase instruments and sheet music. Col. Benjamin Grierson collected $959 in this way for the benefit of the Seventh Cavalry. Musically inclined German and Italian soldiers often made up the bulk of these unofficial bands.

Military bands were typically stationed only at the headquarters of a regiment, such as Fort Laramie (Wyoming), Fort Abraham Lincoln (North Dakota), and Fort Hays (Kansas). For a short while, Fort Hays was the regimental home of the Seventh Cavalry, under the command of Lieutenant Colonel George A. Custer during the winter Indian campaign of 1868. The fort commonly rang to the strains of the rollicking Irish tune of "Garry Owen," which was a favorite of Custer's and became the regimental march.

The lyrics were probably appropriate for the hard-drinking, hard-fighting cavalry. The first verse goes:

> Let Bacchus sons be not dismayed
> But join with me, each jovial blade
> Come, drink and sing and lend your aid
> To help me with the chorus....[19]

Regimental bands were often pressed into service to play at social functions on army posts, such as at dances, balls, and concerts. Military bands also traveled on tours, giving concerts at various civilian locations. The Third Infantry Band at Fort Hays, for example, gave a concert in Denver in September 1872, playing marches, overtures, waltzes, and other light-classical music. Military bands were also available to play at the occasional weddings and funerals that took place at military posts.

NINE

Medicine Shows

Patent medicine shows provided what would at first seem to be a some-what unusual form of entertainment, but was one that was logical, very pop-ular, and widespread in the West. The traveling medicine show consisted of entertainment and sales spiels that were put on for the purpose of selling a particular brand of patent medicine. People came from miles around to enjoy the show. Admission was usually free, but at various times throughout the show, there were breaks in the entertainment to present a pitch for the prod-ucts, similar to commercial breaks in television programs today.

Medicine shows to sell proprietary nostrums were patterned after the older traveling shows that paraded acrobats, clowns, minstrels, and musicians around the country, stopping in small towns to entertain whoever would attend. The result was a combination of Wild West show, circus, minstrel show, and vaudeville program. Patent medicine shows featured any novelty act that might possibly draw an audience to the pitch man. Shows featured such diverse performers as sword swallowers, fire eaters, singing groups, acro-bats, snake charmers, minstrels, musicians with lively tunes, and comedians.

Medicine shows traveled from town to town in wagons and later by train, from about 1850 until the 1930s. The use of patent medicines became very popular in the 1870s, and peaked in the 1880s. Similar to theater entertainment of the early 1900s, traveling medicine shows declined due to competition from the real Wild West shows, and from the arrival of the movies.

The factories for these products were located mostly in the East, but medicine shows traveled widely in the West, selling potions, pills, and other nostrums. Most patent medicines cost around eight to ten cents to produce, but sold for perhaps a dollar a bottle. In the early 1900s, the sale of patent medicines was estimated to be an $80-million-a-year business.

The American medicine show had its origins in the Middle Ages in Europe with traveling troupes that sold patent medicines. In medieval Italy, a performer who sold potions was known as a *mountebank*, which was the name for one who mounted a platform in a public place and attracted audiences by telling jokes and stories. Another Italian name for one who sold drugs in public places was *ciarlatano*, which was later corrupted to the English word "charlatan," for a confidence man who knowingly sold quack medicines. The names mountebank, charlatan, and quack quickly took on derogatory connotations to describe a con man with a fast line of patter who sold bogus medicines.

The name "patent medicine" came from England, where proprietary concoctions were granted a royal patent. Patent medicines were not "patented" in the same sense that an invention was protected by the U.S. Patent Office. This would be a disadvantage for the product, as the manufacturer would then have to publicly disclose the formula. Instead, "patent" medicines were proprietary medicines with the design of the container and design of the labeling on the box or bottle trademarked to maintain brand recognition and prevent others from using the likeness. Indeed, some patent medicines changed their formulation many times over their lifetime, but still maintained the original look of their packaging. Using the term "proprietary" rather than "patent" was desirable for the pitch doctor, because it implied that the medicine could only be purchased from that particular patent-medicine company.

Along with variety acts, many of the same dramatic plays that were presented in American popular theater of the late 1800s were a part of medicine shows. Melodramas such as *Ten Nights in a Bar-room* and *The Drunkard*, were a widespread but unrecognized part of the sales pitch. The use of "educational" temperance plays like these could be used to attract respectable patrons who did not believe in the theater or in drinking. Ironically, many of the potions the audience purchased after the show were strongly laced with alcohol, but taking them disguised as medicine was acceptable, while drinking whiskey was not.

Medicine shows were presented wherever the pitchman could find space available. Tents, the open-air, and the back of a horse-drawn wagon were popular in the summer. In winter, the performers and pitchmen often retreated to the local meeting hall or "open home." Typically there was no entrance fee to attend even these indoor shows, as the organizer expected to recoup all his costs by the sale of medicines.

Some shows were small, featuring the pitchman accompanied perhaps by only a musician with a banjo. Others were highly organized spectacles. The Big Sensation Medicine Show of Nebraska, for example, traveled with a 12-piece band and a tent that could seat an audience of 1,500. The main show might be preceded by a parade through town to draw attention to the evening performance. One of the best places for entertainment in San Antonio, Texas, was the Military Plaza, which was always filled with pitchmen selling everything from food to jewelry to clothing — and patent medicines. It was one of the best shows in town.

The Pitchman

The pitchman, or pitch doctor, was the one who ran the show and performed the sales spiel or "pitch." Pitch doctors were typically older, scholarly looking men, often with white hair and a professional demeanor. They dressed well in a black Prince Albert frock coat and a silk top hat to look the part of an important "doctor," in the manner of the physicians of the day. Many of the salesmen awarded themselves bogus medical degrees and called themselves "Doctor" or "Doc."

Another sales angle was that some pitchmen dressed as Quakers, complete with wide-brimmed, low-crowned Quaker hats, and filled their sales speeches with "thees" and "thous."[1] The impression they tried to convey was that they were honest, God-fearing, religious people who would not cheat their customers.

Early in his career, P.T. Barnum spent some time, probably not surprisingly, as a pitchman, selling from the back of a wagon. He sold Proler's Bear Grease, which was positively guaranteed to raise hair on bald heads. Predictably, the grease did not work and the enterprise collapsed. It did, however, give Barnum experience that he was later able to put to use in his exploitation of humbugs.

Dubious Treatments

The medicine show was intended to bring the people in, after which the sales patter began. Some people attended the shows merely because the salesmen had such an engaging way of presenting the product.

Two popular ingredients dominated patent medicines. One was laxative ingredients, which made the purchaser feel that the product was actually doing something. The other popular ingredients were herbs dissolved in a high percentage of alcohol, often along with a narcotic drug such as opium or morphine, which induced enough relaxation in the user that he was not bothered by his symptoms.

Pitch doctor Wirt Robe toured the state of Washington for years with the Old Wa-Hoo Bitters medicine show. At the time, "bitters" was used as a

Dr. Warren's White Camphor Cream was one of the many patent medicines that were used to cure a variety of ailments (author's collection).

generic term for medicinal alcohol with herbs dissolved in it. When Robe's local county voted to ban liquor, he was left in a quandary. He decided to quit the road, opened up a store called Wirt Robe's Second Class Emporium, and sold Old Wa-Hoo Bitters by the glass as a temperance drink.

The advertising for Warner's Safe Yeast was a classic application of the patent medicine advertising man's credo. First create the fear: "Because Warner's Safe Cure is the only remedy that can effectively expel the Uric Acid waste, of which there are some 500 grains secreted each day, sufficient, if retained in the blood, to kill six men."

Next offer the problem: "Congestion of the Kidneys, Back-ache, Inflammation of the Kidneys, Bladder and Urinary Organs, Catarrh of the Bladder, Gravel, Stone, Dropsy, Enlarged Prostate Gland, Impotency or General Debility, Bright's Disease. This Uric Acid also causes Heart Disease, Rheumatism, Apoplexy, Paralysis, Insanity and Death."

The final step in the pitch was to offer the cure: "WARNERS Safe Cure, by its action, positively restores them [the kidneys and liver] to health and full working capacity, nature curing all the secondary diseases herself, when the prime cause is removed."

It also didn't hurt to add a vague disclaimer: "We guarantee that every case of direct or indirect Liver and Kidney trouble, as above described, can be cured if consumption of the organs has not taken place, and even then benefit will surely be derived."[2]

The Indian Shows

Indian "cures" were considered by many to have mystical powers to heal via herbal formulas handed down through generations of Indian medicine men. As many of these patent medicines were supposed to come from secret Indian remedies, a Wild West image was a popular one with customers, and Indian medicine shows dominated the traveling medicine show circuit.

George Halleck Center was one of the pitchmen who cultivated a Western flavor. Even though his medicine show was mainly limited to travel around southern Illinois, he dressed in the image of Wild Bill Hickok, with long hair, a large hat, and flamboyant western clothing. He married a young woman who had Cherokee ancestry, and who helped to give the show a Western flavor.

Center spent most of his youth working in coal mines before starting to sell herbal medicines at the age of 20. To attract attention, part of his show consisted of a display that exhibited various mammal skulls, along with a stuffed rattlesnake and mounted owls. Though he continued to sell herbal medicines for the rest of his life, he left the medicine show circuit after five years and went back to coal mining.

Two companies dominated the medicine show business. One was the Kickapoo Indian Medicine Company, which heavily promoted an Indian image. The other was Hamlin's Wizard Oil Company, which was more genteel in its approach.

The Kickapoo Boys

The Kickapoo Indian Medicine Company was started by entrepreneurs Charles "Texas Charlie" Bigelow and John E. Healy. They named the company after the Kickapoo Indian tribe of the Indian Territory of Oklahoma, even though there was no connection between the two. They started the company in Boston in 1881, moved to New York in 1884, then moved to New Haven, Connecticut, in 1887. By the late 1880s, the company had over 800 employees.[3]

The traveling show that Bigelow and Healy put on the road resembled, in many ways, the Wild West shows that later entertained in small towns. At various times, their show offered drama, vaudeville, minstrels, singers, dancers, magicians, and burlesque routines, as well as shooting competitions, dog and pony acts, and the exhibition of various circus animals. A typical show featured Indian songs and dances, rifle shooting demonstrations, a contortionist act, a trapeze artist, and a trained dog act. Their sales efforts extended to producing magazines full of their own advertising, such as *The Indian Illustrated Magazine* and *The Kickapoo Indian Dream Book*.

Healy had a background in this type of ballyhoo. He formerly sold a liniment called the King of Pain with a group called Healy's Hibernian Minstrels, who entertained during the pitch show with Irish jigs and songs. The "King of Pain" description was a popular image among medicine show hucksters. It was also used by "Doc" MacBride, who called himself the "Great King of Pain." One of the Kickapoo advertising slogans was: "Genuine Kickapoo Indian Oil: Quick Cure for All Kinds of Pain."

The other half of the Kickapoo partnership, Texas Charlie Bigelow, was the "doctor" and primary pitchman. He cultivated the image of a Western hero, with shoulder-length hair and a wide-brimmed hat. He was attracted to the medicine show business at a young age, at which time he let his hair grow and became known as "Texas Charlie." When pitching in the East, he wore a buckskin outfit to provide a Western image. Performing in the West, he wore the more sedate frock coat of a traditional pitch doctor. He traveled with a Hindu who did a magic act. He also hired two Syrians from a rug store and dressed them as what he thought looked like Hindu priests in order to provide the mystical look of the Far East for his show.

The primary products of the Bigelow and Healy company were Kickapoo Indian Sagwa, a vegetable remedy for the stomach and liver; Kickapoo Indian Oil, for nervous and inflammatory diseases; Kickapoo Indian Worm Killer, for expelling any kind of internal worms; Kickapoo Indian Salve, for skin

Opposite: With the typical hyperbole of medicine-show advertising, this product was touted as the "King of Consumption," and was said to cure all diseases of the chest and lungs (author's collection).

diseases; and Kickapoo Indian Cough Cure, for colds and lung diseases. They also touted Kickapoo Indian Prairie Plant, for "female complaints," which was a delicate Victorian way of describing menstrual pain and related difficulties.

The tale of Sagwa's discovery, as told at the medicine show, was an involved, woeful tale of Texas Charlie lying at death's door with a dreadful fever until an Indian medicine man gave him a good dose of Sagwa.[4] In no time at all Charlie was hale and hearty again, and fully restored to health. Then, of course, with great difficulty he persuaded the medicine man to disclose the secret of Sagwa to him so that he could pass it on to the general public as a boon to mankind. This was much the same sort of story that most of the Indian medicine sellers told. In reality, Sagwa was a mixture of herbs, bark, and leaves, with a healthy dosing of alcohol. In spite of its supposed Indian ancestry, the ingredients were supplied by a commercial pharmaceutical manufacturing company.

A handbill advertising Kickapoo Indian Sagwa claimed that it "is a compound of the virtues of Roots, Herbs, Barks, Gums, and Leaves. Its elements are Blood-making, Blood-cleansing and Life-sustaining." For only a dollar a bottle. The advertising further claimed: "The sciences of Medicine and Chemistry have never produced so valuable a remedy, nor one so potent to cure all diseases arising from an impure blood."

Kickapoo Indian Salve sold for 25 cents a bottle. It was supposedly made from real buffalo tallow, combined with healing herbs and barks. It was advertised as "a perfect cure-all in skin diseases." The handbills make the claim that it was also good for pimples, blotches, corns, burns, and itching piles (hemorrhoids). Indians supposedly hunted wild buffalo on the prairie for fat to make the salve.

The Kickapoo Company heavily promoted their Indian image. The company headquarters in New Haven was even known as the "Principal Wigwam," with an Indian village for performers behind it. In another link with the West, the company persuaded Buffalo Bill Cody to endorse the product.

The Indians in the first Kickapoo show were Iroquois — certainly not Kickapoos. Later, the company used members of the Pawnee, Cree, Sioux, and Cherokee tribes. The Indians were paid 30 dollars a month, plus room and board.

One of the stars of the first Kickapoo show was "Nevada Ned" Oliver, who was studying for the ministry at Yale when he dropped out and entered show business, playing the banjo. Like other pitchmen, Nevada Ned carefully cultivated a Western image, even though he admitted that he had never been within 2,000 miles of Nevada. He performed trick shooting in the medicine shows and, in his spare time, wrote crime novels. As part of his pitch he would have one of the Indians make some profound statement about the product in his native tongue, then Ned would translate it for the audience.[5] Even Ned admitted that he made up the sales spiel as he went along and was pretty sure that whatever the Indians said had nothing to do with the medicine.

Ironically, Nevada Ned became a cocaine addict from selling one of his own patent medicines, a catarrh powder. "Catarrh" was an older, generic medical term that was used to describe any inflammation of the mucus membranes, such as in the throat and lungs. Today it would be lumped in with sinus problems. Birney's Catarrh Powder, which Ned was selling, contained a base of lactose, laced with a healthy dose of 19 grains of cocaine, and a dash of peppermint for flavoring. Admittedly, there was some legitimacy to the concept, as cocaine was used by the medical profession to shrink inflamed tissues and stop sinus drip. It was also used as a casual, but powerful, treatment for hay fever.

Ned demonstrated Birney's remedy to the customers at every show by blowing it up his nose, as directed by the instructions. After this constant exposure, his nose became inflamed and his disposition became very jumpy. When he checked out the ingredients of the powder, he realized that he had become a cocaine addict. He found that he had to drink a pint of whiskey each night in order to get a reasonable amount of sleep. It took him a long time to overcome the addictions to both cocaine and whiskey.[6]

"Indian encampments" toured the country selling the Kickapoo products. These traveling spectacles were so popular that, at one point around 1890, Bigelow and Healy had over 100 Kickapoo shows on the road, some as far away as Europe. The smallest group might consist of only a salesman and a few performing Indians. The largest was the group that set up in Chicago, consisting of 135 salesmen and performers, and two bands playing accompanying music.

In the summer of 1883, one troupe camped out in the Albany circus grounds. Each week the performers put on eight two-hour shows for the price of admission, which was a dime. The performances were pure vaudeville, with songs, shooting exhibitions, and demonstrations of Indian lore. Between all the acts, the audience had to listen to a pitchman extol the virtues of Kickapoo Indian Sagwa. Later shows were expanded into a type of Wild West act, which included bronc-riding, Indian raids on wagon trains, and cowboys to the rescue.

Healy left the company in the 1890s and went to Australia. Bigelow sold out in 1912. The company went out of business in the 1920s.

Hamlin's Wizard Oil

The other giant of the medicine show business was Hamlin's Wizard Oil Company of Chicago. John Hamlin started his career as a magician before going into business with his brother Lysander and peddling patent medicine.[7]

Hamlin's Wizard Oil was touted as a miraculous cure for aches, pains, sprains, and insect bites. The brothers were not bashful about their claims, which included: "The Great Medical Wonder," "There Is No Sore It Will Not Heal, No Pain It Will Not Subdue," and "Magical in Its Effects."[8] Among the more dubious claims were that it would cure pneumonia, cancer, and rabies.

The Hamlin shows featured more refined music than the loud bands of some of the other companies. Part of the show featured a male singing quartet named the Lyceum Four. As a gesture of good will, they sang in local church services, at fairs, and for charity events in towns where the medicine show was performing.

Starting in the 1870s, the Hamlin Company sent 20 to 30 sales teams to the West each year to peddle their products. They sold from wagons that were drawn from town to town. Each team consisted of six men: a driver, the pitchman, and the vocal quartet. The company did not use the Indian show approach but preferred a more refined image. The salesmen dressed handsomely in frock coats, pin-striped trousers, wing collars, and spats.[9] This type of clothing was rare in the West, except among doctors, so it created an impression of stability and professionalism. It was really a type of company uniform and performers had to wear lest they be fined by the company.

The Hamlin Company did not try to make sales under false pretenses, as they wanted to be accepted by the towns they visited and be welcomed when they returned. The shows usually stayed in a town for two to six weeks and tried to participate in community activities. Their sales strategy was to create a demand for their products and then place bottles of Wizard Oil, Cough Balsam, and Blood and Liver Pills in local stores for continued sales after they left.

One promotion the company used was to sell a book of songs titled *Hamlin's Wizard Oil New Book of Songs*.[10] By purchasing copies of the book, people could sing along at the shows and then use them to sing the songs at home after the show had departed. The song book, of course, also contained advertising for Hamlin's products.

Show Tricks

Several tricks of the trade were used to encourage business during medicine shows.

PARADES

One guaranteed way to build an audience for the show was to stage an elaborate parade through the local town when the show arrived. Performers who appeared in the show offered a teaser of their act as they walked or rode on a wagon through town. Acrobats, fire-eaters, and musicians could show just enough to make the onlookers want more. Parades for Indian medicine shows were particularly popular draws, as the sight of "Indians" in full costume was exciting, even to Westerners.

SHILLS

The use of shills was as old as the sales pitches themselves. A confederate of the pitch doctor — the shill — either pretended to purchase the product or "spontaneously" shouted out that he had been cured of some dreadful disease by the particular medicine. This technique was used to get sales rolling and make the prospective purchasers feel that the product was selling so fast that they had better grab a bottle or two. A similar technique was used by gamblers and carnival salesmen.

WORMS

Tapeworm remedies were popular in medicine shows. The pitch was that tapeworms were widespread, living inside the general population, eating them from within and thus threatening their health. This sort of pitch was used to throw a scare into potential customers. Indeed, intestinal worms were not uncommon among rural audiences due to the widespread contemporary practice of eating undercooked meat.

As part of the scare tactics, pickled tapeworms were put on exhibit. They were ghastly looking, white, rope-like specimens, some of which were 50 feet long. The awed prospective medicine buyers were not told, however, that the worms were obtained from the local stockyards. The worms were stored in a clear glass jar full of grain alcohol, prominently displayed near the stage or entrance to the medicine show tent, where the public could see them plainly.

The cure, of course, was to use the salesman's patent medicine. Most of these nostrums had strong laxative powers that would indeed expel everything. Typical was the Kickapoo Indian Worm Killer. Handbills for the product used a classic pitch, starting with a disgusting description of worms and the problems they could cause if not treated. The cure could be purchased by mail for only five dollars. Similar products were David Jayne's Vermifuge (worm killer), and Thomas Dyott's Infallible Worm Destroying Lozenges.

"Doc" Arthur Hammer was a pitchman who touted the innumerable benefits of his worm cure. He was an impressive figure, always well dressed in a frock coat and silk top hat. He is memorable in this context because his thirst for alcohol was so great that he occasionally drank the preservative used in his worm display.[11]

Amateur Dentistry

Another popular attraction to draw customers to medicine shows involved teeth pulling. Watching another person having a tooth pulled, often without any anesthetic, was considered to be great entertainment. There was never a shortage of patients, because most people in the West had bad teeth due to poor or non-existent dental care, and a bad diet. Because the Old West had few dentists, many people were ready to see the itinerant dentists who did come through town. In the mid– to late 1800s, most dentists were located in the East. Small towns in the West were primarily serviced by traveling dentists, who made a regular circuit of areas that had no dentist or doctor to care for teeth. These visits might be only once or twice a year. Even then, much of early frontier dental care consisted of pulling a decayed tooth when the ache became bad enough. Pulling one in public, so that others could stare morbidly at the pain being inflicted, was enough to attract a crowd.

One of the great dental pitchmen was James I. Lighthall, known also as the "Diamond King," who pulled teeth throughout Texas in the 1880s.[12] Naturally he sold patent medicine on the side. He perfected his pitch to a fine art. He was a real showman and, as part of his image, wore eye-catching, spectacular outfits. He would appear on stage to do his work in a jacket encrusted with diamonds, or in a sealskin hat and sealskin coat that had diamonds sewn on the material in the patterns of large stars. Some of the gems were real, others were probably rhinestones. He also had a flashy red velvet suit adorned with buttons made from gold coins.

Lighthall claimed to have spent 13 years among the Indians, learning their secret knowledge of compounding roots, barks, and leaves. He had a traveling troupe of eight men and two women. Like other medicine show salesmen, he sold a variety of products, including his special Snake Oil, otherwise known as — what else? — The King of Pain. Other products were a blood purifier, a tooth powder, and Indian Hair Tonic. One of his potions was made from the bark from prickly ash, poplar, dogwood, and wild cherry, mixed with sarsaparilla root. These ingredients were chopped up and put in a quart bottle, after which the bottle was filled to the top with whiskey. A tablespoon or two of this high-proof concoction, which was recommended before each meal, would certainly put the user in a mellow mood.

To generate attention and attract potential medicine buyers close, Lighthall offered to pull teeth at no charge. Afterwards, he went into a sales spiel for one of his medicines known as Nature's Remedy, a patent medicine which was mixed up by his mother in a barrel. He also sold Spanish Oil for $1 a bottle.

Tooth-pullers often roared out to the patient: "That didn't hurt, did it?" Any reply was muffled by the dentist's constant patter or by loud music from a band playing to heighten the tension and act as a covering noise. Lighthall placed his patients in front of a musician pounding on a big bass drum so that any complaints were immediately drowned out.

One dentist who took public tooth-pulling to the extreme was the famous Painless Parker, who traveled around pulling teeth at medicine shows and a circus. Parker was a legitimate dentist, who started his career traveling through the backwoods of Canada to tend to rural clients. At various times he worked in medicine shows, owned a circus, and was the owner of a chain of dental offices. He was another expert showman. At various times, to attract attention, he blew a cornet outside his office, hired tightrope walkers to cross the street above his building, and pulled teeth on the sidewalk outside his office, accompanied by the music of a brass band. When he owned a circus, his tent was decorated with a definite dental theme consisting of pictures of teeth and advertising for Parker. The circus musicians sat in a bandstand that was shaped like a set of giant dentures. Outside the tent, he set up a clinic manned by dentists, doctors, and nurses. Once, as a publicity stunt, he did dental work on a hippopotamus.[13]

SNAKES

Exotic snakes and lizards of the West were often used a part of medicine shows to attract attention and draw customers the sales pitch. Live or stuffed gila monsters were used by several pitchmen as the beaded, multicolored appearance of these venomous lizards was unusual and dramatic at the time.

Snakes had two primary uses in medicine shows. One was that snake oil was prized as a curative. The other was that snakes held a morbid fascination for many people. As a result, snake acts were popular medicine show attractions.

Snake oil was considered to be a secret medicine of great curative power. Any kind of snake oil was believed to be good, but rattlesnake oil was considered to be among the best. Because of the association of snake oil with dubious claims and even more dubious medicine pitchmen, the term "snake oil salesman" eventually came to have a derogatory connotation. In reality, much of supposed snake oil was a standard commercial type of oil. One was made from a mixture of white gasoline and wintergreen oil.

One popular snake oil salesman was Clark Stanley, who called himself the Rattlesnake King. He started out as a Texas cowboy, but became a patent medicine salesman. He traveled around Texas with a booth that he used to kill rattlesnakes. His gruesome show was a great attraction. He would wade into the booth, which was full of rattlesnakes, and kill dozens of them. He then processed the oil into his Snake Oil Liniment. It was touted as a secret remedy that was supposedly given to him by the medicine men of an undisclosed tribe in the West, and was recommended for rheumatism, cold, aches, and pains. A government analysis of the liniment showed it to be mineral oil, mixed with beef fat, camphor, and red pepper.

To promote snake oil, acts by snake charmers were sure to gather a crowd. If the snake charmer was a woman, the crowds would be enthralled. Popular acts were billed as daring dramas with poisonous, unpredictable rattlesnakes, but the snakes used were typically bullsnakes. Bullsnakes, also commonly known as gopher snakes, are fierce-looking but harmless snakes that look so like a rattlesnake that they are often mistaken for them. The audience certainly could not make the distinction from a distance. A bullsnake was occasionally even billed as a dangerous python or cobra, and the uneducated rural audiences to which the medicine pitchman catered didn't know the difference.

OTHER TRICKS OF THE TRADE

Though patent medicines have a negative connotation as useless nostrums, some of them did have active ingredients that had an effect on the patient. This was promoted by the medicine show pitchman as an effective cure or at least a relief from symptoms. Among others, liniments often contained ingredients that did relieve some pains. Alcohol and opium in some medicines dulled the senses and conquered the racking cough of consumption (tuberculosis), so that the person taking them felt better even if they were not cured. Deafness caused by impacted earwax could be "cured" by dissolving the wax in oil (this is still the remedy of choice today).[14] Tapeworms could be expelled by a strong purgative. Liver pads contained a hot substance, such as pepper, that created a warmth in the skin which provided some comfort, indicating that healing was taking place.

Some of the pitch doctors were clever. "Doc" Will Cooper never said that his medicine, called Tanlac, would cure all the ailments he described, but he did say that it would *relieve* them. His tonic contained 17 percent alcohol, so frequent doses would indeed make the user oblivious to his symptoms — at least for a while.

TEN

Motley Pleasures

Along with popular plays, song-and-dance spectacles, and variety acts featuring conventional actors, actresses, and singers, an assortment of other types of acts toured the West providing entertainment. Almost anything was fair game if it could turn a profit and amuse the entertainment-starved miners, cowboys, and other inhabitants of the wide open spaces.

The Circus

Circuses made an early appearance in the Old West. The first circus performance in San Francisco took place in 1849. Like everything else in gold-rush San Francisco, the price of seats was expensive, costing up to $55 for the best seats.

Circuses had their origins in "hippodrama" or the exhibition of acrobatic feats performed on horseback. One of the earliest of these shows was a performance by a former cavalry officer named Philip Astley, in London in 1768.[1] These equestrian acts, later combined with displays of exotic animals such as camels and zebras, became an early form of what we now call "the circus." Circuses were popular because they featured glamorous performers in extravagant costumes performing daredevil acts, accompanied by strange and exotic animals.

Circuses of the early 1800s traveled the East from town to town in horse-drawn wagons. By the mid–1800s, intrepid performers started to journey as far west as Kansas and Nebraska, which was then considered to be the forefront of the West. The earliest traveling circuses were small in scale, typically offering horseback performers, acrobats, jugglers, trick riders, and acts featuring smaller animals, such as trained dogs and monkeys, because of the difficulty of transporting larger animals for long distances by wagon. It was not until rail

175

A variety of performers played in the West. This act, from an early circus, featured a leopard and its woman tamer in the type of flashy outfit that appealed to males in the audience (Library of Congress).

transportation in the West improved to the point that larger animals, such as elephants and lions, could be easily moved from town to town that they became common in traveling circus acts.

The circuses that traveled the Old West were much like those of today, and featured performances by trained animals, clowns, acrobats, trapeze artists, tightrope walkers, and horseback riders. But, in addition, circuses of the mid–19th century also presented plays, musical performances, and minstrel shows.

Elephants and lions usually featured prominently in the later shows as many people had never seen them before a circus came to town. As an promotional gimmick, it became commonplace for circuses to unload their animals at the edge of town and parade triumphantly down Main Street to the accompaniment of a band. This spectacle provided free advertising for the show and built up anticipation and enthusiasm among spectators to buy tickets to the upcoming performances.

By the 1880s, smart promoters had added women performers dressed in abbreviated costumes and tights to equestrian and acrobatic acts to make the show appear more sensational, and to appeal to the Victorian males in the audience. Sideshows provided customers with a close-up, behind-the-scenes look at caged, exotic, wild animals, such as lions and tigers, from the circus performance.

Finding a suitable place for larger animals to perform was not always easy. One circus that was booked to perform in Leadville, Colorado, found that the weather was extremely cold when they arrived, due to the high mountain air. After a short debate, the manager refused to unload the circus animals unless they could perform indoors. The only building large enough was the Tabor Opera House, which meant that the animals performed on the same stage that had hosted Oscar Wilde and Sarah Bernhardt.

Animal entertainment was not just limited to the circus. One budding entrepreneur brought six camels to Virginia City, Montana, and, for a small price, offered camel rides up and down the street. The rides were popular until a girl fell off one of the animals and was injured. The man left town in a hurry after this. It was just as well. The local wagon drivers were not amused by the camels, because the strange-looking, smelly animals frightened their horses.

Another unusual sort of animal entertainment appeared in Tombstone one day when a man showed up with a bear trailing behind him on a chain. The man claimed that this was a wrestling bear and for a $5 bet contestants could see whether they or the bear would be the first to be wrestled to the ground. Eager bettors lined up with five-dollar bills in their hands. Their first indication that this might not be as easy as it seemed was when the bear stood up on its hind legs to a height of about seven feet. The bear was so big that none of the contenders could lift even one of its legs off the ground. The bear was obviously well trained because, at the owner's command, it lifted each of its opponents up and placed him gently on the ground. The bear and its owner, now somewhat richer with a pocketful of five-dollar bills, left town undefeated.[2]

In the 1880s, when a network of railroads covered the West, visiting circuses became more commonplace in small Western towns. Until this occurred, circuses wishing to travel to the more out-of-the-way towns were often limited by the availability of transportation. The circus that performed in Virginia City, Nevada, in 1864, for example, put this town on their tour schedule simply because performers, crew, animals, and supporting equipment could travel all the way to Virginia City by railroad.

The first circus to travel by rail all the way across the country was Dan Castello's Great Show, Circus, Menagerie, and Abyssinian Caravan — a mouthful of a name. This occurred in 1869, soon after the transcontinental rail lines

Wild Bill Hickok was buried in Mt. Moriah cemetery in Deadwood, South Dakota, after being shot by a drifter named Jack McCall (author's collection).

from the East and the West met in Promontory, Utah. Transportation to towns not yet served by the main railroads, however, was still a difficult issue for the troupe. Castello's circus was able to travel to Cheyenne, Wyoming, on the Union Pacific railroad to perform but, in order to reach Denver, 100 miles or so to the south in Colorado, the troupe spent four miserable days traveling by wagon through the rain. Once they were there, they took advantage of the area, and Castello struggled on by wagon to the nearby towns of Golden,

Central City, Georgetown, and Boulder, before returning to Cheyenne and the railroad. In 1885, more than 50 circuses were touring the United States.

As the railroad allowed rapid and easy transportation around the West, promoters changed their schedules to force patrons to come to them instead of the circus coming to the patrons. Business decisions were sometimes made to omit from their travel schedule towns that did not appear to have enough people to make a stop worthwhile. Instead, eager circus-goers had to travel to wherever the circus chose to appear. Conversely, the convenience of the railroad and the highly organized methods developed to load and unload the circus train made it practical for the show to perform for a single day — if audience attendance could justify it — and still travel to the next scheduled town overnight.

Circuses that traveled the West were not necessarily large. One circus that visited Virginia City, Nevada, in 1870, contained only 22 performers — 21 men and one woman. This circus was small in size for the day, but the miners were so hungry for entertainment that it was very popular. Among the larger ones, the Forepaugh's Monster Railroad Circus, Museum, Menagerie and Elevated Stage had something for everyone. Among the trained animals were 25 Shetland ponies, 25 English greyhounds, goats, a performing bear, and several lions. Millie Zola, the self-styled "Queen of the Air," rode a bicycle, blindfolded, across a wire that was strung 50 feet above the ground.

Another circus of historical interest in the Old West was Mrs. Agnes Lake Thatcher's Hippo-Olympiad & Mammoth Circus.[3] Agnes Lake Thatcher (also known as Agnes Lake) was the widow of circus-owner William Lake Thatcher, who shortened his name to William Lake, and who had started out in circus life as a clown. Show business had always been in Agnes's blood, also. In her youth, she was an accomplished horseback rider, a tightrope walker, a lion tamer, and had even performed as Mazeppa in Germany. William and Agnes both performed on the *Floating Palace* for nine of the years that the showboat plied the Mississippi River. The two eventually started their own circus in 1863.

William Thatcher was, unfortunately, shot to death in Granby, Missouri, in 1869. A man named Jake Killian (also identified in the local paper as Kill-you) had refused to pay for the concert after the show and Thatcher had him thrown out. Killian returned with a gun and shot Thatcher in cold blood. After her husband was killed, Agnes continued to tour with and run the circus alone.

Lake met Wild Bill Hickok for the first time on July 31, 1871, when the circus visited Abilene, Kansas. The two later ran into each other in Rochester, New York, when Hickok was appearing in Buffalo Bill's *Scouts of the Plains*. They met yet again in Cheyenne, Wyoming, and were married on March 5, 1876. Agnes was quite wealthy by this time, as she had sold the circus in 1873.

P.T. Barnum and James Bailey joined forces to create "The Greatest Show on Earth," when the competition between their rival circuses became too intense (Library of Congress).

In July 1876, Hickok went with an expedition of miners to join the gold rush to the Deadwood area of South Dakota, hoping to make a gold strike that would let him retire with Agnes. He was there for only about three weeks before he was killed on August 2, by Jack McCall, an itinerant with a grudge against him, in Deadwood's saloon No. 10 (also called Nutall and Mann's Saloon). McCall claimed at his trial that Hickok was responsible for the death of his brother. No evidence was found to support this. More likely, McCall had lost money to Hickok during a card game the day before. McCall was executed on March 1, 1877, for Hickok's murder.

Agnes later took out a marriage license with a George Carson, but no evidence exists that they married. She preferred to be remembered as Mrs. Hickok.

The lines of Western entertainment sometimes became blurred and circus-type acts were common in variety theaters as novelty acts. Mademoiselle Zazel, a 16-year-old girl, was shot out of a cannon a distance of 60 feet in the Bird Cage Theatre in Tombstone. Instead of using gunpowder, as in a conventional cannon, she was propelled by springs located at the bottom of the barrel. The effect was, nevertheless, spectacular. This act earned her the name of the "Human Cannonball."

Conversely, circuses frequently contained elements of the theater. Sideshows, which offered exhibits of freaks, were simply an updated version of the earlier "educational" museums and their contents. Circus bands performed concerts and led parades through the local town as a form of advertising to draw ticket-buyers to the circus performance, similar to medicine show parades to attract potential consumers.

One type of performance that was missing from many of the earliest circuses was the high-trapeze acts, both because the techniques of aerialists had not yet been perfected and because it was often not possible to rig trapezes in the small tents or theaters of the day. Instead, circuses and variety stage performances featured the forerunners of trapeze artists, known as "leapers." These daredevil performers ran down a ramp and then catapulted themselves off a springboard. While in the air they performed acrobatic maneuvers and somersaults, before they (hopefully) landed safely on a padded mat.[4]

Not surprisingly, these acts turned out to be extremely dangerous for the performers. Many leapers performed stunts that were more and more daring as they tried to enthrall their audiences and outdo their competition, and many were unsuccessful in their attempts. Injuries such as broken legs, arms, and backs were the common result of even the slightest miscalculation. Even broken necks were not unusual. These acts were eventually replaced by trapeze acts, which limited what the performers could do.

One of the most famous circuses in the United States had its origins in the era of the Old West and later became linked with Buffalo Bill's *Wild West* spectacular. The story started in 1859, when a young orphan, James A. McGinness, went to work for Fred Bailey's circus. The two men became very close and, in the mid–1860s, McGinness changed his name to James Bailey, which he felt was a better circus name. He worked his way up through a variety of jobs, and eventually became the manager of the entire circus. In 1876, Bailey also became half-owner of Cooper and Bailey's circus.[5]

By 1880, the combined circus had become a serious competitor for P.T. Barnum's Museum, Menagerie and Circus. The competition between the two eventually became too intense and wasteful, and Barnum and Bailey merged to form what they called "The Greatest Show on Earth." They developed the innovation of three rings with continuous performances in all three. In 1906, following the deaths of both Barnum and Bailey, the circus was bought by the Ringling Brothers, who combined all three shows to create the famous Ringling Bros. and Barnum & Bailey Circus.

By 1910, traveling circuses in the West started to decline in size and scale, and there were fewer on the road. One of the direct causes was that the costs of transportation and operation had risen to prohibitive levels. Another significant factor was that there were too many types of entertainment competing for the potential audience's attention and dollars.

Bulls and Bears

Bullfights, bear fights, and fights between bears and bulls in the Old West were typical early California types of entertainment, having their origins in the time when the region was still a part of Mexico. Bullfights were particularly popular, especially among the Mexican residents. One reason for the popularity of these contests was that spectators loved to bet on which animal would survive the fight.

Even after the initial rush of gold seekers to the Sierra Nevada Mountains in 1849, elements of the Mexican culture remained and were absorbed by the early American settlers. The owners of the 30 saloons built in the mining town of Columbia, California, in the foothills of the Sierra Nevada mountains, for example, commonly staged bull and bear fights. These were very colorful events, with men and women in bright costumes, and Mexican women waving on the matadors with gaily colored handkerchiefs. The object of these animal fights was to make money for the promoters, and many towns built circular arenas with high fences to keep out those who didn't pay.

The spectator sports of bull and bear fights had their origin in the earlier sport of bear-baiting, which originally came to the East Coast of the United

States from England. In California, the "sport" consisted of having a dog harass a bear to enjoy the reaction of the tormented animal.

Mexican *vaqueros* started the spectator sport of rodeo by competing in front of audiences to see who could lasso an angry bull. The extension of this was to rope both a bear and a bull and match the two against each other. This type of fight was easy to stage in the western foothills of the Sierra Nevada Mountains due to the natural presence of black bears and grizzly bears, and because bulls were readily available on local ranches. Grizzly bears were preferred for bear fights because of the animals' bad temper. Contests involving black bears were reported to be less exciting. One variation was to substitute a mountain lion as one of the contestants in the ring.

The methods of staging a bull and bear fight varied, but, as a general practice, the bear was roped or chained to a post in the middle of an arena and given 10 to 20 feet of slack rope or chain with which to maneuver. The bull was driven in to attack it. The reason for this particular arrangement was that a bull fought by charging his opponent and trying to hook it with his horns, whereas the bear attempted to bite and hold on with his teeth while trying to pull the bull down. The bears were also generally chained because of their habit of trying to escape and chase after spectators. Sometimes the bulls were also restrained and sometimes their horns were sawn off at the tip to avoid accidents and to improve the fight.

These different methods of fighting — the bull trying to toss the bear up in the air and the bear trying to drag the bull down — were responsible for the Wall Street descriptions of stock market trends. A bull market goes up, a bear market goes down.

A typical bear fight was staged at Mokelumne Hill, in the Sierra Nevada Mountains, when a bull-killing bear named General Scott (after General Winfield Scott, who led the invasion of Mexico in 1847) was pitted against a large bull. The crowd became so excited by the progress of the fight that they contributed to a collection for a second bull.[6] Both of the bulls were so badly wounded in the ensuing fight that they had to be destroyed and General Scott was declared to be the winner. A few weeks later, the bear was pitted against a third bull. This time, however, the bull gored the bear in the ribs and inflicted serious internal damage from which the bear didn't recover.

Some of the fights were man pitted against bull, and were patterned after Spanish bullfights. The bullfighters who took part in these contests were male. In an unusual performance at the mining camp of Sonora, California, however, a Mexican woman — at least, so described by onlookers — fought and killed a bull. But appearances were not always what they seemed to be. At the nearby town of Columbia, an investigation was made after Señorita

Ramona Perez fought and killed a bull. It turned out that the *señorita* was actually a *señor* in woman's clothing.[7]

Not all of these bullfights were an unqualified success, such as the Mexican bullfight that was staged in Virginia City, Montana, in October of 1864. To add authentic color (and so that he could charge spectators two dollars a ticket), the promoter hired some local Mexicans that he felt could serve as bullfighters. For the animal contestants, he looked around and found what he considered to be mean-looking "bulls," which were actually harmless oxen whose job was pulling wagons. When the event started, the local bullfighters weren't as keen on the idea as they were at first and abandoned the "bulls" alone in the corral.[8]

Other fights were more successful. In the spring of 1884, the cattle town of Dodge City, Kansas, found itself in a financial quandary. The depression of 1883 had caused the economy to slow to a crawl, a quarantine against cattle was depressing the Texas cattle trade, and money for investment was scarce. As a result, to try to boost the town's image, some of the Dodge City business leaders decided to stage a bullfight as part of their 1884 Independence Day celebration. Saloon keeper and ex-mayor Alonzo B. Webster couldn't find any statutes on the books that prohibited such a performance, so he and several fellow businessmen raised $10,000 and set the stage for what they were calling a "genuine Spanish bullfight."

Webster hired five "bullfighters" from Chihuahua, Mexico, including Gregorio Gallardo, a tailor, and Evaristo Rivas, a public works inspector.[9] With superb hyperbole, the local newspapers claimed that Gallardo was the most famous bullfighter in Mexico. Webster delegated D.W. "Doc" Barton, a former drover, to select a dozen suitably ferocious bulls. The promoters built a bullring outside the town with a 100-foot diameter arena and a grandstand that would seat 4,000 spectators. They arranged for appropriate entertainment by Dodge City's Cowboy Band to accompany the event. Webster's advance publicity drew newspaper reporters from as far away as New York City, St. Louis, and Chicago.

In spite of severe criticism, an estimated 3,000 eager spectators showed up on the day of the event. Though this was not as many as the promoters had hoped, they were able to recoup their investment. Harry Bergh, Jr., the president of the American Society for the Prevention of Cruelty to Animals, wired a protest to Governor George W. Glick of Kansas, but he refused to intervene, and the bullfight proceeded as planned. In spite of all this hoopla, the event was not a success. The bullfight ended with one bull being killed in a rather crude manner, and the other four bulls refusing to fight.

Meanwhile, the nearby cattle town of Caldwell, Kansas, had caught wind of the upcoming event at Dodge City. Not to be outdone, they planned their own bullfight.[10] The town went as far as building a stadium but, at the last minute, wiser heads prevailed and Caldwell's Independence Day festivities consisted of only rodeo events. Those who were expecting a bullfight had to go to Dodge City. Caldwell did later stage a bullfight in conjunction with their agricultural fair in October, but the event did not receive any publicity and no contemporary accounts of it have survived.

Bullfighting in the Old West was not over yet, though. In 1895, two Colorado men, promoter and ex–bunco artist Joe Wolfe and Arizona Charlie Meadows, decided that a bullfight would be a good business investment for the mining town of Cripple Creek. The town did not have a suitable arena, but the two found a racetrack four miles away in nearby Gillett. The two promoters rented the racetrack and announced that the Joe Wolfe Grand National Spanish Bullfight Company would present a real bullfight with imported fighting bulls and Spanish bullfighters.

The announcement was greeted by a storm of protest. The secretary of the local humane society wrote to the government in Washington and received an emphatic reply making it clear that no bullfight would take place. Wolfe, who had meanwhile adopted the character of "Spanish José" to promote the event, went ahead with his plans.[11] He modified the racetrack, adding an amphitheater that would seat 5,000 patrons. He put up posters all around the mining district, promoting the event and offering seats at two dollars, three dollars, and five dollars.

The tension grew among those who wanted the bullfight and those opposing it. The bullfighters, hired from Chihuahua, Mexico, arrived on August 23 and Wolfe staged a grand promotional parade through Cripple Creek to heighten interest in the coming event. Unfortunately for the promoters, the fighting bulls had been refused entry from Mexico, and Wolfe had to round up some second-rate local bulls to fill in.

Saturday, August 24 — the highly publicized day of the big event — crowds of people came from the local towns, along with a special train loaded with eager spectators from Colorado Springs and Denver. As the crowd waited for the main event, they could while away their time — and money — in the saloons and gambling halls that surrounded the amphitheater. In spite of the fact that many of the "gamblers" lost all their money and couldn't pay for admission to the bullfight, about 3,000 spectators crowded the benches.

The first bull was duly dispatched after a rather weak performance. Then, at the crucial moment, the local sheriff appeared and arrested Wolfe for cruelty to animals. After a meager fine, Wolfe was soon back in business.

The Sunday performance was a big bust. Less than 300 people showed up. Even so, two bulls were killed after a very lackluster performance. Wolfe canceled the third performance on the basis of lost revenue. But that was not the end of it. Wolfe, Arizona Charlie, and the bullfighters were all re-arrested and taken to jail. They straggled back out as they made bail or paid fines. As a result of the poor receipts for the fight, Wolfe went bankrupt and skipped out to Florida, one step ahead of the sheriff.[12]

And the Other Fighting Animals

Though bear fights and bullfights were the most notorious events, many other animals were pitted against one another in fights for the entertainment of spectators and betting men. Many of the bigger saloons in the larger towns offered cockfights and dog fights. These gruesome animal fights were very popular and attracted large crowds. In 1861, at Sportsman's Hall in Leavenworth, Kansas, the sporting element could enjoy rat killings, raccoon fights, and cock fights.

Cock fighting was an early sport imported from Mexico for the entertainment of bettors. The method of fighting was very simple. The referee announced the names of the two roosters who were to be pitted against each other in a fight, and described their previous wins so that the sporting men in the audience could wager on their favorite bird. Hundreds of dollars could change hands during a well-promoted match. After the betting was complete, the owner or manager of each rooster put his bird on the ground in front of the other one. The roosters jumped at each other and tried to slash their opponent with the razor-sharp spurs on their feet. One bird usually bled to death from these claw wounds and the other was declared to be the winner. If a bird refused to fight — which seldom happened — the other one was declared to be the winner.

Popular also were dog fights, badger fights, and dog versus badger. Badgers, being rather bad-tempered animals with very long claws, were quite capable of killing a dog. Because of this, badger fights were considered to be very entertaining. One observer had this to say about badgers: "When dug or dragged out of his hole he will put up a winning fight against 'most any kind of a dog, and will often hold a whole pack of dogs at bay for hours, so that a badger fight was classed among the best sports of the day."[13]

One animal fight, held in 1866, in Virginia City, Nevada, pitted a 75-pound cinnamon bear against three bulldogs.[14] The event attracted a hundred spectators. The bear won. In 1871, a big wild cat was matched with a bulldog. The dog won.

Denny O'Brien's saloon in San Francisco had a pit in the basement that was used for dog fights and to match terriers against a number of rats.[15] Local street urchins caught the rats underneath the wharves on the waterfront and sold them for anywhere from 10 cents to 25 cents, depending on their size and level of viciousness. The outcome of one match was that a particularly wily 22-pound dog killed 48 rats in under five minutes.

One record of animal fights that has survived listed a bull versus six dogs, a bear versus six bulldogs, a tiger versus a bear, and a bull versus 12 dogs. The admission charge to see all this was a dollar for adults and 50 cents for children. Animal cruelty to create spectacle at these events was the norm. The newspaper advertisement for this particular event stated that "if the latter [a bull] conquers all his enemies, several pieces of fireworks will be placed on his back, which will produce a very entertaining amusement."[16]

Fisticuffs

In the middle of the 19th century, at the same time as the discovery of gold in California, prize fighting became a popular sport and form of entertainment across the country. So, as well as stage entertainment and animal fights, variety theaters and saloons were quick to put on prize fights and wrestling matches.

Boxing matches were popular and prize fights frequently took place as exhibition matches on dance hall and variety theater stages. The sponsors of these matches were often saloon owners. Their primary business reason for putting on a boxing match was to pack spectators into the bar in order to sell more liquor at inflated prices. Though many of the matches were available for merely the price of a drink or two in a saloon, promoters of the best boxing matches might charge up to $25 for a seat. They also quickly realized that if they could start to promote discussions in their saloons among potential attendees ahead of the fight, they could, at the same time, sell many more drinks.

Matches might be staged between two local fighters, or a well-known boxer might come to town and challenge any comers. On rare occasions, two well-known boxers would square off in an exhibition match. The latter, of course, drew the most customers and made the most money for the promoters.

Prize fights were rarely based on boxing skill, but on the endurance of the individual fighters. In 1876, the railroad town of Cheyenne, Wyoming, hosted a prize fight between John Hardey and Enoch Winter. It was an unusually short fight for the time, lasting only 30 minutes. More typical was Hardey's fight against John Shannessy, which lasted for an hour and 43 minutes and went for 126 rounds. A round lasted until one or the other of the fighters was knocked down, after which they rested for 30 seconds. Each fighter was paid $500 for his efforts.

The number of rounds in a prize fight was not necessarily fixed, and boxing matches often continued until one contestant or the other was knocked out. Fights were often quite gruesome, sometimes used bare knuckles, and might include impromptu additions to conventional fighting style, such as chewing on the opponent's ear. In Dodge City, in 1877, two fighters named Nelson Whitman and Red Hanley engaged in a championship prize fight refereed by a Colonel Norton. The two went at it immediately. They fought so vigorously that, as one newspaper reporter commented: "During the forty-second round Red Hanley implored Norton to take Nelson off for a while till he could have time to put his right eye back where it belonged, set his jaw bone and have the ragged edge trimmed off his ears where they had been chewed the worst."[17] Norton refused and told him to fight on. The newspaper went on with great glee to say: "The only injuries sustained by the loser in this fight were two ears chewed off, one eye bursted and the other disabled, right cheek bone caved in, bridge of the nose broken, seven teeth knocked out, one jaw bone mashed, one side of the tongue chewed off, and several other unimportant fractures and bruises."

As a result of the poor combination of drinking and violent visual stimulation, boxing matches in saloons might turn into free-for-alls. After the main fight was finished, spectators worked up by the intensity of a good brawl might climb into the ring and challenge any and all comers to an impromptu match.

This belligerent characteristic among the audience could be put to good advantage. The Topic Theater in Cripple Creek, Colorado, staged a prize fight every Friday night, following the regular show. If no professional fighters were available, Otto Floto, a local promoter, would canvass the local saloons for drunks who were itching for a fight, and pair them off at the Topic. Floto also booked such contemporary boxing notables as Jack Dempsey, Mike Queenan, and Mike Mongone. In 1896, he booked Jim Corbett to fight Billy Woods.

One of the colorful examples of boxers in the Old West was John "Con" Orem, one of the most popular boxers in Virginia City, Nevada. He was also a local saloon-keeper who owned a variety theater called the Melodeon. Orem claimed to be the Middleweight Champion of the United States.[18] Whether he was or not is debatable, but he had indeed fought professionally and his boxing background helped him to keep any rowdy patrons of his saloon in line. Out of five professional fights, he had won two, drew one, and won the other two on technicalities. He fought in Montana professionally six times, winning three, losing two, and being awarded a draw once. Orem had previously fought Enoch Davies in Denver on August 27, 1861, in front of a crowd of 2,000 spectators. After 109 rounds, Davies conceded and Orem claimed the "Championship of Colorado."

On January 2, 1865, Orem fought in Virginia City against Hugh O'Neil, a solidly-built freighter who stood six feet tall and weighed 190 pounds. Conversely, Orem was five feet six-and-a-half inches tall and weighed 138 pounds. A special log building, 80 feet long by 28 feet wide, was erected for the occasion. The building later became Leviathan Hall.

Anticipation for the match mounted and seats sold at ten dollars for a reserved seat and five dollars for a general seat in the pit. To be sure that this event afforded a complete evening's entertainment, the building included a bar, and a band was hired to play music. A special seating section was reserved for any ladies who attended — though, as it turned out, only a few did.

To heighten the suspense in the days before the highly publicized event, a series of sparring matches was arranged by the promoter. This was so that, nominally at least, the potential audience could judge each fighter's style, but in reality, it was to boost interest and attendance at the match. The actual fight went for 185 rounds and lasted for three hours and ten minutes. Officially, each round of the fight lasted for one minute or until one boxer was knocked off his feet. During the course of the fight, Orem used this rule as an excuse 36 times, deliberately falling to one knee to end the round.

Not all of the fight was completely aboveboard. O'Neil kept falling on his opponent when Orem was down, and one time he hit Orem behind the ear after the round was over. A.J. Nelson, the referee as well as the owner of the building, finally stopped the fight and called it a draw. Both men had taken a terrible beating. Orem was carried away by friends. O'Neil went home in a wagon, his eyes so badly beaten that he couldn't see where he was going. For all this punishment, each man received the miserly sum of only $425 after expenses.[19] The next year, Orem participated in a re-match with O'Neil, which Orem won on a foul.

A memorable match in Dawson, in the Yukon Territory, occurred between Frank Slavin of Australia, the British Empire's heavyweight champion, and another Australian, this one named Perkins. Slavin was known as "The Sydney Cornstalk" because he was tall and had very long arms. The fight lasted for 14 rounds. Slavin gave Perkins a severe beating and the man died 18 months later, thought to be a delayed death resulting from internal injuries due to the fight.[20]

Known prizefighters were automatically considered to be tough characters, so boxers often attracted unwanted attention. One night Slavin was drinking in the Monte Carlo saloon in Dawson when a drunk named Biff Hoffman challenged him and knocked him to the floor. Always on the lookout for a good opportunity, a promoter named Wilson Mizner arranged for a match between the two to settle the grudge. The fight was profitable for the promoter, but was not exciting for the audience. Apparently not expecting much of a fight, Slavin entered the ring in a white sweater and trousers, instead of boxing trunks. Slavin's first punch knocked out Hoffman. For this minimal trouble, Slavin picked up a quick $1,000 of prize money from Mizner.

Drunks challenging boxers was not an unusual occurrence. Happy Jack Harrington drank too much one night in Denny O'Brien's saloon on the Barbary Coast of San Francisco and got into an argument with boxer Billy Dwyer. As Dwyer raised his arm to hit Jack, Harrington stabbed him in the stomach with a Bowie knife.[21] Dwyer died shortly afterwards, and Jack was convicted and sent to California's San Quentin prison.

The popularity of boxing matches extended beyond the fight itself. Before a match, speculation ran rife among drinkers in local saloons as to which one of the contestants would win the match and how he would win it. After the fight was over, a similar analysis was carried out in the same saloons in defense of both the winner and the loser. Items for rowdy discussion were usually the respective boxing styles of the two opponents, how the referee performed, if he was fair enough, and an analysis of the referee's decisions that had been made throughout the match. All these topics were the subject of lively alcoholic debates that often became quite heated. Feelings, in fact, ran so high at boxing matches that most promoters banned weapons anywhere in or around the fight locations to prevent the backers of one fighter or the other from starting any violence.

Prize-fighting was not always popular. In Montana Territory, for example, the first legislature banned boxing matches. To the delight of the residents, a later legislature reversed this decision and legalized boxing. But only if the contestants wore gloves. To meet the letter of the law, the participants wore thin leather gloves — not today's heavy padded boxing gloves — thus effectively returning to bare-knuckle boxing.

Boxing was also banned by law in Seattle. There were two ways around this restriction that that were commonly used by professionals who wanted to box. Members of private clubs could spar among themselves, so one way to be in a boxing match was to join a private club. The second loophole was that boxing could be part of the plot of a play. So boxing promoters could put on a play in which a famous boxer, such as John L. Sullivan, James J. "Jim" Corbett, or Bob Fitzsimmons, played the hero, and incorporated a crucial fight that involved a boxing match. The match might be a staged boxing match with gloves or could be part of the resolution of the plot where the boxer fought and vanquished the villain at the conclusion of the play. This met the letter of the law and still allowed a good fight.[22]

These boxers were not always very good actors, but were guaranteed to draw a crowd because of their reputation. Sullivan appeared in an *Uncle Tom's Cabin* touring company from 1896 to 1902.[23] Jim Corbett appeared in several melodramas and achieved modest financial success during the acting phase of his career.

In the course of touring the West, Sullivan and Corbett both appeared in Leadville at the Tabor Opera House. The ropes for the boxing ring they used are still stored in a box in the dressing room area under the stage. Circus and boxing blended when Sullivan did an exhibition tour with the Great Inter-Ocean Circus in 1888.

Wrestling was also pursued as a spectator sport in the West, but did not have as wide a following as boxing. Possibly the lack of attraction was because wrestling was a less aggressive and bloody sport than 19th-century bare-knuckle boxing. In 1884, for example, a wrestling match at the Bird Cage theater in Tombstone resulted in only one throw.

ELEVEN

The Wild West Shows

One of the entertainment influences that promoted the rough-and-tumble image of the Old West and thrilled Eastern audiences were the Wild West shows of the late 1800s. These spectacles included cowboys and cattle, riding stunts, trick shooting, and re-enactments of famous Indian fights.

The Wild West types of shows and spectacles had a long history in the Old West. These shows were promoted as being authentic re-creations of life in the Wild West, as performed by authentic cowboys. This advertising had to be balanced by the fact that these shows had to entertain their audiences in order to attract customers and remain financially solvent. Therefore, the events depicted had to have a certain dramatic quality or they could not hold the paying audience's attention.

P.T. Barnum created a form of staged Wild West show as early as 1843, when he presented a mock *Grand Buffalo Hunt* in Hoboken, New Jersey. The show was not a great success. The 15 buffalo calves used in the show broke through the barriers and escaped from the arena, causing panic among the crowd. The animals escaped into a nearby swamp and only a few were recaptured.[1]

One of the earliest of what could be called the Wild West shows was organized by Joseph McCoy, the founder of the town of Abilene, Kansas, in the late 1860s. In an effort to promote Abilene and its cattle trade, McCoy made a tour of Chicago and St. Louis with three buffalo, an elk, and three wild horses to attract and amuse potential cattle buyers. He also took along real cowboys. Several, in full costume, herded the animals around an enclosure and demonstrated techniques of riding, roping, and capturing the animals. McCoy's showmanship worked well, and, with this prompting, he was able to persuade cattle buyers to come to Abilene to inspect and buy the cows that were for sale.

In 1872, John B. "Texas Jack" Omohundro was hired by Sidney Barnett to stage a similar mock buffalo hunt at his museum. After logistical difficulties with the government and the Indians that Barnett hired, Texas Jack backed out and Wild Bill Hickok took over, staging a spectacle at Niagara Falls. The show featured Indians chasing the buffalo, shooting at them with blunt arrows and finally lassoing them. In spite of its popularity, the show was a financial disaster and soon closed.

An unlikely promoter of a Wild West show was the outlaw Cole Younger. Thomas Coleman Younger — usually called Cole — was one of the James-Younger gang that participated in the bank robbery fiasco in Northfield, Minnesota, resulting in the capture and imprisonment of the three Younger brothers — Jim, Bob, and Cole. Cole was pardoned in 1901 and went into business with Frank James, Jesse James's brother, to form the short-lived *James-Younger Wild West Show.* As part of the terms of Cole's parole, he was not allowed to exhibit himself in return for monetary payment. To get around this restriction, he sat in the stands and allowed the audience to stare at him.[2]

Buffalo Bill's Wild West

What made Wild West shows famous and enduring as an entertainment form was their promotion by Buffalo Bill Cody. During his long career, Buffalo Bill is estimated to have appeared before 50 million people. Over one five-month period in 1885 alone, he was seen by a million people and made a profit of $100,000.

William Frederick "Buffalo Bill" Cody was a genuine product of the Old West. He had been a Pony Express rider, a scout for the U.S. Army, an Indian fighter, and a buffalo hunter for the railroad.[3]

Cody was born in Scott County, Iowa, on February 26, 1846. His nickname of "Buffalo Bill" came from the time he spent as a buffalo hunter, supplying meat for the Kansas Pacific Railroad in late 1867 and early 1868.[4] He served as an army scout for much of the period 1868 through 1876. He distinguished himself when he participated in the Battle of Summit Springs in eastern Colorado on July 11, 1869, after the Indian Tall Bull and his Cheyenne Dog Soldiers captured two white women, Susanna Alderdice and Maria Weichell.[5] During the fight, Cody claimed that he killed Tall Bull, though during the confusion at the height of the battle this could not be confirmed with accuracy.

The other side of Buffalo Bill's fame was that he was portrayed as an exaggerated fictional character in the so-called "dime novels." The invention of the steam-powered rotary press had allowed mass production of printed books at very economical prices, which allowed these lurid fictional accounts of the mythic Wild West to be published and sold for a dime — or even a nickel. These books (called "pulp novels" because of the cheap paper on which they were printed) churned out sensationalized fictional exploits of real people. In one overblown lurid pulp-novel tale, mountain-man Kit Carson was credited with killing two Indians at the same time. The writer described a headlong charge during which Carson avoided the Indians' attempts to dispatch him as he conveniently killed one with a knife and the other with a tomahawk. Carson later said he couldn't recall such an incident.

Buffalo Bill was made famous in the pulp writings of Ned Buntline. Cody first met Ned Buntline on July 24, 1869, while Bill was a scout for the Fifth Cavalry, based out of Fort McPherson, Nebraska. Buntline, whose real name was Edward Carroll Zane Judson, was a dime novelist who wrote over 400 novels and stories, many of them under a pseudonym. Buntline's first Cody story was *Buffalo Bill, the King of Border Men*. He wrote about Cody in 14 lurid dime novels, with titles such as *Buffalo Bill's Best Shot; or, The Heart of Spotted Tail* and *Buffalo Bill's Last Victory; or, Dove Eye, The Lodge Queen*.

The Cody legend continued to be promoted by other pulp-novel writers. One of the most prolific was Colonel Prentiss Ingraham, who wrote over 120 stories about the plainsman and contributed the script of a stage play for Cody. In all, 550 pulp novels about Cody appeared in print.

Cody was nominated as a candidate for the Nebraska legislature in 1872, after which he referred to himself as "The Honorable William F. Cody."

Buffalo Bill as an Actor

In 1872, Buntline persuaded Buffalo Bill and John Burwell "Texas Jack" Omohundro, an Indian fighter as well as an old scouting companion and good friend of Buffalo Bill, to venture into show business with him. Buntline wrote a play based on his novel *Buffalo Bill's Last Victory*. He knocked out the script in four hours and called the result *The Scouts of the Prairie; or, Red Deviltry as It Is*. The play was more music-hall entertainment than legitimate theater. It featured Irish and German racial stereotypes, an Indian kidnapping of the virtuous heroine, and a grand finale in which the rugged plainsmen entered with guns blazing to rescue the heroine, just as she was about to be burned at the stake. In spite of wooden acting and an improbable plot, the drama was a rousing success and played to packed houses.

Part of the script consisted of Buntline talking with Cody and Jack about their exploits. The principals played themselves, supported by a group of "Indians" recruited from locals in Chicago. The show was somewhat loose and amateurish, because Cody and Texas Jack were not experienced actors — or even actors at all. The performance was also marred, in part, by cheap theatrics, such as the use of pieces of red flannel for scalps. When the play lagged, the principals threw in Indian attacks and concluded it with a mock battle with the redskins, complete with war whoops and gunshots. Audiences were more thrilled with the actors than the plot, because Cody was a real Indian fighter and scout, which added to the credibility of the play.

The play opened in Chicago on December 17, 1872, and then went on to St. Louis, Rochester, Buffalo, Boston, and the Midwest. The audiences loved it and Buffalo Bill cleared about $6,000 for the season. The show closed on June 16, 1873.

The play also featured Giuseppina Morlacchi, a ballet dancer and actress who had previously studied dance at La Scala in Italy and performed in Italy, London, and Spain. She played the part of Dove Eye. She was described in a tongue-in-cheek fashion by the Chicago *Tribune* as "a lovely Indian maiden with an Italian accent and a weakness for handsome scouts."[6]

Cody and his buckskin-clad fellow actors toured for the next ten years in various interchangeable shows based on Indian lore and rescuing settlers from Indian attacks. Examples were *The Knight of the Plains, or Buffalo Bill's Last Trail* and *Twenty Days, or Buffalo Bill's Last Stand.* In 1873, Cody formed a show named the *Buffalo Bill Combination*, a traveling theatrical troupe with Texas Jack, Morlacchi, and James Butler "Wild Bill" Hickok.[7] Sticking with a tried-and-true formula, they acted in a drama called *The Scouts of the Plains.* Buffalo Bill, Texas Jack, and Morlacchi all played roles similar to the earlier *The Scouts of the Prairie*, but nobody in the audience seemed to notice or mind. The theatrical Buffalo Bill was so popular that he was the subject of a burlesque named *Bill Buffalo, with his Great Buffalo Bull.*

Wild Bill Hickok joined Buffalo Bill in New York in 1873. Hickok traded yarns with Bill and gave an exhibition of trick-revolver shooting as part of the plot in the play. Hickok, however, was not comfortable on the stage and felt that they were all making fools of themselves. He left the show in 1874.

Texas Jack married Giuseppina Morlacchi on August 31, 1873. In 1876, the two left Buffalo Bill and started their own troupe. Jack appeared in *Texas Jack in the Black Hills.* In 1880 he appeared in *The Trapper's Daughter* in Denver. They went on to Leadville where Morlacci appeared in *The Black Crook* at the Tabor Opera House. Leadville was to be Jack's last stop as he died there suddenly on June 28, 1880, from pneumonia.[8] His funeral was held on the stage of the opera house. Buffalo Bill visited Leadville in 1908 and erected a monument over Jack's grave.

In the summers between acting seasons, Cody guided hunting parties in the West and scouted for the Army. On July 17, 1876, Cody was involved in an Indian confrontation at Hat Creek (also called War Bonnet Creek in army records), near Montrose, Nebraska. This was only a month after George Armstrong Custer was annihilated with his entire command at the Battle of the Little Bighorn during the Sioux Indian Wars. During the Hat Creek skirmish, Cody shot a minor Cheyenne chief named Yellow Hair. Cody scalped the Indian, proclaiming melodramatically that it was "the first scalp for Custer."[9] To capitalize on this event, later in 1876 Cody produced and starred in a dramatization of the Hat Creek Fight called the *The Red Right Hand; or, Buffalo Bill's First Scalp for Custer.* After the battle, the name of the dead Indian, Yellow Hair, was mistakenly translated by an army interpreter as "Yellow Hand," hence the subsequent confusion in names that followed the story, the play, and the recreated battle in later shows.

Cody displayed Yellow Hair's scalp, headdress, and knife in local store windows as part of the promotion for the show. When some complained that the display was too gruesome, Cody displayed them as advertising in theater lobbies and used the real scalp at the climax of the play.

Until 1877, Cody's "Indians" were played by white actors hired as extras, a job also known at the time as "supernumeraries" or "supers." In 1878, Cody hired real Indians from the Sioux reservation as actors in his stage melodramas.

The event that crystallized Cody's thinking about a Wild West show

This Colt .45-caliber, double-action revolver, produced in 1917, had a smooth bore and was used with shot shells for improved accuracy in breaking glass balls thrown in the air, and other trick shooting (author's collection).

occurred in 1882 when Cody organized the *Old Glory Blow Out* in his home town of North Platte, Nebraska, to celebrate Independence Day. He put together a program of riding, roping, bronco busting, and exhibition shooting, all of which turned out to be the forerunner of *Buffalo Bill's Wild West.*

The next year, 1883, Cody teamed up with dentist and exhibition marksman William F. "Doc" Carver to present a shooting show. The show, based on the North Platte celebration, was organized around roping, riding, trick shooting, and attacks by Indians. Doc Carver, a brilliant rifle shot, was nicknamed the "Evil Spirit of the Plains." Perhaps the name was appropriate. When he missed a shot one day, he went into a rage, shattered his rifle over his horse's head and punched his helper in the face. With understated pomp he also dubbed himself as "Wizard Rifleman of the West, Conqueror of All America and Europe, and CYNOSURE of people, Princes, Warriors and Kings."[10]

On May 19, 1883, Carver and Cody opened *Hon. W.F. Cody and Dr. W.F. Carver's Rocky Mountain and Prairie Exhibition* as a Wild West show. Supporting the two were Indians, cowboys, and a band to provide accompanying music. The program included wild animals, wild horses, and exhibitions of riding and shooting. One of the features was trick shooting by the two principals.

One of the popular exhibition tricks was shooting glass balls out of the air. The shooters used smoothbore revolvers and rifles with cartridges loaded with a half-charge of powder and light lead shot, instead of with solid lead bullets. The shot pattern at 20 yards, which was the typical distance for breaking balls, was about three inches across. The use of shot gave the shooter a better chance of hitting and breaking a greater number of balls than he or she would have with a single bullet, and, for the sake of safety, the shot carried over only a very short range. In 1878, Buffalo Bill had accidentally wounded a small boy with his Winchester rifle during a stage show in Baltimore. After this he used shot, because pellets fired from shot shells had a much lower velocity than did a solid lead bullet. The shells were specially loaded with a very light charge of powder, so that the shot would carry only over a short range.

In spite of the advantage of using shot shells, trick shooting was an exhibition of great skill and accuracy. After touring St. Louis and New York, Cody and Carver dissolved the show and parted company

The Wild West

In 1883, Cody organized *Buffalo Bill's Wild West,* which opened in May of 1884 in St. Louis. The playbill called the *Wild West* an "equestrian drama,"

A re-enactment of "Custer's Charge" from Buffalo Bill's *Wild West* during a performance at Ambrose Park in Brooklyn, New York, circa 1894. A painted backdrop in the
background served to set the scene (Denver Public Library, Western History Collection, Nate Salsbury collection, NS-270).

as Cody didn't like the name "show," and felt that the participants were not
"entertainers." For him the re-creation was authentic history and he looked
upon his presentation as a realistic portrayal of life on the Plains. Many of
the Indians in his spectacle had fought against the U.S. Cavalry in the Indian
Wars and the cowboys were authentic working cowboys from ranches in the
West. Most of the performers were men, as winning the West was looked
upon as a male accomplishment, in an age where women were mostly relegated
to the home or menial factory jobs.

In spite of Cody's perception, the *Wild West* was planned as entertainment
and presented only a narrow view of life in the West. The Indians were portrayed as hostile red savages to be fought and vanquished, and did not reflect
any of the more subtle issues of the white man displacing their entire culture
and way of life in the West. As historian Paul Reddin stated: "The Wild West
show reduced the western saga to a morality play in which Cody, along with
scouts and cowboys, represented the forces of good and civilization and Indians
and a few errant white road agents symbolized evil and barbarism."[11]

Interest in the show was fueled by advance agents who posted handbills and posters all over the towns where the *Wild West* was scheduled to appear. The posters contained melodramatic images that served to reinforce the public's misconceptions of the West. Sensationalistic newspaper stories and advertising created more of the same fevered level of interest in the coming show.

In 1884, Cody teamed with experienced actor and showman Nate Salsbury, who acted as the show's business manager. Part of Salsbury's experience came from when he had organized Salsbury's Troubadours in 1875. Both men later claimed to the originators of the idea for a Wild West show.

A typical *Wild West* performance started with the national anthem and a grand procession of all the cowboys and Indians, led by Buffalo Bill. After Cody's introduction, he introduced the first equestrian portion of the program, which consisted of horse races and an exhibition of Pony Express riding, showing how rapidly the riders changed mounts. This was followed by a re-enactment of Cody's duel with Yellow Hand and the famous scalping. Various shooting performances by Johnny Baker (also billed as the "Cow-boy Kid"), Annie Oakley, and Buffalo Bill were next, followed by an attack by Indians on the Deadwood stage which was suitably repulsed by Buffalo Bill and the cowboys.[12] This part of the performance involved an exciting thrill for several volunteers from the audience — often local dignitaries — who were invited to ride in the stagecoach as it careened around the stadium. Then Indians performed horse races, war dances, and riding exhibitions. The program concluded with an attack by Indians on an isolated settler's cabin and a grand spectacle of a battle to defeat the "red savages," in which the entire entourage participated. The scenes were something right out of a dime novel.

Musical accompaniment for the show was provided by a 12-piece Cowboy Band under the direction of William Sweeney. The band dressed in Western style, with chaps, neckerchiefs, big hats, and holstered Colt revolvers. The entire extravaganza was immensely popular and toured America, playing in local baseball stadiums and fairgrounds.

The show was fast paced. The riders and horses always galloped and battles between the cowboys and Indians took place at a fast tempo. Part of the thrill of the outdoor spectacle involved the smells and sounds that accompanied it: the smell of sweating horses, horse manure, and smoke from gunpowder accompanied blood-curdling yells from the Indians, gunshots, and the whoops of the cowboys. This created a mixed background of sensory stimuli that accentuated the sight of the extravaganza.

Exhibitions of shooting skills played a major part in the show. Guns and bullets were featured prominently as the tools that won the West. This was partly because, in the 1880s and 1890s, skill at marksmanship was an extremely popular sport and was considered to be a mark of manliness and respectability.

As a result, the cowboys in the show were all heavily armed and shooting, either as skills of marksmanship or as part of the re-enactments, such as the attack on the Deadwood Stage or the Indian attack on the settler's cabin, forming a noisy backdrop to many of the acts. Cody himself was an excellent shot with revolvers, rifles, and shotguns, and was a featured performer.

Sitting Bull, one of the chiefs of the Sioux Indians, traveled on tour with the *Wild West* for one season, at $50 a week, for four months. The memory of Custer's defeat at the Battle of the Little Bighorn only nine years previously was so recent that his presence wasn't always well accepted by the audience. He was greeted with boos and catcalls at some of the performances. At one performance in Pittsburgh, he was even attacked by the brother of a soldier who was killed in the Bighorn battle.[13] Defending himself, Sitting Bull hit the man with a hammer, averting the attack, but knocking out several of the man's teeth at the same time.

A series of stars toured and performed with the show. Arguably the most famous, besides Buffalo Bill, was Annie Oakley. Oakley was born on August 13, 1860, in Woodland, Ohio, as Phoebe Ann Moses.[14] She started her famous shooting career at the age of 12, when she supported her family by supplying small game — grouse, quail, and rabbits — to a wholesale food supplier for hotels and restaurants in Dayton and Cincinnati. Her big break came in 1875 when she shot in a competition against traveling exhibition sharpshooter Frank Butler. She won by one shot. The two were married a year later, on June 20, 1876, and he became her manager and press agent as well as her husband.

In 1885, the couple joined *Buffalo Bill's Wild West*. Sitting Bull dubbed Annie "Little Sure Shot" as a sign of his respect for her ability. She became a consummate show woman, with a personality and performing style that captivated audiences during her ten-minute trick-shooting act. Her repertoire was amazing. She performed trick shooting from horseback and while riding a bicycle, shot at targets while aiming over her shoulder in a mirror, shot out the flame of a candle, shot a dime out of a man's hand at thirty paces without hitting his fingers, and broke moving targets of glass balls. She was one of the real stars of the show, receiving a salary that was reported to be $1,000 a week. Cody could afford it, though, at a time when the show was netting $1 million a year.

Two other show business characteristics endeared Oakley to her audiences. One was that she wore her hair down at a time when respectable women were not seen in public with their hair long and full. The other was that she wore fancy Western costumes with boots and knee-length skirts when women's legs were traditionally hidden under floor-length dresses.

Annie was in a train wreck in North Carolina in October 1901, and this is generally credited as the reason for her retirement from the *Wild West*. She actually left the show later in 1901, after she suffered severe burns in a treatment bath at a hot springs resort in Arkansas.[15]

Not as well known as Annie Oakley was Lillian Frances Smith, who headlined as a sharpshooter during the 1886 to 1888 seasons and was nicknamed "The Champion Girl Shot." The competition between the two women was intense and Smith left after the 1888 season to pursue her career as an exhibition shooter elsewhere, possibly as the result of a personality clash with Oakley. Other female performers were Della Ferrell and Georgia Duffy, both of whom were trick riders.

Another lesser-known cast member, who was nonetheless a featured performer in the show for ten years and who also appeared as the hero of dime novels, was Buck Taylor, dubbed "King of the Cowboys" long before movie star Roy Rogers was given the title by Republic Studios in the 1940s. Buck Taylor was an authentic Westerner, born in Texas and raised on a ranch where he learned to lasso steers and ride wild horses. Taylor was a trick rider of exceptional skill who could perform stunts such as picking up a coin from the ground while riding at a full gallop. In 1887, author Prentiss Ingraham introduced Taylor to readers of pulp-fiction literature with *Buck Taylor, King of the Cowboys*. Though Taylor appeared in only a few novels, his fictional exploits added to the romance of the cowboy and provided additional publicity for Cody and his show. After Taylor left Cody, he started his own Wild West show, but, by then, interest in such shows was waning and the show closed after a brief run.

In *Buffalo Bill's Wild West*, Cody ritualized the American myth of the Wild West through dramatized and heroic one-sided re-enactments of historic events. He wanted to portray the American frontier history as he saw it, complete with Indian villages, buffalo hunts, Indian attacks and daring rescues, and the recently resolved Sioux Indian war in the Black Hills of South Dakota. The result was elements of rodeo, buffalo stampedes, and trick riding. By 1883 he was already viewing the Old West with nostalgia.

In 1886 and 1887, the show was presented outdoors in summer in an arena on Staten Island, and in the winter in Madison Square Garden. The winter show was revamped into *The Drama of Civilization*, which contained a series of scenes that told the story of the civilization of America from the colonial period to the mining era. Even with the limitations of an indoor setting, the staging of the show included a cyclone destroying a camp on the Plains and a prairie fire. In one sequence Cody wore a yellow wig and played the part of Custer.

The show went to England in April of 1887 and was performed twice for Queen Victoria — the second time it had been presented before members of the royal families of Europe. The *Wild West* was immensely popular, with

From left to right, three of the leading Wild West showmen of the time: Buffalo Bill Cody, Pawnee Bill (Gordon Lillie), and Buffalo Jones (Charles J. Jones) (Denver Public Library, Western History Collection, Nate Salsbury collection, NS-32).

between 20,000 and 40,000 spectators attending each performance. One of the trick-horse riders who performed was Emma Lake, the daughter of Agnes Lake, the woman who was briefly the wife of Wild Bill Hickok. The show returned to tour Europe in 1889–1891. The *Wild West* troupe was in Europe for an extended tour between 1902 and 1906, visiting England, France, Italy, Germany, Austria, and Hungary, among other countries.

During 1893, Cody added Cossacks from Russia (actually trick riders from Russian Georgia, who were billed as "Cossacks"), gauchos from Argentina, vaqueros from Mexico, and Arabian riders. The title of the extravaganza was increased to the impressive-sounding *Buffalo Bill's Wild West and Congress of Rough Riders of the World.*[16] The Cowboy Band was expanded to 37 members.

To give the audience of the era a more thrilling spectacle, a dramatization of Teddy Roosevelt's charge up San Juan Hill was later added. This display had the magnificent title of *Resplendent Realism of Glorious War.* The recreated battle used 600 performers, who fired an estimated 10,000 shots and used 500 pounds of gunpowder.[17]

In 1893, the *Wild West* performed on 15 acres of leased land next to the World's Columbian Exposition in Chicago, attracting as many as 18,000 spectators to each show. Buffalo Bill had hoped to be on the main grounds, but was turned down by the fair committee as being inconsistent with the Exposition. Of the almost 28 million visitors who attended the Fair, an estimated six million saw the *Wild West.*

In 1894, James Bailey (of Barnum and Bailey fame) took over the logistics of management and transportation for the show, and arranged for winter quarters for the performers, in return for a half interest in the show. The *Wild West* had to transport more than 500 people, hundreds of animals, and stage props such as the Indian village, the Deadwood stage, and scenery backdrops that were 200 feet long and 30 feet high. This task required the use of 82 railroad cars.

Bailey introduced techniques of circus management so that the show could do one-night stands. Part of the success of Bailey's methods was due to improvements in transportation that had taken place since the show started and would not have been possible without the expanded railroad system of the 1880s. Likewise, Buffalo Bill's international tours and their success would not have been possible without ocean liners.

Bailey was an important addition. A veteran of circus logistics, he was quite familiar with the problems of moving a large troupe of performers and animals around the country by the easiest and cheapest method. In 1895 the show spent 190 days on the road making 131 one-day stands, and traveling 9,000 miles. In 1896, they performed in 132 locations for 332 performances, and 104 cities in 1897. By 1898, the operation required eight sleeping coaches

Buffalo Bill's coffin was encased in a steel vault under two tons of cement on top of Lookout Mountain, west of Golden, Colorado, so that he could not be relocated to Wyoming, Nebraska, or one of the other states who wanted the honor of having him buried in their communities (author's collection).

for 700 employees, 151 cars for 18 buffalo and 500 horses, 16 flatcars for equipment, and 35 for general baggage. In spite of the success of the *Wild West* and continued good attendance at the shows, Cody ran heavily into debt (with traveling expenses and poor investments) in the early 1900s.

Cody merged his show with *Pawnee Bill's Historic Far West and Great Far East* in 1908. Gordon W. Lillie, who styled himself as "Pawnee Bill," had a Wild West show that contained motley elements from the Far East, including elephants, camels, Japanese acrobats, boomerang throwers from Australia, Bedouin Arabs, and dancers from Ceylon. Buffalo Bill and Pawnee Bill presented their new show under the lengthy title: *Buffalo Bill's Wild West Combined with Pawnee Bill's Great Far East*. It was more popularly known as the "Two Bills Show."

As a result of further financial problems, for the 1914 and 1915 seasons Buffalo Bill and the *Wild West* came under the control of the Sells-Floto Circus, which was owned by Denver newspapermen Harry H. Tammen and Frederick G. Bonfils.

Wild West shows, including Buffalo Bill's, struggled on for the next few years, but by the late 1910s the public had mostly lost their interest in live cowboy performances. The Old West, it seemed, was better depicted in the motion pictures. Elements of the Wild West show combined with the circus and continued on in lesser form, in spite of declining audience interest. Other elements of the Wild West shows, such as steer riding, cattle roping, bucking broncos, and feats of horsemanship, became the staples of rodeo entertainment and and still flourish today.

Cody died in Denver on January 10, 1917, but wasn't buried until June, five months later, on top of Lookout Mountain, west of Denver, at a site that couldn't be reached until the spring thaw allowed the burial site to be properly prepared.

The Other "Shows"

Cody was undoubtedly the king of the Wild West spectaculars, though several other smaller shows with western themes tried to copy his popularity. One later rival to *Buffalo Bill's Wild West* was the *Miller Bros. 101 Ranch Wild West* show. The show was formed by brothers Joe, Zack, and George Miller, the sons of George W. Miller, the founder of the Miller ranch, and Edward Arlington, a circus man. The Millers built a 110,000-acre farming and ranching empire in Oklahoma. Like Buffalo Bill Cody, the brothers wanted to keep alive their nostalgic view of the West, so they conceived a show that featured their view of ranch life. Their approach was different than Cody's and featured mostly riding acts and horsemanship, without Buffalo Bill's emphasis on Indian and frontier elements. After experimenting with several different formats, they opened in Norfolk, Virginia, on May 20, 1907. Over the next few years the Miller Brothers added cowboy stars of the silent screen, such as Tom Mix and Buck Jones.

Tom Mix was an authentic cowboy who had worked at the 101 Ranch and taught himself the skills of riding, roping, and shooting which allowed him to go into the movies and become a cowboy star at Fox Studios. In 1934, Mix went out on his own with a show called the *Tom Mix Circus and Wild West*. The timing was not good. The stock market crash created personal financial difficulties for Mix. In addition, public tastes changed towards the singing cowboy stars and Mix was not able to generate interest in either his show or a re-entry into movies. A lack of cash for entertainment expenditures among the general public during the depression, combined with the advancing age of the star, finished off his career. Mix died in a car accident in Arizona on October 12, 1940.

Bull-roping competitions by Mexican *vaqueros* in early California were the forerunners of today's rodeo events, such as Brahma-bull riding (photograph by Tyler Dingee, author's collection).

A variety of Wild West shows continued through the first few decades of the 20th century, including *Tiger Bill's Wild West, Thompkins Real Wild West and Frontier Exhibition, Buffalo Ranch Real Wild West,* and *Colonel Tim McCoy's Real Wild West.* Actor Tim McCoy later performed a Wild West routine as part of Ringling Bros. and Barnum & Bailey's Circus in 1938; however, it was not successful and closed within a few weeks.

Rodeo

Rodeo derived much of its roots from the Wild West shows. Buffalo Bill Cody's *Old Glory Blowout,* for instance, contained many of the traditional rodeo events, such as bronc-riding and steer-roping. But rodeo as a form of entertainment really began much earlier than this — from the great cattle drives.

The name rodeo comes from a Spanish word meaning "roundup," and that was where most of the skills for this type of entertainment arose. Starting in the 1860s and lasting until about 1881, cowboys drove large herds of cattle from Texas to the railheads in Kansas, notable Abilene, Dodge City, Wichita, and Newton. While on the trail, cowboys had to be able to lasso calves and steers, and break and ride horses. At the rodeo, men pitted their skill in these tasks against others to make this competitive entertainment.

The first official rodeo was probably the one held at Deer Trail, Colorado, on July 4, 1869. A group of working ranch hands gathered from several outfits, including the Hash Knife, the Camp Stool, and the Mill Iron, to show off their skills and compete in a series of events that highlighted what they did every day working with cattle.

Modern bareback riding and saddle-bronc riding events came directly from bronc-busting and the need for cowboys to tame wild or unruly horses so that they could be ridden safely during the cattle drive. Each cowboy needed several horses during the drive, so a suitable string of horses had to be ready for use at all times. In the modern competitive rodeo events, the cowboy has to ride the horse for only eight seconds — though this seems like an eternity for the rider. Breaking a horse on the trail during a cattle drive consisted of riding the horse until either the rider gave out or the horse was tamed enough for a saddle. Similarly, calf-roping (now called tie-down roping) and steer-roping came from the necessity for catching calves and cattle for branding during the round-up.

Modern steer wrestling consists of a cowboy jumping onto a steer from a running horse and wrestling it to the ground. The competitive part is that the contestant with the fastest time wins. Again, this event came from the necessity of capturing cattle. The man who has been credited with introducing bull-dogging into the sport of rodeo was Bill Pickett, one of the performers from the *101 Ranch Wild West* show. Pickett was an authentic cowboy who had worked firsthand with cattle. His technique consisted of jumping onto the back of a running bull from a horse chasing alongside and grabbing the animal's lips or nostrils with his teeth until it submitted to capture.

AFTERWORD

The Stage Lights Dim

The period from 1850 to about 1910 formed the high point of historical American theater in the Old West. It coincided with the stage entertainment that accompanied the flood of pioneers who settled the West during this period and entertained them through their early years. The golden age of theater in the Old West started to draw to a close in the early 1900s as motion pictures started to rise in popularity as a form of entertainment. Stage entertainers were thrust into the background as fickle audiences rushed to see the new flickering images on the silver screen.

Stirrings of the new cinematic industry occurred as early as 1895, when Max Skladanowsky in Berlin and the Lumière Brothers in Paris presented public showings of movies of short subjects.[1] Following their success in Europe, the Lumière Brothers presented a public exhibition of some of their films in the United States at the Eden Musée on 23rd Street in New York. The first films of the Thomas Edison studio were screened on April 23, 1896, at Koster and Bial's Music Hall in New York.

These early films were short subjects, lasting only a minute or two, and depicted common events, such as the arrival of a train in a station, a horse race, a gondola ride in Venice, or a baby eating breakfast. Some were simply visual recordings of static scenes, somewhat like the earlier *tableaux vivant*. An example of this was the Edison Company's one-minute film, *Cripple Creek Barroom*, directed by W.K.L. Dickson. The scene shows six stereotypical Western stock characters, including a gambler, a drunk, and a cowboy, all lounging around a bar presided over by a bartender who looks suspiciously masculine.[2]

These first films were viewed as novelties that were not considered to be a threat to the theater but rather an entertaining addition to variety programs in vaudeville houses. Special visual effects were used to startle and amaze viewers. George Méliès, a French magician and theater owner, developed

One of the first Western movies was a minute-long production titled *Cripple Creek Bar-room*, made in 1898 by the Edison Company. This still photograph shows several different stereotyped Western characters, such as a gambler and a cowboy, lounging around a bar that is presided over by a rather homely female (a role often played by a man in early film productions) (Glenn Kinnaman Colorado and Western History Collection).

many of the techniques of filming that were later adopted by others. His camera tricks, such as double exposure, animation, and altering film speed for slow and fast motion, fascinated his audiences.

Eventually theaters were built specifically for showing motion pictures. These were simple rooms equipped with seats, a screen, and a movie projector. By 1908, there were an estimated 5,000 to 8,000 (and perhaps as many as 10,000) of these nickelodeons, so-named because the cost was a nickel to view the program. "Odeion" derives from the Greek, meaning roofed-over theatre.

As in stage theater, it was not long before cries for censorship arose among moralistic Victorian audiences. One silent film that shocked viewers was *The Kiss*. This short film by the Edison Company featured a 47-second on-screen close-up of a kiss between middle-aged actors May Irwin and John C. Rice, excerpted from a popular play called *The Widow Jones*.

Early motion pictures were filmed from a single point of view, with the camera held stationary. As the popularity of movies increased and filming techniques matured, directors increasingly turned towards telling stories in their films. Though not the first fictional story, one of the more sophisticated films to tell a coherent story by changing the camera position and using editing to narrate and carry the story forward was *The Great Train Robbery*, a western filmed in 1903 in the "wilds" of New Jersey by director Edwin S. Porter for the Edison Company. The movie sparked great interest in movie westerns and the West. In particular, the evolving techniques of movie-making used in this one-reeler showed audiences scenes that would not be effective on the stage, such as the arresting close-up in which an actor pointed a revolver straight into the camera lens and fired several times. The use of a camera close-up gave this particular image a great shock value for the viewers.

One of the players in *The Great Train Robbery* was an actor named Gilbert M. Anderson, who played four separate roles. After the success of the movie, Anderson and George K. Spoor formed a partnership in Essanay Film Manufacturing Company ("S" for Spoor and "A" for Anderson). Anderson couldn't find the type of actor he was hoping for, so he cast himself as the star. To everyone's surprise — including Anderson's — he grew to become immensely popular as an actor and became the first western film star as "Bronco Billy" Anderson.

In the early 1910s New York theater owners saw the need for bigger and better movies to keep their rapidly growing audiences happy. The length of motion pictures grew from one reel to several. Shrewd businessmen, such as Adolph Zukor, Marcus Loew, and William Fox, who came originally from other businesses, saw the vast profit potential for this new medium and became early exhibitors of films in nickelodeons.

By 1912 Mack Sennett was cranking out one-reel slapstick comedies at Keystone Studios, later famous for the Keystone Cops. As the demand for this type of entertainment grew, the makers of movies demanded more money. So, a few enterprising exhibitors decided to also become their own suppliers and organized their own movie production companies. In 1912, Zukor formed the Famous Players company, which later became Paramount Studios. Loew built an empire that he eventually consolidated as Metro-Goldwyn-Mayer, better known as MGM. Fox's efforts grew into the giant 20th Century–Fox studios.

Another who saw the writing on the wall was Benjamin Franklin Keith, one of the creators and driving forces of the vaudeville business. In March 1893 he had opened two B.F. Keith's Theaters in New York and Boston to present variety acts aimed towards family entertainment. The music and acts at his theater were about the same as other theaters of the type, though Keith had insisted that his acts were to be clean and that the women entertainers were modestly dressed. Under this premise, Keith opened a string of theaters that did well. His theater in Boston hosted 25,000 people a week. Through a series of stock manipulations, the Radio Corporation of America (better known by their initials RCA) gained control of the theater chain and formed a film production company under the name of Radio-Keith-Orpheum, which became better known as RKO Pictures.

By the late 1910s, motion pictures had become a respectable form of entertainment. Actors such as Douglas Fairbanks, Mary Pickford, Tom Mix, William S. Hart, Lon Chaney, and Buster Keaton were using sophisticated plots, and eager audiences were demanding more of these feature-length films. In response to this demand, the number of movie theaters in the United States grew to 20,000. Many were extravagant edifices with lavishly appointed interiors that reflected the owners' desire and efforts to draw in the public.

By 1915, directors such as Cecil B. De Mille and D. W. Griffith were filming lavish feature-length spectacles. Mack Sennett's comedy films were spiced by the Sennett Bathing Beauties, and included pioneering stories such as the 1914 feature-length film *Tillie's Punctured Romance*, which set the stage — so to speak — for later popular comedies. Movies became longer and more sophisticated and, by 1920, had essentially taken over from the variety theater as a primary form of mass entertainment.

By the 1930s burlesque and vaudeville still stumbled on in a few remaining variety theaters, but Hollywood films had replaced theater-going as the national entertainment.

Magnificent Opulence

Even after theatrical entertainment started to decline after the beginning of the 20th century, and motion pictures were on the rise as the primary form of mass entertainment, magnificent stage theaters continued to be built. But an eventual transition from stage entertainment to movie theater was inevitable.

The Burns Theater, built in Colorado Springs, Colorado, is a good example of the changeover and the typical progression from legitimate stage shows to vaudeville and then to showing movies. James Ferguson Burns, a successful mine owner who made his fortune from gold mining in nearby Cripple Creek, spent $300,000 to build the Theatre Beautiful, more popularly known as the Burns Opera House or the Burns Theater. The ground-breaking for the building took place in October of 1910, but the theater wasn't completed and ready for a grand opening until May 8, 1912. For audiences, the wait was worth it. The main entrance, lobbies, and foyers were furnished in white Italian marble. The vast stage was 96 feet wide and 69 feet deep, and the seating capacity was 1,400.[3] The theater was opened by the 60-piece Russian Symphony

The exterior of the Burns Theater was faced with Italian marble (Glenn Kinnaman Colorado and Western History Collection).

Orchestra, accompanying a quartet of classical singers. After this grand opening, the theater presented legitimate drama, opera, and concerts.

In the 1920s, the theater offered shows from the Pantages vaudeville circuit on Mondays and Tuesdays, a movie or a traveling show on Wednesdays and Thursdays, and vaudeville shows on Fridays and Saturdays. The theater was closed on Sundays, as theater-going was still not considered proper on the Sabbath.

Like many other theaters, the Burns Theater ended its days as a legitimate theater when it was converted into a movie theater, called the Paramount, in February of 1928. Part of the contract stated that it could not be used at the same time for legitimate stage drama presentations. In 1933, the building became the Chief Theater. The theater was demolished in March 1973.

Chapter Notes

PREFACE

1. John M. Burke, publicist for Buffalo Bill's *Wild West*, in 1895, quoted in Reddin, *The Wild West Shows*, xiii.

CHAPTER ONE

1. *Sacramento Daily Union*, December 8, 1856.
2. Noel, *The City and the Saloon*, 18.
3. Jan MacKell, *Brothels, Bordellos, and Bad Girls: Prostitution in Colorado, 1860–1930* (Albuquerque: University of New Mexico Press, 2004), 109.
4. Program for the Elks Opera House, Leadville, Colorado, November 12, 1903.
5. S.D. Trav, *No Applause — Just Throw Money* (New York: Faber and Faber, 2005), 100–101.
6. Because this group of miners came west in the California gold rush of 1849, they were given the generic name of "Forty-Niners."
7. Manifest Destiny was a 19th-century doctrine that it was the God-given duty of Americans to spread westward and colonize the entire continent from coast to coast.
8. Barsness, *Gold Camp*, 223. The use of topical references in local towns is still included in some road shows. This was done, for example, by a touring company of the musical comedy *A Funny Thing Happened on the Way to the Forum*. The basic plot revolves around a bordello that moves in next door to the residence of a respectable couple in ancient Rome. When the play came to Colorado Springs, Colorado, in the early 2000s, the script incorporated references to South Tejon Street, which, at that time, was a cruising ground for local ladies of the evening.
9. John Hanners, *It Was Play or Starve* (Bowling Green, OH: Bowling Green State University Popular Press, 1993), 12.
10. Joan S. Reiter, *The Women* (Alexandria, VA: Time-Life Books, 1978), 137.
11. Jeremy Agnew, *Brides of the Multitude: Prostitution in the Old West* (Lake City, CO: Western Reflections, 2008), 128.
12. Amelia Jenks Bloomer was an advocate of women's dress reform. Citing the need for bodily freedom during exercise and similar activities, she developed her namesake "bloomers," which were a type of baggy trousers, gathered at the ankle and worn under a short belted tunic. The garment was moderately popular for riding a bicycle, an activity that became a craze in the 1890s. Mrs. Bloomer's bloomers did not achieve the same popularity, however.
13. The term "slapstick" derives from the prop that stage comedians used to hit one another, and was made from two pieces of wood. Slapsticks made a sharp, slapping noise that sounded much more severe than it actually was.
14. Robert L. Brown, *Saloons of the American West* (Silverton, CO: Sundance Books, 1978), 37.

15. *Montana Post*, March 10, 1866.

16. Tucson *Star*, October 19, 1882. The "bald-headed age (next to stage)" was a whimsical, generic term commonly used to refer to the baldheaded dirty-old-men who were reputed to frequent the front rows of theaters, just below the stage, often armed with opera glasses in order to better view the showgirls in the chorus.

17. Allan G. Bird, *Bordellos of Blair Street* (Pierson: Advertising, Publications & Consultants, 1993), 118.

18. Marvin Gregory and P. David Smith, *Mountain Mysteries: The Ouray Odyssey* (Ouray, CO: Wayfinder Press, 1984), 40.

19. Joann Levy, *They Saw the Elephant: Women in the California Gold Rush* (Hamden, CT: Archon Books, 1990), 138.

20. Susan L. Johnson, *Roaring Camp: The Social World of the California Gold Rush* (New York: W.W. Norton, 2000), 139.

21. Brown, *Saloons of the American West*, 115.

22. Larry Barsness, *Gold Camp: Alder Gulch and Virginia City, Montana* (New York: Hastings House, 1962), 75. Alum is a white crystalline substance that occurs naturally as the mineral Kaolinite. It is used as an astringent in the leather and textile industry, and also in medicine.

23. The carbon arc spotlight emitted a continuous electric spark, or arc, between two carbon electrodes that were slightly separated (in a manner somewhat like the spark of an arc welder) and thus gave off an intense white light. The carbon electrodes, which were about the diameter of a pencil, continually burned away during use, so a small electric motor was used to advance the electrodes slowly towards each other, in order to keep the light constant. The initial arc was created by momentarily touching the carbon electrodes together then separating them, hence the term "striking an arc."

24. Keith Wheeler, *The Townsmen* (Alexandria, VA: Time-Life Books, 1975), 183.

25. Robert G. Athearn, *The Coloradans* (Albuquerque: University of New Mexico Press, 1976), photo group 3, #11.

26. Blair, *Leadville*, 65.

CHAPTER TWO

1. "Mlle." is the abbreviation for Mademoiselle, the French term of address for unmarried women and equivalent to the English Miss. "Mme." is short for Madame and is applied to married women as the English equivalent to Mrs.

2. The name "fandango" was used in Nevada at the time to describe any large meeting.

3. Lawrence W. Levine, *Highbrow/Lowbrow: The Emergence of Cultural Hierarchy in America* (Cambridge, MA: Harvard University Press), 18.

4. Robert C. Toll, *On with the Show: The First Century of Show Business in America* (New York: Oxford University Press, 1976), 154.

5. Odie B. Faulk, *Tombstone: Myth and Reality* (New York: Oxford University Press, 1972), 117.

6. Brown, *Saloons of the American West*, 40.

7. The blackface minstrel show style of entertainment continued sporadically into the 1970s, sometimes seen at charitable benefit shows by service clubs.

8. The author remembers as a small boy being part of the chorus in a minstrel show performed at a school concert. Another recollection from the event was how difficult it was to wash burned cork from his face.

9. This name was the origin of the term "Jim Crow laws" to describe segregation or discrimination against Negroes.

10. This peculiar musical device was first used because something was needed to form the rhythm accompaniment, and the drum was not considered at the time to be a suitable instrument for stage entertainment.

11. This type of rapid-fire verbal humor was carried over into vaudeville and radio by the likes of the Marx Brothers and Abbott and Costello.

12. This female costuming of males was referred to as being in "drag." One explanation for

the name was because the long train of a fancy gown was "dragged" across the stage by the actor. Another explanation was that the weight of the train of the dress was similar to the drag, or brake, on a stagecoach.

13. Not all cross-dressing male performers were so demure. In 1881, at the Bird Cage Theatre in Tombstone, three men dressed in women's underwear with tights underneath pranced around the stage, each trying to outdo the others in obscene actions. This type of act was not unusual for the vulgar, low-class variety theaters.

14. Toll, *On with the Show*, 258–259.

15. Ibid., 97.

16. Bars and saloons have often been associated musically with the honky-tonk piano. This sound was originally not desirable. It occurred when a piano aged and the wooden hammers hardened, thus creating a distinctive, tinny sound when they hit the strings. When this sound became artistically desirable, it was sometimes created deliberately by forcing carpet tacks or thumbtacks into the ends of the piano hammers to make a hard surface and create the honky-tonk sound.

17. Brown, *Saloons of the American West*, 117.

18. Barsness, *Gold Camp*, page 215.

19. Frank Rahill, *The World of Melodrama* (University Park: The Pennsylvania State University Press, 1967), 244.

20. Toll, *On with the Show*, 151.

21. A. H. Saxon, *P.T. Barnum: The Legend and the Man* (New York: Columbia University Press, 1989), 62.

22. Asbury, *Carry Nation* (New York: Alfred A. Knopf, 1929), xv.

23. Ibid., 240.

CHAPTER THREE

1. Don Russell, *The Lives and Legends of Buffalo Bill* (Norman: University of Oklahoma Press, 1960), 258.

2. Queen Victoria's reign was from 1837 to 1901.

3. Hanners, *It Was Play or Starve*, 3.

4. John S. Haller, Jr., and Robin M. Haller, *The Physician and Sexuality in Victorian America* (Urbana: University of Illinois Press, 1974), 51.

5. Charles Darwin, *The Descent of Man, and Selection in Relation to Sex*, Vol. II (London: J. Murray, 1871), 327.

6. Frank Ryan, *Darwin's Blind Spot: Evolution Beyond Natural Selection* (Boston: Houghton Mifflin, 2002), 38–39.

7. Agnew, *Brides of the Multitude*, 36.

8. Don B. Wilmeth and Tice L. Miller, *The Cambridge History of American Theatre*, Vol. II (Cambridge, MA: Cambridge University Press, 1993), 447.

9. Robert C. Allen, *Horrible Prettiness: Burlesque and American Culture* (Chapel Hill: University of North Carolina Press), 74.

10. Penelope Byrde, *Nineteenth Century Fashion* (London: B.T. Batsford, 1992), 66. The Grecian Bend style became such a fashion craze that it was the subject of several popular songs, such as "The Grecian Bend Song," "The Grecian Bend Mazurka," and "The Grecian Bend" (humorously subtitled "She Stoops to Conquer"), the latter being a schottische in the form of a song with chorus.

11. Agnew, *Brides of the Multitude*, 52.

12. Much hysteria surrounded White Slavery, the term given to the crime of innocent white women being kidnapped and forced into prostitution. As part of the folklore, procurers were supposedly scouring the countryside offering gullible young girls jobs as actresses. Lurid rumors spread about how these women were drugged, beaten, and abused, only to awaken as prisoners in brothels. Self-proclaimed authorities bandied about figures of up to 80,000 women being forced into white slavery each year, without any basis for their statistics.

13. Ernest A. Bell, *Fighting the Traffic in Young Girls* (Chicago: G.S. Ball, 1910), 230.

14. George J. Kneeland, *Commercialized Prostitution in New York City* (New York: The Cen-

tury Company, 1913). According to the author, of 1,106 prostitutes in New York and Philadelphia, 88 of the women claimed to be in "theatrical work."

15. Pierre Berton, *The Klondike Fever: The Life and Death of the Last Great Gold Rush* (New York: Alfred A. Knopf, 1958), 384.

CHAPTER FOUR

1. Allen, *Horrible Prettiness*, 51.

2. Neil Harris, *Humbug: The Art of P.T. Barnum* (Boston: Little, Brown, 1973), 33.

3. The name "freaks" was not used at the time as a derogatory term for people with biological deficiencies, but was used to distinguish those who chose to exhibit themselves for money in museums like Barnum's. Barnum called them "living curiosities."

4. Jeremy Agnew, *Medicine in the Old West: A History 1850–1900* (Jefferson, NC: McFarland, 2010), 139–140.

5. Harris, *Humbug*, 168.

6. Tom Thumb's real name was Charles Sherwood Stratton. He was a genuine midget (a normally formed, but small, human being, as opposed to a dwarf, who had a normal upper torso, but a deformed lower one), who was only 25 inches in height, at the age of five. Barnum added six years to his supposed age, gave him a new name after a midget from the King Arthur legend, dubbed him "General," and toured him around the country. He was one of Barnum's most popular attractions.

7. Kenneth Jessen, *Eccentric Colorado: A Legacy of the Bizarre and Unusual* (Boulder, CO: Pruett, 1985), 124.

8. An exhibition of living pictures was presented as far back as the late 1700s, at the Palace Theater in London. The concept was apparently considered too much ahead of its time for staid London audiences and was rapidly closed by the authorities.

9. Hanners, *It Was Play or Starve*, 14.

10. This technique, now called "freeze-frame," is still used in motion pictures and television.

11. Some things never change. In 1997, the author observed an act put on for a convention meeting at one of the major hotels in Las Vegas, Nevada. It consisted of several women behind a backlit translucent screen apparently performing a striptease, followed by exotic dancing. Due to clever stage lighting, the illusion of the silhouettes was that they looked like they were dancing naked.

12. These body stockings were also known as "fleshings," "fleshing tights," or "flesh elastic," and sometime nicknamed "symmetricals"—because they were. Incidentally, the leotard, as these figure-hugging garments were also known, was developed by Jules Léotard, a French circus performer and trapeze artist, who wanted to show off his manly assets for the females in his audience.

13. Arthur H. Saxon, *Enter Horse and Foot: A History of the Hippodrama in England and France* (New Haven, CT: Yale University Press, 1968), 173.

14. Allen, *Horrible Prettiness*, 113–114.

15. Gender role-reversal has continued in the traditional British Christmas children's pantomimes, such as *Cinderella*, *Mother Goose*, and *Puss-in-Boots*. The heroine is played in conventional manner by a female in a dress. The leading male role — or "principal boy" — is played by another, taller female (with shorter hair) in tights, an abbreviated tunic, and high-heeled boots or shoes. The part of the female comedy lead — a motherly type, traditionally called The Dame — is played by a man in a wig, heavy make-up, and outlandish dresses.

16. The Blondes were described by some sources at the time as "whores." (See Chapter 3 for a discussion of this terminology.)

17. The cancan has become identified today with a specific piece of music: "The Infernal Galop" from Jacques Offenbach's *Orpheus in the Underworld*.

18. Even more scandalous, when the cancan originated in the variety halls of Paris around 1830, was that often the dancers didn't wear underwear, which was not unusual for women until the 1850s and the introduction of crinoline skirts. Price (1998, page 97) has asserted that women in the Wild West who performed the cancan were generally prostitutes and often danced without

underwear. This is almost certainly an overgeneralization; but, if this took place, it would have made the performance quite crude.

19. The Barbary Coast in San Francisco was named for the area in Northern Africa that stretched from Tripoli to Morocco, and was notorious for pirates and thieves. In San Francisco, the namesake Barbary Coast was located just north of Portsmouth Square and centered between Stockton and Montgomery Streets. It was lined with saloons, gambling dens, low-class variety theaters, and houses of prostitution. The main area extended for three blocks or so along Pacific Street, known locally as "Terrific Street."

20. Herbert Asbury, *The Barbary Coast* (New York: Pocket Books, 1947), 101.

21. Faulk, *Tombstone*, page 127.

22. Agnew, *Brides of the Multitude*, page 129.

23. Toll, *On with the Show*, 222.

24. Around the same time, the role of women was also changing. They were entering the workplace, they were demanding the vote, and they were taking their place as equals to men in society.

25. Wilmeth, *The Cambridge History of American Theatre*: Vol. II, 36.

26. Ibid., 61.

27. Larson, Erik. *The Devil in the White City* (New York: Crown, 2003), 248.

28. Berton, *The Klondike Fever: The Life and Death of the Last Great Gold Rush* (New York: Alfred A. Knopf, 1958), 321.

29. Allen, *Horrible Prettiness*, 265.

30. Graeme Cruickshank, "The Life and Loves of Letty Lind," *Gaiety*, Issue 22, 2007, 4.

CHAPTER FIVE

1. As one of the prominent mining boomtowns in the Sierra Nevada Mountains of California in the 1850s, Placerville was no stranger to excitement. Originally named Old Dry Diggings, the town was renamed Hangtown to commemorate various hangings that took place there. To change the town's image, the residents rechristened the town with the more genteel name of Placerville, in 1854.

2. Josiah Gregg, *Commerce of the Prairies*, Vol. I (New York: Henry G. Langley, 1844), 242.

3. James O. Pattie, *The Personal Narrative of James O. Pattie* (Philadelphia: J.B. Lippincott, 1862), 110.

4. Robinson had the title of "Doctor" because he had previously been associated with a drugstore.

5. Levy, *They Saw the Elephant*, 130.

6. Asbury, *The Barbary Coast*, 22.

7. The price of gold at that time was fixed by the government at $16 per ounce. This lady was making a good income, as the wages paid to a miner were $3 a day. The prices of everything in gold-rush San Francisco were high. Eggs were $4 a dozen, flour was $2 a pound, and potatoes were $30 a bushel.

8. Levy, *They Saw the Elephant*, 129.

9. Wilmeth, *The Cambridge History of American Theatre*, Vol. I, 410.

10. Asbury, *The Barbary Coast*, 14.

11. Works Project Administration, *San Francisco*, 136.

12. Asbury, *The Barbary Coast*, 14.

13. Asbury, *The Barbary Coast*, 117.

14. Toll, *On with the Show*, 183.

15. Asbury, *The Barbary Coast*, 109–110.

16. Wilmeth, *The Cambridge History of American Theatre*, Vol. I, 411.

17. Though a popular and prolific novelist and playwright of his time, Edward George Bulwer-Lytton's florid turn of phrase eventually fell out of style. He is mostly remembered for the opening line of his 1830 novel *Paul Clifford*, which began, "It was a dark and stormy night." Unfortunately for the novelist, this distinctive style of writing has been memorialized in the annual Bulwer-Lytton Fiction Contest, which is sponsored by the English Department of San Jose State University in California. Entrants are charged with composing the worst opening sentence of an imaginary novel.

18. "Washoe" was a generic nickname used to describe the mining district surrounding Virginia City, Nevada.
19. Murray Morgan, *Skid Road* (Seattle: University of Washington Press, 1982), 119.
20. Ibid., 120.
21. Berton, *The Klondike Fever*, 130.
22. Ellis Lucia, *Klondike Kate: 1873–1957* (New York: Ballantine Books, 1962), 50.
23. Berton, *The Klondike Fever*, 377.
24. Ibid., 377–378.
25. Ibid., 379.
26. Lucia, *Klondike Kate*, 76.
27. Morgan, *Good Time Girls*, page 146, gives Pantages's first name as Percales. Given Pantages' illiteracy and the hazy nature of his early life — he was not even certain of his own birth date — either name could have been a written representation of what he called himself.
28. Lucia, *Klondike Kate*, 78–79.
29. Berton, *The Klondike Fever*, 375–376.

CHAPTER SIX

1. Mark Twain, *Roughing It* (New York: Harper & Brothers, 1899), 147.
2. Estelline Bennett, *Old Deadwood Days* (New York: J.H. Sears, 1928), 105.
3. Bennett, *Old Deadwood Days*, 111–112.
4. Agnew, *Smoking Gun*, 180.
5. Richard Erdoes, *Saloons of the Old West* (New York, Alfred A. Knopf, 1979), 175.
6. In placer mining, pans or simple sluice boxes are used to wash gold flakes out of the sand and gravel of creeks and dry streambeds. Hard-rock mining, by contrast, involves blasting deep shafts and tunnels in solid rock to dig out the gold-bearing ore.
7. Blair, *Leadville*, 70.
8. Ibid.
9. Erdoes, *Saloons of the Old West*, 148.
10. Blair, *Leadville*, 71.
11. The collapse of silver mining in the West had several causes. Basically, silver mining in the 1880s became so prevalent that the value of the precious metal dropped. As an attempt by mine owners to shore up the price, the Sherman Silver Purchase Act of 1890 specified that the government would continue to buy a fixed amount of silver at a fixed price each year. As silver mining expanded, even more silver flooded the market. The price was inflated by guaranteed government purchases, while the real value of the metal dropped. To try to correct this and other financial problems in the nation, President Grover Cleveland asked Congress to repeal the Sherman Act, which it did in 1893. This kicked the artificial prop out from under the silver mining industry and the price of silver immediately dropped to less than half of its inflated price. Mines couldn't produce at these lowered prices so most of them closed, throwing thousands of miners out of work and creating a depression in silver mining camps.
12. Robert G. Althearn, *The Coloradans* (Albuquerque: University of New Mexico Press, 1976), 41.
13. Forbes Parkhill, *The Wildest of the West* (New York: Henry Holt, 1951), 65.
14. Palace Theater playbill, August 2, 1880.
15. Parkhill, *The Wildest of the West*, 67.
16. Clark Secrest, *Hell's Belles: Denver's Brides of the Multitudes* (Aurora, CO: Hindsight Historical, 1996), 137.
17. Saxon, *P.T. Barnum*, 228.
18. Jan MacKell, *Red Light Women of the Rocky Mountains* (Albuquerque: University of New Mexico Press, 2009), 70–71.
19. Adobe was a popular building material in the Southwest because it was readily available — and cheap. Adobe bricks, also called "dobie," "adobys," or "Spanish brick," were unfired bricks made of local mud (with straw as a binder) that was dried in the sun. Adobe bricks were typically about a foot long, ten inches wide, and four inches thick.
20. John M. Myers, *The Last Chance: Tombstone's Early Years* (New York: E.P. Dutton, 1950), 54.

21. Roger A. Bruns, *Desert Honkytonk* (Golden, CO: Fulcrum, 2000), 72.

22. Ibid., 3.

23. Ibid., 70.

24. Faulk, *Tombstone*, 117.

25. One early short cheesecake movie that was made by the Edison Company started with a woman fully dressed in a skirt, blouse, and hat swinging on a trapeze on a stage in front of two male viewers. As she swung, the woman adroitly removed articles of clothing, until she finished the act in circus tights. Given the woman's smooth performance, this was obviously a well-practiced act.

26. Faulk, *Tombstone*, page 109.

27. Toll, *On with the Show*, 68–69.

28. Ibid., 69.

29. Leland Feitz, *Myers Avenue* (Colorado Springs, CO: Little London Press, 1967), 14.

CHAPTER SEVEN

1. James, *The Roar and the Silence*, 208.

2. Works Project Administration, *San Francisco*, 135.

3. Archer B. Hulbert, *Forty-Niners: The Chronicle of the California Trail* (Boston: Little, Brown, 1931), 189.

4. Berton, *The Klondike Fever*, 378.

5. Levy, *They Saw the Elephant*, 129.

6. Lyman, *The Saga of the Comstock Lode*, 209–211.

7. Asbury, *The Barbary Coast*, 103.

8. Cy Martin, *Whiskey and Wild Women* (New York: Hart, 1974), 82.

9. Drago, *Notorious Ladies of the Frontier*, 45.

10. Ibid., 47.

11. Martin, *Whiskey and Wild Women*, 85.

12. Lola Montez's house in Grass Valley still stands today, at 248 Mill Street. The building houses the Grass Valley Chamber of Commerce and a small museum with Lola Montez-related artifacts. Lotta Crabtree lived nearby, at 238 Mill Street, which is now an apartment building.

13. Harris, *Humbug*, 132.

14. Toll, *On with the Show*, 42.

15. Lyman, *The Saga of the Comstock Lode*, 285.

16. Toll, *On with the Show*, 211.

17. Lyman, *The Saga of the Comstock Lode*, 289–290.

18. Asbury, *The Barbary Coast*, 127.

19. George D. Lyman, *The Saga of the Comstock Lode* (New York: Scribner's, 1934), 296.

20. Toll, *On with the Show*, 211.

21. Drago, *Notorious Ladies of the Frontier*, 123.

22. The public loved clothing that was endorsed by theater stars. Sarah Bernhardt was involved in the promotion of several models of corset, one of which was named after her. The designs of her shoes were also very popular.

23. Flowers were used as tokens of Victorian ideals, in a symbology sometimes called "floriography." Daisies, for example, represented purity and innocence; red roses symbolized love and passion; sunflowers symbolized pure and lofty thoughts.

24. Keith Wheeler, *The Townsmen* (Alexandria, VA: Time-Life Books, 1975), 183.

25. Parkhill, *The Wildest of the West*, 38–39.

26. Toll, *On with the Show*, 301.

27. Lucia, *Klondike Kate*, 70.

28. Ibid., 71.

CHAPTER EIGHT

1. *Wood River Times*, January 11, 1882.

2. J. Lee Humfreyville, *Twenty Years Among Our Hostile Indians* (New York: Hunter, 1903), 465.

3. Hiram N. Chittenden, *The Yellowstone National Park* (Cincinnati, OH: The Robert Clarke Co., 1905).

4. Delmont R. Oswald (ed.) *The Life and Adventures of James P. Beckwourth as Told to Thomas D. Bonner* (Lincoln: University of Nebraska Press, 1972), 107.

5. John K. Townsend, *Narrative of a Journey Across the Rocky Mountains* (Philadelphia: Henry Perkins, 1839), 75.

6. Maguire, *A Rendezvous Reader*, 166.

7. Ethyl alcohol, or ethanol, was — and is — the basis for alcoholic beverages. The "raw" alcohol used by the trappers was 100 percent ethanol. Most hard liquors today, such as whiskey, gin, or vodka, contain about 40 percent alcohol (80 proof).

8. Agnew, *Brides of the Multitude*, 115.

9. Rufus Sage, *Wild Scenes in Kansas and Nebraska, and the Rocky Mountains, Oregon, California, New Mexico, Texas, and the Grand Prairies; or, Notes by the Way* (Philadelphia: G. D. Miller, 1855), 132.

10. James H. Maguire, Peter Wilde, and Donald A. Barclay (eds.), *A Rendezvous Reader: Tall, Tangled, and True Tales of the Mountain Men, 1805–1850*), 174.

11. Francis F. Victor, *The River of the West* (Hartford, CT: Columbian, 1870), 110.

12. Maguire, *A Rendezvous Reader*, 43.

13. Lavine, *The Games Indians Played*, 10.

14. Guy Logsdon, *The Cowboy's Bawdy Music*; in Harris and Rainey, *The Cowboy: Six-shooters, Songs, and Sex* (Norman: University of Oklahoma Press, 1976), 132.

15. Barsness, *Gold Camp*, page 93.

16. Edward M. McFarland, *The Midland Route: A Colorado Midland Guide and Data Book* (Boulder, CO: Pruett, 1980), 84.

17. James, *The Roar and the Silence*, page 211.

18. Baseball was reportedly the invention of Abner Doubleday, in 1839, but it is more likely that it evolved from the English game of cricket.

19. http://en.wikipedia.org/wiki/garryowen.

CHAPTER NINE

1. Armstrong, *The Great American Medicine Show*, 176.

2. All quotes are from advertising handbills for Warner's Safe Yeast.

3. Armstrong, *The Great American Medicine Show*, 178.

4. Ibid.

5. Calhoun, *Medicine Show*, 33.

6. Ibid., 82.

7. Anderson, *Snake Oil, Hustlers and Hambones*, 112.

8. From an advertising poster for Hamlin's Wizard Oil.

9. Anderson, *Snake Oil, Hustlers and Hambones*, 112–113.

10. Ibid., 114.

11. The alcohol used to preserve these specimens was typically grain alcohol, which is one name for ethyl alcohol, the alcohol in whiskey and other alcoholic beverages, so Hammer could ingest it with relative safety. Methyl alcohol, used in automobile antifreeze, is poisonous. So is propyl alcohol, which is used in rubbing alcohol.

12. Anderson, *Snake Oil, Hustlers and Hambones*, 136.

13. Armstrong, *The Great American Medicine Show*, 181.

14. Ibid., 175.

CHAPTER TEN

1. Lewis, *From Traveling Show to Vaudeville*, 109.

2. Faulk, *Tombstone*, 126.

3. "Hippo" was commonly combined with and added to circus names, in the sense of "horse," to emphasize the equestrian acts. In this definition it is not a shortened form of hippopotamus. Small circuses presented in theaters or opera houses were sometimes called "horse operas."

4. Toll, *On with the Show*, 65.
5. Ibid., 62.
6. Johnson, *Roaring Camp*, 181.
7. Ibid.
8. Barsness, *Gold Camp*, 213.
9. Vestal, *Queen of the Cowtowns*, 238–240.
10. Dykstra, *The Cattle Towns*, 176.
11. Sprague, *Money Mountain*, 180.
12. Ibid., 185–187.
13. Will E. Stokes, *Episodes of Early Days* (Great Bend, KS: self-published, 1926), 116.
14. James, *The Roar and the Silence*, 209.
15. Asbury, *The Barbary Coast*, 111.
16. Albert A. Fossier, *New Orleans, the Glamour Period, 1800–1840* (New Orleans: American Printing Co., 1957), 464.
17. Dodge City *Times*, June 16, 1877.
18. Barsness, *Gold Camp*, 217.
19. Ibid., 221.
20. Berton, *The Klondike Fever*, 379–380.
21. Asbury, *The Barbary Coast*, 111.
22. Morgan, *Skid Road*, 121.
23. Rahill, *The World of Melodrama*, 252.

CHAPTER ELEVEN

1. Rosa, *They Called Him Wild Bill*, 162.
2. Wayne M. Sarf, *God Bless You Buffalo Bill* (East Brunswick, NJ: Associated University Presses and Cornwall Books, 1983), 109.
3. The accepted account of Buffalo Bill's service with the Pony Express comes from his autobiography, published in 1879. In 2005, historian Louis Warren questioned the reports that Cody actually rode for the Pony Express and concluded that this story was apocryphal.
4. At that time the Kansas Pacific Railroad was named the Union Pacific, Eastern Division. The railroad had no corporate connection to the Union Pacific, but was later absorbed by it.
5. There were several militant groups within the tribal structure of the Northern Cheyenne, who lived along the North Platte River in Nebraska and the Yellowstone River country of Montana, of which the Cheyenne Dog Soldiers were the most aggressive. Their attitude was that it was better to die young fighting in battle than to grow old and die a natural death.
6. Enss, *Buffalo Gals*, 9.
7. A "combination" was a traveling show troupe put together to present one play. A stock company, by contrast, had a rotating inventory of plays that they presented, and thus often stayed at one theater for an extended time.
8. Pneumonia was a common disease in high-altitude mining towns, such as Leadville, Colorado, at 10,200 feet. In the time before modern antibiotics, there was often no recovery from the disease.
9. Russell, *The Lives and Legends of Buffalo Bill*, 231.
10. Reddin, *The Wild West Shows*, 59.
11. Ibid., 76.
12. Though claimed by show publicists to be the actual stagecoach that ran from Deadwood to Cheyenne, and recovered after it was left rotting on the prairie following an Indian attack, the vehicle was actually ordered from the Black Hills and Cheyenne Stage Line specifically for the show.
13. Sitting Bull was not a direct participant in the Battle of the Little Bighorn. He stayed behind at the Indian village to help protect the women and children. He was killed in a fight when Indian police came to arrest him on the Sioux reservation on December 16, 1890.
14. For reasons that were never made completely clear, Annie changed the family name to Mozee and her own surname to Oakley.
15. Wilson, *Buffalo Bill's Wild West*, 142.

16. The name "rough rider" was a generic old-time cowboy term that was applied at the time to any genuine expert horsemen.

17. Reddin, *The Wild West Shows*, 125.

AFTERWORD

1. Peter Cowie, *Seventy Years of Cinema* (New York: A.S. Barnes, 1969), 16.

2. In the first motion pictures, as in earlier burlesque acts, men often dressed as women to play female roles.

3. Boyer, *The Burns Theatre*, 2.

Bibliography

Agnew, Jeremy. *Brides of the Multitude: Prostitution in the Old West.* Lake City, CO: Western Reflections, 2008.

_____. *Life of a Soldier on the Western Frontier.* Missoula, MT: Mountain Press, 2008.

_____. *Medicine in the Old West: A History 1850–1900.* Jefferson, NC: McFarland, 2010.

_____. *Smoking Gun: The True Story About Gunfighting in the Old West.* Lake City, CO: Western Reflections, 2010.

Allen, Robert C. *Horrible Prettiness: Burlesque and American Culture.* Chapel Hill, NC: The University of North Carolina Press, 1991.

Anderson, Ann. *Snake Oil, Hustlers and Hambones: The American Medicine Show.* Jefferson, NC: McFarland, 2000.

Anderson, Patricia. *When Passion Reigned: Sex and the Victorians.* New York: Basic Books, 1995.

Armstrong, David, and Elizabeth M. Armstrong. *The Great American Medicine Show.* New York: Prentice-Hall, 1991.

Asbury, Herbert. *The Barbary Coast.* New York: Pocket Books, 1947.

_____. *Carry Nation.* New York: Alfred A. Knopf, 1929.

Athearn, Robert G. *The Coloradans.* Albuquerque, NM: University of New Mexico Press, 1976.

Barsness, Larry. *Gold Camp: Alder Gulch and Virginia City, Montana.* New York: Hastings House, 1962.

Bell, Ernest A. *Fighting the Traffic in Young Girls.* Chicago: G.S. Ball, 1910.

Bennett, Estelline. *Old Deadwood Days.* New York: J.H. Sears, 1928.

Bernstein, Joel H. *Wild Ride: The History and Lore of Rodeo.* Layton, UT: Gibbs Smith, 2007.

Berton, Pierre. *The Klondike Fever: The Life and Death of the Last Great Gold Rush.* New York: Alfred A. Knopf, 1958.

Berton, Mme. Pierre. *The Real Sarah Bernhardt, Whom Her Audiences Never Knew.* New York: Boni and Liveright, 1924.

Bird, Allan G. *Bordellos of Blair Street.* Pierson, MI: Advertising, Publications & Consultants, 1993.

Blair, Edward. *Leadville: Colorado's Magic City.* Boulder, CO: Pruett, 1980.

Boyer, Robert V. *The Burns Theatre: From Beginning to End.* Colorado Springs, CO: Pikes Peak Area Theatre Organ Society, undated.

Brown, Dee. *The Gentle Tamers: Women of the Old Wild West.* Lincoln: The University of Nebraska Press, 1968.

Brown, Robert L. *Saloons of the American West*. Silverton, CO: Sundance Books, 1978.

Bruns, Roger A. *Desert Honkytonk*. Golden, CO: Fulcrum, 2000.

Byrde, Penelope. *Nineteenth Century Fashion*. London: B.T. Batsford, 1992.

Calhoun, Mary H. *Medicine Show: Conning People and Making Them Like It*. New York: Harper & Row, 1976.

Carlyon, David. *Dan Rice: The Most Famous Man You've Never Heard Of*. New York: PublicAffairs, 2001.

Chartier, JoAnn, and Chris Enss. *Gilded Girls: Women Entertainers in the Old West*. Guilford, NE: TwoDot, 2003.

Chittenden, Hiram N. *The Yellowstone National Park*. Cincinnati, OH: The Robert Clarke Co., 1905.

Clokey, Richard M. *William H. Ashley: Enterprise and Politics in the Trans-Mississippi West*. Norman: University of Oklahoma Press, 1980.

Cowie, Peter. *Seventy Years of Cinema*. Cranbury: A.S. Barnes, 1969.

Culhane, John. *The American Circus: An Illustrated History*. New York: Henry Holt, 1990.

Darwin, Charles. *The Descent of Man, and Selection in Relation to Sex*, Vol. II. London: J. Murray, 1871.

Dary, David. *Cowboy Culture: A Saga of Five Centuries*. New York: Alfred A. Knopf, 1981.

_____. *Seeking Pleasure in the Old West*. Lawrence: University Press of Kansas, 1995.

Drago, Harry S. *Notorious Ladies of the Frontier*. New York: Dodd, Mead, 1969.

Dykstra, Robert R. *The Cattle Towns*. New York: Alfred A. Knopf, 1968.

Eales, Anne B. *Army Wives on the American Frontier*. Boulder, CO: Johnson Books, 1996.

Ellis, Amanda M. *The Strange, Uncertain Years*. Hamden, CT: Shoestring Press, 1959.

Enss, Chris. *Buffalo Gals: Women of Buffalo Bill's Wild West Show*. Guilford, CT: Two Dot/Globe Pequot, 2006.

Eppinga, Jane. *Tombstone*. Charleston, SC: Arcadia, 2003.

Erdoes, Richard. *Saloons of the Old West*. New York: Alfred Knopf, 1979.

Faulk, Odie B. *Dodge City: The Most Western Town of All*. New York: Oxford University Press, 1977.

_____. *Tombstone: Myth and Reality*. New York: Oxford University Press, 1972.

Feitz, Leland. *Myers Avenue*. Colorado Springs, CO: Little London Press, 1967.

Fowler, Gene (ed.) *Mystic Healers and Medicine Shows*. Santa Fe: Ancient City Press, 1997.

Furman, Evelyn E. *The Tabor Opera House: A Captivating History*. Aurora, CO: The National Writers Press, 1984.

Gabor, Mark *The Pin-up: A Modest History*. Köln: Benedikt Taschen Verlag GmbH, 1996.

Glenn, Susan A. *Female Spectacle: The Theatrical Roots of Modern Feminism*. Cambridge, MA: Harvard University Press, 2000.

Gowans, Fred R. *Rocky Mountain Rendezvous: A History of the Fur Trade Rendezvous*. Provo, UT: Brigham Young University, 1976.

Gregory, Marvin, and P. David Smith. *Mountain Mysteries: The Ouray Odyssey*. Ouray, CO: Wayfinder Press, 1984.

Haller, John S., Jr., and Robin M. Haller. *The Physician and Sexuality in Victorian America*. Urbana: University of Illinois Press, 1974.

Hanners, John. *It Was Play or Starve: Acting in the Nineteenth Century American Popular Theatre*. Bowling Green, OH: Bowling Green State University Press, 1993.

Harris, Charles W., and Buck Rainey (eds.) *The Cowboy: Six-shooters, Songs, and Sex*. Norman: University of Oklahoma Press, 1976.

Harris, Neil. *Humbug: The Art of P.T. Barnum*. Boston: Little, Brown, 1973.

Havighurst, Walter. *Annie Oakley of the Wild West*. Lincoln: University of Nebraska Press, 1992.

Holbrook, Stewart H. *The Golden Age of Quackery*. New York: Macmillan, 1959.

Humfreyville, J. Lee. *Twenty Years Among Our Hostile Indians*. New York: Hunter, 1903.

James, Ronald M. *The Roar and the Silence: A History of Virginia City and the Comstock Lode*. Reno: University of Nevada Press, 1998.

Jessen, Kenneth. *Eccentric Colorado: A Legacy of the Bizarre and Unusual*. Boulder, CO: Pruett, 1985.

Johnson, Susan L. *Roaring Camp: The Social World of the California Gold Rush*. New York: W.W. Norton, 2000.

Kasper, Shirl. *Annie Oakley*. Norman: University of Oklahoma Press, 1992.

Larsh, Ed B., and Robert Nichols. *Leadville: U.S.A.* Boulder, CO: Johnson Printing, 1993.

Lavine, Sigmund A. *The Games Indians Played*. New York: Dodd, Mead, 1974.

Levine, Lawrence W. *Highbrow/Lowbrow: The Emergence of Cultural Hierarchy in America*. Cambridge, MA: Harvard University Press, 1988.

Levy, Joann. *They Saw the Elephant: Women in the California Gold Rush*. Hamden, CT: Archon Books, 1990.

Lewis, Robert M. (ed.) *From Traveling Show to Vaudeville: Theatrical Spectacle in America, 1830–1910*. Baltimore: Johns Hopkins University Press, 2003.

Lucia, Ellis. *Klondike Kate: 1873–1957*. New York: Ballantine Books, 1962.

Lyman, George D. *The Saga of the Comstock Lode*. New York: Scribner's, 1934.

MacKell, Jan. *Brothels, Bordellos, and Bad Girls: Prostitution in Colorado, 1860–1930*. Albuquerque: University of New Mexico Press, 2004.

_____. *Red Light Women of the Rocky Mountains*. Albuquerque: University of New Mexico Press, 2009.

Maguire, James H., Peter Wild, and Donald A. Barclay (eds.) *A Rendezvous Reader: Tall, Tangled, and True Tales of the Mountain Men, 1805–1850*. Salt Lake City: University of Utah Press, 1997.

Martin, Cy. *Whiskey and Wild Women*. New York: Hart, 1974.

McFarland, Edward M. *The Midland Route: A Colorado Midland Guide and Data Book*. Boulder, CO: Pruett, 1980.

McMurtry, Larry. *The Colonel and Little Missie*. New York: Simon & Schuster, 2005.

McNeal, Violet. *Four White Horses and a Brass Band*. Garden City, NY: Doubleday, 1947.

Miller, Ronald D. *Shady Ladies of the West*. Los Angeles: Westernlore Press, 1964.

Miller, Nyle H., and Joseph W. Snell. *Great Gunfighters of the Kansas Cowtowns, 1867–1886*. Lincoln: University of Nebraska Press, 1963.

Morgad, Dale L. *Jedediah Smith and the Opening of the West*. Lincoln: University of Nebraska Press, 1953.

Morgan, Lael. *Good Time Girls*. Kenmore, WA: Epicenter Press, 1998.

Morgan, Murray. *Skid Road*. Seattle: University of Washington Press, 1982.

Myers, John M. *The Last Chance: Tombstone's Early Years*. New York: Dutton, 1950.

Noel, Thomas J. *The City and the Saloon: Denver, 1858–1916*. Lincoln: University of Nebraska Press, 1982.

Parkhill, Forbes. *The Wildest of the West*. New York: Henry Holt, 1951.

Powell, Kerry (ed.) *The Cambridge Companion to Victorian and Edwardian Theatre*. Cambridge, MA: Cambridge University Press, 2004.

Price, David. *Cancan!* London: Cygnus Arts, 1998.

Pullen, Kirsten. *Actresses and Whores: On Stage and in Society*. Cambridge, MA: Cambridge University Press, 2005.

Rahill, Frank. *The World of Melodrama*. University Park: Pennsylvania State University Press, 1967.

Reddin, Paul. *The Wild West Shows*. Urbana: University of Illinois Press, 1999.

Reiter, Joan S. *The Women*. Alexandria, VA: Time-Life Books, 1978.

Rosa, Joseph G. *They Called Him Wild Bill: The Life and Adventures of James Butler Hickok.* Norman: University of Oklahoma Press, 1974.

Russell, Don. *The Lives and Legends of Buffalo Bill.* Norman: University of Oklahoma Press, 1960.

Ryan, Frank. *Darwin's Blind Spot: Evolution Beyond Natural Selection.* Boston: Houghton Mifflin, 2002.

Sage, Rufus. *Wild Scenes in Kansas and Nebraska, and the Rocky Mountains, Oregon, California, New Mexico, Texas, and the Grand Prairies; or, Notes by the Way.* Philadelphia: G.D. Miller, 1855.

Saxon, Arthur H. *Enter Horse and Foot: A History of the Hippodrama in England and France.* New Haven, CT: Yale University Press, 1968.

_____. *P.T. Barnum: The Legend and the Man.* New York: Columbia University Press, 1989.

Seagraves, Anne. *Daughters of the West.* Hayden, ID: Wesanne, 1996.

_____. *Women Who Charmed the West.* Hayden, ID: Wesanne, 1991.

Secrest, Clark. *Hell's Belles: Denver's Brides of the Multitudes.* Aurora, CO: Hindsight, 1996.

Slide, Anthony. *The Encyclopedia of Vaudeville.* Westport, CT: Greenwood, 1994.

Smith, Duane A. *Rocky Mountain Mining Camps.* Lincoln: University of Nebraska Press, 1967.

Sprague, Marshall. *Money Mountain.* Boston: Little, Brown, 1953.

Toll, Robert C. *On with the Show: The First Century of Show Business in America.* New York: Oxford University Press, 1976.

Toms, Don. *Tenderloin Tales.* Pierre, SD: State, 1997.

Townsend, John K. *Narrative of a Journey Across the Rocky Mountains.* Philadelphia: Henry Perkins, 1839.

Trav, S.D. (D. Travis Stewart). *No Applause—Just Throw Money.* New York: Faber and Faber, 2005.

Twain, Mark. *Roughing It.* New York: Harper & Brothers, 1899.

Vestal, Stanley. *Queen of the Cowtowns: Dodge City.* New York: Harper and Brothers, 1952.

Victor, Francis F. *The River of the West.* Hartford, CT: Columbian, 1870.

Warren, Louis S. *Buffalo Bill's America: William Cody and the Wild West Show.* New York: Alfred A. Knopf, 2005.

West, Elliott. *The Saloon on the Rocky Mountain Mining Frontier.* Lincoln: University of Nebraska Press, 1976.

Wetmore, Helen C. *Buffalo Bill: Last of the Great Scouts.* Stamford, CT: Longmeadow Press, 1994.

Wheeler, Keith. *The Townsmen.* Alexandria, VA: Time-Life Books, 1975.

Wilmeth, Don B., and Christopher Bigsby. *The Cambridge History of American Theatre. Volume One: Beginnings to 1870.* Cambridge, MA: Cambridge University Press, 1998.

_____. *The Cambridge History of American Theatre. Volume Two: 1870–1945.* Cambridge, MA: Cambridge University Press, 1999.

Wilmeth, Don B., and Tice L. Miller. *Cambridge Guide to American Theatre.* Cambridge, MA: Cambridge University Press, 1993.

Wilson, Robert L., and Greg Martin. *Buffalo Bill's Wild West.* New York: Random House, 1998.

Works Project Administration. *San Francisco: The Bay and Its Cities.* New York: Hastings House, 1947.

Yost, Nellie I. *Buffalo Bill: His Family, Friends, Fame, and Fortunes.* Chicago: Sage Books, 1979.

Zamonski, Stanley W., and Teddy Keller. *The '59ers: Roaring Denver in the Gold Rush Days.* Denver: Stanza-Harp, 1967.

Index

Numbers in *bold italics* indicate pages with photographs.